HOME OF MIST

A HOME OF MIST

THE WAR OF OBSIDIAN AND MIST

TWO

CHARLES R. BURGUNDY

A Home of Mist
Copyright © 2025 Charles Burgundy

All rights reserved. No part of this publication may be sold, transmitted, reproduced, or stored in a retrieval system without the prior written consent of the publisher, except in the case of brief quotations embodied in critical articles and reviews.

This is a work of fiction. Names, characters, places, and incidents are products of the author's imagination or are used fictitiously. Any resemblance to actual events, locales, organizations, or persons, living or dead, is entirely coincidental.

ISBN: 978-2-9591370-4-4

charlesrburgundy.com

PREFACE

As this is now the second book I release, I have made this one decision: I would much rather take all the time necessary to release something I'm proud of instead of hurrying a result I would be unhappy about.

Many parts of this second book were written before the first few chapters of The Fracture of Shackles. They were some of the first pages I wrote, in fact. But as the story became clearer and more polished, those chapters, too, needed to be improved on, and so I rewrote them time and time again.

I faced a few challenges in that process. Some scenes would just not have the tone I wished them to have, or sometimes I felt like a character was inconsistent throughout the book, to name just two that came to mind.

But eventually, with time and effort, everything became as excellent as I could make them be. It is hard to ever claim that perfection was reached, but I am nevertheless proud of the final result—and so, at last, comes this second book, and I'm excited that you now get to read it. I hope you enjoy *A Home of Mist*!

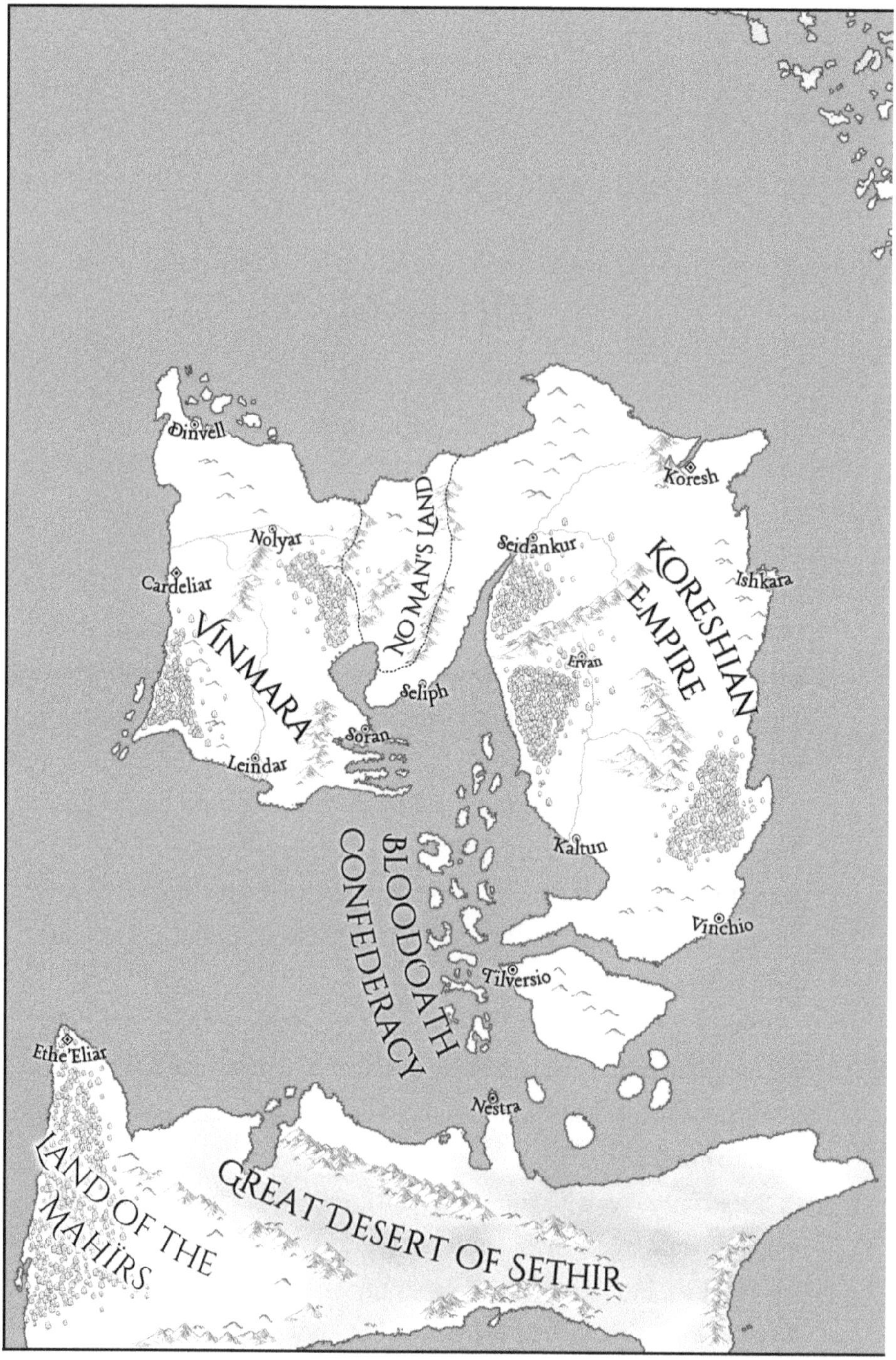
Ðinvell
Nolyar
Cardeliar
VINMARA
Soran
Leindar
NO MAN'S LAND
Seliph
Seidankur
Koresh
Ishkara
KORESHIAN EMPIRE
Ervan
Kaltun
Vinchio
Tilversio
BLOODOATH CONFEDERACY
Nestra
Ethe'Eliar
LAND OF THE MAHÏRS
GREAT DESERT OF SETHIR

KULMANDR

Jolskar Runval

ILLMERIA

Naila Asharsai
Kashpur

Mistport
The Fortress

CHAPTER 1

SECRETS IN THE OLD TEMPLE

A gentle rain helped extinguish the last flames lit by the recent battle. As the sounds of combat became more and more distant, a few of the inhabitants dared to look outside their windows or open their doors to observe the aftermath of the carnage. Broken shields, weapons, and bodies covered the ground, and the great gates of the Fortress lay shattered.

Valirian sighed, shaking his head. Would Adiloka's folly cause Illmeria's doom?

A short and sturdy man approached, trotting towards his general. In spite of his headache, Valirian forced a stern expression and straightened his back. "What is the situation, Sergeant?"

"My General, the last Northerners within the city walls have surrendered, and we are gathering them to the central plaza." The sergeant's face was marked by the exhaustion of a long day, yet his eyes showed great relief, for the Fortress had been saved.

Valirian glanced behind the man. Not so far away, Mistian soldiers returned to the city after pursuing the few Northerners who had attempted an escape. Amongst them, he had hoped to see the War Hero,

Syrela, for he very much preferred her capture to her death. Her life, doubtlessly, was most valuable for the Queen's plans. "What about the Blade of Illmeria?"

Hesitant at first, the sergeant bowed slightly, his eyes closed. "I'm sorry, My General. We didn't manage to capture her. As we reached their camp, the Northerners did their best to delay us and buy the War Hero enough time to flee."

Though Valirian frowned slightly, he nodded. It was perhaps preferable for her to live and escape rather than die, for she knew better than anyone in Illmeria how to fight—and defeat—the Koreshians. In time, her help could prove crucial. "Very well. Every Mistian has fought bravely tonight. Send couriers to the nearby villages, and to Ilmassar, and spread the news of our victory here. Send a courier to Mistport, too. We must ensure that the city is not facing any immediate threat."

The sergeant acknowledged his orders with a nod, and Valirian turned towards Xelya.

Thoughtful, the Queen contemplated the burnt and damaged roof of the Tower. Fortunately, it seemed, the light rain had been enough to extinguish the flames, preventing any further spread of the fire, though it had nevertheless destroyed the top floor entirely. The Illmerians must have attempted to assassinate her by setting it ablaze with a projectile or magic.

Valirian approached her, careful not to step on a dead soldier. His lips pursed as he stopped and took a moment to gauge the extent of the battle. At least a thousand bodies lay dead on the plaza, Northerners and Mistians alike.

"It seems I was correct in taking precautions," said Xelya, her eyes not moving from the Tower. "Though nevertheless upsetting, nothing of value was lost. The books and most of the furniture had been moved to the basement in advance."

Her words reassured him, for he had begun to feel at home in the Tower, and knowing the Sovereign had taken adequate measures to safeguard all their belongings helped him remember it was merely a matter of time before they returned there. "A wise choice, My Lady," he said. "However, the question of where we will rest tonight remains to be answered."

"Indeed, though I have the answer," she said with a slight smile. "There is an old temple, not so far away. It is spacious enough and has been carefully kept in good condition, though it has not been used in years. We shall use it as our temporary headquarters."

"How far away from the city is it?"

"It is deeper in the mountains, to the north-east, though not very far. Perhaps some half hour away."

After such a day, Valirian was unwilling to take any unnecessary risks. He glanced at his troops; he and the Queen would need an escort. "Let me ask ten trusted soldiers to guard us on the way there. I fear the possibility of some Northerners having escaped into the mountains." Though he had at first expected her to be too prideful to accept the proposition, she simply nodded, perhaps too exhausted to waste the little energy left in her to debate such a small detail.

"There is one thing I would like to do before we depart," said Valirian. He looked down, his lips pursed, and Xelya nodded. It was as if she knew what was on his mind.

The two walked a few steps back together, where, minutes before, Valirian had defeated Syrela. There was Ayun, his lifeless body still warm. No doubt did Ayun's spirit smile at them from the Beyond, yet the thought only brought a bittersweet smile to their lips. His sacrifice, in the end, had not been in vain, yet Valirian collapsed to his knees next to his old friend. How he would miss his wisdom, his comforting words, his sense of honour and duty.

Carefully, he grabbed the old man's head in his hands, shutting his eyes and closing his mouth. For many long seconds, he tried to keep himself from crying, yet tears rolled down his cheeks. For Ayun, in honour of his memory, Valirian would continue the fight.

"Thank you, Ayun," he whispered. "You have been like a second father to me." He crossed the old man's arms on his chest, a tradition in Mistian culture for warriors fallen in combat. In spite of his tears, he felt a warmth in his heart, a strange solace that only seemed to grow stronger as he stood up. "I will protect Illmeria. As you have for your entire life, I will protect Illmeria and defend its people."

A minute passed. Only as Xelya turned her attention to the soldiers who had gathered in the centre of the plaza did either move. "We will honour his memory in due time," she said. "His, and the one of every brave man who fought and died to defend the Fortress."

Valirian approached his men, returning mere moments after, followed by ten of them. The guards were all young, yet each had followed him in every battle, having shown their talent and loyalty to their general. They first headed to the Tower, asking the servants for some food for them all, as well as some clothing, before going on their way, out of the city.

The path up the hill was long, or so it seemed to the exhausted group, and little was said, yet they eventually arrived at a somewhat isolated part of the mountains. Devoid of vegetation beyond some short grass, and with a side partially protected by cliffs, the area seemed easy to defend, as if a fort should have been erected in place of the humble temple. It was made of simple stone and wood and lacked any of the decorations or symbols of other similar edifices around the Fortress.

"We will keep watch in front for the night, My General," said one of the men.

All bowed before the Queen as she set foot within the temple's small garden, and only her Advisor followed her. The night had been long, and so it was with a great sigh of relief that both of them nearly collapsed onto the two chairs in the main hall, resting their sore arms on the table between them. Before Valirian could protest, Xelya used the little energy left within her to light the many candles of the room, all with a snap of her fingers, surrounding them in a warm red light. There, for quite some time, the two sat, too appreciative of their only brief moment of calm to disturb it—though something felt odd to Valirian. Left alone with his questions, he could only wonder about the events of the day, the Sovereign's honesty, and what the future entailed. Certainly, she, too, had much on her mind, yet a part of him forbade him from fully appreciating the calm, memories of Alexar resurging as he dared glance at her.

"I do not doubt that much time will need to pass before you, too, will find me worthy of your trust," said Xelya. "However, in a time when most would have seized an occasion for revenge or acted for their own gain, you chose to spare me." Though she spoke with the same confidence and calm so characteristic of her manners, her eyes stared at the floor, and her visage was devoid of its usual pride.

Slowly, he nodded. Naturally, she could end his life the very next morning, once she had rested. A mere word of hers could annihilate his efforts, had she been lying about her true intentions, yet it was a risk he was willing to take.

With his eyes now used to the dim light, he observed the state of the temple. Indeed, it had been carefully maintained. Beyond the thin layer of dust on most of the furniture, all was kept to a respectable minimum, with a few chests of drawers and candlesticks all around the room, keeping the decoration simple. There was an undeniable practicality that had been the focus in the arrangement and furnishing of the temple. The entrance, the large room they sat in, had a ceiling some twenty feet above them. Flights of stairs on the left and right sides of the room led to an upper platform, where three doors led, Valirian guessed, to three bedrooms.

"Let us not spend the night sat here," said Xelya, standing up. "The bedrooms are upstairs, with one leading to a small garden and hot springs."

Though not explicit, the offer made Valirian chuckle. A hot bath was more than welcome, his sore muscles begging for an occasion to relax. He headed upstairs, followed a few seconds after by the Lady. He opened the central door for her and let her enter.

She rapidly inspected the room—furnished with a large bed with two bedside tables next to it, a closet, a table, two chairs, and a chest of drawers, atop which sat a dusty mirror—and nodded. "This place is just how I remember. For the longest time, this is where I lived. In the adjacent room, more specifically."

Thus was explained the remarkable state of the temple. Though it had certainly not been used for quite some time, the Lady would never allow for her childhood house to fall into neglect.

With a swift movement, she dusted off the mirror, looking at herself with a slight frown. "It seems that a new armour will be required." The areas around her elbows and shoulders had been quite noticeably damaged, the thick gambeson having suffered in her duel with Syrela.

"It will be arranged, My Lady," said Valirian. "I will ask for an armour of steel to be made for you."

Xelya let out a laugh and smiled. "Steel armours befit those pikemen in the front line or cavaliers such as you. I appreciate the thought. However, it will only serve to exhaust me, reducing the usefulness of the most valuable of my protections: my powers."

Valirian knew not how to answer, so he nodded and shrugged. "Then I will arrange for a new gambeson to be made for you."

Xelya invited him to take a seat, then detached from around her waist the small pouch she had been carrying and placed it on the small table. Inside was some much-needed food: bread, dried meat, and two apples. Under the weak light of three candles, the two shared their meal, barely enough to satiate their hunger for the time, yet it gave them the energy they had been so dearly missing.

"There are the hot springs you mentioned," said Valirian, looking through the window just above the bed. The transparent water that had pooled in the rocky formation reflected the moon, giving him just enough of a glance. It was vast, though certainly not more than a few feet deep, and only a few rocks in the centre stuck out of the water.

"Indeed. The monks who built this temple two generations ago chose this place wisely." With her food finished, she stood up, slowly heading to the wooden door at the back of her room.

"After such a day, nothing compares to a warm bath," he said. As if to emphasise his point, he stretched his sore back, impatient to remove his armour.

"Indeed," she said. "Let me enter first, and follow me in a few minutes."

He promptly closed his eyes and shook his head at her words. "My Lady, I would not dare!"

"I trust your sense of decency, Advisor. There are plenty of rocks behind which we may hide ourselves, and there is much I would like to discuss."

Thinking it unwise and unnecessary to disagree with her on something so petty, he nodded and headed to one of the other bedrooms. It was not without a smile that he removed his armour and left it on the floor. Partially covered in blood and with various marks of battle, it had certainly saved his life that day. He took a brief moment to himself, breathing in deeply. Never before had he worn his armour for so long, for he had barely removed it the night prior, preferring to keep some of the pieces on to save him time come morning.

He then headed to the garden, where it took him a moment to notice the Lady's presence. She was almost entirely hidden behind a few rocks, only the top of her head visible from the entrance. He approached the water with hesitant steps and tested it with his foot; all too used to the cold water of his own baths, he feared scalding himself. At first contact, all apprehension vanished, and his expression shifted, a slight smile appearing on his lips. Warm, the bath would be a well-deserved reward after such a day. He entered the water and slowly headed to the rocky formation, though keeping a reasonable distance from the Lady.

Long minutes passed. It all felt out of time to the both of them. Yet twice did Xelya attempt to break the silence, and twice did she stop herself, unsatisfied with the words she had almost uttered. "What compelled you to act today may forever stay a mystery to I," she eventually said. "You may attempt to find the most exact words yet may never truly be able to explain what made you spare me. However, allow me to explain why I may have seemed so unjust with you." At first, his silence made her clench her fists, and she looked down at the water, wanting to avoid his sight, blaming her exhaustion for her perceived inability to find the right words.

In truth, he knew not how to respond, understanding the importance of the moment. "My Lady, there is no anger in me any longer, though I am more than willing to listen to what you wish to share."

"It is the least I can do. There is no doubt that I had feared your betrayal, just as I feared anyone else's. You, simply, were the only person capable of truly threatening my power." She turned slightly to see him partially. Their eyes met, and on his lips was a slight smile. Her fists relaxed, and she took a deep breath. "Even amongst the Mistians, many fear me—and feared what I would become after I seized power. Such a fear I can only understand, for to their eyes, those events indeed can only be a young student killing her masters to gain power. None heard, or saw, what betrayal I witnessed.

"Those monks, my masters, had indeed taught me all, from the art of ruling to the intricacies of magic. Yet many forget that the one who found me, the man who brought me to them and raised me as his own daughter, was their very own leader, the grandmaster of the order."

He was surprised at her mention of events seemingly so taboo that all Mistians spoke of them as if Xelya herself could always be listening. He understood this; she had taken a necessary decision that day, or at least she had seen it as such, for she would otherwise not speak of betrayal so lightly.

"He was calm and wise, albeit strict, and commanded their respect," she continued. "He saw in me the next Sovereign of the Fortress—that was no secret—and perhaps some of them did grow jealous. However, none would dare contest the wisest and most powerful amongst them. Disagreements, and doubts, only appeared after his death, now almost four years ago.

"His death was soon followed by another. The second oldest brother of the order, both the logical successor and the grandmaster's right-hand man, passed away a mere month after. Though I do not doubt that the grandmaster's death was of natural causes, I am quite certain that his right-hand man's sudden illness was no mere coincidence. Soon after, the remaining monks and I would struggle to ever align, and instead of preparing me to rule, as had wished the late grandmaster, they pushed me further and further away from power until the Koreshians invaded."

She paused, toying with a small pebble between her fingers. She remembered very well the day the rumours of war and destruction reached her ears, the feeling of powerlessness that overwhelmed her and filled her with rage. That memory made her lips purse and her fist close around the pebble. "The news of their invasion, and the fall of Mistport, caused unprecedented panic amongst all Mistians, and a solution needed to be found, quickly so. Imagine, thousands and thousands fleeing from the war, speaking of imminent destruction and of bloodthirsty brutes that no power could stop. The Fortress was on the brink of revolt." She threw the pebble, and her eyes turned to her Advisor. "To those idiots at the top of the Tower, I was to be their salvation."

Rarely did her voice betray any emotion, yet in her tone was something that made Valirian shiver.

"They had planned to trade me to the Koreshians in exchange for sparing the Fortress. It would have been my fate had I not begun spying on them during their council sessions. The anger I felt at that moment is one I hope to never feel again, for I felt capable of making the Tower itself collapse. And so I entered the council room where they had been discussing—and left none of them alive."

Her gaze remained on him, and he looked down. How could he not understand her reaction, he who had seen for himself the horrors of slavery? "My Queen. I do not know one of your subjects who would hold the true motives of your actions against you."

"I know, Valirian. I know," she said, letting out a slight sigh. "Yet I cannot simply announce the true reasons behind my actions. Mere words will ring hollow. I merely wanted you to know and understand." She mostly disappeared behind the rocks as she massaged her arms in the warm water. "Do not bother yourself so much with formalities when we are in private. You may call me by my name, so long as only the two of us are to hear it."

His eyes widened. Such was not an honour of which many could boast, nor one to be taken lightly. "Thank you, Xelya."

The Lady reappeared, and her eyes turned to him once more, visibly pensive.

Xelya still had so much on her mind, so much she had not yet told him—some things better left unsaid for the time being, even—yet she knew not where to begin. "I hope you now understand why I feared betrayal. I could hardly trust my former masters. How could I trust the Mistians or a foreigner? My power was then based on fear, on the raw, powerful magic I possess, and so I could not tolerate any form of insurrection, no matter how well-intentioned. At least so I thought."

He nodded. A weight seemed lifted off his chest as he remembered his earlier doubts. He need not fear her any longer. "I understand. Let this stay in the past, for your power no longer needs to be as such: you have fought bravely to defend the Fortress, and together we triumphed over the War Hero herself. You have earned their respect and admiration."

CHAPTER 2
A MATTER OF HONESTY

How much time had passed? Valirian rubbed his dry eyes and through the curtains attempted to see the sun. Still hidden behind the mountains, it was far from its zenith; perhaps an hour or two had passed since dawn. He winced at the sight of the wound on his arm. The makeshift bandage he had made from cloth had mostly fallen off during his sleep, revealing a cut, though thankfully one not too deep. Hoping not to have failed in his duties towards the Queen, he hurried to get dressed and dusted off the mirror in his room.

Yet he stopped himself in his hurry, taking a moment to observe what appeared before him. It had been weeks since he had last seen his own reflection so clearly. A brief moment of surprise was his first reaction. Twice, he blinked. What had once been a frail, pale young man was no more. His skin had regained its liveliness. Weeks spent campaigning and training outside had given it a slight golden tint, and his body had grown stronger, forged by the hardships of battle. Above all, his visage had transformed. No longer was he a boy. His eyes looked forwards unashamed, and his slight frown, calm yet stern, reminded him of Ayun's usual demeanour. Deep in thought, he realised that his voice, too, had deepened. He spoke more slowly and stumbled less on his words. He smiled as he looked back on what he had been able to achieve, of whom he had become, a slight nod to conclude his silent reflection.

He got dressed and stepped out of his room, then headed outside. He concluded that Xelya was more than likely still resting, as he had not seen her inside and the soldiers had confirmed they had not seen her exit the temple—all for the better. He informed the guards he would return with food and to tell the Queen if need be. It was nearly an hour before he returned, followed by three servants carrying more than enough supplies for every single man, as well as some food for Xelya and him, something the Lady doubtlessly awaited.

Careful, Valirian softly knocked on the door to her room, a basket in his hand. "May I come in, My Lady?"

A few seconds passed without an answer.

"Yes, you may," she said, her voice still hoarse and low.

As he entered, he could not help but look away, for the Sovereign had her attention turned to the mirror before her, her fingers holding a comb. With a few precise movements, she carefully finished preparing herself. Her skin—so pale the day prior, bruised and not without a few superficial cuts—had regained its vigour, and her magic had healed the other marks of battle.

At his embarrassment, her lips formed a slight smile, and she invited him to sit down at the table nearby. Only then did she notice the bandage on his arm, stained by his own blood. "How tired must I have been not to have noticed such a deep wound earlier." With a slight frown, she studied it from afar.

Valirian shrugged. The wound was hardly painful after the night, and though he had lost some blood, his life was far from threatened. "This is a result of my fight with Syrela. I knew I would not be victorious if I attempted to fight on her terms, so I attacked her with a dagger hidden in my belt. The element of surprise was enough to wound her and force her to retreat."

"A smart decision, I must say," said Xelya. "Yet I will not allow your carelessness to risk an infection. Your presence is too valuable at the Fortress." She shook her head as she stepped closer, kneeling at his side as she carefully removed the cloth. Thankfully, the cut did not appear to be all too serious, though it was in no way the benign matter her Advisor seemed to make it.

"My Lady, you need to keep yourself . . ." he said, yet as she stared into his eyes, he dared not continue.

"Do not move. I am rested enough to use my magic again, and I will not allow you to take foolish risks."

Though hesitant, he nodded. She whispered a few words, and a soothing warmth spread through his arm, his wound closing in mere instants. Soon, the heat dissipated, the tingling ceased, and her spell ended. "Thank you, Xelya," he said, looking down.

She let out a soft chuckle. As he looked up, she was already sat on the opposite chair, taking some food out of the basket he had brought.

"There is much we need to discuss," she said. Her night of peaceful rest had filled her with energy like no other, yet it had only been in the morning, as she awoke, that she truly grasped the importance of their victory and its implications. War against the Northern Alliance was no longer a fear or a prospect—it had become a reality. It was only by great fortune that the first battle had been a major success in her favour, and there was no time to waste, for they risked being outnumbered should they wait for too long. "The past few days have doubtlessly been unexpected, to say the least. However, we must decide on a course of action," she continued. "As war is a path we are forced to follow, we must act while the advantage is ours."

Countless ideas rushed through his mind, and he leaned forwards. "For the immediate future, we should focus our attention on what needs to be rebuilt. The army has lost its two captains, yet our soldiers have never been so numerous. On the other hand, the gates and many other buildings have suffered damage."

She nodded and smiled at his enthusiasm. "I shall then focus my attention on the reconstruction of the city. You know your men well. Choose from amongst them a few captains to assist you."

"May I suggest, My Lady, that you first focus your attention on the industrial district?" he asked. "Many will join our army, and we will need all the resources possible to ensure that each of them is well-equipped."

Though the prospect was enticing, she did not share his enthusiasm for the power of their army. In a prolonged war, would they truly stand a chance against the alliance? "Advisor, what resources are at our disposal at the current time?"

"We have more than enough gold in our coffers to pay our men and keep our economy afloat," he answered. "With the bountiful spring harvest, and the promising summer harvest, as well as the trading possibilities offered by our control of Mistport, we should be capable of sustaining a war, even should our army double in size." Only after he spoke did he remember the uncertainty: had Mistport, too, been besieged? "Should Mistport still be under our control, of course," he added, though still hopeful.

"Let us hope so. If so is the case, then let us send merchants to Tilversio. There is no doubt our goods will interest them." Xelya turned her head to the window, letting out a slight sigh. "Though news of Mistport cannot arrive too soon."

Neither expected the city to have fallen, but neither could deny their distaste for the unknown: such a sudden attack from Syrela, at the head of such a large army, had left them undeniably disoriented.

"However, with the resources at our disposal, we are in a position to expand our power and influence," she continued. "If we do not seize the occasion, our enemies will recover and eventually break us. The Grasslands and Heartlands are too populated for us to risk a drawn-out war." With her food finished, she stood up and took a few steps to the mirror. "We should attack in the Grasslands at the soonest. Once a few of the major towns are under our control, Lady Adiloka will be forced to negotiate with us."

Valirian listened in silence. While he did agree it was the time for action—or, rather, it would soon be—he judged it foolish to attack the Grasslands. Too daring, it would also drag all of Illmeria into a bloody, fratricidal war. Yet he slowly nodded.

Xelya frowned and took a few steps. She towered over him, staring right into his eyes. "Advisor, have I not made it clear that from now on, I desire nothing but your honest opinion, or are my words so untrustworthy to you?"

Valirian chuckled, looking down at the table. She was right. "Forgive me, My Lady. I believe your words, and I did not mean to doubt your honesty." He stood up. His slight smile seemed to make her frown vanish.

"I have allowed you to oppose my decisions in private, should you judge your objections justified," she said. "Now, Advisor, tell me what your thoughts truly are."

"I believe that we do not need to risk invading the Grasslands and committing ourselves to a costly war—and possibly exposing our armies to a trap, too—to gain an advantage," he said. "Simply taking control of the Islands would give us such an edge, without the risks of a direct assault."

His regained confidence made her smile as she reflected on his proposition. There was much merit to it, and though she was far from convinced, she could understand his position. "It is something we must discuss further, in time. For now, let us focus on the immediate." She headed out and, with a simple gesture, invited him to follow her.

"I can give my recommendations for the promotion of two or three sergeants. It may perhaps help you in your task."

As they headed down the stairs, he answered with a nod, curious of the names on her mind.

"Very well," she said. "Expect a letter shortly, Advisor, and if you must find me, I will be at the Tower to determine what areas are in need of repairs."

"Understood, My Lady," he said.

After a brief discussion with the guards positioned at the entrance, the group headed back to the city, sharing few words along the way, for the Lady and her Advisor saw it unfit to discuss strategy before their subordinates. They agreed to meet again at noon, to discuss the matter properly, then parted ways.

The silent emptiness that Valirian found as he entered the captains' quarters was crushing. For weeks he had grown accustomed to opening the door and being welcomed by the warm smile of Ayun or a nod of acknowledgement from Yuzsan. Yet in spite of that emptiness, he hesitated not as he got to work with a stern frown. This was the beginning of a new chapter, and he would be at the centre of it. The first step would be to count the remaining soldiers, for the two battles of the days prior had certainly dwindled their numbers, yet the results were a pleasant surprise. Within the walls of the Fortress, some six hundred men still stood battle-ready, and a hundred would soon heal from minor wounds. Added to them would be the soldiers positioned in the surrounding villages and forts, Ilmassar, and, hopefully, Mistport. With those together, they would surpass a thousand men with ease, a figure much higher than at first anticipated.

"Alright, let's not wait any longer," he said to himself as he sat at his desk. The Queen's recommendations were not long to arrive, for a servant brought them in the following hour. There was, he realised, a necessity to increase the number of captains. Where two would certainly be enough for some four hundred men, the army had now surpassed a thousand in number and would continue to grow. Some more help would be necessary.

First on the list was a sergeant named Xilto. Though being recommended by the Queen herself was doubtlessly impressive in itself, more remarkable was the man's loyalty through time, for he had been at the defence of the Fortress for nearly two decades. It was only natural, as an encouragement for soldiers to be loyal and aim for excellence, to promote him. Valirian was most familiar with the other name in the short missive. Sergeant Akior was the one who had led the defence of the northern gates during Syrela's siege. He was a remarkable example of leadership, commanding platoons in the various skirmishes that occurred in the streets of the city. Both of them were veterans, Xilto being way above forty years of age and Akior, though some years younger, had just passed thirty-five. It was what Valirian sought first and foremost in those meant to advise and assist him; few could claim to have any amount of experience comparable to them, which made them most suitable for the position. Yet beyond the two obvious candidates, Valirian found himself uncertain.

"My General, if I may," said Xilto, "there are two sergeants that Akior and I are familiar with and have earned our respect. Sergeant Zelshi and Sergeant Aaposhi."

Had it been any other person's recommendation, Valirian would have doubted their true motives. Personal interests and favours were something to be cautious of. However, he knew Xilto: he was a man of honour, respected as such by every soldier. "Bring them to me," said Valirian. "I shall then take my decision."

Many minutes passed before both arrived at the captains' quarters, and after a long discussion, the answer became apparent. Zelshi had made a name for himself as perhaps the most talented warrior of the army, yet such a status he had earned through an unparalleled sense of discipline, and he held a sense of idealism very much reminiscent of Ayun's. Aaposhi was admired by his peers for the way he inspired his men, leading them fearlessly into dangerous charges though not lacking in tactical abilities, as he had shown during the reconquest of Mistport, notably. Though the two were younger than both Xilto and Akior, being in their early thirties, they both had served in the militias of Mistport before coming to the Fortress.

All five gathered and held a prolonged discussion on the various matters at hand, coming to an agreement in regard to organisation, training, and the general direction to be followed from there. They concluded that, unless it was absolutely necessary, the army needed to avoid battle for the following weeks.

Noon soon arrived, however, forcing them to pause their work for the time. Valirian had to return to the Tower, as he had promised Xelya, though he intended to take care of one final detail before meeting with the Lady again. The ten men who had followed and guarded them throughout the night were officially assigned to the Sovereign's personal guard. He also doubled their number to ensure the Queen would be protected at all times. The battle had made him realise that, more than the Mistlands, it was her the Northerners feared, and though assassination attempts were uncommon in Illmeria, and though the Sovereign was no easy target by herself, he preferred leaving nothing to chance.

Once that matter had been taken care of, he hurried up the stairs and headed to the dining room, slightly worried he was late. The morning had been perturbed by the late hour at which both had awoken. Yet there he instead found the Queen, aided by a dozen workers, repairing some of the damage that had been done to the room and cleaning the remaining debris. Though the ceiling had been almost entirely destroyed, most of the furniture seemed in a decent state, if not almost intact, a most pleasant surprise.

"My Lady," he said as he entered, bowing down as she turned to face him.

"My Advisor is on time, as per usual and as expected," she said. "It is only a matter of minutes before our meal is served. You may take a seat."

He nodded at the invitation. The many workers there, seemingly done with their work, headed out of the Tower. For a minute or two, he simply inspected the large oak table in front of him, mostly unscathed in spite of the events of the past day. A few dents, slight and far from one another, were visible, and more irregularities could be felt under his careful touch, yet they did not render the furniture unusable. Seconds after, as a thick, white tablecloth now covered the wood, everything felt and appeared intact, indistinguishable from before, leaving him to wonder if those dents had not been present before the siege even happened. The quality of the table nevertheless impressed him, his eyes now drawn to the rest of the room as he truly gauged the damage the Tower had suffered.

As he had first thought, the entirety of the highest floor had been destroyed by the fire; what debris remained of it had been magically transported by Xelya to the ground far below. When it came to the floor they both sat at, the wall behind the Sovereign's usual seat had been the most severely damaged, almost entirely destroyed, yet to Valirian's surprise, everything else seemed in a relatively unaffected state.

The Tower had resisted beyond his expectations, and he could not help but feel impressed—yet also curious. His time with Xelya, an outstanding magic user, had made him quick to suspect magic even in some seemingly inconspicuous and banal things. The Tower, after all, was mostly built out of wood, yet it seemed to have suffered minimal damage. His silent inspection came to an end as the Sovereign took her seat to his left and servants entered the room, carrying platters of food.

"Have you taken your final decision in regard to your captains, Advisor?" she asked, bringing soon after a glass of wine to her lips. As she breathed in its delicate aroma, her lips formed a slight smile.

"Yes, My Lady. Your recommendations have been most helpful, for both Xilto and Akior have been promoted. I also decided to promote two other sergeants. Namely, Zelshi and Aaposhi." As Xelya raised an eyebrow, he thought it wise to explain his reasoning. "Our army has grown in size, quite significantly so. It will only continue growing larger, as hundreds of volunteers are arriving to the Fortress. I thought it preferable to plan ahead for the future."

Satisfied, the Lady nodded, yet Valirian's sudden hesitation did not escape her eye, and she frowned. "Is there something else you wished to say?"

"My Lady," he said, "I do not mean to impose any decision on you, yet I have appointed the soldiers that guarded the temple last night as your personal guard so as to ensure your protection at all times."

Pursing her lips, the Queen shook her head; her eyes stared right into his. "I am more than capable of defending myself, Advisor. Our soldiers are better used elsewhere." For her every movement to be watched in such a manner was inconceivable, an inconvenience that would prove both ineffective and tiresome.

"It is wiser, My Lady," he insisted. "I do not doubt your abilities in combat, but having such a guard would act as a deterrent against most assassination attempts, as well as keep you safe in battle."

With her duel against Syrela all too recent, she sighed. She lacked the desire to fight the decision. "So long as they do not prove too limiting. I will not tolerate being slowed down."

He repressed a smile, amused at the assumption that his young and well-trained elite soldiers would be unable to keep up with her. Above all, he was pleased that she accepted, albeit reluctantly. It was wise to say no more, though, and so a few minutes passed, Valirian judging it preferable to let the Lady speak first, for there was no need to risk angering her.

"Let us discuss strategy," she eventually said. Before continuing, she glanced at him, studying his reaction. Thoughtful, he stared at the mountain peaks behind her. "You and I both agree that allowing ourselves a few weeks of preparation is necessary. Likewise, we are in agreement that we must now take the initiative and assume the offensive."

Valirian nodded. In truth, their only disagreement so far had visibly been on deciding their future target.

"Very well," she continued. "With the Northerners' recent defeat and the heavy losses incurred, I do not wish to give them the slightest of chances to recover. We must attack them in their most vulnerable area."

Indeed, the Northerners had lost thousands of soldiers in their recent attack on the Fortress. However, Valirian was unconvinced; in the time it would take the Mistians to prepare their counteroffensive, the Northerners would have had more than enough time to regroup and ready themselves.

"Yet their most vulnerable area is also the one they are more likely to defend," he answered. "They will have enough time to gather a large army, but that army will be incapable of attacking us on our soil, for they would lack the supplies to do so. A disadvantage they would not suffer in the Grasslands."

The Lady swirled the little wine left in her glass, finishing it soon after. "Yet it would be the best way to press our advantage. We cannot underestimate their capacities in the long term, unless we take control of their crucial supplies of grain. It is a risk, admittedly, but one worth taking."

In spite of his disagreements, Valirian understood her reasoning. For the longest time, the Lady had obtained advantages over whichever opponents she had by taking risks. She understood that herself very well, and he knew there was a very reasonable chance for her plan to succeed. Yet he saw another occasion to obtain an advantage over the Northerners, one that would avoid such risks—and an unimaginable bloodbath.

"Such an approach would prove costly for both sides," he said. "With an indirect offensive, and some smart diplomacy, we could have similar effects without weakening ourselves. The Northerners are not the only threat our men will face on the battlefield." Even though the Queen seemed less worried by the Koreshians than he was, she would not ignore the prospect of a future invasion. The threat they represented was very much real, and she did not disregard his warnings. "Should we expand our influence to the Islands, and bring under our control the city of Sanadra, we would control the seas. Their only major port would be Kashpur, which would be an easy target for the large fleet we could build. We would control all commerce done in Illmeria, while preventing our opponents from ever crossing the Sea of Tranquillity again."

Xelya looked down. She had a slight frown, and he repressed another smile. Whether she agreed or not, he had at least made her hesitate—a victory in itself.

"I fear the Northerners would prove themselves very unreceptive to diplomacy," she eventually answered. "Unless we were to obtain another victory, one of equal significance at least. Hence why I am willing to take a measured risk to end this war rapidly."

He nodded. The Duchess, Lady Adiloka, was not known to be easily swayed, and he knew that negotiations with her would certainly be a delicate matter.

Xelya stood up, inviting her Advisor to do the same. "There is much left to reflect on, still. However, we have more than enough time to take a decision."

He nodded, following her out of the room. In spite of their failure to agree on a strategy to follow, for the time being, Valirian could not hold back his smile any more. Both of them had, in the end, openly discussed the matter, and though she still seemed somewhat stubborn in his eyes, she had been willing to listen. The night, perhaps, would bring the counsel awaited by both, and certainly, they would reach an agreement by the end of the week. For the time, there was much work left to do, and the two swiftly returned to their duties.

CHAPTER 3
A LIGHT AGAINST PAST SHADOWS

"Form ranks! Two steps forwards!" Xilto's voice echoed through the training grounds, each command followed by the footsteps of some two hundred soldiers clad in heavy armour.

From a little further behind the old captain, Valirian observed, nodding to himself. That day already, over eighty young men had arrived at the Fortress and taken up arms. Doubtlessly, more would follow. Though his presence was hardly needed, he had preferred supervising the various drills for the time being, occasionally exchanging a few words with Zelshi or Akior. There was little he had to say about the methods of the newly promoted captains. All had diligently followed his instructions, and though that had made his afternoon quite uneventful, time seemed to pass rapidly.

Not very far, perhaps a ten-minute walk, Xelya supervised the reconstruction—or, more accurately, assisted in them with the use of her magic. At first, Valirian had advised against it, not wanting her to waste her powers merely to save some minutes of work, but as it was a trivial matter, he soon came to accept it; if the Queen thought herself capable of helping, so be it.

There was, in truth, little to worry about. The economy was flourishing, and the second harvest of the year, set for the sixth or seventh month, seemed very promising. The more Valirian reflected on the matter, the less plausible the prospect that Mistport had fallen. Why would the Northerners not concentrate their forces on the Fortress first? The capture of the south would have certainly meant the surrender of the rest of the Mistlands.

Eventually, he headed to the Tower, where Xelya had preceded him by merely a few minutes, though that time, they had agreed to head to the old temple to dine. Less crowded and active, there they would at last enjoy some quietness.

"There is something important I must do before we head to the temple," she said. "Follow me."

Without another word, and leaving her personal guard at the entrance, she led Valirian up the stairs of the Tower, a pain he had wished to have avoided, yet he refrained from protesting. As the Lady pushed open the door to the library, his reluctance was wiped away by a wide smile. Filled with countless bookshelves, well-lit, and built almost entirely in a beige wood, the room appeared even larger at first glance. On two levels, the bookshelves of the second level connected by small bridges, there were easily thousands of volumes in the room alone, covering subjects from architecture to botany, folktales to military history.

Xelya laughed at his silent admiration. "By all means, visit, explore. Let us find a few tomes each. We will read them together and discuss their content."

Going their separate ways, they spent many long minutes exploring the library, yet with each step, at every new title, Valirian could not help but be surprised. Vinmaran history, it seemed, was better recorded in the Sovereign's library than in his own homeland. A treatise on strategy written by a Vinmaran general of old was his first pick.

His second, an account of various battles and wars between Vinmara and Koresh. Lastly, he chose a book written by an Illmerian monk on magic. The subject, still mysterious and foreign to him, was one that Xelya could easily explain, even if only on the surface. Having grown up in Vinmara, he hadn't had any contact with magic until Koresh, where magic seemed infinitely more present than in his old homeland. Yet as he arrived in Illmeria, the omnipresence of magic there had made Koreshian sorcerers appear as a rare exception in comparison.

As he grabbed the last book, he winced. Tarasmir's glowing red eyes appeared, for just a second. He paused in his movement, scanning the room around him to reassure himself. That sight had only been in his mind, just a memory that resurfaced. That encounter had been all too close for his taste. It had left an everlasting mark on his mind, evidently. The memory of the Koreshian Emperor's aura only seemed to have grown more vivid as time passed. Tarasmir had doubtlessly mastered his art; everything in him seemed in perfect order, very much like everything around him had to be.

With a deep sigh, Valirian pushed himself to grab the book.

"I am not surprised in the slightest, Advisor," said Xelya with a slight smile as she saw his selection of books. She, on the other hand, had chosen two tomes: an Illmerian account of the Koreshian invasion and a treatise on the various monastic orders of Illmeria and their fighting techniques and magic. "I am most impatient to read them all. Let us wait until we have arrived at our destination, however."

With a nod, Valirian led the way, and the two began their long way down the stairs. Behind him, Xelya observed her Advisor. Thoughtful, she had come to realise how little she knew of him, how much still made no sense to her. How had a foreigner, from a land so far away, found himself in Illmeria against his will? How had he mastered the Illmerian tongue? Where had he learnt all his skills? In the past, in an attempt to explain all she still ignored, she had come up with a thousand possible answers, yet now she intended on asking him directly, once the two arrived at a calmer place.

Soon, the quietness of the temple replaced the sound of the guards' heavy boots and the occasional discussions between the Advisor and his men. Much to her liking, Valirian knew when to respect the silence, and so, without a word, they both headed to her room, a bag of food and the many books with them.

"For a long time," she said, "this temple was the home of the grandmasters of the monks. It is here that each of them would go to meditate on important decisions, such as whether to go to war or whom to designate as their successor."

In some inexplicable way, there indeed was something special about this place. Everything seemed quieter. Something powerful, yet beyond Valirian's ability to comprehend. "One cannot help but feel at peace here," he answered.

The two ate a simple meal, just enough to resource themselves after the day. With her food finished, Xelya stood up, glancing outside at the hot springs. "Let us take a bath, just as last night. We will read afterwards."

Having finished his food, Valirian headed to his room to prepare himself, joining the Lady in the water some moments after.

"I have been wondering much about you, Advisor," she said. "About how a young slave, captured by bandits, seems to know so much about so many varied subjects. Certainly, not every commoner in Vinmara has mastered Illmerian as well as you. Am I correct?"

His foot had barely touched the water as she spoke, making him pause for a moment. Her praise made him smile, his chin high as he chuckled. Indeed, learning Illmerian had been a significant challenge; after all, it shared very little in common with his mother tongue. Yet as memories flooded his mind, he felt unable to hold back a sigh.

"It seems a lifetime ago, now," he answered. "As you guessed, I was born in a noble family, though one of rather minor importance, in spite of our wealth. My father was a renowned warrior, or so I like to believe, and, having proven his worth in many battles and commanding armies against Koresh, he earned himself an estate.

"As peace followed the wars in which my father earned his fame, he met my mother and married her. We lived in the countryside not far away from the capital, though I had never gone there until I became an adult." All traces of a smile faded as he spoke of a time he had only heard of from his father, who himself seldom ever spoke of it. Valirian's mother died in childbirth, and his father, deeply in love, had never remarried. A cold void had doubtlessly been left in his heart, yet he had held on to the hope of seeing his son grow up and become a great man in turn. However, to both of them, the memories of the one who had given her life so that Valirian might live were forever bittersweet, a heavy weight his father preferred not to talk about. "Forgive me. This is no easy subject for me. I may need a second to find my words."

Her only answer was a simple nod. Whether he spoke or sat in silence, Xelya preferred to listen, to allow him the time to think. Though she knew not the cause of the pain he felt, she understood.

"It's in that estate that I grew up," he eventually continued, "and my father ensured that I would receive the best education possible. For that, I was given a tutor, an old but wise man named Lenhart, who was a savant and a scholar with impressive knowledge of countless subjects. He played with my curiosity perfectly, always finding ways to awaken an interest in the subjects he would teach me about, which is precisely why I found such a passion for languages at an early age."

The memories of childhood brought a smile back to his visage, a heart-warming sight to Xelya, who turned to face him so she might hear him better.

"It is from him that I learnt Illmerian—but also Koreshian and

Kulmandran. I never understood why stories of 'tall, blond giants that lived in the frozen archipelago of Kulmandr' enthralled me so much as a child, but it certainly made me an interested student.

"Eventually, however, as I became a teenager, my father required that I be taught two subjects he thought crucial: administration and the art of war. I turned out to be a much worse student in sword-fighting than I was in mathematics. However, I excelled in all things related to administration.

"It certainly disappointed my father to see his son incapable of wielding a weapon properly, but he found comfort in knowing that I could eventually administrate the family estate and make it prosper. How foolish of him, it seems." Though he allowed himself to laugh at his conclusion, and though Xelya reciprocated, he couldn't help but pause, taking a deep breath in an attempt to alleviate the burden he felt in his chest. It was only by a miracle that he had been given a second chance, yet it did not erase his mistakes—or their consequences.

"You must have cherished your childhood very much," she said.

"Indeed, My Lady," he answered with a joyless smile. For a brief moment, he closed his eyes, focusing on the warm water caressing his skin. "One day, my father died on the battlefield. He had perished a hero, or so they told me, yet no amount of heroism could console me at the time. Only the company of my old mentor could. Yet we must all bend to the laws of time, and no matter how much I denied it, Lenhart was ailing and soon passed away. All of the estate had fallen ill, in fact, but while I recovered in a matter of days, his body did not have the vigour of his youth any more." With some water in his hands, Valirian washed a few tears away, rubbing his cheeks for a moment.

Xelya seemed hesitant, taking a few seconds before speaking. "What about your mother?" She did not want to cause him pain, but she feared she had already guessed the answer.

"She gave her life to give birth to me," he answered.

Xelya nodded and looked down. She found no words to answer, even as a long minute passed.

"I then made a decision I still regret to this day," he said. "As I had no reason to stay behind—at least, so I thought at the time—I chose to sell my father's estate and everything I owned that I could not bring with me. I dreamt of following in my father's footsteps, of adventure and heroism. I bought a ship, a sword, and an armour, and with a few companions, I set sail to protect the innocent and fight the unjust.

"It was undoubtedly an admirable goal, and I had no other intention than to imitate the man who had given me life. However, it is quite obvious that things turned in my disfavour. A few days after my nineteenth birthday, the pirates of Bloodoath captured me, and I was sold to Koresh." For a second, he was hesitant to continue—after all, there was little more to add. More importantly, he preferred not revealing he had been a slave to Koresh's most cruel general, lest she begin to suspect him once again.

"Well-educated, I naturally served as a scribe for quite some time," he said. "Then as a weapon-bearer as the Koreshians invaded. When they were defeated at the battle of Kashpur, I stole a horse and fled, only to be captured by bandits." With perhaps his first genuine smile in some time, he turned to her, letting out a slight chuckle. "You know the rest, My Lady."

Reciprocating his smile, she nodded. There was something deeply impressive in his story, for though he had lost everything at a young age, he had continued fighting. Her smile widened as she realised that, in some way, she had granted him an opportunity to right the wrongs, that in spite of her past mistakes, she had helped him find a purpose once more. He had become a reminder of her goals and what she fought for; it all confirmed that making him her Advisor had been the correct decision.

"Your story only brings one question to my mind," she said. "What is your age, exactly?" The mention of his nineteenth birthday had implied his relative youth, yet his short beard and his facial traits made him appear quite older than her, by maybe five or six years. Or was it his foreign blood that gave her that impression?

"I am almost twenty-one years of age, My Lady."

Her eyes widened in spite of her smile. Though to most Illmerians he appeared a few years older than her, it was in reality the other way, for she had passed her twenty-fourth birthday mere weeks before, though without much celebration. "You are a brave man, Valirian. Do not feel ashamed of yourself, nor of your past."

Her words of encouragement were unexpected yet heart-warming. Feeling a rush of heat to his face, he bowed his head low. "Thank you, My Lady."

Sinking lower into the water, they both found a moment of peace in the warmth of the hot springs. For Valirian, a weight had been taken off his chest, and her show of sympathy, though surprising, had made him appreciate her company. Undoubtedly, the Lady was not accustomed to such discussions, a result of her martial upbringing; raised to be the Sovereign, she had certainly been expected—and trained—to control her every emotion and hide them as much as possible. At that moment, he realised how little he truly knew her, how he had assumed much about her, for so long, yet he began to see, slowly, a little more of who she truly was.

"Xelya, may I ask you something?"

Though she showed not her surprise, she turned around to face him, her curiosity doubtlessly piqued. "You may ask, Valirian."

"Your powers," he asked. "Were you born with them, or did you develop them over time?"

For a short moment, she thought of her answer. He obviously knew very little, if anything, of magic, as highlighted by his choice of books. She needed to be precise, yet not so much as to leave him confused. "In some way, both. Every person is born with a varying affinity to magic, but that affinity is nothing without training. Some have great potential from birth but must tap into that potential and learn to harness it. As such, one could spend an entire life attempting to control magic but fail to do so, for their potential is non-existent, while another could express their powers while absolutely untrained."

As if her answer explained many of the questions in his mind, he nodded slowly, stroking his chin with his hand. "But what does determine one's potential?"

"For all the sages, monks, and scholars have been able to observe: ancestry. It seems that something in the blood determines one's powers, though there is doubtlessly some luck involved, too." Taking a brief pause, she observed her own reflection in the water, lost in the purple glow of her own eyes. "We know very little. Some old folktales say that magic was created by Nav himself and given to us by the spirits. Some others claim that it is the blood of the Mahïrs, who arrived here centuries ago, that give us any power. Some combine the two together. Maybe it is neither."

"I assumed that your eyes, and the colour of your hair, were a result of your affinity with magic," he said. "Am I wrong?"

Turning to him once again, she smiled. "You are correct, though these are not the only effects of magic on my body. Magic also seems to affect one's mind, notably with keener intellect, but yet again, powerful magic users, in whom the changes would be noticeable, are too few to truly confirm those ideas."

"Does magic affect the way one ages, too?" he asked.

She laughed, amused by the politeness of his question. "I would answer that I do not know yet, for I am only twenty-four years of age. However, it should be expected, for the most proficient of magic users are capable of living longer, sometimes well over a century."

Realising the clumsiness of his question, Valirian profusely apologised, yet it only seemed to amuse Xelya even more.

"Worry not. No offence was taken," she said. "Should I conclude that you thought me much older, however?"

"Perhaps a few years older," he admitted. "But I did not expect you to be over thirty." Her explanation reminded him of the Sorcerer-King, founder and first Sovereign of the Fortress, or so told the legends. Any mention of him in any of the many books he had read seemed clouded in mystery, and yet all sources agreed he had ruled the Mistlands for over a century. However, some scholars had begun to debate his very existence, claiming that old knowledge was, for the most part, lost and the little that remained was exaggerated in many ways.

"Magic can influence one's thoughts, too," she said. "And though it is possible to resist it with training, a mage can influence another person's mind." A shiver in her spine made her shift uncomfortably, and something weighed in her chest as memories she preferred to forget returned to her. Though weeks had passed, and in spite of her many attempts, never had she been able to truly bury them; thoughts of the day she had attempted to use her magic on Valirian always returned to haunt her. What had originally been some mere discomfort at the thought of using the magic, which required some close physical contact with the target no less, had left an unbearably bitter taste in her mouth after her failed attempt. It had been out of pragmatism, out of necessity, or so she had convinced herself, yet nothing justified such cruelty—but she felt unable to admit her fault.

"If magic is so powerful as you make it seem," he said, "then it is good that only one sorcerer in Koresh rivals your capacities."

Though she had heard many rumours regarding Tarasmir, the confidence with which he spoke those words made her smile. "How would you know, you who knew nothing of magic mere minutes ago?" she asked with a slight chuckle.

Her question made him frown. For a moment he considered simply laughing with her and feigning ignorance, but he saw no harm in speaking of his encounter with Tarasmir. "My Lady, with all due respect, in my time as a slave I met the Emperor of Koresh, though briefly. As he approached me, there was this . . . vision I saw, and of all the mages I encountered, only yours was as perceivable, clear, and powerful as his."

All amusement vanished from Xelya's expression, and her eyes widened. For a few seconds, she frowned, deep in thought, and only after quite some time did she turn to face her Advisor again. "You have seen my aura? And the Sorcerer's, too?"

"Well, I have, yes," he answered. "Is there something strange about that?"

Once again, thoughts rushed through her mind as she tried to make sense of this, though this time, her answer came sooner. "I should not have been so surprised. Only experienced and trained mages and those who have had no contact with magic until late in their life can perceive a mage's aura. This is a rare ability in Illmeria, where most grow up in frequent contact with monastic orders or have some form of affinity with magic themselves, even if minimal." It was indeed no surprise, then, that he—a young Vinmaran noble who grew up on a secluded farm in the countryside, far away from the large cities—had unintentionally developed such an ability. In fact, very few were those in Vinmara who had any affinity with magic.

"Do you remember his aura?" she asked.

He closed his eyes and nodded slowly. He took a deep breath as he recalled his memories, taking some time to find the words to describe them. Nodding once more, he ignored a shiver in his spine as he turned to Xelya. "Tarasmir's aura is the one you would expect from a cynical and calculated emperor. It is dark, cruel, but orderly. My first glimpse felt like a whiplash. Then all I could see was a powerful red and something tall, impressive, and majestic on a black throne."

Her silence would certainly leave him uneasy, but how could she reply? Duels of magic had nothing comparable to them. Some could be over in mere instants. Others took hours to resolve, and often did both mages lose their lives. The description he had given of the Emperor indeed depicted him as a formidable foe. "No matter," she said. "Illmeria will triumph, regardless of the challenges."

At her confidence, he smiled. Regardless, he could only place his trust in her abilities should the two ever face on the battlefield. "Why don't we head back inside and read one of the many books we have on Koresh?" he suggested.

As she agreed, he stood up and headed back to his room. A few minutes having passed, he knocked on the Lady's door, entering once she allowed him in.

"Please, take a seat," she said, the five tomes on the table in front of her, waiting for him to be seated before continuing. "Out of all the books, there is one I very much look forwards to reading with you." She showed the one at the top of the pile: the account of the Koreshian invasion.

Carefully, he opened it, skimming over the first few pages. It was, it seemed, a faithful account written by a monk who had followed Syrela and her forces for the entirety of the war. The rapidity with which the book had reached the Sovereign's library impressed him. It seemed almost abnormal, in fact. "How come such a book can be found in your library?"

"A mere coincidence," she said. "One of the Northerners had it in his tent, and one of our soldiers found it there. They rightfully thought it wise to bring it to I."

Together they read, at first almost amused by the preface, for the monk hid not that he saw in Syrela the one who would unite Illmeria against its enemies—a statement that doubtlessly awoke much anger in the Duchess, for the monk had been forced to flee Kashpur soon after. It seemed, however, that the War Hero herself appreciated little the flattery, as the book was banned from amongst her men, though visibly, some of her soldiers disregarded the restrictions and preferred to see the Blade of Illmeria rule instead of Lady Adiloka. Soon, their amusement turned into a keen interest in the tales of battles and strategy narrated in the book, for the War Hero had left nothing to chance in her skirmishes with the Koreshians.

The tale proved to be most interesting to Valirian, who greatly appreciated viewing the war from an Illmerian perspective. Very few details seemed to be missing, and none of great importance, yet what impressed him most was how each action of the Koreshians had been carefully reported, how Syrela always was aware of the intentions of her enemies. Occasionally, he would add a comment, telling how the Koreshians had viewed their failure in the Northlands or explaining the soldiers' discontent towards their high command as the War Hero felt forever unreachable.

"The Koreshian general, Alexar, had to enforce strict measures to prevent any rebellion," he said. "Though it hardly bothered him, and it did not surprise his men either, for he was known to be cruel, and to him, the end always justified the means."

Though Valirian's lack of sympathy surprised Xelya very little, the anger with which he spoke of Alexar made her raise an eyebrow. Certainly, her Advisor had personally been the victim of his cruelty, she concluded.

For many more minutes, the two continued their read, and Valirian could only be amused by how masterfully Syrela had toyed with Alexar, outmanoeuvring him on every occasion. To conclude the evening, they read the last part of the book, the Battle of Kashpur—or the "Battle of the Pearl," as the author had named it. Valirian had the widest of smiles as he read those pages, though yet again, a part of him felt indebted to Syrela for her victory; he dared not imagine his life had he stayed a slave of Koresh.

"I imagine the high command was very much frustrated at their repeated failures," she said. "They took a risk by attacking Kashpur, as they found themselves outmanoeuvred in the Northlands."

Valirian chuckled as he remembered the anger on Alexar's face the day he had thought himself catching the War Hero's army off-guard, only to find the camp entirely deserted. Not a single thing had gone in the Koreshian's favour. "Indeed. It was anger that brought him to the Northlands in the first place. To him, it was inconceivable that an army of trained Koreshian soldiers had met such fierce resistance that reinforcements needed to be called. Now, it feels like it had been an intentional trap by Syrela."

Closing the book carefully, he placed it next to the pile, satisfied. "Likewise, every soldier knew that the attack on Kashpur was an act of desperation, and though they thought victory possible after the first hours of battle, Syrela's sudden arrival destroyed all hopes they might have had." In reality, he knew little of the soldiers' mindset regarding this exact battle; he preferred using it so as to avoid any further explanation of his relation to Alexar.

"This general you mentioned, Alexar," she asked. "There is no mention of him after the failure in the Northlands. Did he survive?"

"I can only hope he suffered a painful and agonising death," he said. "However, I do not know. Maybe the War Hero killed him. Maybe the Emperor punished his failure by death."

Stroking her chin, Xelya frowned. He had painted the Koreshian army in a particularly negative light, yet this same army had conquered a vast empire in recent times. Complete incompetence could not bring so many victories.

"Koresh relies on swarming tactics," he answered as she asked him about it. "Their large empire provides them with large quantities of troops and more than enough equipment. It does not matter if they are often under-trained. Only the Grey Giants, their elite forces, are truly a problem on the battlefield."

"What is the secret, then, behind Vinmara's success against Koresh?" she asked. "Vinmara is no larger than Koresh. Is better training really sufficient?"

"Well, it is a difficult question for me to answer," he said. "I would imagine so. However, it would be foolish to claim that Vinmara has been having the upper hand in the past decades. No major amount of territory has been lost, yet the wars have hardly been going in their favour."

"I suppose we will find our answer in the books we will read in the following days. However, I suppose that should an army stand their ground and resist the initial charge, the Koreshian troops will begin to lose their morale."

"That would correspond with the stories told by my father. Often, the Koreshians merely failed to take a position rapidly, and that sufficed to make them retreat and scatter, leading to heavy losses as the Vinmaran cavalry would give chase."

"Then I can imagine that our troops are trained accordingly," she said.

Confident, he answered with a nod. "We still lack a large cavalry. However, our troops have proven their discipline both at the Battle of Mistport and at the Battle of the Fortress. It is why keeping them well-paid is of the utmost importance. The Koreshians are conscripts who are forced to fight, and most won't risk their lives in battle if the occasion to flee is presented."

A few moments of silence followed. Xelya reflected on their discussion. War at such a scale would leave little room for error, and she could not deny her own inexperience. In fact, only one person in

Illmeria could truly claim to have any, making the War Hero's life all the more valuable. "I appreciated our discussion. However, we should head to sleep. Much awaits us tomorrow."

CHAPTER 4

TWO EMERALDS IN A CAGE

"Deep breaths, My Lord," said Zelshi. "Pay attention to your breathing more. You need to be in control all the time."

Valirian followed the captain's instructions, and time seemed to slow. Firmly gripping the wooden sword in his hand, he then stretched. Little time had passed since the break of dawn, and although he had shared a meal with the Queen, his body felt numb, as if he had not quite left his bed yet.

"My General," said Akior, "I suggest that you begin with a quick jog for a few minutes. It'll get you in the right conditions."

He did as advised. After he discussed the day's tasks with the Lady, she had suggested—or, rather, politely demanded—that he return to his old routine of practice so as to keep himself battle-ready, something he had, in truth, yearned to return to for quite some time. Xilto and Aaposhi, both natural leaders with more experience than the other two captains, would supervise the army drills, while Zelshi and Akior would assist Valirian in his practice. Indeed, while Zelshi was a fantastic warrior, Akior was attentive to the smallest of details yet knew to focus on what was essential.

"Your strikes are more precise when you have the advantage, I have noticed," said Akior. "But when Zelshi gains the upper hand, you begin to panic."

Valirian nodded. The words might seem harsh, but he doubted not the captain's intentions. He made the various remarks his priority, and Zelshi, visibly reading his fellow captain's mind, always seemed to put Valirian in perfect practice situations.

"There, perfect!" said Akior.

Finally! It had taken quite some time, but Valirian had struck Zelshi's exposed neck, winning an otherwise hopeless duel—the first positive in what had been a rather disappointing morning. Yet even Zelshi allowed himself a slight smile at his general's progress.

The two combatants returned to their positions. A long hour had passed already, yet it had felt like seconds to Valirian, especially as he looked back on his own progress. He might have lost most of the duels, and felt embarrassed on a few occasions, but he had much greater confidence in himself as he entered the following sparring match. That day had perfectly illustrated the necessity of regular practice, even if it cost him his pride.

Another long fight, this one decided by an inch as Valirian barely missed the captain's wrist. He removed his helmet, looked up to the sky, cloudy and grey, and took a few deep breaths. He grabbed a cloth to wipe his forehead, wishing some rain would cool his burning skin, while Zelshi drank the entire contents of his waterskin.

"My General, you clearly know how to fight," said Zelshi. "I'm not surprised that you beat the War Hero herself."

Valirian's eyes widened slightly, and his attention jumped from one of the captains to the other, not knowing what to answer.

"Have you not defeated Syrela in a duel at the Battle of the Fortress?" asked Akior.

"I wounded her and made her retreat," said Valirian. "However, she was exhausted from the battle, and we did not capture her. It hardly counts."

The two captains looked at one another with a chuckle, and Akior bowed with a wide smile. "My General, I don't think any mortal man could defeat the War Hero otherwise. Had she been capable of using her magic fully, we would be bowing before her instead."

"It was brave, My Lord," said Zelshi. "It earned your men's respect. Well, even more than before. The War Hero is sometimes called by the Northerners 'She Who Has Never Lost a Battle,' a statement true until she crossed paths with you."

Valirian chuckled. That he had been the one to take away that title from her made him smile, yet he knew he might not be so lucky should they duel once more. "Then let it be a reminder to our men of what it is to act when necessary, for that is bravery in essence: doing what is needed, regardless of the danger. It will be a lesson they will need to remember should we ever fight Koresh once again."

The two captains nodded, yet their attention turned to something behind the Advisor. A young man approached them with rapid steps, though the closer he got, the more often he seemed to glance behind. With a few slow steps, Akior went to meet him, and the young soldier stopped himself and bowed low, catching his breath.

"Do you bring any news to us?" asked the captain.

The young man nodded, turning his attention to Valirian. "My General, a courier bearing the Mistian banner says he has news from a group of our soldiers. The sergeant that leads them asks for your presence and said it's important. Something you would be pleased by."

As he turned to his captains, Valirian frowned, yet their expressions betrayed the same surprise. It was no common protocol for a sergeant to ask for a general's presence directly, yet it was no alarm either—the young soldier's message seemed to indicate good news.

The three men exchanged a nod, and Valirian turned to the guard. "Very well. Captains, assist Xilto and Aaposhi in their task. I will return once my attention is no longer needed. If it is a matter that requires your presence, too, you will be informed."

Without another word from any of them, Valirian followed the young man to the northern gates, though as he headed there with rapid steps, the guard was soon forced to catch up. He glanced behind at the training ground. That sudden interruption of his training was no small matter, as he had wished to continue sparring for quite some more time. He expected the sergeant who had dared to call for him to have a very valid reason to do so. It was a bold demand to summon one's general in such a manner. Yet deep in his thoughts, he struggled to establish what could justify such a thing.

Had the news been of Mistport—very unlikely, as he expected the courier he sent there to return that evening rather than so early in the day—certainly, the message would have been different: more pressing and less positive if the city had been attacked or a simple, unimportant report otherwise.

On his way to the northern plaza, Valirian was surprised to meet Xelya, followed by her personal guard, her visage marked by a slight frown. The Queen was ready for any possibility, it seemed, and as they shared a brief glance, it became clear the message had been worded differently when brought to her. She certainly seemed to expect some sort of trouble.

"My Lady, do you know the motives of such an urgent request?" he asked.

"I intend to discover them very shortly," she said.

"I believe there is no reason to worry. Had it been worrying news of Mistport, for instance, the message would have undoubtedly been more pressing."

Letting out a sigh, Xelya nodded, turning her attention to the plaza further to her right. "Let us hope so. Let us hope, too, that whatever the matter, it is worth the disturbance."

The small group continued their rapid march through the street until they entered the plaza. Near the broken gates, a small troop of soldiers waited, a wagon of supplies dragged by two horses following them through. Visibly, the men had not slept for some time. Perhaps they had marched for the whole night. Some seemed wounded. Others had their armours damaged.

Turning to one another, Xelya and Valirian raised an eyebrow before returning their attention to the group. As the two approached, the sergeant leading those men removed his helmet and headed to the wagon of supplies. A hidden stash of weaponry? Weapons left behind by the Northerners in their hurried retreat? Valirian's thoughts raced as he sought to make sense of the situation, and his eyes moved not from the young sergeant.

With a strong, confident movement, the young man removed a large cloth that covered the entire cart. The reveal left Valirian even more perplexed than he was before. Instead of a pile of crates, or perhaps swords and spears gathered in a bunch, there was nothing but a single iron cage. A crazy idea traversed his mind, one the Lady seemed to share as they both once again turned to one another. Valirian felt his heart race as the sergeant hurried to approach them. He recognised him: Cadmael, the young man whom he had put in charge of Fort Seaguard, one of the most promising elements of the army.

He was a tall man, slightly taller than his general, yet his face was round, juvenile, and joyful in spite of the clear fatigue that marked it, and his brown-orange eyes sparkled with excitement as he adjusted slightly his short black hair. In spite of the wound on his left arm, he had his hands behind his back, his chest put forth, and walked with his head held high, a wide smile appearing on his lips as he bowed before the Queen and her Advisor, only a few steps separating them.

"My Queen, My General!" he said. "I am Cadmael, sergeant in charge of Fort Seaguard. I want to apologise for the interruption, but I think the occasion is justified." The young man turned to Valirian and cleared his throat. "And I also know that leaving my post is not wise, but I couldn't miss the opportunity."

"I remember you very well, Cadmael," said Valirian. "The Queen and I are both very much impatient to see why it was such a necessity to interrupt us in our duties." His curiosity on the edge of turning to frustration, he turned his attention to the cage and slowly walked to it.

"Let's not wait any more, then," said the young sergeant. Understanding he had taken enough of their time, he turned around. "Follow me." He took rapid steps towards the cage, soon after followed by Xelya.

They were only a handful of steps away from the cart as both the Lady and her Advisor stopped in their tracks, any smile, frown, or raised eyebrow vanishing from their visages. Xelya's eyes widened as she stood there, and Valirian laughed. From inside the cage, two sparks of emerald looked up.

"My Queen, My General," announced the young man. "I present to you the Blade of Illmeria, the War Hero herself, Lady Syrela."

CHAPTER 5
A TENDENCY FOR STUBBORNNESS

There was Syrela, in the cage, silent and immobile. Although Valirian could not exactly distinguish the facial traits of the mysterious warrior he had fought two nights before, he knew the sergeant's words were true. Still wearing her thick, green gambeson, she sat curled up, her two emerald eyes shining behind the metal bars. She observed, doubtlessly with some apprehension, the scene unfolding mere steps away from her.

"Excellent work, Sergeant," said Valirian. He had been quick to find his composure, or at least it seemed so on the surface—countless emotions collided within him. His heart raced and he felt the urge to laugh and jump, yet his eyes constantly shifted to the cage, looking for any serious wound on the War Hero's body. "There is much we will have to discuss. For now, you may rest. Head to the captains' quarters and show them this ring." From his finger, he handed Cadmael the silver ring set with a single amethyst, the one the Queen herself had given him as a symbol of his new authority in her name. The young sergeant bowed before his general as he was handed the ring, and taking it with great care, he did as he was told.

Xelya, having stayed a few steps behind, seemed finally capable of moving. She had mustered the strength to hide her surprise, her shock, yet the thousands of questions that rushed through her mind doubtlessly rushed through her Advisor's. She approached the iron cage with slow steps. From the gates, a few Illmerian prisoners entered the city: the War Hero's personal guard, certainly. She paid them little mind, quickly returning her attention to Syrela.

"She is deserving of respect," said Valirian. "Let us send her to the Tower's underground, a place more suited for her." His words, though spoken to Xelya in a low voice, seemed to have been heard by the War Hero, as her expression shifted to a frown and her lips pursed. Beneath the Tower, Valirian knew, was a room that was both relatively isolated and rather spacious, traditionally used for prisoners of high importance. Certainly did Syrela ignore the details, however, and she imagined herself sent into a dungeon to be forgotten there.

The soldiers that had followed Cadmael were laughing and joking in low voices, in spite of their exhaustion. Valirian turned to them. "Bring the other captives to the prisons and serve them food. Afterwards, you may rest for the day, though your presence may be required to narrate your story."

A small crowd had gathered around the plaza, though the Advisor's men had prevented any curious spectator from approaching the perimeter too closely. Xelya glanced behind herself. What had to be discussed could not be in public. "Let us return to the Tower. Bring the War Hero with us."

* * *

"What an unexpected turn of events!" she said, allowing herself a laugh as the two had finally entered the dining room. Valirian joined her in her laughter, though unlike her, he took a seat at the large table.

Admiring the mountains for a few moments, still smiling widely, Xelya took a deep breath, regaining her composure. "To think that I had been prepared for the worst. Who could have imagined! This makes our victory all the greater." She turned around and sat, hearing servants arriving from the stairs, though the hint of a smile never really left her lips. "It is still difficult to truly believe."

He agreed with a nod and let out a chuckle, though more at her disbelief than at the situation. All of the Mistlands had been aware of the attack on the Fortress, and Syrela had been wounded and quite severely weakened. For his men to capture her was indeed fortunate but far from unbelievable.

"What should we do with the sergeant, Cadmael?" he asked. In truth, the two of them had already reached the same conclusion.

"It is only natural to reward heroism in some manner, at the very least," she answered.

"Indeed, and our army could certainly use a fifth captain. It would show our men that loyalty and heroism are deserving of a reward."

With the hint of a frown, Xelya turned to her glass of wine. "Let us be careful in that regard. I do not wish for our soldiers to take too many liberties and disobey orders. Rewarding the sergeant's work is only fair, yet let us not allow indiscipline to rule our ranks."

Valirian rubbed his chin. The Lady was more reserved and stricter by nature; he understood very well her wise warning. Soldiers needed to follow orders for tactics to be efficient rather than mask disobedience with heroism in seeking their superiors' good graces. But would that truly be the message such a promotion would give? Had Cadmael truly disobeyed his orders? He had, after all, been given the task of protecting Fort Seaguard and its surroundings. Had he not done so?

"I do not believe that such an issue will arise," said Valirian, "though it is wise indeed to stay careful. Sergeant Cadmael followed orders above all. It is merely a matter of how we portray his actions."

She nodded. His judgement on the matter was worth trusting. "Perhaps it is his young age, and his immaturity, that worried me first and foremost. I do not doubt that, in time, he will be a crucial addition to our army's command. However, I suggest that you mentor him personally, for the time being."

"As you wish, My Lady," he said. There was a slight pause in their discussion, and the two reflected in silence. Valirian imagined all the ways the War Hero's capture might have unfolded; he was certainly impatient to hear the young man's tale. "Even wounded, Syrela is doubtlessly a challenging opponent. Defeating and capturing her is no small feat. I wonder how talented with a blade he truly is." At her lack of an answer, Valirian turned to Xelya. In her glass, she swirled her wine, yet her eyes stared into the distance.

She remembered their disagreement of the previous day on the strategy they ought to follow. She reminded herself of the arguments of either side: a reasonable discussion, but nevertheless inconclusive. "Lady Syrela's capture might be the only victory we ever need over the Duchess."

The statement rang undeniably true. His eyes widened, yet the more he reflected on it, the more obvious it was. She was the Duchess's only experienced general. While it was overly optimistic to imagine Lady Adiloka surrendering at the news of the War Hero's capture, Syrela had most likely proven herself crucial in the war against the Stormians. Her political importance could not be understated either, for she had certainly helped ease some of the tensions within the Northern Alliance. Now the Duchess would struggle to keep the Northlands under her control. Could the unruliness of the Northian nobility be used by the Mistlands?

"As such, I believe your diplomatic approach to be more suited to the conflict," continued Xelya. "It is indeed preferable to use our advantage to expand our influence to the Islands and then use our dominant position to force a favourable treaty from the Duchess."

The Sovereign's sudden change of mind left him speechless, yet he allowed himself a smile after a few moments, honoured by the trust she placed in his ideas. "I believe that our approach should always aim to crown you Queen of a truly united Illmeria. An Illmeria where all agree to see you as their rightful ruler, something that only peace can achieve."

At his words, she raised her chin with the slightest of smiles. It was to be so, doubtlessly: an Illmeria that stood united against their enemy.

"What shall we do with the War Hero?" asked Valirian. Though his mind was not without an idea on the matter, he wished to hear the Lady's thoughts.

"I fear, Advisor, that not much can be done currently," she said. "She must naturally be treated with respect, even if simply for the fact that nobody in Illmeria would allow for the War Hero herself to be gravely insulted, humiliated, or tortured. However, I doubt that she sees either of us in a positive light." Though he had not quite clearly spoken his mind, Xelya had easily guessed his idea, yet she feared for his hopes to be misplaced.

"Let me personally bring her some food after our meal," he said. "Allow me to talk to her. If we sway her in some way, even by earning her respect or her sympathy, it will only be for the better. We are bound to fight Koresh side by side, and even if she never fully supports us, it is better not to keep her as an enemy."

Xelya shrugged. In spite of her scepticism, there was no reason to stop him, for, at worst, he would merely be wasting his time. "Illmerians have a tendency for stubbornness. And amongst them, Northians are the most stubborn, for they live in conditions harsher than most of Illmeria, rarely ever seeing the light of day. Be careful."

He repressed a smile. Amusingly, the warning was fair, and Valirian had many times been able to see for himself the stubbornness of which she spoke, in his troops and in the Lady alike.

"As you discuss with her, I shall ask for Sergeant Cadmael's story," she said. "I shall interrogate his soldiers, too, so as to obtain more details on the matter. It will be a fair test to discover the young man's worth."

"A wise choice, My Lady. I shall join you once my discussion with Syrela is over. Hopefully, I will be back in time for us to make the final decision regarding Cadmael together."

Nodding as to conclude their discussion, Xelya gave a few commands to the servants to rearrange the room in a more suitable way for the official audience soon to be held. The white tablecloth was to be removed and her throne elevated by a few feet of height and moved further back in the room.

Valirian had gone to the kitchen, intending to bring Syrela a meal worthy of her stature. According to his demands, the cooks prepared a traditional Northian meal: wheat noodles served in a broth, with onions, carrots, and thin slices of venison. The Northlands, rougher and colder than the Grasslands, and in great part too forested, had little farmland on which to grow wheat. As such, wheat noodles were considered a luxury—a detail Valirian knew would not go unnoticed by Syrela. Yet it was more than a calculated decision; he felt the need to honour her.

Alone, he headed downstairs to the underground of the Tower, the first time he had gone there. Although he had known of its existence, never had he been curious enough to explore the area, as there was in truth little of interest to be found. It was a rather small part of the whole edifice, a few rooms where some food was stored in colder temperatures. He had only learnt of the cell's existence through his readings over the months, as a Sovereign of the Fortress had arranged its creation for the son of his rival, the ruler of Mistport. That underground, in fact, differed quite significantly from the rest of the Tower in the materials used; the walls and floor were built in the same dark stone as the thick walls of the Fortress, yet the stone had been cut and polished rather than seemingly carved from the mountains themselves.

His hand caressed the stone. Cold, regular, smooth, yet with a few imperfections, it was an admirable piece of work, but one undeniably non-magical. The doors to all but one of the rooms were made of the same wood as the ceiling—the same wood used for the rest of the Tower—a rather comforting feature in its familiarity. At the bottom of the stairs, Valirian entered a corridor perhaps fifteen steps in length. There were five rooms visible to him: two on either side and one at the end. That last room was his destination, where iron bars replaced the wood, a gate with a lock instead of a door with a handle. There was little of note in those other rooms. From the ceiling hung dry, salted meats, and large wooden barrels of alcohol or sacks of grain were stored against the walls. In one were clothes, napkins, covers, anything made of fabric. The only exception was the last room on the left, which was empty yet kept carefully clean. Certainly, its floor and ceiling had been dusted mere days before at most. Valirian headed to the cell door and grabbed the key hanging from the wall to the right of it.

CHAPTER 6

BENEATH THE TOWER

Neither Valirian nor the young woman, sat cross-legged on the other side of the room, uttered a word. Yet she had not pretended to ignore his presence, nor had she looked down at his entrance. Rather, she stared into his eyes, emotionless, her back straight and her chest forth in spite of her wounds. Though Syrela had suffered two consecutive defeats, she seemed unperturbed. Her eyes moved not as Valirian studied her, curious to see what hid beneath the mask of iron she wore in battle.

The paleness of her skin worried him—even for a Northian, whose skins tended to lighter tones compared to other Illmerians, she was particularly pallid. The lack of sleep and food had visibly weakened her. Her oval and regular visage was marked by a few bruises and scratches, a few small cuts scattered on her jaw. At the sight of the food he carried, a frown darkened her expression. Her thin nose gave her prideful look an air of elegance, her dark red lips pursing as he sat across the low table that separated them.

"Have you got no better use of your time than coming here to eat?" she asked.

Valirian placed the bowl before her, not turning his gaze away. As he had hoped, her frown vanished, though she did not immediately begin to eat, and her attention once more turned to him. Only then did he dare look into her eyes, thin and almond-shaped, and stare into the green shine of her irises.

Her aura, though not as perceptible as Tarasmir's or Xelya's, felt strangely more familiar. He saw a shape standing proudly on a hill, a spear in hand. Before it, a cloud of darkness tried to climb uphill yet seemed to stop at the shape's very feet, its presence alone enough to make the cloud retreat, in spite of the cloud's endlessness, for it covered the vast plains below and into the horizon, far beyond what Valirian could see. The little scenery not hidden by the cloud was clear and stable. Above, the sun and moon were in an endless dance, and as day turned to night and night to day in a matter of instants, the shape moved not. Its stare was enough to deter the dark cloud from challenging it.

He dared to look into the eyes of the shape, and a powerful emotion filled his heart, one he felt quite incapable of describing with words. His mind recalled the tales his father told him as a child, of his battles against Koresh, and he remembered the battle of Kashpur, the charge Syrela had led, the hope she had given her men—all of that, it was as if he had relived it in a single second.

He looked away as Syrela briefly glanced at the food before her, then studied from afar the wounds on her body. The damage on her left shoulder and her left flank—the wounds left by his stabs—seemed less severe than he had at first believed, but more concerning was the deep cut on her right leg, as well as another, albeit shallower, on her right arm. It impressed him that, in spite of them, she was still conscious—or alive, even—for she had doubtlessly lost much blood.

Slowly, Valirian stood up, his hands behind his back. He quickly inspected the room. It had been kept clean, much like the other rooms of the underground—only the cushions the War Hero sat on had been dirtied, for her armour was covered in dust, mud, and blood. The room was otherwise minimalistic, for it was a cell first and foremost. There was a bed in the corner, with a mattress and covers, a bedside table next to it, and a chest of drawers.

"You will be treated with respect, and so will your men," Valirian said. "Worry not, you are a fellow Illmerian general and the War Hero herself."

Though with some difficulty, Syrela stood up. Only then did he properly gauge her height: she towered over him by quite a few inches, himself not a short man in any way. Her body was one of a warrior, yet even with her strength, she lacked not in agility: thin, flexible, and powerful, as he had himself witnessed in battle.

"You speak as if you were an Illmerian yourself, one of my people, that I have sworn to protect," she said. "You are nothing but a mercenary at the service of a dangerous queen."

Valirian frowned, yet his only answer was to sit across the table once again, pointing at the food waiting for her. He hid a slight smile as she sat down after a short moment of silence. She untied the string knot of her ponytail, letting her black hair fall loosely on her shoulders, and began to eat, though not without some hesitation.

She had undeniably hit a sensitive spot with her accusation, yet he had forced himself not to react too harshly. He was to tread carefully, both in words and expressions. "I, just as you do, serve Illmeria. I am no mercenary. Greed and lust for power are not my motives. Rather, I fight for justice and to protect Illmeria."

His words made her chuckle, though her lips pursed and she turned her head away from him. "You are one whose tongue is sharp, an opportunist who has an ease with words and uses it to manipulate others and to avoid getting yourself in trouble."

He bit his tongue. About to burst, he stopped himself and instead closed his eyes and took a deep breath. His expression softened, though it lost not its sternness. He leaned towards her. For once, he seemed to tower over her. "I have seen what Koresh has done to this land, War Hero. I know our enemy better than you, in fact. Long before the invasion, I had been a slave in their accursed city, and even before, I was an enemy of theirs." Returning to his original position, he sighed, closing his eyes. He expected her to speak, yet she kept silent.

"I have seen Illmerian villages burnt to ashes," he said. "I have seen innocent farmers slaughtered with their entire families. I was there when Naila was set ablaze—and I saw your heroism on the fields of Kashpur." He reopened his eyes. Unexpectedly, Syrela seemed attentive to his words, though she certainly had some reserve. "Much like all of Illmeria, I, too, rejoiced at their defeat. And for that, I must thank you, personally. Without you, there is no doubt I would still be a slave to cruel masters. You have given me a chance to escape and fight Koresh once more." In spite of her harsh judgement of his character, he allowed not for himself to forget the respect he had for the War Hero. She was the reason he was free.

"If what you claim is true," she said, "then why choose to fight under the banner of such a ruler, who usurped her position by force? And if you were given no other option by the Queen of Mists, then why refuse to side with the Duchess when given the occasion? You are no fool. You and I both know this: without your intervention, the Sovereign would be awaiting trial for her crimes."

He held back a smile. Indeed, it was he who had triumphed that day; without him, there would have been no victory. He leaned forth again. "I suppose you would be correct, in some sense. Without my army's arrival, the Battle of the Fortress would have been yours, yet what legitimacy would I then have in ruling the Mistlands had I accepted your offer? You accused me of opportunism, yet fighting for an oath I wilfully took is more honourable, more just, than the betrayal you proposed."

He shook his head, then leaned back with a slight smile. "I understand why you see things the way you do. Tell me, however, Lady Syrela: who ruled Illmeria as the Koreshians invaded? Who proved powerless before the horrors they committed, incapable of fighting against an invasion on their own soil?

"The Duchess, while undoubtedly a talented politician and a well-intentioned ruler, showed herself unprepared for an invasion once already. What guarantee is there that she will have the wisdom to be prepared for any eventuality? Had it not been for you, there is no doubt that Koreshian would be spoken in Kashpur at this present time." Though his critique was harsh, his words were only met with a frown, far from the anger he had expected Syrela to display.

"The Duchess is the one that gathered the vast army that defended Kashpur," she answered. "Had it not been for her actions, Illmeria would have fallen. The oath you swore blinds you to the truth."

"It is not only by virtue of my oath that I serve the Queen. At the crossroad of Fate, I saw that Adiloka had many times proven her inability to protect Illmeria. She, alone, could have prevented the disaster had she been wise enough to act rather than comforting herself in the traditions that nearly led this land to its doom. If you desire peace, you must stand ready for war—but you know that, don't you? Now tell me, who is better prepared for war: your army or ours?"

She shook her head with a sigh. Her arms crossed, but with a shrug, she looked away.

He smirked for a brief second. "Do you think that a wise and just ruler should attack a rival without first attempting to negotiate? Do you not think that sending her best general in a particularly risky assault in hopes of assassinating said rival—and by using lies and deceit against I, the Queen's Advisor, no less—is what a cold and cynical ruler would do? All of that without even dirtying her own hands!"

She jumped to her feet, suppressing a wince, and looked down at him. "Don't you dare insult the Duchess!"

He was unfazed. They stared at one another until her wounds forced her to sit down. He took a deep breath, letting a few seconds pass. "Do you believe that this assassination attempt was just and honourable? For what else could this assault be? If you had intended to capture the Queen alive to put her on trial, as you claim, you would have acted accordingly when that no longer was an option. In other words, you would have ordered your troops to retreat as soon as my army arrived rather than risking your own life to take down the Sovereign."

"I did what I had to do, given the situation," said Syrela. "Had I known the result in the end, believe me, I would have ordered a retreat. Those soldiers were my men, not yours. Their deaths weigh on my conscience."

Valirian shook his head and let out a loud sigh. "What you had to do? The Duchess's incompetence and arrogance doomed thousands to die, and you defend her character to the bitter end, while the Lady overthrows weak monks who preferred bowing down to Koresh, and you swear an oath to end her life?"

For a moment, he thought Syrela about to jump at him and strangle him—even weakened, she could very well succeed, or so it seemed. Yet she instead took a deep breath. "I took no such oath, stranger. Had you known who the Blades of Illmeria are, you would know that we are permitted to swear but one oath: to defend Illmeria."

"Is this, then, how you view this oath of yours? Leading an assault that did more to help Koresh conquer Illmeria than any of their generals' pitiful strategies?"

"You defend your Queen as if she was beyond reproach," she said. "Yet you and I both know this, and more than anyone else: rulers are inevitably flawed. I chose the lesser of two evils. I fight for Illmeria, above all."

He shrugged and looked down, slowly shaking his head. In truth, he held back a smile. He thought of her answers, then looked at her. Strangely, her expression was neutral, and she raised an eyebrow.

"I believe you when you say you swore no oath to kill the Queen," he said. "And I do believe you are sincere when you say your only oath is to Illmeria. I know you to be honourable. Yet I beg of you to understand me: you did not hesitate to lead thousands of men to their deaths in that battle, men that could have proven crucial for the next war against Koresh. All of that in an effort to kill her!"

She let out a loud sigh and looked down. He saw her jaw clench as she slowly shook her head.

He looked down, too, then stood up. For a brief moment, he considered ending the discussion there and walking out, but a thought crossed his mind. "Or perhaps you did hesitate," he whispered. "And perhaps you were not listened to. I doubt that you, out of anyone in Illmeria, would ever forget who the real enemy is." Slowly, he stood up, taking a step towards the door. "For my part, I believe to have chosen the only path that will save Illmeria. You have seen my men in action, their discipline in battle, and the quality of our weapons and armours. When Koresh comes, the Mistlands will stand ready."

"I fear that your Queen will only bring ruin to Illmeria if her power is allowed to grow," Syrela finally said. "What good is there in a victory against Koresh if we are to be ruled by another tyrant?"

He almost chuckled as he remembered Xelya's warning: Illmerians had a tendency for stubbornness, indeed. While there admittedly was some truth in the War Hero's response, never had Xelya proven tyrannical, beyond her paranoia towards him. With her subjects, she was strict, demanding, sometimes harsh, but never unjust. "What leads you to believe that she is a tyrant? Do you not think that the rumours you might have heard about her could have been twisted, exaggerated, or baseless?"

She shrugged, which made him sigh. She took a bite from the slice of meat in the bowl before her, and his attention shifted to the small window. A shadow would occasionally pass, yet the rather thick glass would distort it, giving the impression that giants walked outside.

He turned to her, and again, their eyes met. He forced a smile before looking down. "That oath I made, to serve and protect Illmeria, was to an old friend of mine. A mentor, who taught me the true meaning of righteousness and justice."

Raising an eyebrow, she straightened her back and placed the near-empty bowl of food back on the table.

"That friend, Captain Ayun, helped me realise the importance of my position," he continued. "That I had a duty to even oppose Xelya and tell her the truth if need be." The Lady's name had escaped his lips, something he had hoped would go unnoticed by the War Hero. But such was doubtlessly not the case, for Syrela's eyes widened.

"After your duel with the Queen, I was given the occasion to take her life," he said. "I will forever remember that moment. She was defenceless, my weapon was drawn, and the thought came to mind. Yet I saw in her a just and good ruler, the one who would bring peace and prosperity to Illmeria. In virtue of that oath I swore to my mentor, I spared her. I have her trust, and she has mine. She is just as essential to the survival of Illmeria as you are. Let us not stay enemies."

She shrugged. "May I meet this friend of yours, the captain you mentioned?"

Valirian's lips formed a joyless smile, making her look down.

"What happened to him?" she asked, her voice a whisper, her eyes not daring to look at him.

"He was the warrior that fought by my side against you." He turned around, hiding a tear from her as he took a deep breath. His eyes

A HOME OF MIST 65

wandered to the walls, the ground, the ceiling. He waited until the pain he felt in his chest was gone before turning to face her. "Lady Syrela, there is one thing I wish to ask you."

The sudden change in tone, his words lacking the assurance that had become so seemingly usual of him, made her raise her head. She expected him to continue, but he seemed uncertain of his own words. "You may ask."

"During your victory at Kashpur," he asked, "did you capture, or kill, the Koreshian general?"

She closed her eyes, sighing loudly as she shook her head. "In spite of my best attempts, his elite forces prevented me from reaching him personally. We never fought against one another, even after I had killed the last of his bodyguards. Once the battle was over and we gave chase, he had already departed the Koreshian camp by ship as we reached the shore."

He looked down and bit his tongue, his fists clenched, yet he forced a slight smile as he bowed. "Thank you."

She only answered with a nod. Both had certainly wished for the answer to be different. She knew not the details, but how could she not understand his desire for revenge after having herself witnessed the Koreshian general's cruelty?

Valirian turned around, called a few servants, and ordered them to fill a bath for the War Hero, as well as to bring her a set of fresh clothes. Soon, he had disappeared.

* * *

Syrela let out a sigh. Valirian was long gone, and so were the servants who had filled a wooden basin in the adjacent room. Surprisingly, he had left the gate wide open behind him. He feared not an escape attempt, but was there any reason to? More than the unlikelihood of success, would she even attempt it in the first place? What outcome awaited her, if not being stuck in the Mistlands, struggling to find the food to survive?

Slowly, she stood up, wincing at the pain in her wounded leg. With every movement, her entire body seemed in agony, yet she got herself to the room to her right. Drawing upon what little strength she had left, she removed her gambeson and entered the lukewarm water.

Her assumptions about Valirian had been proven wrong—or seemed so at the very least. It was difficult to imagine someone unaffected by the horrors of the Koreshian invasion yet capable of so vividly recalling the most horrible of details. "Why must all men of honour be so blinded?"

She sighed and shook her head. There was one thing she felt obliged to admit: the Queen of Mists did not represent the same threat as Koresh, neither in power nor in the destruction she'd unleash. Perhaps the issue was indeed better solved diplomatically; too many lives had been sacrificed in this fratricidal war already. Yet her mind could not find peace, even at the thought of successfully convincing the Queen's aide to negotiate with the Duchess.

What would happen to her home? The war with the Stormians was ongoing; in fact, skirmishes had become more frequent just before her departure. Would Naila, the Northern Star, still stand at her return? Would Adiloka hold on without her help? And what if Koresh invaded at this exact moment? She did not doubt that Valirian would free her, allow her to take up arms to help in the war, but did they stand a single chance against this invading empire?

Her heart raced. She closed her eyes in an attempt to calm herself down, but cold sweat began to pearl on her forehead; the more she sat there, the worse her migraine felt. She washed the sweat away with water, shaking her head, her jaw tightly clenched as she let out a cry and slammed her fist against the wooden basin.

She needed to keep herself calm. All was not doomed, or so she had to hope. Already before had she faced dire situations. She regulated her breathing, her eyes closed, and she relaxed her muscles—yet to no avail. Her heart still raced; her migraine left her not. She had failed those she had sworn to protect, failed in her duties as Blade of Illmeria. She stayed there, immobile, for what seemed like an eternity.

CHAPTER 7
BLACK FLAG AND ESCAPE

"Impressive tale, young boy!" said Xilto.

Cadmael had just finished narrating his story to the captains. At first, they had thought him to be the bearer of some message, yet the sight of the Advisor's ring quickly raised a flurry of questions that he had promptly answered to the best of his abilities. In spite of his sleepless night and his headache, he spoke with passion, as if merely sharing his tale sufficed to fill him with energy. Joking and laughing with him, the captains had invited him to share a meal with them, and so he felt at ease to talk openly and honestly. None doubted that, soon, he would be one of them.

"I can't believe the War Hero is now our prisoner," added Akior. "The Queen and the General gotta be celebrating right now!"

The captains, too, had celebrated, offering the young man some greywheat beer. In spite of its bitter taste, the drink had filled Cadmael with a confidence that had transpired in his storytelling.

"You must be a talented warrior to defeat the War Hero," said Zelshi. "I wonder just how good you truly are." His slight smile left little ambiguity, and all turned to the young man, waiting for his answer.

So far, Cadmael knew, very few had been able to defeat Zelshi in a duel. However, he believed himself to stand a chance. "It wasn't really a fair fight. She had been wounded during the Battle of the Fortress and for some reason did not carry her blades with her. I guess she lost them during the battle, too."

"The Advisor wounded her twice. That's why she retreated," said Xilto. "Still, I wouldn't want to be the one to fight her, even if wounded."

"We have some time before we go back to work," said Zelshi. "Let's see what you've got."

The young man chuckled and stood up. Soon, all five of them had gone outside. Cadmael knew he was far from his peak, tired and having just eaten a copious meal. Nevertheless, it was an offer he simply could not refuse: Zelshi was known as the greatest warrior in the Mistian army. An occasion to compare to him—to be able to hold, or even defeat him, in a duel—was a dream come true.

Without much thought, the captain picked up a practice sword.

Cadmael hesitated. First, his hand reached for a sword, too, yet he reconsidered: the spear, the War Hero's weapon of choice, was also his best weapon. He grabbed a long staff with a smirk, alongside a shorter sword. Even if tired, he knew his own strengths, and he stood prepared, some fifteen steps from his opponent. Looking at one another, they exchanged a nod. Under the eyes of the three others, their combat began.

They whispered a few words amongst themselves as they watched the combatants closing the distance, slowly. Now only ten steps separated them. Zelshi attempted a charge, and so Cadmael dashed to the right, avoiding with ease his opponent's attack. His counter-attack, a swift thrust of his spear, was, however, easily deflected by the captain, who once again stood ready, a few steps away. In this brief pause, Cadmael seized the occasion, attacking Zelshi's legs and dashing to the left, hoping to force his opponent further away. The tip of his weapon slid against the captain's armour, yet it seemed enough to force him back.

Once more, Zelshi charged, yet this time Cadmael deflected his blow and, with the other side of his staff, pushed the captain back. A few swift steps were then enough to create some distance between the captain and him. For just an instant, Cadmael doubted his own strategy, yet Zelshi seemed slower, less reactive, than he himself was. Using the little time he had gained, he dropped his spear, drew his sword, and, with a rapid jump to his left, avoided his opponent's next attack.

Now in closer range, he was the one on the offensive. He smiled as he dashed forth and attacked the captain's right arm, hoping to land a blow that would end the combat. Instead, his opponent's sword hit his left arm, and he cursed. He knew not whether to blame his tiredness or the food he had eaten, yet his movements were clumsy, imprecise. But he would not give up; this was far from over. He thought of being victorious, of the glory it would earn him, and it made his heart palpitate.

He frowned, prepared for Zelshi's next attack. He would not let him win. Defeat, especially if he did not land a single blow, was inconceivable. The captain stepped forth, and at the last moment, Cadmael avoided his weapon. Now was the time! He attacked at an angle, and their swords clashed. The opening was perfect. With a single thrust, he landed a hit on Zelshi's chest.

The captain dropped his weapon, his eyes wide. For a second, he seemed paralysed. Then he chuckled, soon joined in his laughter by his fellow captains and the young man himself. "Never in my entire life have I fought someone who jumps around so much. Look at you, able to beat me even after a long and exhausting night!"

The two combatants bowed as the others approached, though

Cadmael could not help but think back on the duel: too many times had he allowed his strikes to be imprecise or his movements too slow. He might have won in spite of the circumstances, but he had to improve. "Thank you, Captain. It was no easy victory. You even landed a hit on me. I thought I was going to lose at that moment."

With a chuckle, Zelshi placed his hand on the young man's shoulder. Yet all smiles disappeared as a member of the Queen's guard approached the group.

"By order of the Queen of Mists, Sergeant Cadmael is summoned to the Tower. The Queen herself desires to speak with him."

The captains answered with a nod, and Akior whispered a few words of encouragement as Cadmael followed the man back to the Tower. He knew very well he had no reason to fear—certainly the Queen merely desired to hear his story—and he had no reason to feel ashamed either, yet the mere thought of climbing the Tower to meet the Sovereign made his heart race. The general appeared a much more familiar figure, and though he lacked not in discipline and authority, he nevertheless appeared more understanding, closer to his men than the Queen. Why was this air of mystery around her so overwhelming?

Cadmael shook his head. Above all, he would need to speak slowly and clearly. He repeated the story to himself, his thoughts focused on the approach of the War Hero's camp that night, how he and his men had to stay composed as they prepared to attack. Reminding himself of his victory, he smiled and straightened his back. The thought of meeting the Queen still made his jaw clench, yet he would go there without hesitation.

* * *

Finally, the promising sergeant had arrived. He was some twenty steps away from the throne, and beyond a few of his companions, the room was otherwise empty. Xelya eyed him, her visage expressionless. The young man had dared not to look into her eyes, focused on keeping his breath under control, and he bowed low. She repressed a smile: his efforts to appear confident were endearing. Above all, he had been wise not to speak first. Good. In normal times, she would have summoned the sergeant into her office, just as she had done with Valirian a few months prior, yet this new setting, this large and empty room, had something her office could never truly replicate.

"Sergeant Cadmael."

He bowed again. He seemed to hesitate on whether he was welcome to speak. "You asked for me, My Queen?" There was the slightest of stutters in his first few words.

Leaning forth, she inspected the few soldiers who had too been summoned. Nothing unusual: they were young, exhausted, sometimes bruised or wounded, but never anything severe. "Indeed, for I have been most curious about your tale, as it has brought the Blade of Illmeria herself into our custody." She glanced at the door behind the small group. Valirian was doubtlessly still discussing with Syrela. His return could never be too early.

"My Queen," said Cadmael, "we first heard of the siege of the Fortress from the general himself, who took a part of the troops under my command to free the city. With fewer men, I decided to stay ready and increased the patrols in the area, just in case we would catch some survivors during the aftermath.

"Two nights after, a courier on his way to Mistport told me of our victory at the Fortress and that the Northerners were on the run. I told my men to keep their guards up because we did not know exactly how many of them there would be in the region." As he paused, the men around nodded at his words, and so, with a hand gesture, Xelya invited him to continue.

"Then, the afternoon of the next day, one of my scouts reported a small battalion of Northerners headed roughly towards us. He told me that some of them were wounded and that they were led by a tall woman that we all assumed was the War Hero. I thought that, in some way, she planned to escape by sea and that I needed to act quickly. I also thought it was better to try, but have her escape anyway, than to let an occasion like that go, so for the rest of the afternoon, I made four of my scouts follow her from a distance, just to see where exactly she was going. Every hour, one of them would come back and give me a report, and that would allow me to make a decision on when to attack or if calling reinforcements was possible. This lad over there was one of them." He pointed at a young man, short and slender. He was perhaps even younger than the sergeant himself.

Visibly, he appreciated very little the attention, his focus shifting from the Queen to Cadmael as he seemed speechless. "We followed them for hours," he stuttered in a voice barely audible to the Sovereign. "It was easy to hide in the hills and forest." His sentence over, he looked down.

At the sight, Xelya had to repress a smile. "Very well. Continue your story." There were many reasons to be pleased: his tale had, until then, shown some careful planning but also some reserve about taking unnecessary risks—though, she knew, he had not lacked time to embellish the story.

"To be honest, My Queen, I was scared of facing the War Hero in a frontal battle," said Cadmael. "Everyone knows how deadly she is—we have all heard many stories, after all—and at that point, I didn't know she was wounded. So I thought that the best option was to attack at night. We were a bit more than twenty at the fort, and they were maybe ten at best, so we had our chances if we attacked at the right moment.

"They were going to the eastern coast, south of the fort. It's one of the rare areas where the cliff breaks into a small beach, which confirmed that they planned to escape. It was almost night. It was now or never, so I took my men and led them in an assault. Their position was well-hidden, behind rocks and all, but incredibly hard to defend. I think they mostly hoped that nobody would see them. I positioned a few archers on the cliff above them and led the rest in a charge.

"We quickly defeated them, except the War Hero, who took quite a while to beat, even wounded. We were ten on her, and she still killed three before I landed my first hit on her right leg. In spite of that, she continued fighting, but thankfully, she was unable to continue for too long, and from there, we got her under control."

To his right, his second-in-command nodded. Xelya had expected the young man to brag, or exaggerate, yet his report seemed plausible and surprisingly humble. She rubbed her chin as she silently repeated to herself a detail or two, her eyes not moving from the young sergeant, who hesitantly bowed his head. There was something missing, though not something deliberately omitted by Cadmael: if Syrela had attempted to escape by sea, surely she must have possessed some means of transport to rally the Grasslands, other than a small rowing boat or an improvised raft.

"Were there any ships in the creek?" asked Xelya. "Whether they be far away from the shore or being boarded when you arrived."

For a moment, Cadmael stood silent. His eyes widened, and he seemed unable to stay put as he rubbed his forehead. "Forgive me, My Queen. I forgot to say, but as we left, I remember seeing something in the distance. A shape in the mist. I swear that shape wasn't there when we approached their camp, but I feel like a ship was approaching as we left. I didn't stay around to investigate, mostly because we weren't many, and we could have been heard by other survivors. We hurried to the Fortress after the battle because of that." The young man let out a sigh as the Sovereign nodded, his muscles relaxing.

Xelya frowned and looked down, however. The sergeant's story had raised many questions, though she blamed him not for lacking the answers. What exactly was the War Hero's plan? It seemed odd, especially as it had failed, yet it was undeniably imaginative and well-prepared. Regardless, there were huge implications, for if what the young man had said proved to be true, all of Illmeria would soon be aware of Syrela's capture. It sadly meant the element of surprise was soon to be lost. She had intended to keep the Duchess uncertain about Syrela's fate for as long as possible and act in the meantime. Would Adiloka hurry to save her most valuable asset? Did she even have the men to attempt such folly? Xelya clenched her fist at the thought of another battle against the Duchess so soon after the first one. It would be costly—unnecessarily so.

"Forgive me, My Queen, if I made a mistake," said Cadmael. "I thought it correct to take no risks in my position."

Her attention returned to the young man, and she allowed herself a slight smile. "You committed no such mistakes. Such an occasion was not to be missed, though I hope Fort Seaguard remains under our control. You took measured risks and did the crown a great service by capturing the Blade of Illmeria."

Bowing low, Cadmael stuttered as he thanked the Queen.

Yet Xelya's mind returned to the unsolved riddle of Syrela's escape. Certainly, some elements must have been missing. "Do you believe that the War Hero and her men attempted to contact, in any way, the ship in the distance?"

Visibly more at ease, Cadmael reflected for a few moments, exchanging a few words in a low voice with his men. "I think so, My Queen. Further away from their camp, maybe some seventy or eighty steps away, on the other side of the creek, there was a single black flag next to a lone campfire. It might not be much. However, that's all we can remember."

With a slight smile, she nodded; that was all she needed. Unusual, Syrela's plan of escape had the advantage of limiting a large army's chances of capturing her, but perhaps having incomplete knowledge of the region, she had not taken the fort into account. Creeks of that kind were rare in the Mistlands, as most of the coastline consisted of sharp cliffs, and even a slight miscalculation of the fort's true position could explain the events of the past night. Xelya could not blame her for her precaution, however, for most of the Northerners had been captured, and the rare few who had escaped were forced into hiding in the wilderness—hardly a desirable outcome.

Her attention turned to the door behind the small group, and she began to tap her fingers on her throne's armrests. When would Valirian arrive? She had much to share with him, and she also wished to hear the results of his discussion with Syrela. Such situations made her wish for an easy method of communication between them—yet telepathy, the method favoured by mages, generally required both parties to be capable of magic, and in that regard, her Advisor lacked any potential. Beyond his surprisingly developed ability to perceive auras, even with training, he would not even succeed at the simplest of tricks.

Footsteps, coming from the stairs, dragged her out of her thoughts. Hopeful, she leaned forwards and watched the entrance. Cadmael and his men turned to face the door and bowed as their general entered the room with a wide smile.

Valirian bowed before the Queen, then hurried to join her at her side. The two whispered a few words to one another as she quickly narrated the story to him, though she purposefully omitted the details about the ship and the flag.

"Is that all?" he asked with a frown.

"Not quite," she answered, "but we shall discuss the rest in a more private setting."

Nodding, he turned to the young sergeant, who beamed as his general gestured for him to kneel. "The Queen and I are most pleased with your actions, Sergeant Cadmael. You have shown bravery, intelligence, and good leadership. You are officially promoted to the rank of captain."

"Thank you, My Queen, My General," he said. "I swear to serve Illmeria and the Queen of Mists loyally and with honour." He struggled to keep his calm, stuttering slightly as he spoke. Finished, he let out a sigh. With a gesture, the general invited him to stand up, and Cadmael stepped forwards to return the ring to the Advisor. "I will not disappoint," he whispered to his general.

Placing his hand on the young man's shoulder, Valirian nodded. With the Queen's approval, he turned to Cadmael's second-in-command and promoted him to the rank of sergeant. "Very well," said Valirian, addressing them all. "Take your leave and rest for the day."

CHAPTER 8
A MISTRUSTFUL DECISION

Valirian let out a sigh, and Xelya stood up from her throne, taking a few steps around the room; she had been sitting still for far too long. Beyond the two of them, the room was now empty.

"How has your discussion with Lady Syrela gone?" she asked.

He smiled. "It seems she had her doubts about attacking the Fortress. I am rather certain that such a decision came directly from the Duchess, and the political tensions between her and Lady Adiloka have certainly not helped. Sadly, she still is very much hostile, or so it felt. Especially towards you."

Xelya shrugged. The news hardly surprised her. Still, in spite of her scepticism, it could prove worthy of her Advisor's time.

"She lacks the ease with words of a politician, as expected of a warrior like her," he said. "She speaks with surprising honesty and genuinely believes that Illmeria can be saved from Koresh."

"It surprises me not," said Xelya. "Though sending an entire army to their death, the way she did, is hardly adequate preparation for the invasion she claims to fear so much."

He chuckled, though with a joyless smile. He could not help but constantly wonder, how much time did they have before Koresh returned? He bit his tongue and briefly glanced at the set of stairs. "My priority was to change her mind on your person, My Lady."

At first, Xelya's eyes widened, yet her expression soon relaxed into a smile. "Courageous of you to attempt such a difficult feat. Do not bother yourself too much with such things, however. Your time is better used in discussing a truce with the Duchess."

"I beg to differ, My Lady," he answered. "Your actions will prove your righteousness. I may only pave the way, for you hold the power to change her opinion. Let us both visit her, later today, so that you may use your powers to heal her wounds."

Deep in thought, Xelya stared into his eyes. For a second, conflicting ideas threatened to overwhelm her mind, but she brought silence. Earning the War Hero's respect was a political advantage, no doubt, but there seemed to be something more to his insistence. "If you are to fight a battle, fight it to the end. Let us invite her to dinner, too, more than merely visiting her."

Valirian forced a smile, finding himself speechless. He hadn't expected her to be so dismissive of the idea—or had he misread the Sovereign's tone?

Xelya laughed and took a few steps towards her Advisor. "There was no sarcasm in my words. If our goal is truly to change her mind, then let us not stop halfway. There are more than enough occasions for us to discuss strategy privately."

Her words made him think. The idea had seemed too ludicrous to be meant seriously at first, but her argument rang true. "It is indeed a wise proposition, My Lady. However, I do suggest patience. We should give the War Hero some rest, to recover from her defeat, before inviting her. Perhaps it would be more appropriate to wait for tomorrow's dinner."

"Then so be it," she said. "I find it also appropriate to grant her a few liberties: she will have access to my library, and she will be allowed to walk around the Fortress, so long as a handful of soldiers follow her. However, before visiting her, let us discuss a few details." She returned to her throne, and her Advisor sat next to her.

"A few details?" he asked. "I suppose you mean regarding the captain's story?"

She nodded and with a few words explained what she had earlier omitted: the flag, the ship, and her own theory.

"What a strange escape plan," he said. "Why would she give such strange instructions rather than retreating to the original landing?"

"That location is known by our soldiers. I suppose she wanted to avoid returning there. It does imply, however, that she considered the possibility of a defeat, and quite seriously so." Once more, she stood up, inviting her Advisor to follow her as she headed to the stairs. "If it had not been for a fortunate turn of events, as well as an unexpected display of talent from the young captain, Lady Syrela's plan would have been successful, and she would have escaped our grasp."

Together with his earlier discussion with the War Hero, that information only raised more questions, to which Valirian found no satisfyingly certain answers. Had Syrela reluctantly agreed, or had she been sent against her will to the Mistlands? Had she just been particularly cautious, or had she thought it to be a suicide mission? As the two walked down the stairs together, he shrugged. For now, those questions would be left unanswered. A few minutes passed, and few words were exchanged, only some thoughts and details on their incoming discussion.

Her Advisor's slight smile, full of confidence, irked her, though she showed it not. Perhaps, as he had met the War Hero before, he needed not to think much about his words, yet such was not Xelya's case. Her thoughts raced, and as only the long corridor separated them from the

War Hero, she bit her tongue and frowned. She would not allow her uneasiness to show. Her fists clenched, and she walked slowly, forcing Valirian to slow down behind her.

Syrela was sat on her cushion, just as when he had visited earlier, though she wore a fresh set of clothes, and her body had been cleaned of the dirt and blood. She was impassive, immobile beyond her eyes, which met the Sovereign's.

"It is an honour to be able to greet you in person, Lady Syrela," said Xelya. "Allow me to repeat what my Advisor has doubtlessly told you: you will be treated with all the respect due a person of your quality."

The War Hero frowned. For a moment, she studied Valirian before her sight shifted back to the Queen. "All that had to be said has been said. Why come here and bother me?"

Xelya's expression stayed neutral beyond a slight smile as she stepped closer. "There is no need for such rancour between us. It is only right that your wounds are healed."

Syrela moved not as Xelya knelt at her side and placed her hands on her right shoulder. The War Hero closed her eyes as the Queen whispered a few words. Her body tensed, and she bit her tongue, prepared for a pain that never came. As a gentle warmth entered her and filled every fibre of her being, her muscles relaxed, though she kept her eyes closed. Her magic now over, the Sovereign stood up and took a step back, letting Syrela reach for her arm and massage where there once was a cut. She still felt tired, and her body was certainly still sore, yet there was no denying that she had indeed been healed. She reopened her eyes, shifting her attention to Valirian, who stood still, his arms crossed as he leaned against the wall.

"May you rest well, Lady Syrela," said Xelya. "Tomorrow will be a more appropriate time to discuss. Let us not stay enemies, for there is no enemy other than Koresh."

Not waiting for an answer, the two of them left, carefully locking the door behind them as they headed to the small garden outside. There, they parted ways after discussing their plans for the rest of the day. Left with little time, they agreed to oversee various affairs before meeting at the temple directly.

CHAPTER 9

NIGHTMARES OF FIRE IN A GOLDEN CAGE

With a loud sigh, Syrela pushed aside the food she had been given: some rye bread—more common in the Mistlands than the barley bread she was used to—a bowl of vegetable soup, and two slices of braised pork. Though nothing seemed appealing, her lack of appetite was certainly not because the food lacked in quality. Had she not, after all, eaten dry bread for a week when supplies had begun to run low during the Koreshian invasion? She glanced through the small window of her room, beyond the iron bars. The sun had long since disappeared behind the tall mountains of the Fortress, leaving her alone in the world, her only company the weak flame of a candle.

It all appeared a pale copy of the quietude she found in her temple's garden, where, alone, she could meditate for hours unbothered. That temple, her mind seemed to always return to it. The reconstruction should be over by now, yet she was so far away. Would it still stand when she finally returned? She had trained herself to never surrender, never abandon a just fight, and never lose hope. Many times, she had pushed on in spite of the circumstances and the enemies she had fought. It was what had earned her the titles she had proudly borne into battle: the Never-Vanquished, She Who Has Never Lost a Battle. Even in the previous months, as a few setbacks had made her troops lose ground to the Stormians, she had triumphed over them in a crucial battle, and much of what had been lost was promptly retaken. Now those titles made her sigh. She shook her head, trying to repress tears.

How would the war go without her? The thought of Naila's fall made her migraine return. A single mistake and a single defeat had been all it took for her efforts in the north to be annihilated. In spite of their disagreements, Adiloka had often listened to her suggestions and trusted her leadership. Why had she not heard her advice this time? Had it not been for the Mistian forces being split as she arrived, she would have stood no chance; her army was terribly unprepared for a siege of such a scale. The only result had been this unbearable shame and the death of some four thousand of her men. The people had lost its hero; the soldiers, their general; the Northlands, its defender. The Duchess would not succeed in a war fought on two fronts, and things would only worsen should the Koreshians return. It seemed none in Illmeria believed them to be a threat any more. Only Valirian shared her worry, or so he claimed.

"Even if his intentions are good, that changes nothing," she said, sighing again as she stood up. She could not bear staying in this cell. Was there any hope of escape? She had carefully studied the Fortress and its fortifications during the siege. She knew them well, and even with such knowledge, she doubted her chances. The walls were tall, the cliffs of the mountains too sharp, and the entrances were constantly guarded. And even were she to succeed in escaping the city, where would she go? All in Illmeria, from Ilmassar to Asharsaï, would recognise her glowing green eyes, a colour too unique, a glow too recognisable. It would take days, in the best case, for the Mistians to find her again, and that was without considering her chances of crossing the Sea of Mists.

She shook her head, taking a glance at the dark corridor just outside. It was empty. The glow of her eyes might often be a disadvantage, but it also greatly helped her see in the dark—perhaps their only advantage. Her hosts had not been particularly careful. She knew where the key was, and so she easily made it fall on the hard floor, in spite of her tiredness and the effort required to use any magic. It echoed, loud and clear, and she waited for a few seconds. Silence. With a slight chuckle, she brought it to herself and opened her cell. She was thankful that Valirian had the presence of mind to grant her clothes that suited her: a pair of thick trousers and a long shirt rather than a cumbersome dress. Made of linen, her clothes allowed her all the freedom of movement she desired, though she had wished for something slightly warmer for the night.

Slowly, she made her way across the corridor and headed up the stairs.

"Halt!" said one of the two soldiers guarding the entrance. The man blocked her way with the shaft of his spear, and though he seemed surprised to see her out of her cell, he showed no hostility.

"You are not supposed to leave your room, My Lady," said the other guard.

"I am aware," she said. "I do not mean to escape. I simply need to get some fresh air. I can't stand staying in that room for so long."

The two men glanced at one another. Then both nodded. "We'll have to follow you, My Lady," said the second. "But feel free to walk around the garden outside."

She nodded and led the way. Forcing a smile, she took a deep breath. The air was colder than she had imagined, but it mattered not. Her hands caressed a flower bud, and she studied the plant's unusual leaves, surprised by their waxy texture. Certainly, that sort of bush was specifically adapted to the Mistlands and the strange climate here. A few steps behind her, the two soldiers were alert, almost startled by any of her movements. In other circumstances, it would have certainly amused her.

"Are you supposed to allow me so much freedom?" she asked.

"Well, we were not given precise orders," answered one of them, after a few seconds. "But the general told us to treat you like a respected guest, and I don't think you're foolish enough to try and escape."

She took a few steps to a small stone bench in the middle of some bushes. Sat there, she observed the Tower and pointed at its burnt roof. "Tell me, where does the Queen reside since the Tower is so damaged?"

"The Queen and her Advisor both reside in a temple just outside the city," said the guard. "The top floor burnt, so they moved there."

She raised an eyebrow. The Lady and her Advisor had shared the upper floor? She had expected the Queen's aide to have his own mansion somewhere in the city, yet such was not the case—unless that manor had been damaged in the battle, too. And earlier, her name had escaped his lips, something very much uncommon, for even she, the War Hero, did not call the Duchess by her name, even in private. He certainly did have some real influence, for the structure of his army was very much akin to that of the Vinmarans, and his tactics resembled those she had read about in Vinmaran books. If only her influence had been the same in the north! There, the many nobles had turned the affairs of armies and command into a political matter, without mention of the traditionalists who refused to see a peasant take up arms and defend what was theirs.

"Are you volunteers?" she asked the guards.

Without hesitation, both nodded. "Many of us joined the army because of what happened in Mistport. Many of us lived there, or had family there, and when the Koreshians destroyed the city, we fled to the Fortress, hoping to find a leader that would keep our land safe."

"We are part of the Queen's guard," said the other. "We were picked by the general for our loyalty and our bravery."

Slowly, she stood up from the stone bench and headed back inside. "And so, you are paid by the crown, and you do not have any other occupation?"

The soldiers chuckled. "No, My Lady. The general ended the time of the militia. Every man in the army is paid a salary, and every soldier has only one job: to fight for the Queen of Mists."

It was no surprise that, with their land threatened, they had risen to fight and defend what they held dear—she had seen it, too, after all—and it surprised her not, either, that the stigma around a commoner taking up arms did not exist in the Mistlands. However, an army made of professional soldiers, paid and equipped by the crown, was a luxury even Koresh lacked—and something she, again, had lacked the power and support to create.

Once inside, she handed one of the guards the key to her cell, her hunger too pressing to ignore any longer. Finishing her food rapidly, she then headed to sleep, collapsing on her bed. Her thoughts wandered, and she remembered the sergeant who had captured her: Cadmael. Doubtlessly, he was a great warrior, and the thought of meeting her end by his blade was almost appealing, a most honourable death. It would have spared her from powerlessly watching her land fall into ruin as one conquering army or another would eventually cause the collapse of the Northern Alliance.

She was all too aware of her political importance for anyone in Illmeria. The Duchess relied on her, the Queen sought to use her capture to her advantage, and Duke Zheraï of the Stormlands would have done so, too. She stared at the ceiling, empty-eyed, until her body could no longer hold. She fell asleep, her rest troubled by incessant nightmares. There, she would see the streets of Kashpur covered in bodies as Koreshian soldiers surrounded her and forced her into chains.

CHAPTER 10
MATTERS OF AFFINITY

"You may enter, Advisor," said Xelya. Valirian entered; after sharing a meal and taking a bath, they had agreed to read together.

"Advisor, now that the amount of prominent magic users at the Fortress has doubled, I believe it is time for I to teach you the basics of magic in greater detail." With a gesture, she invited him to sit to her right so that both could see the open book on the table before her.

"I suppose that makes me your apprentice, then," he said with a smile.

She laughed and turned to face him slightly. She looked into his eyes, as if she'd get a different result than in the past. "My friend, as much as I wish that such could be the case, I fear I would more easily find fish high in the clouds than magic in your entire body."

The answer made his eyes widen. His mouth slightly ajar, it took a second before he burst out laughing. "I thought so, though I had not expected to be told in such a way."

"Pleasantries aside, those are indeed the tough laws of magic.

Some are born with a high potential, yet for others, magic is a faint whisper, barely audible even with much training."

He nodded and turned his attention to the book. It described what the author had named "affinity."

"There are various levels of affinity, as you can see," explained Xelya. "The lowest affinity with magic allows the mage to manipulate the elements surrounding us. Metal, stone, but also fire, water, and air. Such is the magic that the War Hero uses to manipulate her blades, for instance.

"A stronger affinity allows the creation of those physical elements, though rare are those capable of creating metal or stone through magical means. Rather, those mages often use their powers to create water, or fire, to serve their goals."

"I suppose that an example of this would be the Stormcallers of the Stormlands, correct?" said Valirian. "Warriors capable of using the magic of thunder in combat."

"Indeed, and most magic users rarely develop a greater affinity, whether by lack of practice or by lack of potential. Our knowledge of magic is very much imperfect, and accessibility to the little knowledge we do have is greatly limited."

His attention returned to the book on the table. It amazed him that, in spite of the many Illmerian monks who had dedicated their lives to the study of magic, few had actually written tomes on the subject, and those rare books were also hard to find. Many questions—such as the origins of magic or the reasons a certain being possessed a greater potential than another—were still very much left unanswered.

"Do these questions often cross your mind?" asked Valirian after sharing his thoughts.

"In some ways," she said. "For the origins of magic, it is, in Illmeria at least, often believed to be a gift from Nav himself. It would be strange for the Great Spirit to give such a gift to our enemies, however.

I may not be able to explain everything, but that cannot be all there is to that matter. Were I to possess all the answers, I would understand myself better, yet I have come to accept that not everything will be known and that too much is expected of I to allow myself too much time to ponder those questions."

He nodded. Indeed, he had never, until then, considered that she must not see herself entirely as human. At the very least, she must be thinking herself to be unlike her peers. It could easily be a burden as much as a gift in many regards, and perhaps, too, it explained her fears of the past.

"The most powerful of mages are capable of manipulating magic itself," she continued. "They can use the energy within themselves to cast powerful spells. Those may appear, for instance, as bursts of flames, but the nature of those flames, being magical, renders them inextinguishable by normal means.

"One of the greatest affinities one can develop allows for the manipulation of life itself. Though it does not allow one to bring back the dead from the grave, it holds great power. This is the sort of magic I use whenever I heal your wounds." In truth, that sort of affinity allowed for so much more, in indirect and often unsuspected uses. The magic of influencing thoughts, mind-reading, and manipulation all originated from there—yet on that she shared nothing.

"So, those with the greatest affinity with magic can heal or wound others just like that?" he asked.

"The greatest categorised affinity. Forget this not: mortal minds have a tendency of categorising everything, of labelling everything, for else, we struggle to understand it. We do not create boundaries to magic with this classification, only boundaries in our mind to how much we can comprehend.

"Mages and sorcerers of powers beyond what you have read here have existed in times long past. The Sorcerer-King, a name I know you to be at least familiar with, is one such example. The extent of his powers has been long forgotten, but I know of at least one form of magic beyond what this book speaks of: the capacity to absorb and manipulate the magic not within one's body. Everywhere around us, there is energy. More or less, depending on the place, but that energy is often out of a mage's reach."

He raised an eyebrow. It seemed unimpressive, presented likewise. However, as a frown appeared on Xelya's visage, her stern expression deterred him from asking further questions.

"Lastly, there is more than merely affinity to magic in this categorisation," she said. "There is also a matter of intensity. Some, though only having a very low affinity, are capable of feats unimaginable by those with higher affinity but weaker intensity.

"Think of it like so: if a mage were to create a pebble out of thin air, that would be the second step of affinity, while if a mage were to lift a mountain off the ground, that would be the lowest affinity possible. However, it is quite clear which of the two is the most impressive. That is what intensity is, though of course this example is a mere exaggeration. And once again, mere mortal classification."

Valirian turned the page of the book and briefly skimmed it. Much of what was said there had already been explained in greater detail by Xelya, and so he chuckled. "It seems that this book was not of much use after all."

"Indeed," she said. "I prefer it that way, however. I am certain of what I speak of, and I hope that I made myself clear to you."

CHAPTER 11
"IT WOULD HAVE BEEN MORE BEARABLE FOR HER TO DIE"

The land was still covered in grey, for the pale rays of dawn hadn't yet appeared from behind the mountains, yet Valirian hurried out of bed to get himself ready for the day. "Good, there is more than enough time." Done, he left his room. To his surprise, he found Xelya outside, fully dressed and ready herself.

"You woke up earlier than I expected, My Lady," he said, bowing before her.

"You woke up earlier than I expected, Advisor," she answered, making him chuckle. She had, in fact, been awake for longer than him, although only by a matter of minutes, and had feared having to wait for him. He followed her to the table just outside her room, which a few servants had set there the day before so the two might share meals together more comfortably.

"I will oversee the reconstruction of the Tower's uppermost floor," she said. "I suppose that your morning is already planned out?"

"It is. The army will stay my focus for quite a few more days, as we both agreed that there is little time to waste before we make our next move."

"Indeed," she said. "Advisor, I will ask of you to return to the Tower earlier than usual today. It would be more appropriate for you to be the one to personally invite Lady Syrela. Also, it may be the right time to mention our willingness to negotiate with the Duchess."

"Before we make our next move?" he asked. "Do you not fear that she will see it as hypocrisy if we take over the Islands militarily?"

She considered his remark but eventually shook her head. "The Islands are neutral ground. In fact, the historical claims would suggest that they indeed belong to I. It will be easy to remind both the War Hero and the Duchess of my rights to them. Though we may get a reaction for the capture of Sanadra, quite far north and strategically close to Kashpur, it will be nothing too outrageous."

"I will trust your judgement if you think it does not compromise the negotiations. We stand to gain too much to simply risk everything for a few islands."

"It is merely a matter of not acting in any way that would directly threaten the Northern Alliance," said Xelya. "Sanadra is no minor town. It is worth treading that line carefully for it."

Satisfied with their discussion and their meal finished, they both stood up and headed to the city, where they parted ways to attend to their respective duties.

* * *

"Raise your weapon slightly higher, My General," said Cadmael.

Merely a few minutes after Valirian's arrival at the training grounds, the young captain had already defeated him twice. Had it not been for Zelshi telling him of his defeat against an exhausted and sleep-deprived Cadmael the previous day, the Advisor might have given up on practice that day.

"Are you certain that such small details will significantly help me?" asked Valirian.

Lowering his sword, Cadmael raised his eyebrows and briefly shifted his attention to Zelshi, to the side, who observed in silence. "My General, only practice and the correction of a few details will make you better. I'm in my prime. Do not let my young age and my speed discourage you. I was able to beat that old fuck even without sleep yesterday." He chuckled, and Zelshi joined him in his laughter.

Valirian, too, laughed, though for far different reasons; Cadmael was hardly younger than he. It was his foreign appearance that made the captain think otherwise, but the young man was even possibly a year or two older.

"Alright, let's go!" said Cadmael.

This time, their duel lasted many more minutes, though the conclusion was no different. Still, it was enough for Valirian to feel satisfied with himself. The training continued for a long hour, and though he never won against his sparring partner, it mattered little to him, as he had rapidly realised he would never be the young captain's match. It was enough to know that he had the young man's loyalty and admiration and that he had learnt much from those sessions. Cadmael proved a better teacher than at first imagined, though Zelshi's presence helped the young man in that regard. It was good to surround him with his more experienced peers, and in time, Valirian would personally mentor him.

Their sparring session over, he headed to his office, a small room in the captains' quarters, where a pile of letters had built up as a result of the previous day's activity. The majority bore good news—such as a report from the courier sent to Mistport, confirming that the city was under no threat—and the rare few with any trace of negativity only reported some minor problems. He put the read letters in meticulous piles on his desk, yet the much larger pile of unreads seemed endless. In truth, his attention was less and less needed on the administration of the Fortress; the economy was flourishing, and the military was receiving a sufficient flow of supplies. He could now delegate so that he might focus his attention on matters of greater importance, such as the construction of a fleet. It was a process he had already initiated, just before the beginning of his first campaign, and it would prove crucial for any operations in the Islands. In mere days, the harbour of Mistport could build enough ships to support his army for the next campaign.

"It's noon, My General," Akior informed him.

Valirian glanced through the small window of his office to confirm. Time had passed rapidly. The rest of the letters could wait. In fact, he would certainly delegate the unnecessarily laborious work to some scribe right that afternoon. He remembered that Xelya had asked for him to personally invite Syrela, and he nodded to himself. Thoughts raced in his mind, and he considered all of her possible reactions, yet he felt incapable of reaching a satisfying conclusion for each case. Much rested on how he approached her, and he would be allowed no mistake. Perhaps he was too pessimistic. Perhaps a victory against Koresh was still possible without the War Hero and her support, but he preferred not entertaining the thought too long. She still was their best hope.

Yet in all this affair of diplomacy, what truly motivated them to engage in possible peace talks with Lady Adiloka if not their own gain? Were the negotiations just another tool of power to Xelya and him? He sighed and shook his head. The peace talks needed to happen, no matter what; the siege of the Fortress was a fratricidal battle not to ever be repeated.

"My General, I . . ." One of the guards posted at the top of the stairs hesitated. The two soldiers exchanged a nod as Valirian waited for them to continue. "Lady Syrela left her cell yesterday night. But she didn't attempt to escape."

Valirian frowned, his sight shifting from one of the guards to the other. What nonsense was this?

"I don't know how she got the key, My General, but she went up the stairs to us," said the soldier. "She said she wanted to take a walk outside, and since she was already out, we figured we would allow it but keep watch on her. She returned to her cell after some fifteen minutes."

Valirian's frown vanished, and his eyes widened. He had not been foolish enough to assume that such a simple gate would stop the Blade of Illmeria, should she desire to leave, but the scene described seemed almost amusing. "No doors nor locks can truly hold back the War Hero. This is why you were told to guard her, soldiers. Lady Syrela is to be allowed in the perimeter of the Tower so long as you follow her."

The men nodded and saluted their general. Certainly, they had been unsure of how to react, but there had been no harm done. What good would it be for her to leave the Fortress, anyway? She would not stay hidden forever, even in the wilderness.

As he headed to see the War Hero, he slowed his steps so as to avoid making any noise. The key to the cell was where he had left it, and he opened the gate with great care, lifting it ever so slightly so that it did not scrape the ground.

Syrela was sat on her bed, her eyes staring at the wall before her. Valirian's heart sank. Her skin had grown even paler, heavy eyebags and dark circles surrounding the unmoving green sparks. Was it not for the rare blinking, one could have almost mistaken her for dead.

"Lady Syrela . . ." he said, approaching her slowly. She moved not, as if he did not exist to her. He looked down. For a few seconds, neither moved, until he sat at the end of her bed.

"I envy my ancestors who died an honourable death on the

battlefield," she said. "You are a man of honour and a talented warrior. I should have accepted my defeat that night."

"An honourable death would have meant the loss of Illmeria's greatest defender, My Lady," he said. "Those left behind would only hold on to a memory of what you represent, without your guidance to help."

"Lord Valirian, Illmeria's greatest defender died in that battle, regardless of whether I lived or not. It would have been more bearable for her to die an honourable death."

He sighed, and once more he looked down. That cell, so deprived of light, reminded him of that day at the hands of those pirates of Bloodoath. Only the stench of mould was missing.

"You want me alive because you hope I can save this land from Koresh, but you know better than anyone that I can be defeated," she said. "Because of my own failures, my city will fall and my people will be ruled by a Stormian. If I cannot defend my own home, how can I defend the homes of others?"

He bit his tongue, refraining from shouting. He wished to tell her a thousand words, but none would come out. "Was it not the Duchess's orders for you to come here?" he eventually asked.

She sighed. "It would be all too easy to blame every strategic shortcoming on her. I am not one to do so. It was my duty as Blade of Illmeria to refuse this attack. I am the protector of this land, and in that sacred duty, I failed."

He quieted the storm in his own mind. He looked at her for a few seconds, studying her pale visage. "A few years ago, a young boy departed Vinmara on a quest for justice and with dreams of glory. He left to follow in the footsteps of his father, who died an honourable death in battle."

She frowned. Such was hardly an appropriate time for a fairy tale. Yet, about to speak, she understood. She leaned forwards, waiting for him to continue.

"Without guidance, it did not take long for him to meet a fate none would envy," he said. "Slavery to Koreshian masters. An absolute dishonour and humiliation for a young Vinmaran noble. Having seen the Koreshian war machine in action, he had given up all hope. Worse than slavery, he would have no other choice but to willingly serve his masters. Yet a bright light, like no other, came from the hills, and her bravery alone sufficed to give him the hope for justice he had long lost." He fell on his knees at the side of the bed, his eyes staring deep into hers. Long seconds passed. "Lady Syrela, all hope is not lost. I beg of you, do not give up. The fight against Koresh is not over, and we may still win it!"

She turned her head and sighed, wearing a slight frown. "Do you think I would have triumphed had the spirits not smiled upon me that day? My dishonour is great enough. I will not add to it by joining the Sovereign, as you wish me to, even if you claim there is no other way to defeat Koresh. Do not mistake the respect and sympathy I have for you as approval. I have more than enough reasons to be loyal to the Duchess."

He stood up and took a deep breath. He needed to contain himself. Was his anger even truly justified? Deep down, it had indeed been his hope that she would join the Queen and him, though he doubted he would succeed, but with the War Hero's support, the Mistlands would indeed be unstoppable.

"Forget loyalty, forget this matter of honour, forget those petty disagreements," he said. "This is a fight for Illmeria so that those who come after us may have hope!" He turned, his arms crossed as he stared at the wall. "The Queen and I have decided to negotiate with the Duchess. There is one thing, above all, that unites us. So let us not compromise all of Illmeria for a matter of internal rivalry."

Slowly, she turned to face him, studying him for a few moments. "You and I are the only two in Illmeria who seem to truly grasp the imminent threat of a second invasion. Yet here we are: you are merely an Advisor, and I am a prisoner in a land far away from my home."

"Yet we both have the ear of our lieges," he said. "Do not give up. We may convince them to cooperate in spite of their stubbornness."

Her lips gave the hint of a smile, and she nodded.

"Let us be hopeful, else we have nothing," he continued. "You have my word: I will do all I can to ensure that we negotiate a truce, arrive at an agreement, and that neither of our sides sheds any more Illmerian blood until the war against Koresh is truly over."

She straightened her back and sat on the edge of her bed.

"I hope that this agreement lasts and that no war is needed even after our victory against Koresh," he said. "But if we must meet once more on the battlefield, and if I must meet my end by your blade, so be it. A man can only run from his destiny for so long. For now, let us rather work together." He offered her help to stand up, and she reached for his hand.

She massaged her forehead, as if it would alleviate her painful headache. "I barely slept last night. I fear for Illmeria. Should Koresh invade, it would be a matter of weeks before the Northlands are burnt to the ground. The Duchess stands no chance. Our enemy won't repeat the same mistakes twice."

About to speak, he stopped himself; he needed to tread carefully. "From what I saw, Illmerian soldiers were under-equipped and under-trained. As a foreigner, I was quite surprised to discover that Illmeria was quite some time behind both Koresh and Vinmara in terms of weaponry."

She nodded. She knew those to be problems but had lacked the ability to put forth any of the solutions she had imagined. "Illmeria is not a nation of warriors."

Such a statement was true even for the Mistlands. In the Stormlands, the "warrior caste" simply included many more than in the rest of Illmeria. Yet what she had witnessed in the Mistlands, this army, trained and organised by Valirian, reminded her of tales she had grown up reading and admiring, the tales of the Mistian revolt that overthrew the malevolent Sorcerer-King. They were doubtlessly a proud and strong people, a people that even a powerful tyrant with magical powers had not been able to suppress into slavery.

"Lady Syrela, my first intention was to invite you to our table," he said. "The Lady and I thought it to be more fitting." Her sight shifted around the room. He easily understood her hesitation, so he bowed his head slightly, waiting for her answer.

"I accept your invitation, Lord Valirian," she finally said, forcing a slight smile.

He chuckled as he led the way. "I am no lord, though I am of noble blood. Simply call me Valirian." He had not expected her to accept the invitation, yet it was an undeniable relief that she had. Though she was still very much pale and tired, there seemed to be a new glow to her expression, a heart-warming sight.

He went up the stairs with his head held high as Syrela followed him closely. That day had been an important step for Illmeria, and though much remained to be done, he couldn't hold back a smile. Certainly, he needed to temper Xelya's approach somewhat, for she would seek to defend her own interests above all once the time for negotiations came, but he doubted not his ability to do so.

CHAPTER 12

A PAWN'S WORTH

The food had been served for quite some time already. Where exactly could Valirian be? Xelya tapped the table's edge with her fingers, her eyes constantly shifting from the food before her to the entrance of the dining room, and she took a deep breath. Her Advisor could certainly be stubborn, too, on occasion; he indeed fitted Illmeria. She leaned back in her throne with a slight sigh. Food was not a matter of the highest importance, after all.

Finally, footsteps reached her ears; the time had come. With a slight smile, she stood up, more proper to welcome her guest, displaying her most regal dress of fine black and purple silk. "Welcome! Please, take a seat."

The slight nod that Valirian gave served as a sufficient apology, so she returned to her throne and invited them to begin their meal as they so wished. "I am pleased to see that you have accepted our invitation, Lady Syrela." Bringing her glass of wine to her lips, she seemed unbothered by the War Hero studying her expression.

"Just as your invitation had a motive, so does my agreement to it," answered Syrela. "Your Advisor has spoken of possible negotiations between the Duchess and the Queen of Mists." The War Hero's sight promptly shifted to Valirian, who seemed to be content letting the Sovereign answer.

"Do not mistake the honour I judged fit for the Blade of Illmeria for cold cynicism," said Xelya. "Though I indeed intend on making an offer for a truce with the Duchess so that a common ground may be found." Syrela's directness had been unexpected, though far from shocking. There was a certain honesty to leaders of men that was undeniably pleasant. Xelya saw Syrela's attention shifting to Valirian, then the plate of food before her. "I merely thought the time to be right to finally hold a conversation with you, War Hero, who seems so quick to judge me."

"I will hold my judgement for the time being," said Syrela. "It is not my duty anyway. I simply hope that my presence here can help make those negotiations happen." Lacking any visible response from the Sovereign, she shifted her attention back to the Queen's aide, yet she closed her eyes and took a deep breath. "I am no fool. I know most of the attention will be on me during the peace talks. The Duchess will want my return, and you will negotiate me to the best of your abilities. If you are, however, genuine in your intentions of saving Illmeria, then let me ask this: there is much more than my freedom on the line, to me, as a personal matter. The Northlands is my home, and Naila, my city. I do not trust the Stormians, nor their Duke, and I fear for my land. If you find it within yourself, then consider making a concession so that I may defend what I hold most dear."

Xelya glanced at her Advisor, who gave her a slight nod. "Be reassured, Lady Syrela, our intention is to release you. We have no more reasons than you to risk the safety of the Northlands, whether in case of a Koreshian invasion or from any other threat."

Syrela nodded, her eyes still closed. She held back a sigh, then turned her attention to the red liquid in her glass. Wine was uncommon in the Northlands, for grapes in Illmeria only grew in the Grasslands—never had she tasted any alcohol other than barley beer. Slowly, she brought the crystal cup to her lips. The perfume was pleasant, though quite strong, reminiscent of so many aromas, familiar yet indescribable. She took a sip, finding with much surprise the taste milder than the beer she had grown to despise in the Northlands, though she frowned at the sensations.

"Does My Lady not drink?" asked Valirian, raising an eyebrow. "Let me ask a servant to bring you something else."

"No need," she answered. "I had not expected the taste, but it's far from unpleasant." More accurately, however, she did not want to seem impolite—nor did she desire to explain her hatred for beer, the only drink she and her men had available during some of the rougher days of the Koreshian invasion.

"I suppose you don't intend to sit idle at the Fortress as you wait for the Duchess's answer," said Syrela. "What are your plans in the meantime?"

"Do the best we can to prepare our army for the war to come," said Valirian.

"We also intend on restoring order on the Islands," said Xelya. "Banditry and isolation have been issues that have plagued the region for far too long."

Though the Queen's honesty was unexpected, Syrela showed no reaction. It was Xelya's openness, more than her plans, that left her without an answer. The Islands, sparsely populated and far away from the Grasslands, were, after all and for the most part, seen as an extension of the Mistlands by the rest of Illmeria. The only concern was Sanadra: the city was dangerously close to Kashpur and provided a perfect naval base should the negotiations fail or the Duchy of the Pearl otherwise enter a war against the Mistlands in the future.

"We intend to ask for parts of the Grasslands," said Xelya. "I aim to make the Mistlands fully independent from the Duchess. Therefore, we need to secure a sufficient supply of grain for my people."

The War Hero's eyes widened, and she studied Xelya's expression. Was the Queen testing her reaction? "The Duchess will never accept ceding land," she eventually said.

"Then I hope the war against Koresh makes her see reason. The Mistlands will account for most of the steel production for the Duchess's army, and I have no doubt my soldiers will prove crucial in battle, too."

Syrela shrugged. It was no use discussing the matter much longer. In the end, Lady Adiloka herself would make the decision—unless the Mistlands were to force her hand through war. "Let's hope that a compromise can be found regardless."

They soon after finished their meal, and little more was said. Syrela returned to her cell, though she was allowed to pick a book from the library, to keep herself occupied for the day.

"She knows that our demands might make the Duchess heavily reliant on our economy," said Valirian.

"Indeed," answered Xelya.

He turned to her and looked down. He had much to say, but it seemed as if no words would escape his mouth.

"Yes, Advisor?" she asked.

"My Lady," he said. "For the good of Illmeria, we should accept Lady Syrela's request. As in showing goodwill by freeing her."

Xelya frowned, and she leaned forwards. Visibly, she expected him to continue.

"She is a major asset in the negotiations, and I believe that Your Grace, a better diplomat than I, will certainly find ways to obtain a favourable treaty from the Duchess," said Valirian. "Yet I can only understand Lady Syrela. Let us not risk her ire by holding her here against her will too long, while her homeland is in grave danger."

"Is it by mere calculation that you suggest freeing her?" asked Xelya.

Valirian shook his head, which made her eyes widen. "I will not lie to you, My Lady. She has my sympathy. I need not remind you that I owe her my freedom as much as I owe you. Additionally, she is a fierce warrior. If the Duke of Storms reveals himself a threat to us, or if the Koreshians are to invade, her presence on the battlefield would play in Illmeria's favour."

"Then let us hope that Lady Adiloka is not too stubborn," said the Queen. "It would be hardly reasonable for I to simply relinquish one of the greatest advantages in my favour out of mere sympathy."

He nodded. Her reaction surprised him little. How could she be blamed for defending her—and her people's—interests first and foremost? The centre of power in Illmeria had always been Kashpur. The Mistlands, in comparison, were hardly ever considered of any importance.

"Advisor, how much time until you believe your troops and yourself ready to depart to the Islands?"

"A matter of weeks," he answered. "Maybe two or three, for a few more vessels need to be built."

"Excellent," she said. "There is much left for us to do, then. Let us return to our duties."

CHAPTER 13
THE EMPEROR'S SHADOW

"Your tea, My Queen." The young servant brought the kettle and a box of leaves to the low table and left.

Xelya was alone. Things felt colder that night, the first she would spend at the Tower rather than at the old temple. Her Advisor would not quite yet return there, even though she had rearranged the rooms with him in mind. Indeed, he had left, earlier that day, for Mistport, where he would depart with his army.

Taking a few leaves from the box, she placed them in a small pocket of fabric, which she then submerged. Tea-making was an activity she never left to anyone else, not even her most trusted servants, for she found something strangely calming in the simple process, and her delicate taste never seemed satisfied by anyone else's. She brought the cup to her nose, breathed in the subtle aroma, and opened a book.

She sighed. Reading now felt different; she had become all too used to her Advisor's company. She shrugged and closed it. She would allow herself to go that day without her usual reading.

Eight hundred men had followed Valirian, a number in itself impressive, but she had been left speechless when he had informed her that those men only accounted for about half of their total troops, and that did not include the recruits still being trained. They would near three thousand men in a matter of weeks, so long as Aaposhi and Xilto faced no particular issues and so long as the production of weapons and armours could proceed apace. Zelshi, Cadmael, and Akior had all three followed the Advisor, as their presence was hardly needed at the Fortress, yet their absence helped not in this odd sensation of emptiness that seemed so omnipresent now.

"Too hot," she whispered as her lips touched the liquid, putting down the cup on its small plate. Next to the plate were two silver pendants, a small purple diamond set in each. Carefully, she took one in her hands and studied it. It was precisely what she had asked for. She had given one of the smiths the task some twelve days ago, just after Valirian and she had dined with Lady Syrela for the first time. Now was not quite the time—she was too tired anyway—but they would certainly fit the idea in her mind.

She glanced to her right and stood up, observing the city from the balcony. The sun was hidden behind the mountains, though it had not quite disappeared behind the horizon, painting the cloudy sky orange. Could it really be so late already? Footsteps, from the stairs, made her turn around.

"My Queen," asked a young woman, "how many shall we serve for dinner tonight?"

Xelya glanced at her. "It will be Lady Syrela and I only tonight."

The servant bowed and left without another word. Xelya glanced at her tea, and she once more tested its temperature. Slightly too hot for her taste, but cold enough not to scald her tongue. She drank the cup's contents. Valirian had insisted that she frequently dine with the War Hero, and though she doubted it would have much impact, she had agreed out of politeness. She had some time before having to head downstairs to the dining room, but even if she needed to be early, she felt no need to hurry there. Whereas her Advisor had seemingly earned the War Hero's respect, Syrela could be tiresome on occasion, in spite of her attempts at hiding her mistrust. It was good that, at the very least, Valirian had her respect, even if Xelya couldn't deny that a thought, on occasion, traversed her mind and briefly worried her about her Advisor's loyalty.

She shook her head. Her trust could not be blind, but she could not allow herself to fear and doubt him baselessly.

* * *

Dinner was served. The smell of grilled fish soon filled the room with its pleasant perfume. Leaning back in her throne, Xelya moved not her eyes from the entrance. It was simply a matter of time before the War Hero arrived.

"Good evening," said Syrela with a slight bow.

"Good evening, Lady Syrela. It is always a pleasure to have you at my table. Please take a seat!" Oddly, in Syrela's refusal of unnecessary and forced politeness, there was something that put Xelya at ease. The War Hero's lack of a smile was, in itself, an honest answer. "The courier with the letter destined for Lady Adiloka has left today, with my Advisor. Let us hope that the Duchess's answer is quick to arrive."

"Let us hope so indeed," said Syrela. "Though forgive my impoliteness, but for what reason has it taken so long for a mere letter to be sent?"

"Apologise not, Lady Syrela. Your concern is only fair, though the reason is quite simple: until recently, we had no ships ready to be sailed."

"Is Valirian also crossing the Sea of Mists to deliver the letter?" asked the War Hero.

"My Advisor has gone to the Islands with my army. His campaign there should not take long, hopefully no more than two weeks. His presence would be appreciated at the negotiations."

Syrela nodded in agreement. It was too important of an event for him to be absent. Yet the War Hero smiled as she once more turned to Xelya. "I must say, I did not quite believe the rumours of the Queen of Mists taking a foreigner as Advisor at first. He must have asked a high price, given his knowledge and skills."

"There is something quite inexplicable in that regard," answered Xelya. "He seems very much uninterested in money. I twice offered him a large house to live in, in the centre of the city, but each time he refused." Syrela's eyes widened, and Xelya nodded.

"Then did he just offer his services to you?"

"In some ways," said Xelya. "He had been captured by slave traders, and when my men caught the bandits, they mistook him for a Koreshian soldier. He proposed his services for me to spare his life, though I had no intention to take it from him." Syrela seemed to reflect for a moment, and Xelya studied her closely. What could leave her so thoughtful?

"How did he then arrive to Illmeria? Certainly those bandits did not capture him in his homeland."

"Has my Advisor not told you that himself?" Xelya found it hard to believe that such an important matter—his time of slavery in Koresh—would be left out of any of their discussions.

Syrela seemed unsure. "I do not believe so. Or perhaps he alluded to it, but I forgot."

Xelya repressed a smile, as she understood the War Hero's intentions.

"I had imagined he would have told you, out of anyone, for he was one of the Koreshian slaves that escaped captivity after your victory at Kashpur. It was by mere misfortune that he ended up captured, once more, and brought to the Mistlands." As the War Hero only answered with a nod, Xelya allowed herself a chuckle. "I first tasked him with administrating the iron mines of the Fortress. Then, as he proved his talents everywhere he seemed to go, I eventually concluded that he deserved to become my Advisor."

"Understandable," said the War Hero. The Sovereign leaned in her direction with the hint of a smile, gazing directly into her eyes. Syrela raised an eyebrow, feigning surprise—yet her heart was racing, and she bit her tongue.

"Lady Syrela," said the Queen, "I fear you to be a poor liar. Honesty and directness suit you far better."

The War Hero stayed completely immobile for an instant, though she eventually frowned, daring to meet the Sovereign's eyes.

"I know my Advisor," said Xelya. "He has doubtlessly told you what I have just told you. Likewise, I find it hard to believe that you would be so unsurprised by him being a former Koreshian slave, especially if he owes you his freedom." Xelya straightened her back, wearing a slight smile. "I suspect that you merely did not trust his story and, as such, tried to find confirmation. Quite foolish, for if he had indeed lied to you, he would have at least informed me of it. But such lies would not last for long, as it would be too difficult to keep such a web of lies consistent. Thankfully, any of our veterans can confirm the story."

Syrela looked down for a moment but then chuckled, though without a smile. "Do not dare accuse me of lies, Queen of Mists. Nothing I said was untruthful, even in my quest for confirmation."

Xelya nodded. Perhaps she had been too harsh in her words. "Forgive me, Lady Syrela. I meant not to accuse you." Slowly, she stood up, taking a few steps towards the window behind her throne. Night had fallen on the city, only the dancing light of a few lanterns outside. "Likewise, nothing of what either of us said was untruthful. He indeed was a runaway slave, once more captured by bandits and freed by myself."

There was a strange expression on the Queen's visage as she sighed. Syrela, though still sat on her chair, turned to face her. "Is it true, then, that your life was in his hands during the aftermath of the battle two weeks ago?"

Xelya froze. She frowned and clenched her jaw, but she shook her head with yet another sigh. How could Valirian share such information—with a rival, no less? She turned to face Syrela, her fists clenched behind her back. "He spoke the truth, though I had wished for him to keep such a story to himself. I will make sure to obtain an explanation from him. In time." Telling a lie had crossed her mind, but she refrained. "What did he tell you?"

"That, after the battle, he could have taken your life. That he had the occasion if he had indeed judged you a danger, but he had chosen not to," explained Syrela.

Xelya felt her muscles relax, and she nodded slowly. Perhaps she had reacted too quickly. But her eyes widened. What if she did share the story in its entirety? What would the War Hero find to say? "We may trust one another now, but such was not always the case. His rapid rise in popularity made me doubt my choice to grant him any responsibilities, and one of the reasons I made him my Advisor was precisely so I could keep him under control and closely watch his every move.

"That made him fear being truthful with me, and I trusted not his intentions. Our rare disagreements never ended constructively. I suppose he grew tired, or began to think his life at threat, and that day, after the battle, he decided to act. As he said, he could have ended my life. But he chose not to. By doing so, while I was powerless, the perfect occasion to seize power, he proved his loyalty." Xelya returned to her seat, closer to the War Hero. "I know, Lady Syrela, that though you have kept your judgement for yourself, you condemn my rise to power—amongst, certainly, other things. Yet he, who has served as the highest and most powerful person in my realm, who knows my intentions and goals better than all, condemns me not."

Syrela shrugged, and for a moment, she seemed to reflect on the Queen's words. "Does he perhaps ignore that you seized power by overthrowing your very own masters? Such is not the way of rightful rulers. And what, other than actions, should one be judged on?"

The War Hero certainly expected anger, but Xelya would show none. Or maybe Syrela would imagine those words to make her reflect on her actions, as if she had any reasons to feel remorse for those fools' fates, for Xelya stayed silent for a long minute. "Amusingly, he is the only one to know the truth. Though there is still much I have not told him."

"You would claim that their death was necessary and that you did what was needed," answered Syrela.

Xelya shrugged. Why be bothered by this scepticism? Her thoughts wandered for a moment. Only after another minute did she turn her attention back to the War Hero. "Lady Syrela, as a magic user, I suppose that you are familiar with the more theoretical part of magic."

Syrela nodded, though with a frown.

"You have then certainly read some of the treatises on the matter," continued Xelya. "Including the more obscure conjectures that our knowledge is limited and affinity only reflects what we have been able to observe for certain."

"It is oral tradition in the Northlands," answered Syrela. "The most powerful wizards of old could manipulate magic outside of their own bodies, and we, the Blades of Illmeria, descend from one such wizard."

The Sovereign nodded but said no more. Syrela reflected, then sighed loudly and rolled her eyes. "You are not suggesting that a few senile monks at the top of a tower had developed such an affinity, are you?"

A laugh escaped Xelya, and she shook her head. "With what you claim to know, you must as well know that the most powerful mages of the ancient times could absorb the magic within others, as well, and gain power that way. They certainly would have been more than just a few senile monks, had they been able to."

As the Queen stood up, Syrela clenched her fists and bit her lip, ready to jump from her seat. Was the Sovereign threatening her? Yet the Lady instead closed her eyes and lowered her head. What had so suddenly overcome her? Syrela relaxed and stood up, though with a deep frown.

"You have certainly also heard that the Emperor of Koresh is a powerful sorcerer indeed," said Xelya.

Syrela nodded. Suddenly, her eyes widened, and thoughts raced in her mind.

"I see that you begin to understand the implications," said Xelya. "You will doubt my words—that is no surprise—and I will admit, I have no proof that Lord Tarasmir indeed is capable of such a feat, but I will take no risk, though I have to ask of you one promise: do not inform Valirian of it. I doubt much good would come from him learning this. That is the only detail I intentionally kept from him."

Slowly, Syrela nodded. "You have my word, but why keep it from him?"

Xelya shrugged. "As I said, I doubt much good would come from it. It would make him worry for no good reason. For the possibility to become an issue, it would require our absolute defeat against Koresh anyway. He is very much uneducated about magic, though I have taught him some of the basics. Trust me, it is better that way."

As to reaffirm her answer, Syrela nodded again.

"Very well," said Xelya. "Then let me explain my reasons and why Tarasmir is relevant to the matter. The monks planned on making a deal with the Koreshians: to trade me in exchange for sparing the city."

She told Syrela about her rise to power and spoke in great detail of her mentor's death, the presumed assassination of his successor, and the conflicts between the remaining monks and her. To Xelya's surprise, she found in the War Hero an attentive ear, whose eyes were riveted on her, and not once was she interrupted.

"What makes you think they would have succeeded and traded you to Koresh?" eventually asked Syrela, the Lady's story now over.

"I imagine they misjudged my power. I cannot say for sure. It is not as impossible as it seems, however. I caught them unaware when I attacked them in the council room."

Syrela looked down, staring at the table.

Xelya sighed, shaking her head. "Lady Syrela, I do not claim that no other solution was possible. I could have run away, for instance, but would that have been the right thing to do in such times? I do not claim with certainty, either, that Lord Tarasmir knew of my existence and sought to absorb my power. I am merely saying that such was a possibility.

"Lastly, I do not claim that I seized power for absolutely selfless reasons and that I never intended to rule. I believe myself to be the rightful Queen of Mists. Yet my actions are not as unjust, and unjustified, as you seem to think."

Syrela walked to the open window and glanced at the city below. Her hands behind her back, she felt her jaw clench. Suddenly, she turned around and gazed into Xelya's eyes.

For long minutes, both stared into one another, searching for something, anything, that could be unearthed in the other's aura.

Eventually, Syrela sighed. She had found nothing of note, and most certainly neither had the Sovereign. Her mind was flooded with memories, rumours, echoes. She looked up once again. "You have given me much to reflect upon, Lady Xelya. Perhaps, though, I misjudged you."

CHAPTER 14

WISHFUL THINKING

The sky above was clear, and the farmlands before Valirian were flat and vast. Those were perfect conditions for his army. He smiled, studying the horizon just a little longer. It had been ten long days since his departure from the Fortress, both exhausting and exciting, for the deployment of those eight hundred men on the Islands had brought a wide array of unexpected challenges. As a response to piracy and banditry, various local lords had risen up and sworn to defend their land—hardly more than a handful of villages in most cases. Often, at the sight of the Sovereign's army, those lords immediately submitted. Sometimes, they asked for a local group of pirates to be dealt with, but none were foolish enough to attempt resisting for the sake of a worthless title.

"I can't believe we're almost done," said Cadmael. "I thought it would take us at least two or three more weeks."

Valirian chuckled. "It seems that we may return home earlier than expected." Truth be told, he, too, had been quite surprised by their efficacy. The campaign had been relatively peaceful and little blood had been spilt, for most of the locals saw in the Queen of Mists and her men liberators rather than conquerors, which allowed him to split his army more than he at first imagined. He was originally reluctant to send the young Cadmael on missions alone, but the new captain proved more than capable in his various tasks, quick to learn from Valirian or from Zelshi and Akior.

There was one last target for his army, and all he awaited was Zelshi's arrival. The captain was to rejoin the main army sometime in the afternoon, and together, they would march north to the city of Sanadra, the only major city in the Islands. It was closer to Kashpur than it was to the Fortress, and that in itself explained both its importance and the possible challenges to be encountered. Perhaps the Duchess had sent some soldiers to defend the city.

"My General!" said a scout. "Captain Zelshi and his men are here."

"Perfect," answered Valirian. It was still early in the afternoon, and maybe a few hours separated them from the city. If conditions were as favourable as they appeared, they might reach it before the end of the day.

"My General," asked Cadmael, "can we really capture a city with less than a thousand men?"

"The cities of the Mistlands and the Stormlands are unlike those of the Northerners," said Valirian. "They do not have the tall and thick walls of the Fortress or of Mistport."

"Do they not need them?" asked the young man. "They would fall in a couple of hours to any army!"

"Precisely. Wars in those parts are extraordinarily rare, and in their rare occurrences, battles happen outside of the cities, and the defeated side must accept the winner's conditions." The prospect of battle rejoiced him not, especially as he would expect the defenders to fight in the streets rather than outside in an open field, risking many innocent lives. Times had changed, he feared. The Koreshians had broken many delusions. "Hopefully, negotiations prove a more efficient weapon today than the sword." He turned his head. Down the hill, to his left, Zelshi approached on his horse, his men having rejoined the main force.

"My General," said the captain with a bow.

"You are here earlier than expected," said Valirian. "Good. Let us not wait a minute, and we may reach Sanadra before nightfall."

The captain nodded, and at his general's command, all began to march forth. In the distance, on a hill to the north, one could see the city, just a few hours away.

"Is the plan just to surround the city and then prepare an attack if they refuse to surrender?" asked Cadmael.

Valirian shook his head. "I doubt a thousand men would be enough to surround a city of such size. But we should still be able to intimidate them with our approach." No matter the words he told himself, he lacked the heart to fight a battle in the streets of the city, and he knew his men would, too. The Battle of the Fortress had been different. Sudden, unexpected, forced. They had defended their homes, and perhaps it had been the Northerners who had lacked courage instead.

"A fair warning to the citizens once we arrive should be enough," said Akior.

"Such was the plan, Captain," said Valirian. "I hope to be faster than the Duchess, however. If only the War Hero's capture could have been kept secret a little longer!"

Their discussion ceased as they entered the farmlands around the city. Strangely, the farmers and peasants fled not at their approach, nor did they celebrate their arrival. It was indifference and curiosity. Certainly, they had heard rumours of the Mistian army approaching, yet what exactly went through their minds as they eyed the columns of soldiers passing through? Some raised eyebrows. Children observed, eyes wide open. Old men grumbled a few words to themselves. Only some three hundred steps separated them from the city.

It was as defenceless as Valirian had described it, and he shivered at the thought of a Koreshian army attacking it. Even in small numbers, a direct assault would result in a massacre.

"They don't look like they're preparing for battle," said Zelshi.

Valirian agreed, and he felt not the need for caution as some fifty men approached from the city, bearing a standard unfamiliar to him: a large blue fish that devoured its own tail fin, on a field of white. They were doubtlessly militiamen, but despite their bravery, certainly none were foolish enough to fight the Mistian army in an open field while so heavily outnumbered. A middle-aged man, stout and short and in rich clothing, was at their head, and as his companions stopped, he continued marching forwards. Valirian nodded to the three captains, signalling them to stay behind as his horse trotted to meet the man, who stopped a few steps away from him.

"Welcome to Sanadra," said the rich man. "I am Aknoc, lord-mayor of this beautiful city." As Valirian removed his helmet, the man studied him, his orange eyes nervously observing his every move. "You must be Lord Valirian, Advisor to the Queen of Mists. What brings you here to me?"

"I am indeed My Lady's Advisor," he answered. "Fear not, for our intention is not to wage war against you nor your people."

"What is then the meaning of such an army approaching our peaceful city?" asked the man.

Valirian glanced at Sanadra. From the edge of the city, atop the hill, a small crowd had gathered, observing the discussion from afar. He dropped from his horse and took a few steps towards Aknoc until he was only one step away. "We bring not war here, but war has been brought to Illmeria. I, too, wish things were different, yet the peaceful time Illmeria had hitherto enjoyed is over."

The man paled. "Is that a threat?"

"It is not," answered Valirian. "We do not wish to spill the blood of any Illmerian. Yet when Koresh invaded, it left on this beautiful land a scar that none should ever forget, and we can only prepare ourselves for their eventual return. Make no mistake: it is in your best interest, and in the interest of your fellow citizens, to submit to the Queen of Mists, for she shall protect this land and its inhabitants." His words, spoken aloud, reached the ears of the militiamen behind their lord-mayor, some of whom nodded.

Yet Aknoc sighed and shrugged. "Your offer is not surprising. I knew of your intentions when you arrived, and I knew what you'd ask for." He turned around. He, too, observed the crowd that had gathered at the entrance uphill for a few moments before directing his attention back to Valirian. "See, it's a matter of days, at most, before Lady Adiloka sends me another letter asking for us to submit to her and join her 'new Illmeria,' under her protection. It would be maybe the sixth or the seventh. I lost count a week ago, when the last one arrived.

"I am not an idiot, and rumours spread rapidly. Rapidly enough, at least, for me to have heard of the Duchess's defeat at the Fortress and of the War Hero's capture. I don't doubt your words. I know you would, in the end, protect my city against the Koreshians, were they to return one day. But I'm no fool. I know you also intend to use Sanadra against the Duchess, too."

"I suppose that you are determined to keep your neutrality," said Valirian. "That you refuse to intervene in this Illmerian war being waged by the Duchess."

The man nodded and shrugged. He let out a sigh and looked down as Valirian kept his silence. "We care not for this war. None in Illmeria do, outside of the Queen of Mists and the Duchess of the Pearl."

For a moment, Valirian knew not what to say. His sight shifted between the lord-mayor and the city, and he rubbed his chin. "We will protect your people by building fortifications and garrisoning men here. The Queen has chosen to attempt negotiations with the Duchess. We aim to end this war."

Once more, the man sighed, shaking his head. "See, your words are no different than the Duchess's, at least not in their intentions. I'm sure that your walls would do us good in the end, but you are mistaken to think that we will accept out of enthusiasm. This is why I have continuously refused Lady Adiloka's request." Detaching the long cape of red velvet on his back, he handed it to Valirian. "I have no way of stopping you from seizing control, and I do not want to see bloodshed. Do not mistake this for my approval, though. I will retire from political life but will certainly not support your endeavours in Sanadra."

A second passed before Valirian took the mantle, though he wore it not around his neck.

"Do you sincerely believe that the Koreshians will return?" asked Aknoc.

"There is no doubt in my mind. Vinmara has fought against their empire for generations now. They are not quick to give up."

"And they won't give up or be defeated so easily this time, I suppose," continued Aknoc. "Especially now that the War Hero is your captive."

"We would not keep her our prisoner if Koresh were to invade," retorted Valirian. "We want Illmeria's safety above all."

Aknoc chuckled. "See, I doubt that. You aren't an idiot. I am certain of that, Lord Valirian. You know how important she is and how much the Duchess would give to have her back. Without her, she's nothing."

"You may doubt my words. That changes not the truth. I have no reason to lie to you, especially as you already gave me control of your city. Lady Syrela has my respect, more than just as the War Hero."

The man answered not. For a few moments, he simply looked at his city. Valirian had imagined the crowd would have slowly dispersed as Aknoc handed his mantle, yet it only seemed to grow larger. How populated really was that city? Children began to play in the fields nearby as their initial curiosity about the Mistian soldiers began to fade and not much seemed to happen.

"You have mentioned negotiations with the Duchess," Aknoc eventually said.

"Indeed I have."

"Do you not fear that your takeover here will impact them?" asked the man. "Lady Adiloka won't see too kindly to a Mistian stronghold so far north."

"It will doubtlessly have an impact, but she is quite forced to negotiate with us," answered Valirian. "She needs Lady Syrela back, and her position is unfavourable. We do this because we do not want to wage a war against our Illmerian brothers."

"Yet you will ask for more than simply a truce, won't you?"

Valirian looked away, yet Aknoc's eyes continued studying his visage. "We are not responsible for this war. We are not the ones who attacked first. And above all, we are not the ones who failed to protect our people against the Koreshians. I could have chosen either the Lady of Mists or the Lady of Pearls, believe me. But I do not trust Lady Adiloka."

Aknoc rubbed his chin. Doubtlessly, the man held the Duchess in high regard. On the other hand, perhaps he, too, was critical of her.

He certainly had valid reasons for both, or so thought Valirian. Yet in the end, he regretted not his choice. From Xelya alone came the hope of victory. Perhaps a war fought on the same side, against the Koreshians, would be enough to keep a durable peace in Illmeria—but would a divided nation stand a chance against another invasion in the far future? Was there any hope beyond an Illmeria united and ruled by Xelya?

Valirian looked at the mantle in his hand, then at Aknoc. "It is in nobody's interest to prevent you from administering this city. Take back your mantle and serve your people."

The man shook his head and turned his back to the coat. "There are more than enough competent administrators in this city, and I am getting old. I have governed this land for fifteen years. It would not be right for me to submit and keep my position. Give it to someone else."

Valirian shrugged and turned around. He handed Zelshi the mantle and jumped back on his horse. "So be it. You have my word: your people will be safe, and my men will not shed blood unless it is to defend themselves."

Aknoc nodded. He had a joyless smile that soon vanished. "That won't be needed. I have told my men not to fight if you did not attack. Farewell, Lord Valirian." Alone, he returned to the city. His militiamen approached the Mistian army.

"Captain Zelshi," said Valirian, "I will entrust you with the city for the time being. Keep the mantle and oversee the elections. Focus on building proper walls and making this city ready to handle a siege. Also, train those militiamen and any recruits willing to join our army."

"Yes, My General!" said the captain. He shouted a few commands, and some two hundred men followed him into Sanadra alongside the militiamen.

The result had been as hoped: the city was now under the Queen's control, and no blood had to be spilt, yet Valirian eyed Aknoc one last time. He would pose no threat, even though he seemed loved by his people. Certainly, many would follow him if he desired to attempt overthrowing Zelshi, but he knew better. No, what bothered Valirian was deeper—why was he so attached to neutrality? Did he not see that inaction would lead to Illmeria's doom? Perhaps it was good that he refused the mantle once more and instead retired. Peace required more than wishful thinking.

CHAPTER 15
ONE SAME WILL

Soldiers gathered from around the plaza, forming ranks at Aaposhi's command. From far above, on the Fortress's tall walls, Xelya observed and counted. She could not even see the pavement of the plaza, hidden beneath her troops. "Six divisions. That would be three thousand men without Valirian's own troops." Her sight shifted to Xilto, a few steps to her left. In spite of his stern expression, he stood straight, his chest forth as the Queen inspected him. "That is more than my Advisor had at first anticipated. Does my army lack equipment, and are we to expect the number of volunteers to continue growing?"

"The army has everything it needs, My Queen," answered the captain. "As for the volunteers, that's impossible to say, but I personally don't think so. Unless we are attacked again, the amount of daily recruits should go back to something more reasonable."

She turned northwards, to the hills and fields outside the Fortress. The inspection had left her satisfied. Soon, they would need to leave and meet with the Duchess. The time and place had been decided, though she wished to await her Advisor's return before leaving. A courier from Mistport had informed her of his imminent arrival, and she expected him that very day.

"Good evening, Lady Xelya," said Syrela.

"Good evening," answered the Queen. "I had not expected you here."

"I hope I do not intrude, or that my presence here is not mistaken for spying. Those were not my intentions."

A slight chuckle escaped Xelya, reassuring the two guards following the War Hero that no mistake had been committed.

"Valirian is to return today, I heard?" asked Syrela.

"Hopefully. I desire not to make Lady Adiloka wait, yet if we are to arrive on time, our departure must be tomorrow in the morning. My Advisor returning late would delay us."

"Why not leave now and meet him in Mistport?" the War Hero asked. "We would gain time and save him some unnecessary travel."

"A few internal matters require his presence here before we leave. Though it is a possibility I considered, I had to dismiss the option, unfortunately."

Syrela answered with a nod and turned north, leaning on the crenellations.

"Captain Xilto, the men may rest for the time being," said Xelya. She then dismissed the two guards that had followed Syrela, commanding them to return to the Tower. There, the War Hero and she waited in silence, and many long minutes passed. A gentle breeze was blowing, and Xelya took a deep breath, allowing herself a smile as she closed her eyes. "This sight doubtlessly captures something the balcony of my Tower does not."

"The sight from the mountains must be breathtaking," said Syrela.

"If one is prepared to face the cold, then the sight of the Mistlands covered in snow, from the cliffs, is something quite incomparable. Especially under a full moon."

Syrela's eyes widened. "You have gone there during winter, at night? Is it not dangerous?"

Letting out a slight laugh, Xelya nodded. "Indeed, when I was much younger. The cold never bothered me much, and I had warm clothing. I know those mountains and the woods well."

"Then, hopefully, in a different time, I, too, hope to explore them."

A banner, in the distance. The two leaned against the crenellations, as if they had forgotten the reason of their presence until that moment.

"Not one moment too soon, spirits be honoured," said Syrela. "I was starting to believe he decided to take some rest in Mistport." Following Valirian were some nine hundred men, though many seemed like untrained recruits rather than soldiers. For a moment, Syrela found herself speechless.

"He may be the first general in Illmerian history to always return with more troops than when he left," said Xelya. With a simple gesture, she invited Syrela to follow her down the walls to the plaza.

"The size of your army gives me hope, Lady Xelya," said the War Hero. "With peace, we may stand strong enough to defeat Koresh."

A few steps away, soldiers opened the gates, letting the Advisor and his men in. He shouted some orders to his troops, and Cadmael took over their supervision as Valirian dropped from his horse and met with Xelya and Syrela.

"My Lady," he said with a bow. For a moment, he hesitated. Why was the Queen alone with the War Hero, without any of her bodyguards? The informality of her welcoming surprised him, too, but he brushed away the thoughts and refrained from asking any questions. Did any of this truly matter?

"It is good that my Advisor has returned," said Xelya. "I have heard of your excellent work in the Islands, which I had wished to reward with some much-deserved rest. Sadly, we have little time."

Raising an eyebrow, Valirian chuckled and followed the Lady as she led the way to the Tower. "I see that the reconstructions have been completed in my absence."

"Indeed," answered Xelya. "Here and everywhere in the Fortress, though the city had, in truth, suffered very little from the battle." All three headed up the stairs to the dining room with little more said, only exchanging a few pleasantries on their way, waiting until they were seated for him to narrate his adventures.

"It must have felt strange to lead such a large army to deal with a few ill-equipped pirates," said Syrela.

"In some way, though I had already gotten used to the thought with the previous campaign around Mistport," he answered. There was a pause as the servants brought dishes to the table, and the smell of roasted venison soon filled the room.

"We have an important matter to discuss, Advisor," said Xelya. "The Duchess has agreed to negotiate with us and has offered to meet on the sacred hill of Jalhi in four days."

He nodded. The name felt oddly familiar. He searched his memory for many long seconds before his eyes suddenly widened. "Jalhi? Is it not in the south-western parts of the Grasslands? Arriving there in four days will not be easy."

"Which is why the both of us were waiting for your return, earlier," said Syrela. "We need to leave tomorrow in the morning if we are to arrive on time."

From her sleeve, Xelya pulled out the letter and handed it to her Advisor.

"Her terms are reasonable," he said after reading it. "She asks for the army accompanying us not to exceed five hundred men, and the location is only an hour away from the shore. I doubt Lady Adiloka would be foolish enough to try anything anyway." The missive was, quite strangely, long. It thoroughly detailed many of her demands, such as the War Hero's presence, but also his, named specifically, a rather odd request as he recalled the letter the Duchess had sent him shortly before the Battle of the Fortress.

"Very well, then let us leave tomorrow morning," he said, handing back the letter to his Queen. "I suppose we will discuss some of the matters tonight, My Lady?"

"Indeed, though it is a matter of formality first and foremost," she said.

Valirian's attention shifted to Syrela, whose eyes were looking down as she otherwise sat immobile, struggling to eat. He bit his tongue, repressing a sigh. Never before had she been so far away from Naila, nor for so long, and the sight of her city, burnt to the ground by the Koreshians, had certainly never left her mind. How could he not understand? "Could there be any hopes for negotiations with Lord Zheraï of the Stormlands? Their warriors could certainly prove useful against Koresh."

Syrela shrugged and sighed, shaking her head. "I fear that the Duke is opposed to the very idea of diplomacy. Lady Adiloka and I have on many attempts tried to find a compromise, yet his refusal goes so far as to not even bother sending letters in reply. The Duchess even once suggested that I marry him to end that pointless war."

"I doubt that such a political marriage would have sufficed to bring peace," said Xelya. "In truth, he would have certainly used it to strengthen his own position."

With a slight smile, Syrela laughed and nodded. "I would have never given my approval anyway."

"So be it, then," said Valirian. "In the end, a war might still be waged amongst Illmerians." Though he knew little of the Duke, it was easy to imagine that, as the leader of one of the largest clans of the Stormlands, his ambitions were not merely set on his own region. Strangely, the Duke had been one of the few clan leaders that had not united against the Koreshians at the Battle of the Blue Ford—the battle that saw the invaders repelled from the Stormlands, though at a high cost. Instead, it was that exact opportunity he used to unite the Stormlands under his rule, as many other clan leaders had perished in the battle or had seen their clans weakened, leaving Zheraï's army as the most powerful force.

"I would have never imagined that the most important decisions of the Mistlands were taken while sharing such good food," said Syrela, having managed to finish her plate.

Xelya laughed, finishing her glass of wine at the remark. "Such fine dishes help my Advisor and I in making wiser decisions." She stood up from her seat. Valirian and Syrela both followed her out of the room soon after, though she suddenly stopped at the stairs. "Something pressing requires my attention, though I would have loved to accompany you to your room, Lady Syrela."

"I appreciate the thought, Lady Xelya," she answered.

Valirian exchanged a quick nod with the Lady and followed Syrela down the stairs into her room. He was quite surprised to see the stone cell greatly embellished: a few sheep pelts covered the ground, there was a fine cloth on the low table, and the shelf on the far left corner was filled with books.

"Did you expect your Queen not to treat a high-ranking Illmerian general with respect in your absence?" asked Syrela before his speechlessness. She struggled to hold back a laugh.

"I guess my expectations were slightly unfair," he said. Their smiles vanished, and for a second, neither spoke. "It was an honour to have you as our guest, in spite of the circumstances."

"I had much time to reflect," said Syrela. "It may have pained me terribly to stay here, for I still worry about my home, but perhaps my judgement of you was quite unjust." She sighed and turned to him, looking down as he silently nodded. "Valirian, you have earned my respect. I know the negotiations to come will not be easy, and I know Lady Xelya will aim to gain from them, but I do not doubt your honesty in wanting to save Illmeria."

"We will find a solution," he answered. "She is not as stubborn as she may seem, and she does not ignore the outside threat."

She forced a slight smile as she nodded, and he turned around. Yet barely outside the room, he faced her once more and bowed. "Thank you, Lady Syrela. Earning the respect of the person who saved my life is worth more than all the gold in the world."

* * *

"I will certainly miss the hot springs of the temple," said Xelya.

She leaned back in her armchair and toyed with something in her palm, which Valirian could not see. "Why not build a palace there, fit for your grandeur?" he asked.

"Only when Koresh is defeated for good, when we have truly obtained this era of peace Adiloka desperately chases after," she said.

He sat next to her as she poured them both some tea, and as they shared a drink, he told her in greater detail of his campaign in the Islands, no longer needing to omit some of the more delicate points of strategy.

"For how long do you suggest Zelshi to stay in Sanadra?" she asked.

"It will depend on his own reports," said Valirian. "I suppose that in a month or two, he will be able to return after handing over the governance to a local administrator."

She finished her cup and opened her palm, inspecting whatever it was she held there. "Advisor, there is an important matter I wished to discuss with you." She handed him something: in the shape of a tear, a small amulet, the size of a thumb and set with a purple diamond at the centre.

There was a slight glow to the gem, and he felt as if mesmerised as he stared, his eyes unable to move, and he swore he heard a distant song. He shook his head, his heart racing for a short moment, but he calmed himself and nodded, eyes closed. "The magic caught me by surprise."

"I enchanted those amulets for the both of us this afternoon," she said as she revealed the one she had been wearing around her neck, "so that we may always communicate with one another when needed."

He took the amulet in his hand. Once more, he heard the song, yet it was distant, soft, and pleasant. With a slight smile, he wore it around his neck.

"If land separates us, all you must do is place the diamond in contact with a mirror," she said. "I will do so, too, and I will appear on the mirror's surface, allowing us to communicate in spite of the distance. Do know its limits, however: it is costly. As such, the longer the distance, the more time will pass before we will be able to communicate again. It may need more than a week if we are to be very far away."

His eyes widened, his mind struggling to grasp all the ways they could use such a tool. Letters could be lost or intercepted and could take significantly longer to reach their destinations than this trinket would need to recharge.

"Let us agree to contact one another at sunset when a shorter distance separates us, shall we?" she asked.

"Of course, My Lady," he said.

Xelya gazed at the amulet around his neck and clutched at hers. She had a slight frown when she looked him in the eyes. "The amulet has another power. Should we make eye contact, we will be able to enter one another's minds and communicate telepathically." She sighed, allowing herself a slight nod. "The thought is frightening."

"Indeed. But you have my trust." Certainly, it would be of great use in many situations—such as delicate negotiations. With a smile, he turned to Xelya, gazing into her eyes.

"*Like that?*" he asked.

She laughed. "*Indeed.*" For a moment, there was silence. Glimpses of images flooded their minds, each all too aware of the other's mental presence. Xelya looked down, and a brief moment after, as she turned her head, the telepathy ended.

"We . . . will need time to get used to it," she said.

He could not disagree, remembering his past experiences with such magic, yet it bothered him no more. His own willpower, he had come to understand, had twice saved him from a terrible fate, and no longer did he need to mistrust her.

"I have noticed that you and Syrela have solved some of your disagreements. Am I correct?" he asked.

"You would be. I do not know the extent of her trust. However, she appears to no longer see in me a tyrant I abhor."

"I believe so, too," he said. "She will be a powerful voice for peace at the negotiations."

Xelya rubbed her chin, pensive for a few moments. "Would you advise me to pursue peace above all, Advisor?"

"Without a doubt."

"Then so be it," she said. "If you believe that only a truce can save Illmeria, then I will do all I can so that there may be peace, at least for the time being. You have my word."

CHAPTER 16
STORM AND STARFALL

A bed of soft green leaves, a gentle wind. Xelya opened her eyes. All around her, a forest of tall green trees. She got up, trying to study her surroundings, peering deeper into the woods, yet there was nothing but darkness wherever she looked. The trees, the shrubs, the bushes—all created a seemingly impenetrable barrier around the strange clearing she found herself in. In only one place, there was a sort of path between the trees, a trail. Her legs moved as if animated by a will of their own, leading her further in. They moved with confidence, more than she'd ever dare have, disregarding the ambient dimness.

It dawned on her. A strange presence, everywhere, one all too familiar yet nameless still. She bowed her head, felt all warmth leave her body, and trembled. It was in everything around her, even the leaves she stepped on, yet she could tell it drew closer.

"Go forth and witness," it whispered. Its voice was like a thousand echoes, yet crystal clear.

Xelya shivered but nodded. It was a whisper she had heard before, countless times, but never had she dared ask its name, and again she would not. As she now felt capable of using her own legs, and though, at first, still hesitant, she moved forwards to the path.

With each step, the wind seemed to blow stronger, and as she arrived in a clearing, its force was such that she struggled to stand straight. There, the forest gave way to a hill, atop of which was a star. The hill was far away, yet even from there, she could distinguish the intricate runes carved on the star, but she could make not any sense of it, for it was written in a script and language foreign to her. It was none of the known languages, not even the strange language of the Mahïrs. That she was certain of.

On the flank of the hill, to her right, was a tall wall of natural rocks. On the other side of that wall, a gathering of grumbling clouds, with lightning arcs hitting against the wall, to no avail. Yet as her legs stepped closer, the wall turned. In a single second, it had moved before her. In the following second, it was rushing at her.

Xelya gasped and tried to move, but her legs answered not. The collision with the wall pushed her, and she fell on her back. Though her vision blurred for a brief instant, and her entire body felt numb, hardly any pain followed. Before her, the wall turned to dust, carried away by the wind.

As the wall stood no more between it and the stars, the gathering of clouds roared, deafening like thunder, and a shape, resembling the head of a dragon, emerged, its maw open wide. Lightning bolts were fired, and a storm set ablaze the star, which burnt bright for many long seconds before it was no more. And the forest, from the smallest tree to the tallest, bowed before the dragon. Only then did Xelya stand up, though the roaring celebration of the beast deafened her, silencing even the wind.

A bed of warm linen blankets, the blue light of the moon. Xelya opened her eyes, clutching at her pillow, biting her tongue. She sat on the edge of her bed and massaged her temples, shaking her head.

Outside, the moon was high. It was a full moon, and so as she opened her window, she could see the shapes of the buildings and temples beneath her. Her city, her home. She sighed, her muscles relaxed, yet she kept staring at the moon. She was still, beyond the gentle breeze lifting her white hair, until her eyes widened. Her fists clenched, her jaw dropped, her skin paled, and she turned around to face her bed and closed the window.

It all made sense, now.

* * *

Taking a deep breath, Valirian smiled. A few steps to his right, Syrela repressed a shiver. The particularly thick mist seemed to make it worse for the War Hero, and so he offered her a coat. Nearby, Aaposhi shouted orders to a few hundred men, while on the other side of the plaza, two sergeants oversaw the workers preparing the supplies. For Valirian, about to once more leave the Fortress, just hours after his return, there never was a moment to rest.

"We should be on time," he told Xelya, who answered with a quick nod.

Their horses were ready. Soon, they rode out of the city at the head of a small army. Cadmael had volunteered to lead those men, and it had taken little convincing from the young man for Valirian to agree. What better occasion to gain experience, after all?

"I've never seen Mistport with my own eyes," said Syrela. "Last I heard, the city had been ravaged by the Koreshians."

"It has been mostly rebuilt," said Valirian, "though it is true that still many districts feel rather empty."

Indeed, as they approached the city the following day, it was a bright spectacle that awaited Syrela. Though the roofs were hardly different from the rest of Illmeria in style, curved inwards and made of slates, their colour—red, orange, or light brown—together with the city's many gardens, gave life to the otherwise light grey stone used everywhere else. Even from a distance, one could see the harbour buzzing with activity as merchants from Tilversio and Nestra sailed far to the east to do their commerce.

"Are Tilversio and Nestra not city-states under Koreshian dominance?" asked Syrela as they made their way to the harbour.

"Not exactly. Koreshian influence would be more accurate," answered Valirian. "They enjoy a degree of freedom, as they are not part of the empire proper. They come here to buy the purple dye otherwise so rare in their land, as well as silk—to later sell them to the nobility and elites in Vinmara or Koresh."

The War Hero's frown made Xelya and him laugh.

"Indeed, Lady Syrela," said Xelya. "It does mean that, indirectly, the Koreshians finance my army through this lucrative trade, all unbeknownst to them."

Syrela laughed at the thought, and as the soldiers loaded their supplies into six vessels, she observed with a smile the transactions and discussions amongst the merchants. "It will only take us a day to cross the Sea of Mists, correct?"

"A day and a night," answered Valirian. "Though we may only arrive in the early afternoon, for our destination is a little further west. So long as, of course, the winds stay as favourable as they appear to be."

A long hour after their arrival, it was time to board, and so, early in the afternoon, they set sail northwards. Alone on deck, Valirian breathed in deeply. The sun, very low on the horizon, gave the sea a deep crimson colour, the waters below calm—almost abnormally, or so one unused to sailing the Sea of Tranquillity might think. He headed to the Lady's cabin and smiled as he pushed open the door, joining Xelya at her table as she poured herself a cup of tea.

"I am thankful we are merely sailing the Sea of Tranquillity and no other," she said. "I know not how well I would handle the high ocean otherwise." She poured him a cup, too, and handed it to him, and he gladly accepted. "You seem in a great mood today, Advisor."

"I cannot help it," said Valirian. "I have many memories of Mistport, yet seeing the city so lively and prospering soothes the more painful ones."

She smiled, bringing the cup to her lips, yet she stopped herself. For a second, she seemed to hesitate.

"Is there something wrong, My Lady?" he asked.

She shook her head but spoke not. She put the cup on the table and leaned towards him. "There is something we must discuss, Advisor. See, recently, some information arrived from spies I have in the north of Illmeria."

His jaw dropped, and his thoughts raced, fearing the worst. About to speak, he leaned forwards.

"It is not Koresh. Not yet, thankfully," she said. "Though it is not something of minor importance either. Some few days ago, Naila fell to the Stormians. In a crushing defeat, in spite of numerical superiority, the Northern Alliance lost control of the city."

Though he relaxed, he kept a sombre expression as he nodded. "And you fear the War Hero's reaction."

"Her love for her home is no secret," she said. "I fear she will see us as the cause for the city's fall. It is not absurd to suggest that, had she been there, she would have defended Naila successfully."

"I understand very well," he said. "Though we can feign ignorance, trying to hide the fact will do us little good. She will sadly find the truth all too soon."

"Let us hope for the negotiations to be unaffected by it," she said with a sigh. She leaned back in her armchair and closed her eyes. There was no knowing the War Hero's reaction. In an instant, all efforts to achieve peace could crumble.

"At least the Duchess stands to lose a lot should the information spread," said Valirian. "It is also in her interests to keep it a secret, though from us instead."

"Let us hope so," she said. "Let us not mention the city directly, nor discuss the war in the north too much anyway. For I, it will be a matter of discussing my sovereignty in the Islands and obtaining concessions in the Grasslands." Before her Advisor's hesitance, she frowned. "Do you have any objections?"

"The Duchess does not have my trust," he said. "I doubt she would be foolish enough to refuse a truce, but I fear that anything more will be inconceivable to her."

Xelya shrugged and took a sip of tea. A war against Koresh, she trusted, would strengthen her more than Adiloka, even if her troops were to do most of the fighting. "If Lady Adiloka is so blind as to refuse any reasonable proposal, then once Koresh is defeated, I will be justified to take by force what is rightfully mine. I doubt that, once the war is over, her stance will be left unchanged."

He chuckled. There was no doubt the war to come against Koresh would further ruin Adiloka's image in the eyes of the Illmerian people. "I suppose we shall see tomorrow."

CHAPTER 17
OATH-BREAKER NO MORE

It felt like an eternity since Valirian had last set foot in the Grasslands. Though the less inhabited parts in the south-west had suffered little, he doubted not that, across the hills, many scars from the invasion were still visible. From a small mound, he supervised the landing. He heard the occasional laugh from the men as they set camp, while some others would sing or whistle as they worked. The location was perfect: near the coast, at the mouth of a small river, on a slightly elevated position. The camp would be protected from any possible attack. Only an hour separated the landing area from the sacred hill of Jalhi. Even from there, Valirian could feel something strange—as if some magical energy was in the very air he breathed.

"Is this something to be worried about?" he asked Xelya.

The Queen shook her head as she studied the hill, further in the distance. "Jalhi has been revered as a sacred place for times immemorial. What happened here, the reasons for this magic to be felt so distinctly, are unclear, yet even six hundred years ago, there are records of ceremonies being held here, specifically because of this magic's strange omnipresence."

"Legends in the Northlands are that a great battle happened here, a long time ago," said Syrela. "Not one tale says the same about said battle, yet it is very possible that some mages did indeed fight."

The three soon rejoined the army, down the small hill. There was no reason to wait any longer. With Cadmael having chosen eleven of the Queen's guard to follow him, the group headed to the sacred hill. There, at the centre of six obelisks, a stone table, ancient and worn by the weather. It had doubtlessly witnessed centuries, perhaps millennia. The slight traces of magic that could be felt from further away had now become a tangible energy, one almost capable of forming an aura yet all too distant, too ancient, to be clearly visible to Valirian.

"Lady Adiloka must have been informed of our arrival," said Syrela. "Here she is."

From the other side of the hill, a large group approached. Its size, though perhaps three times theirs, worried them not; most seemed to be mere nobles and courtiers who had certainly earned the right to attend the negotiations by their position. At their head, the Duchess, slow and affirmed in her steps. On her head sat a crown of gold, set with many diamonds and gems, the largest of which was a rose diamond two inches in size, at the centre of a lotus of gold just above her forehead. Beneath, her black hair had been tied in an intricate knot behind her head with a golden hairpin, while her ample clothes of rose and gold were stitched with countless pearls. The slight frown on her visage highlighted the rose glow of her eyes, revealing her affinity with magic. For many long seconds, she stood across the table, observing Xelya without a word. Perhaps only two steps behind her, three noblemen, clothed in silk tunics of various colours, whispered a few words amongst one another—certainly the Duchess's husbands, following the old Illmerian tradition that allowed powerful rulers to marry more than once as to secure the realm's stability.

Valirian dared peer into Adiloka's eyes. He was drawn in, pulled into a magnificent garden where fruits were made of gold and flowers of crystal. The perfume was rich, powerful, and sweet, reminiscent of incense, too, in many ways. At the centre of the garden was a dais, on which stood a throne made of rose gold. A shape draped in fine, white cloth sat on it, a necklace of thousands of pearls around its neck; it thoughtfully contemplated the sky above, a turquoise with clouds of gold. Yet Valirian could distinguish little more details of the shape, for her head and chest were clouded in grey smoke. Only as the shape turned to face him, revealing two pink eyes behind the veil of smoke, did the vision end.

"I must say that I am delighted that you have accepted to negotiate," said Xelya. "Let us hope that we find an agreement, Lady Adiloka, Duchess of the Pearl."

"My agreement to those negotiations had been given before the news of Sanadra's annexation," said the Duchess. "What is the meaning of this, o Queen of Mists? Why has the Mistlands dared expand so far north if you claim to want peace?"

At the Queen's side, to the left, Valirian glanced at Syrela: a few steps away, with two soldiers guarding her, her attention shifted from one lady to the other.

"It is merely a defensive precaution, Lady Adiloka," answered Xelya. "A natural reaction at your sudden and unjustified assault on the Fortress. My city." Taking a step forwards so that only a few inches separated her from the stone table, she raised her chin. "Contrarily to yours, my men shall not assault Kashpur, even though it is perfectly within our capacities. Be assured of that." At her words, the three consorts turned silent, though Adiloka only raised an eyebrow.

"A truce between our two realms will require many guarantees for my agreement," said the Duchess. "Amongst the most important ones will be the immediate return of the Blade of Illmeria."

"We intend not to keep the War Hero as our captive. She will play a crucial role in the imminent war against Koresh. However, I likewise have conditions for my agreement."

Adiloka turned to her consorts and exchanged a few whispered words. Further behind, the nobles that attended the negotiations murmured amongst themselves. Eventually, the Duchess's attention returned to the Queen. "What are your conditions, Lady Xelya?"

"The Mistlands promise to stand with the Northern Alliance and the rest of Illmeria should Koresh attack. Likewise, I expect the Northern Alliance to come to our aid against the invaders if need be. It is only united that we may win this war.

"In exchange for our help, I demand that you recognise the legitimacy of my rule over the Islands, including the city of Sanadra. Additionally, I ask that parts of the south-eastern Grasslands be granted to my realm. My army is large and well-equipped, capable of challenging the invaders on the battlefield. There is no doubt that a great part of the war effort will be sustained by us."

The deep frown and pursed lips of the ducal consorts made Valirian take a step forwards. He could not blame Xelya for defending her interests, but he hoped to see her show some goodwill.

"Need I say that such conditions are unacceptable?" said Adiloka. "The Illmerian army is larger than the Mistian army, and my realm more populated than yours. Additionally, I do not wish to risk making myself indebted to the Mistlands by accepting your military help under any conditions. We have defeated the Koreshians before. We will do it again, should they return."

Valirian glanced at Syrela. Her fists were clenched, and her eyes were closed. Had Xelya's demand angered her? Losing her favour could prove a major thorn in their side.

"I am merely demanding guarantees for lasting peace in Illmeria," said Xelya. "We do not wish to prolong that war, and your attack on the Fortress was a foolish endeavour that cost all too many Illmerian lives."

"A truce is acceptable," said the Duchess. "However, no Mistian soldier shall set foot in my realm. That is out of the question. We will discuss cooperation against the Koreshians if the question becomes relevant." She turned around and spoke a few words with her consorts.

The Lady and Valirian looked into one another's eyes. The connection was instantaneous, which almost startled him. "*She must intend to gain time,*" he said. "*If we liberate Syrela, a truce would allow her to take Naila back.*"

Xelya nodded. She thought it unlikely that Adiloka would break the truce once the Stormlands were defeated, especially as Syrela would stand against another attack on the Mistlands. As such, liberating the War Hero was not quite out of the picture yet. "*We must at least secure a concession on the Islands and our sovereignty,*" said Xelya. "*We will be able to control trade and rule the sea, which is a significant advantage.*"

It surprised Valirian not that Xelya had asked for so much. Adiloka would try to appear stronger than she was, even though the Mistlands had the stronger position, so her refusal of some demands was hardly surprising. His worries were more directed at Syrela, who visibly struggled to keep her calm.

"In exchange for the Blade of Illmeria's freedom," said Adiloka, "we will recognise your rule over the Islands, with the exception of Sanadra, which must stay neutral in all political matters for the time."

Without hesitation, Xelya shook her head. "The city of Sanadra has wilfully submitted to my rule. There is no reason for their independence."

Valirian glanced at Syrela. Xelya needed to make a concession, for the good of Illmeria, even if it appeared less than ideal. "*Agree to free Syrela. Not for Adiloka, for Illmeria and for her.*" For a second, there was no answer from the Lady. Valirian felt his heart skip a beat.

"So be it," she said. "*I will trust your advice.*"

"I accept, however, to free the War Hero," said Xelya. "I intend not to keep her a prisoner any longer."

For a few moments, Adiloka reflected in silence. She seemed hesitant. Perhaps, in the end, she would agree to give up Sanadra. "Then what guarantee do I have that, once the occasion presents itself, you will not launch a naval invasion from the Islands?"

"If I were to wage a war against you, Lady Adiloka, I would have struck now rather than negotiate. Without your best general, and after a major defeat at the Fortress, I doubt that your army would be capable of defending Kashpur."

"You cannot even defend Naila against the Stormlands!" shouted a voice from behind.

Startled, all turned to face him. It was one of the nobles, further back. Already, a handful of men had silenced him and forcefully dragged him down the hill. For a minute, there was silence.

"This is not good," said Xelya.

Valirian turned to Syrela. The War Hero took a deep breath and stepped forth. The two guards attempted to stop her, yet her magic kept them away. With a hand gesture, Valirian told them to stand back.

"Lady Adiloka," said Syrela, "is what this man claims true?"

A second passed. Sights shifted from Syrela to either ruler, and the War Hero's sight turned to Valirian. The rage in her eyes made him shiver.

"It is," began Adiloka, "though it is nothing but a set—"

"And yet you refuse any assistance against them," continued Syrela, interrupting the Duchess. "And underestimate once more the Koreshian threat, in spite of all my warnings."

There was a deep echo in her voice, and Valirian swore that her eyes glowed with even greater intensity. Quite inexplicably, he felt his legs struggle to keep balance, yet the ground shook not. Fearing to lose his footing, he grabbed the edge of the stone table.

"Likewise, I had more than once warned against an attack on the Mistlands, in spite of my personal disagreements with the Queen of Mists," added Syrela. "Yet it is now clear as to who stands for Illmeria and who stands for their own gain. Your orders to attack the Mistlands resulted in the loss of Naila, but directly and above anything else, in the loss of thousands of Illmerian lives as well, both amongst your people and Mistians." She turned around and walked to Valirian's side, and their eyes met again before she turned back to face Adiloka once more.

"As the Blade of Illmeria, I am forbidden to swear any oath but the one I swore before the spirits. And though I betrayed not that principle, may Nav unleash his anger upon me if I allow the alliance between you and I, Duchess, to stand any longer, for it is a clear betrayal of my one and only oath. Illmeria's best interests are no longer of concern to you. Spirits be honoured, that which you had tried to hide from me was revealed at the perfect moment."

The nobles that had followed Adiloka murmured again in spite of the consorts' attempts to keep them silent.

"Lady Syrela," said the Duchess, "your decision is a true tragedy. What has led you to take such a dark path?" Her voice was weak, and she seemed paler.

Syrela's lips pursed. She turned her head and sighed, then headed down the hill to the Mistian camp.

"Those that truly wish to save Illmeria are welcome to follow the War Hero's example," said Valirian. "Do not fear an attack from us. We wish not a war with our Illmerian brothers."

"Thus are concluded our negotiations, it would seem," said Xelya.

CHAPTER 18

THE YOUNG BOY'S TALE

"Hurry up, we are packing!" shouted a sergeant. "The sooner this is over, the faster we go back!"

At their return to the camp, Valirian had immediately ordered their departure, to the surprise of the sergeants, who had expected to stay for at least a few days. On the way to the large red tent set up for the Queen, he spoke little to her. She, too, seemed to prefer waiting for a more private setting.

Finally, Xelya could allow herself to laugh. She sat down with a wide smile. "Quite an unexpected turn of events. I expected not the negotiations to be so easy." Calm quickly returned to her visage.

To her left, her Advisor was deep in thought. "Though they have politically turned to our advantage, Lady Adiloka's incompetence and stubbornness are hardly causes for joy," he said.

"Indeed, unfortunately," she answered. "Though it strengthens us, she is considerably weaker than we thought. She finds herself hardly capable of defending her own realm—and not simply against us, but against the Stormians and the Koreshians, too."

"She represents no threat to us," said Valirian. "Let us not wage war against her. We have better uses for our resources."

Xelya nodded and stood up, taking a few steps towards him. "Lady Syrela's decision won't stay as a mere rumour for long. But above all, I worry for her. I very much understand what Naila represents to her." She placed her hand on his shoulder, and he smiled, as if dragged out of his contemplation. "Please, go and see her. You may be able to give her some hope."

"You are right. I shall." He left at once, wasting no time. Yet his hurry vanished as the War Hero's tent stood before him. What was he to tell her? Did she even wish to see anyone? Was it wiser to let her rest for the day? He bit his tongue and let out a sigh. Eyes closed, he took another step forwards. "Lady Syrela, may I enter?"

A soft, barely audible "yes" was all that reached him. He glanced around, ensuring he had not misheard, before lifting the tent's fabric and entering. Not a candle had been lit, nor was there a lantern around, so it took his eyes a moment before they could distinguish anything.

Syrela was sat on the ground, cross-legged, her eyes closed and her muscles clenched. She was visibly attempting to control her breathing. "Valirian, tell me honestly. Did you know of Naila's fall?"

He froze. Then he looked down. He sat to her side and slowly nodded. "We—or rather, Xelya—learnt of it just before our departure. I suppose a report of some spies of hers reached her in Mistport just before we embarked. She told me on the ship, but we did not know how to, or if we even should, announce it."

She opened her eyes and gazed into his. She forced a smile and placed a hand on his shoulder. "Little escapes the Sovereign's eyes, it seems. Thank you for being honest with me." She looked down and hid her face in her hands. Her tears fell onto the ground below, and for many long seconds, not a sound escaped her until she struggled to breathe. "That young Vinmaran boy you told me about, how does his story end?"

He sighed. "Still a few pages need to be written before it ends, though I wish I knew what was to be written on them."

"Yet he was freed. He saw Good where many saw none, even though Koresh tried to break him." She looked up, though still tearful, and took his hands in hers. "I do not know Koresh as much as you, but I have seen enough to know that most would have lost themselves in all they'd have witnessed. Where do you draw your strength? How did you find in you the ability to stay true to who you are?"

Had he? He bit his tongue, ignoring a painful lump in his throat and repressing some tears. He clenched his fists and shook his head. "Maybe you overestimate me, My Lady."

"No," she said. "I know you are a good man. No one evil could have shown mercy like you have."

"It is only the fear of repeating the same failures of the past that keeps me on the path of righteousness. I wish I had a better answer." He stood up, wiping a few tears with the back of his hand.

"Then I will earn my redemption, too, and make amends for my own blindness and all it caused."

"It is not your fault," he said. "Had I known of Naila's fall, I would have freed you unconditionally, at my own risks if I had. I'm sorry, Syrela."

She moved to her bed, in the back of the tent, and found a handkerchief. She breathed in deep a few times. Even though much still weighed on her heart, something had been lifted. She found the strength to smile. "I had feared the fall of Naila before I even left for the Mistlands. The prospect of peace briefly helped me forget it might happen, but we cannot escape reality forever." She turned to face him again. "I don't regret my decision of today. I know it's the best way to save Illmeria, and though I have failed my oath before, I will try to make amends for as long as I breathe."

Syrela opened her arms. Without a second thought, he wrapped his around her. Their tight embrace lasted for mere seconds but brought a wide smile to Valirian. "You have my word, Syrela. Your home will be rebuilt, and I will fight until my last breath to keep it safe."

* * *

Their return to the Mistlands surprised much the locals and those who had stayed in Mistport, yet their surprise turned to deafening cheers as they saw the War Hero in her green gambeson, wearing her mask of iron and her armour, behind the Queen and to the Advisor's side.

In the north, she was doubtlessly cursed as a betrayer, but that thought bothered not Syrela. Even after a sleepless night of reflection, she regretted not her choice. She would bear all insults and judgements to save Illmeria. The rumours had spread rapidly, as if the entire city was there to see her arrival. Her name was chanted, and soldiers bowed to her. She bit her tongue. Would those she had fought mere weeks before truly follow her into battle, into the greatest perils? Much was to be done before she deserved their admiration. A sigh of relief escaped her as they left the city behind and took the road to the Fortress. With time, their excitement would thankfully fade. Soon, they had returned to the Tower's familiar dining room.

"With this task over, it now seems as if a thousand more are to be taken care of," said Xelya. "I understand that you both believe the Koreshian invasion to be imminent. Am I correct?"

Their eyes met. Both Syrela and Valirian nodded together.

"Indeed," he said. "My Lady, given that a single victory is all that saved Illmeria from slavery under Koresh, I fear that a year is all they would need to muster a large enough army for another war. They are hardly deterred from their ambitions."

"This time, however, they will not make the same mistake," said Syrela. "They know that Kashpur will struggle to defend itself if they strike there with full might. I hope Lady Adiloka will be wise enough to gain time and allow its citizens to flee southwards, but we should not expect her to delay the Koreshians for long."

Xelya nodded, then stood up. In front of Syrela, she opened her hand, a silver ring in her palm. "Then let us make it official. Lady Syrela, you have earned my trust. Your knowledge of strategy and experience against Koresh are second to none, and your bravery and skills are unequalled in Illmeria. I name you general, a rank shared only by my Advisor himself."

As she took the ring, Syrela bowed her head.

With a slight smile, Xelya returned to her seat. "If you are both in agreement, then prepare my realm for war. Establish a battle plan. Organise my army. Prepare what must be prepared. It is not a war we may lose. On my end, I will do all in my power to ensure that we stay informed of any developments in the north. Likewise, we will quickly learn of Koresh's return, I can assure you."

Though there would be much work, and though it remained unclear when the next invasion would occur, having an experienced general by his side gave Valirian confidence. "Good. We will need to act quickly once the invasion begins."

Soon, their meal was served, and little more was discussed. It was agreed that Syrela was to rest in the vacant room, upstairs of the captains' quarters. It was just above the large council room, where sovereigns of the Fortress would discuss all affairs of war with their captains, generals, and councillors. For two generations, both had been unused.

"Valirian, I will wait for you in the council room, early in the morning," said Syrela. "For now, I am quite tired. I wish you two a pleasant night."

Having finished their food, the Queen invited Valirian to follow her upstairs so that they might share some tea before sleep. Knowing that, for once, he was not required to leave and that duty did not call him away immediately gave him the widest of smiles.

"I very much understand your good mood, my friend," said Xelya. Closing her eyes, she leaned back in her seat, reciprocating his smile as she sat down.

"We will not have many occasions to relax like this, indeed," he said. For a few moments, the thought of even pouring the tea into their cups appeared a bother. "Xelya, I . . ." He paused. It was as if he had forgotten his own words, but as she opened her eyes and leaned towards him, he took a deep breath. "Thank you for putting your trust in me during the negotiations. Sincerely. I could feel that you thought against what I proposed, so . . . It means a lot."

With a smile still on her lips, she placed her hand on his. For a brief second, she looked down, then poured them both some tea. "In the end, it seems your optimism brought us good Fortune. There are lessons to learn from your idealism, I have come to observe." She brought the cup to her mouth and savoured the warm liquid, enjoying the whistle of the wind through the tiled roof.

"To think that some six months ago I was forced to sleep on some rocky ground," said Valirian.

"I shall never regret ambushing that group of marauders, all those months ago," said Xelya.

He chuckled. "Nor do I regret my services to My Queen and Illmeria. I have grown attached to this land."

CHAPTER 19
COLD AND LONG-AWAITED

It had been three weeks since the negotiations. The Mistlands prospered through the trade of rare and luxurious goods—the fine silk and the purple dye produced by the musakin, above all others—as the more ambitious merchants from the west brought much gold to the crown and its subjects. But all understood the time for preparations had come: a war was to be fought, and every man, woman, and child was to be ready; none from Ilmassar to Mistport ignored it. Most of those days Syrela and Valirian spent in the dimness of the council room. Maps, books, open and closed, and various reports covered the large circular table. Often would they eat there, and once, Valirian found Syrela asleep on the ground as he arrived early in the morning, having collapsed from exhaustion while drafting a battle plan.

She accepted his warnings and showed more care for her own well-being, yet he could only understand her diligence. Neither knew how much time they had been allotted. As such, neither thought it wise to waste it. In the evening, Valirian returned to the Tower. Often, though not always, Syrela declined the invitation for dinner, and though her absence saddened Xelya at first, she soon understood not to see any harm in it.

She, too, after all, had busied herself with various tasks. She and her Advisor had agreed that all matters of administration, commerce, and logistics would be of her resort directly. In truth, those tasked with the most work were doubtlessly the smiths; with the news of Syrela's new allegiance, many young men rushed to the Fortress to join the army. Some even crossed the Sea of Tranquillity by whichever means they had, for many militiamen who had served under the War Hero during the Koreshian invasion sought to follow her into battle once again.

"With seven thousand men, we have to think of supplying," said Valirian. "I'm quite certain that with our defences, the Mistlands could withstand an invasion, and both the Fortress and Mistport could hold against a siege. But we need to plan for operations of reconquest."

Syrela frowned, unrolling yet another map in front of herself and studying it for a few moments. "Your concerns are valid. We need to determine our goals and, from there, a strategy. We have spent enough time thinking about the Mistlands. We need to anticipate the Koreshian invasion of the Northlands, Grasslands, and Heartlands."

Leaning in, he answered with a nod. He knew the War Hero had much more to say on the matter.

"Worry not. We have enough time," she continued. "My plan was to discuss the subject this afternoon anyway, but I don't think myself capable of staying inside this building much longer." She straightened her back and glanced at the door. The lack of windows in that room had certainly taken a toll on her. "Let's head outside. We might even have the occasion to spar against the captains." At her words, a thought crossed her mind, and she smiled. Though Valirian raised an eyebrow, he said not a word and followed her outside. Neither of them had taken any time to spar since they began war preparations, and she had not held a weapon in over a month, for neither practice nor battle.

"It would be a shame for Illmeria's greatest warrior to lose her edge," he said. "Do you even remember which side of the blade is sharp?"

She rolled her eyes with a laugh and opened the door that led to the training grounds outside, where Cadmael and Zelshi sparred against one another while the other three watched. The duel neared its end, as the young captain clearly had the upper hand, and only seconds passed before he struck his opponent on his left side.

"Have our generals decided to join us in our sparring?" asked Xilto as he bowed before the two.

"I'm impressed by how long you can stay inside a room, My Lady," said Zelshi. "But it's not a bad idea to focus on something else once in a while."

Without a word, Syrela nodded and headed to the weapons rack. She grabbed a long staff, weighing it in her hand for a few moments. "It has been quite some time indeed. The Advisor and I shall spar first. Neither of us have had much practice recently, and neither of us are warmed up. It should be more fair that way."

Valirian chuckled, knowing the War Hero believed not a single word of what she said. She certainly meant to use him as adequate practice for herself: an opponent competent enough, but not so good as to defeat her so that she might have a greater chance at defeating the more trained captains. "Very well," he said. "Ready yourself, Lady Syrela."

As she was taller than him, and quite significantly so, her advantage of a greater reach was only amplified by her use of a spear against his regular sword. He needed to close in quickly. Some ten steps separated them, a particularly short distance, yet she seemed content to merely study him. He thought it wise not to leave her too much time to think or prepare, and so he rushed.

Dashing to her left, the War Hero kept her distance and had threatened to end the duel in mere seconds, for her weapon only narrowly missed his neck. He attempted again. This time, she landed a strike on his arm as she dashed to the right. Could he ever catch her? She took a step forwards and thrust; he thought it his chance and attacked. Yet while his weapon only missed by an inch, he felt a violent force push against his chest, knocking him to the ground. Out of breath, he saw his vision blur for an instant. Syrela had knelt next to him and helped him up.

"My apologies. I knew that feint would get you," she said. "I did not quite measure the force of my blow, however."

Once more on his feet, he let out a sigh. Had he not known the War Hero's reputation, he would have felt ashamed before his captains.

"Do not feel embarrassed, my friend," she said in a low voice. "You are a talented fighter, smart and quick to react. Just a little predictable sometimes."

"The fight was never fair," said Cadmael. "There is no such thing as 'out of shape' for a warrior like you, General Syrela."

To Valirian's surprise, the War Hero answered with a slight smile. Slowly, she nodded. "It is not entirely false. Perhaps you believe yourself a more fair opponent, then?"

As Cadmael smiled, Valirian's eyes widened. He repressed a laugh as the two took slow steps towards one another, taking positions across the training ground—Syrela wanted her revenge! The young captain had earned quite a reputation during his time in the army, after all. She held no anger or bitterness towards him, he knew, yet her pride had doubtlessly led her to seek battle with him. Clearly, Cadmael, too, had yearned for another occasion to duel the War Hero.

The young man's eyes studied her posture closely. All amusement had vanished from his expression, and the two circled one another.

Syrela took a step forwards. The combatants were dangerously close, yet she waited. She would wait for him to strike first. Perhaps his assault would betray his overconfidence. Perhaps he expected an easy victory after having defeated her before.

He attacked not. For the time, he continued studying her. He was more thoughtful than he had at first appeared. Eventually, he took a step forwards. The slightest of movements meant the other would be within reach.

As she had hoped, he was first to attack, striking at her left leg, missing narrowly. He would soon discover that she was easily his match in speed. She struck twice, attacking his left side and forcing him to take a step back to avoid her blows. Though she had expected his speed, she could not deny being nevertheless impressed by his swift reactions, but things were precisely the way she wanted: she was on the offence.

He distanced himself, enough to be just out of reach, doubtlessly testing her—or perhaps daring her. He wanted her to continue her assault, certainly, but she would not fall for his trap. Instead, she had forced him back. Though not by much, it was still a victory. Seeing her reserve, Cadmael was the one to attack this time, yet she easily dashed to her right and pivoted around him, forcing him to dash backwards to avoid her thrust. Some seven steps separated them. Both had time to think. Cadmael dropped his staff and unsheathed his sword, and Syrela mirrored him. If he so wished to test her in closer combat, so be it—but her tactics would change.

Her weapon drawn, she charged the young captain, and twice their blades clashed. Her third blow landed, and she smiled. She had been the first to land a hit, albeit only on his left arm. She took a step back, avoided an attack, and struck again. In spite of the blow, he had not lost courage. Quite the opposite. She aimed at his neck, hoping to end the duel, but a rush of pain in her right leg made her wince.

He had hit her. Now was not the time. Quick! In spite of him landing his strike, and though he had avoided her previous attack, his defence was open. Redirecting her strike, she lunged, her blade finding the young man's chest. Silence. All were immobile. The duel was over.

"General Syrela, you are a warrior like no other exists in this world!" said Cadmael, bowing low before taking a few steps back.

Syrela bowed, too. Never had someone been such a challenge to her since her childhood. "They say you are the greatest fighter in our army. I now see why."

Though he still struggled to catch his breath, Cadmael laughed. Receiving such a compliment from the War Hero made his heart race, and his vision briefly blurred at the sudden rush he felt from it.

"Outstanding performance, Lady Syrela," said Xilto, the other three captains approaching and congratulating her, too.

"I hope this is far from the last time you and I get to spar, Captain Cadmael," said Syrela.

Once more bowing low, Cadmael knew not how to answer. "Of course," he eventually stuttered.

The scene made Valirian chuckle. He, too, approached Syrela, holding back a laugh. "I learnt much from observing you two. I certainly hope to see you spar again."

Satisfied, Syrela let out a sigh and turned to the captains' building. "Perhaps we should then make a habit of sparring with the captains. Ideas are clearer in my mind now. Let us head back to work."

As the captains bowed one last time, the two soon disappeared behind the heavy wooden doors.

CHAPTER 20

THE UNSEEN MAGIC

"Is your quest for vengeance satisfied?" Valirian asked. Now that they were in private, he had the widest of smiles.

Syrela stretched and let out a laugh, then shrugged with a smirk. "The thought did cross my mind. But though a little overconfident on occasion, Cadmael is neither a fool nor an idiot. He has my respect."

Valirian looked down, thoughtful, and his expression shifted to a frown. She knew some thoughts weighed on him, and so she moved to his side.

"My friend, tell me honestly," he said. "Were you holding back against me?"

A short moment passed. She knew not how to answer. "I did prolong the duel by not attacking one of your weaknesses. In the heat of the moment, I was not sure how to act."

He sighed. How could he blame her? Being defeated in mere seconds, even by the War Hero, was humiliating. Yet the truth rejoiced him not, either.

"I can mentor you," she hurried to say at his sigh.

Shaking his head and pursing his lips, he straightened his back and glared. "Do not treat me as you would a child, Lady Syrela."

She looked down. He took a deep breath, and as she glanced at him, he seemed to have relaxed. "I'm sorry. I spoke without thinking, and I understand your frustration. Please, allow me to practice with you."

"Thank you," he said. "I have never been an outstanding warrior, in spite of my best efforts. I know I got lucky at the Battle of the Fortress."

"You did what you could, given your situation. You attempted something knowing you wouldn't succeed in most other scenarios. It was quite smart." The memory made her shiver, and she shook her head. "That battle is not my greatest achievement. Let's not linger on the subject too long, even if, spirits be honoured, all things ended relatively well. We have quite some work ahead of us."

Having turned their attention to the table, they had soon pushed to the side the less relevant maps, the older reports, and all other unnecessary encumbrances to make room for the large map of the north of Illmeria, representing the Grasslands, Heartlands, Northlands, and even parts of the Stormlands.

"Our defences in the Mistlands are ready," said Syrela. "Now, let's see: the Duchess will have some men, and we can expect Kashpur to be an early target." Placing a few wooden figurines on the map, she showed a possible situation where the Koreshian troops landed on the western shore and headed directly towards the Pearl of Illmeria.

"We might struggle to arrive in time to save the city," said Valirian. "The Duchess does not have enough troops to resist until we intervene. We would need to have our army prepared and already in the Grasslands before they arrive, something she would not tolerate."

Syrela rubbed her chin. The thought of stationing an army there, regardless of the diplomatic uproar it would cause, was increasingly appealing. She hesitated until she shook her head. "Sadly, you are right. As painful as it is, it would be wiser to stay in the Mistlands and in the Islands. We cannot risk Adiloka making a foolish last stand against our army, hoping to defeat us. Thousands could die." She placed a few figurines just outside the map, to the south, where the Mistlands would be. "Let us assume the worst scenario. Last invasion, they sent four armies, one of which headed to the Mistlands. This time, their repartition will doubtlessly be different, but we can expect their forces to be similar or even more numerous. We should be expecting six armies, at the very least, perhaps even eight, bringing the Koreshians to some thirty thousand at most. More would be impossible to reasonably supply. Comparatively, we are outnumbered three or four to one. Therefore, we must find a way to split their forces."

In spite of his best attempts at gathering a large army, being so vastly outnumbered left him uneasy. Had he failed at his duty? Should more men be recruited and trained? How many more soldiers could reasonably be battle-ready before the invasion?

"Our goal should be to defend the Illmerian people, first and foremost," she said. "Land may be retaken and cities rebuilt. That matters not. If we cannot make it to Kashpur fast enough, then let's hope that Adiloka would gain enough time to allow her people to flee southwards. We'll be able to protect the refugees better then."

Valirian leaned over the map, studying it closely. The level of detail and precision in the work of the Illmerian monks had always amazed him; they were nothing like the maps made in Vinmara or Koresh. "We could hold a line from the western hills to the sea in the east," he said, pointing on the map. "If we position along the right rivers, we will be able to split our men into large enough groups, and the Koreshians won't be able to cross without being seen."

Taking a few of the Mistian pieces, Syrela positioned them as he had proposed. Splitting command efficiently would be the main challenge, but the idea seemed reasonable.

"I worry that this does not answer how we defeat the Koreshians, though," he said. His lips pursed as he stroked his beard, but Syrela's calm made him raise an eyebrow.

"Have you forgotten the first invasion?" she asked. "We know the land better. With a bit of creativity and some mobility, we can easily overcome their numerical superiority."

"Do you not think that they will be prepared for the tactics you used the first time? Especially as I suspect the same general to lead the invasion—if he has not been executed for his incompetence, of course."

"Oh, but tactics are not a worry for us," she said. "Surely indeed, they shall not fall to the same tricks twice. They will come prepared, with more supplies and better organisation, and they will strike more strategic locations with more soldiers. Yet they cannot ignore the Mistlands. I may not know this land as well as my home, but I know enough to be certain that an army stuck in the forested hills between Mistport and the Fortress is exposed to all sorts of ambushes. Taking a battle where the advantage of numbers is nullified is not the difficulty."

"Well, what will be the difficulty?"

"It will rather be predicting where the Koreshian army will strike after they take Kashpur. I worry not that our soldiers in the Grasslands could be caught, but more that they strike the Mistlands from an angle we did not predict. This is why we spent so much time preparing our defences."

He nodded, better understanding Syrela's near-obsession with large networks of scouts and outposts along the western and northern shorelines of the Mistlands. Thankfully, the sharp cliffs made it difficult, if not impossible, to land in most areas.

A HOME OF MIST

"Did I ever tell you how we managed to so accurately predict the invaders' every move during the first invasion?" she asked. "I had hidden a network of spies in the trees, and with a simple system of ropes, one could alert another of their army's presence, and the information could reach me within an hour at most."

He was hardly surprised. After all, he knew she must have had a clever solution. With a leaf of paper and a small piece of string, she showed him her trick in just a few minutes. It relied on a relatively simple code, with knots made in the string to communicate basic information from just a glance. It simply required equipping the scouts with a strange device Valirian had never seen before: two lenses in a wooden tube, called "long-sight" in the Northian dialect. Though relatively uncommon, as its use was limited to spotting small game from a greater distance, those hunters who had one gladly gave it away for the cause.

"It might be worth trying to equip some of our scouts with them, then," he said, "especially those on outposts near the sea. It might allow them to more easily spot ships in the distance."

"Perhaps, but the mist might limit the tool's effectiveness. Regardless, it's worth a try." Syrela's attention returned to the map in front of them. "I will lead our forces in the Grasslands. You will control our defences in the Mistlands from Mistport. The refugees can be transported via ship from the Grasslands to a safer place, such as the Fortress."

He did not object, trusting her ability to improvise better than his. Should the Koreshians move southwards after their capture of Kashpur, her leadership would be needed to gather the troops and win an important battle.

"Very well," he said. "And once the majority of refugees have been rescued, we regroup our armies and wait for the Koreshians to make a mistake?"

"In some sense," she said. "It will greatly depend on what strategy they then follow, but they will attempt an attack on us at one moment or another. If we encircle them, for instance, we have a chance." She sighed, pushing aside yet another report. "Sadly, we have no easy strategy for this war. We have to hope for a favourable battle and, from there, retake most of what was lost."

Satisfied with their guideline, for the time being, they spent most of the afternoon discussing details and various possible scenarios. Leaning over the table for so long had made their backs sore.

"I suggest we stop for today," said Syrela, massaging her temples. Her headache was slight, but it certainly could worsen.

"Agreed," he said. "Let us continue tomorrow." He opened the door, then followed her out of the building. It was getting darker, but the sun hadn't yet set. "Xelya will expect us in about an hour. Will you join us for tonight?"

For a brief second, she hesitated. "I should accept. I have kept myself in that room for far too long. I need some rest."

Valirian smiled. Though he understood her drive to work and prepare for the war to come, her visage had grown pale, and her eyes seemed tired. "I have an idea," he said. "Let us find your armour."

She raised an eyebrow but followed him without protesting. Together, they headed to the basement of the Tower, where Syrela's armour had been stored. Too damaged to be comfortable to wear, it had only been used as a symbol as they returned home from the negotiations.

"It definitely needs repairs," she said, inspecting the iron mask. At some point, it had suffered a pretty heavy shock. As such, some of the iron protecting the forehead had been bent.

"More," he said. "It can be improved." Taking the various parts and her four blades in his arms, he tried his best to carry them. Syrela laughed at his well-intentioned attempt but took some of the more encumbering parts off his shoulders.

"See, I know that the gems are helping you control your weapons, for instance," he said, "even if I don't know all of the intricate details. But in Koresh, Vinmara, and more recently the Mistlands, we temper the metal in a different manner and use different processes that turn iron into the much more solid steel."

She raised an eyebrow. She had heard much about this "steel" since her arrival at the Fortress, but she had at first thought it a Mistian word for iron, as if the two were synonyms in the dialect.

"And with all due respect," he added, "there are a few exposed areas in your armour."

That, however, she had long ago noticed. Mistian armours protected their wearers much more efficiently. "Indeed. The previous Blades of Illmeria, much like I, relied on their magic to protect themselves against blows but also arrows fired by the enemy."

They headed to the industrial district together, on occasion attracting the attention of passersby, curious at the sight of the War Hero and the Advisor carrying something visibly heavy.

"The magic is thankfully not in the metal," she said. "I'm quite surprised that someone who is neither a Northian nor a magic user knows that. Has Xelya told you so?"

He chuckled and shook his head, which made her all the more curious, but though she ignored the source of his knowledge, she asked nothing more.

"Then it means we should be able to take the gems and inlay them in another armour, correct?" he asked. "And likewise for your blades." Her nod confirmed all he needed to know.

"The four gems allow me to use my powers to their full extent," she said. "With them, I can control my blades just as well as if I carried them with my hands. It takes a lot of mental practice, but it proves particularly deadly on the battlefield."

From his limited understanding of magic, it seemed fairly logical. Rather than activating Syrela's magic, the gems served as catalysts, strengthening her already powerful telekinetic powers. "Then allow one of the most talented smiths of the Fortress to forge an armour fit for the War Hero herself," he said.

They had arrived before a large building, from which only a pale red light emanated. From the chimney on its roof escaped thick black smoke. It was a place familiar to Valirian, who had often worked with the master smith during his first days at the Fortress. "Good evening, Tremoc!"

The smith's jaw dropped at his unexpected guests, and he left on his anvil the thick prong and the cold metal bar he had planned to work on.

"Who's there, Master?" asked the smith's apprentice, who dropped the broom in his hands at the sight.

"My Lord!" said Tremoc. "And the Blade of Illmeria! How may your humble servant be of help?"

"Lady Syrela needs a new armour."

The smith hurried to make room on a table so that they might drop their burden and began to study what had been brought to him.

"It's a very specific order," said Valirian. "It needs to follow many requirements, and only a master blacksmith could suffice."

Tremoc bowed low, speechless as he returned his attention to the blades and the armour that had been brought to him. "You honour me, My Lord! You've come to the right person." With a hand gesture, he commanded his apprentice to bring him his magnifying glass. "I suppose there is more to it than just 'an armour that fits the War Hero'?" he asked, noticing the green gems.

Syrela nodded and explained in greater detail all she needed—from the gems' role to her fighting style and the freedom of movement she required from the armour. As she spoke, the smith began to draw on a piece of parchment. Soon, there was on it a first sketch of the finished armour as he envisioned it. Valirian spoke little, only giving an occasional piece of advice to Syrela on some minor details. She knew very well what she needed and what was possible.

"My Lady knows armours and smithing very well!" said Tremoc. "Better than my own undisciplined apprentice." At his words, the young boy raised his head and hurried in his cleaning work, as if he had begun to fall asleep. After a few more details were settled, the smith lifted in his hand one of the blades. Slightly curved and without a guard, the edge had begun to rust. Thankfully, on each of them, the gem was intact.

"The blades shouldn't take too long," he said. "The armour will take longer, of course, but I will do it as fast as possible. Me thinks some twelve days." Despite his old age, his beard grey and thick, the man seemed full of energy and confidence, barely capable of containing his excitement at the thought of working on such a project.

"You will be richly compensated for your work," said Valirian. After brief salutations, he and Syrela turned around and left.

The forge was out of sight when she stopped and turned to him. "Thank you. I hadn't thought of my own armour with all the preparations. I appreciate that you helped me with it."

He couldn't hold back his smile, but he looked down, not knowing how to answer. "It was my pleasure. Shall we head back to the Tower? Let us not make Xelya wait."

* * *

"Ah, finally!" said Xelya, standing up from her seat with a smile. "Had I not grown accustomed to it, I would have begun to fear having to dine alone tonight. Please, take a seat."

"My apologies," said Valirian. "Some important affairs delayed us."

Raising an eyebrow, Xelya shifted her sight from one to the other as they took their seats. "And what might that be?"

Valirian and Syrela exchanged a brief glance. It was as if each expected the other to speak.

"Well," said Syrela, "we had realised my armour needed some improvements, so we headed to one of the smiths to see it improved."

Xelya laughed. The answer surprised her not—in truth, she had seen the two carrying something, from a distance, at her return to the Tower. "That explains the strange murmurs I heard just minutes ago."

Without much discussion, the three of them too hungry to speak quite yet, they shared a meal of roasted pork and cabbage.

"Have you decided on a strategy?" asked Xelya, the meal almost over.

"For the most part," said Syrela. Explaining their plan, she emphasised the important role of the preparations, as they could not predict how many would flee southwards to the Mistlands—preparations the Queen herself would handle.

"I see," said Xelya. "That will indeed strain our economy, but that is to be expected with war."

"We should be capable of handling it," said Valirian. "We are fortunate to have stockpiled a lot of grain from the spring harvest, and the summer harvest is about to begin."

"Hopefully," said Xelya. "My worry is not grain, nor is it gold. Neither should prove a problem, even in a prolonged war. And we have ample supplies of iron and coal. We can certainly equip a few thousand more men." She rubbed her forehead. There was so much to take into consideration, so many details to remember and take care of. "I'm uncertain about our stock of timber, amongst other things. Especially if you plan on fortifying your positions in the Grasslands, Lady Syrela."

"Then let us divert the timber used in shipbuilding," said Valirian. "Our fleet is large enough for our plans. Hoping to defeat Koresh at sea would require unreasonable numbers of ships."

Xelya sighed, massaging her temples. "Lady Adiloka does not realise the catastrophe she is heading into, does she?"

Evidently, the Duchess did not—and it weighed on Syrela's heart. She shook her head. "I considered a pre-emptive attack on Kashpur. Some three thousand men, from Sanadra to there, to depose Adiloka. Sadly, it would do more harm than good. She is not alone in thinking the way she does. Beyond her yes-men, many genuinely believe in the same delusions."

Syrela's descriptions of Adiloka's court had always bewildered Valirian. How could they be so content, so certain of their own safety? From their palaces, the Northerners' nobility had not seen the war themselves; they ignored the fate Syrela had saved them from. "The people will not be so blind," he said. "Let us simply hope that they can be protected, that they will be warned of the next invasion in time for them to flee."

Little more was said that dinner, and with their food finished, they headed to their respective room. As per their habit, or at least as often as they found time to do so, Xelya and Valirian shared some tea before heading to bed, and though they were often silent, they appreciated the moment of peace.

"Do you believe we have a chance?" she asked.

He stared at his own reflection in the cup. "I can only believe. Do what I think is right and believe." His hand gripped tightly the armrest, and he closed his eyes, letting out a sigh. Yet as he opened them, there was a slight smile on Xelya's lips, one that made him raise an eyebrow.

"My friend, you have done admirable work," she said. "You have taken into account every detail, every aspect of strategy known to you and Lady Syrela. But there is more that you have yet to observe, and in that regard, I ask you to trust in me."

He smiled, he felt his muscles relax, and slowly, he nodded. "You have my trust, Xelya."

CHAPTER 21
TO FACE THE INEVITABLE

A waveless sea, an impenetrable mist, the gentlest of breezes. Xelya looked down. Her bare feet walked on the water without disturbing it. She could see nothing around her, and in spite of her steps forwards, nothing appeared any more clearly.

The nameless presence. Here it was. She felt something crawl on her back, yet as her hand reached to grab it, she found nothing.

"Understand," it whispered.

She shivered, and a powerful gust of wind dispersed the mist. The starry sky above was absolutely clear, and the flawless surface of the water reflected it perfectly. The stars shone like a million diamonds, bathing the endless sea around her in their blue glow. To her surprise, neither the gust of wind nor the gentle breeze had disturbed the breathtaking spectacle, and she admired it for many long minutes, making her even forget the strange presence on her shoulders.

The wind blew stronger, making her heart race. Even then, the sea was unperturbed, but a smell of smoke and char filled her nostrils, forcing her to cough. She peered into the distance, and countless vessels approached rapidly, carried by the increasingly powerful wind. Their hulls were covered in human skin, and the water turned crimson. Twisted laughter came from the ships' crews, and a powerful wave knocked her on her back. She felt herself sink, for a brief second, so she thrashed around, hoping to keep herself above the sea of blood—to no avail. As she was dragged lower and lower, a titanic shape loomed far on the horizon. It had a lion's head made of a polished black stone, and a crimson fire burnt in its eyes.

Xelya opened her eyes; sweat pearled on her forehead. She glanced around her room, and her breathing slowed down as she found it perfectly normal.

"Do not flee from your destiny."

She froze; her heart stopped. It was the same whisper that had spoken in her dreams. Only then did the presence on her shoulders, which she had not even noticed as she woke up, vanish entirely. She no longer felt it near her, but its words echoed in her mind.

* * *

The news had spread like wildfire. All in the Mistlands had dreaded the coming of that day, but there was no escaping it. In less than a week, all knew: war had come.

"Thankfully, all Tremoc needed for my armour were those sixteen days," said Syrela. Minutes before the report on Koreshian troop movements in the Grasslands had reached her and the Advisor, the blacksmith had brought his finished work. But however outstanding it might be, she could hardly spend much time admiring it; already, she had gone back to the battle plans they had drawn in the past weeks.

"I'm equally thankful," said Valirian. "I dare not imagine scholars having to write how Illmeria fell because the War Hero could not go to battle as her armour had not yet been repaired."

A brief chuckle escaped her, yet she bit her tongue and took a deep breath. She glanced at the report one more time, then put it down on the table. "The time has come. Let's hope our preparations were adequate."

Valirian took the report in his hands, reading it once more, as if he needed confirmation of what had been before his eyes mere seconds before. Thankfully, their scout had been quick, and only some four days had passed since the Koreshian landing, but that swiftness hardly brought any reassurance before the severity of the news. As he and Syrela had feared, they were headed directly to Kashpur. Once they had taken the Pearl of Illmeria, Ksadnivi would soon follow. Even more worrying, Zheraï, the Duke of the Stormlands, had seemingly sworn fealty to the Emperor of Obsidian, certainly with hopes of being spared.

"We have to trust ourselves now," said Syrela. "The Koreshians are particularly dangerous in siege warfare, but facing them in an open field would also be foolish. We have to wait for a mistake—and strike. Once we have triumphed in one major battle, we may retake most of the lost land. Any attempts before that would be doomed to fail."

Before the Advisor could reply, rapid footsteps from outside the room caught their attention. The doors were slammed wide open as Xelya entered, followed by the captains. "It is good that the war council was quick to gather. There is absolutely no time to waste."

"Indeed, My Lady, there is no time to waste," said Valirian with a bow.

Carefully stacking the maps on top of one another, Zelshi made some room at the centre of the table so that a larger map of Illmeria could be unrolled. Unlike the others, which had been marked with various arrows and circles of charcoal or chalk, that one had been intentionally kept intact.

Valirian cleared his throat. He glanced at those gathered around the table. All had their attention turned to him—good. "Even if we are to assume minimal resistance from the Duchess, and even if we assume the Koreshians take no stop nor detour on their way to Kashpur, we have some three days to take positions in the Grasslands." Three days was a pessimistic estimation. Thankfully, the Koreshians were more likely to take five or six, giving the Mistians more than enough time. To his left, Syrela approached and leaned over the table. In a few minutes, Valirian had explained the strategy they had established together, and she answered some of the questions the captains had concerning a few details.

"So, we shouldn't take a fight against the Koreshians unless we are one hundred percent certain it's a small group that won't receive any reinforcements?" asked Cadmael.

"Precisely," said Syrela. "The invaders do not wish to prolong the war, so they will strike rapidly, but they might leave themselves exposed by doing so."

"And we are to consider the Stormians enemies, too," said Zelshi. "That dog Zheraï will get what he deserves."

Syrela's lips pursed as she nodded. Never had she imagined the Duke capable of making such a despicable decision. In spite of the war that had opposed them, she had imagined him to be deserving of some respect, regardless of the absurd ambitions that motivated him. The news had been more of an annoyance to Valirian, who ignored the exact capacities of the Stormian army, but Syrela's tales had helped reassure him.

"It is not something we shall worry about," said Xelya. "Such an alliance is not one to last, and we know their numbers to be low compared to those of the Koreshians. I am doubtful of the impact this will have on the war. Additionally, let us not forget this: the Stormians did not predict the invaders' arrival more than we. Negotiations must have been extremely recent and carefully kept as secret as possible.

Many of their soldiers are doubtlessly still garrisoned in the cities further north or in their own land. We are unlikely to meet them on the battlefield, at least not until we reach Kashpur. It should not, and must not, affect our strategy."

Syrela and Valirian looked at one another, and both nodded. The Queen's predictions were most certainly correct, in great part at least.

"So be it," said Syrela. "Thankfully, many militiamen and soldiers from the north rallied to us in the past four weeks. Out of our nine thousand men, let's send seven thousand to the Grasslands. I will lead them. Captain Zelshi, Captain Cadmael, and Captain Akior will follow me there. Captain Xilto, your presence will be useful at the Fortress: you know the city's defences better than anyone. Captain Aaposhi, follow the Advisor to Mistport and assist him in both the defence of the city and in logistics."

All in agreement, the captains bowed, and the discussion returned to details and numbers. It was decided that a thousand men would defend the Fortress, and another thousand would defend Mistport. It would be barely enough, at least should the Koreshians attack with the forces expected by Syrela and him, but Valirian felt confident in his ability to repel or, at the very least, delay the invaders. The entire city had once been turned into a battlefield and defeated the Koreshians; if it must be so, they would do it again. Soon, the captains had left to oversee the preparations. No time was to be wasted.

"Spirits be honoured, the Mistian cities are well-fortified," said Syrela. "I doubt we would stand any chances were they any more exposed."

"A thousand men to defend Mistport might prove difficult," said Valirian. "It could be costly, even if we were to eventually triumph."

"It is a shame that we must split our troops," said Xelya, "but the risks are measured, and we have little choice in the matter."

"Indeed," said Syrela. "Hopefully, we have taken adequate

precautions to defend the Mistlands. If the Koreshians attempt to land, we will see them ahead of time."

* * *

It was not without a slight smile that Valirian watched the Mistian ships set sail to the Grasslands. Though the front line was across the Sea of Tranquillity, where Syrela led seven thousand soldiers, he ignored not the danger of his own position. Were the Koreshians to attack the Mistlands, Mistport would be their first target, and the city was easy to surround in spite of its defences. If they were too numerous, the city could fall—and it would be his end. Yet all was not hopeless. Even then, Syrela would certainly retake Mistport; the Illmerian army would avenge their fallen brothers. It was pointless to flee from what was to come. He had understood this: in a war, Fate, and Fate alone, decided who lived and who died.

He wandered on the docks. There, an eternity ago, or so it felt, his companion Yuzsan had sacrificed his life in battle. He walked to the castle, where his chambers were and where Ayun had come to discuss with him. During his lifetime, the old man had never realised how much he had influenced Valirian. Would he have made the right decision, had the old captain not advised him that night? Perhaps not. Perhaps he would have doubted. He smiled: their spirits had never left him. They would fight by his side as they had in the past.

* * *

The calmness of the sea, normally so soothing to Cadmael, did little against the thoughts in his mind. Once again, he tried to take a deep breath, hoping to slow down his racing heart, but its effects were short-lived. Many he had known had lost their lives in the battle of

Mistport: nephews, uncles, friends. His world had been shattered in one night.

He turned around, taking a few steps across his cabin. He remembered what Valirian had told him, all the advice he had been able to gather from his general about the Koreshians. His solace was knowing that, in this war that had finally come, he would stand and fight rather than watch from afar, powerless.

He slammed his fist against his desk, letting out a grunt, before heading out of his cabin. He would not be able to find any sleep in those conditions. What good did it do to stay inside? War, true war, he had only seen from a distance, heard about through tales of his superiors or fellow captains. He knew not what awaited him. Yet his generals had trusted him. If the War Hero herself believed in their victory, then so should he.

"Unable to find some rest, Captain?" asked Syrela.

Her voice startled him, but as he realised its origin, he silently cursed at himself and shook his head. "Sadly."

Syrela smiled, and she took a deep breath. "Me neither. It is hardly a surprise."

"Are you afraid, My General?" he asked.

For a moment, she answered not, staring at the horizon. Her magical eyes allowed her to see the outline of the Grasslands. Were it daytime, so would the young captain be able to see it. "Do not be ashamed of your fears, young man. It will be your first true battle, after all. You are a brave warrior; you will overcome any fears." She shook her head as she turned to face him. "No, I am worried. The invaders will spare no one. Neither the young nor the old will find mercy. And I know where they are headed. I beg the spirits of Illmeria to protect Kashpur if possible."

Finding no words to answer, Cadmael nodded, and for a few moments, he stayed by her side. He glanced at her and put his chest forth, his head high. He would fight side by side with the Blade of Illmeria herself, under her command, following her example of bravery and honour.

"Attempt to find some rest, Captain," she said. "Each hour you sleep may help you save another life."

He agreed and turned around, heading back to his cabin.

"We will triumph," she said. "We will triumph and Illmeria shall be safe."

Before he could answer, she had disappeared into her cabin, and so, according to her advice, he attempted to sleep. It was shortly after dawn that he awoke, just as the army prepared to land on the shores of the Grasslands. According to the War Hero's plan, they would first build a small fort near the landing site before heading further north, to the strategic locations—as it had been agreed upon during the war council. Yet Cadmael desired nothing but to ride north, alone if need be. It felt like each minute spent inactive could cost the life of another Illmerian.

"Captain Cadmael, lead a small reconnaissance group to the north," said the War Hero. "If it is possible, gather information from locals or refugees about the front." She took a few steps forwards so that only he would hear. "I understand your impatience, but do not let it lead you to any rash decisions."

"Yes, My General," he said. As he rode northwards at the head of a dozen soldiers, he forced himself to slow his breathing, and once in position, he waited. He watched: in the distance, behind a hill to the north, a column of smoke. A group of villagers marched southwards, and soon, they would cross the bridge he and his men guarded. "We are men at the service of the Queen of Mists," he said to them. "Head south and you will find refuge."

Their faces lit up, and they thanked the young man profusely as they crossed the bridge. Beyond, the plains seemed calm, though it did little to reassure Cadmael. The Koreshian army was still expected to be much further north, perhaps laying siege to Kashpur or Ksadnivi. Why so much smoke?

"What is the news in the north?" he asked one of the village elders.

"The invaders are going to Kashpur," said the old woman. "They are probably already attacking the city." She came closer, her voice low. "They are too many. The battle won't last long. Everyone is fleeing south."

Cadmael needed to keep his calm. He repeated Syrela's words to himself, silently. It was as the War Hero and the Advisor had imagined. His lips pursed as he nodded. Then he turned to his men. "Sergeant, you and your men will set camp here. I need to return to the general. Avoid any confrontation. Guide any refugees to our landing area. Keep your eyes open, especially at night. We don't know where the Koreshians might exactly be."

He jumped on his horse. Soon, his men had set up a small camp, but he had already left. He did not bother to turn around once as he rode as fast as he could. His men were unlikely to face any threat, not in the immediate future. At least the invaders' progress did not exceed expectations, but it left the Mistian army little time to act. They needed to take positions immediately. He galloped throughout the night, ignoring his own exhaustion, until the fort was in sight. He dropped from his horse with a slight smile—it was shortly before dawn.

CHAPTER 22

A MORNING OF GREY AND RED

Silence. There was something beautiful in the grey minutes before dawn, the pale rays of the sun not daring yet to show themselves. The cold morning air filled Syrela's lungs, and a gentle breeze caressed her skin as she stretched her muscles. She got dressed and tied her hair behind her head. The day would be doubtlessly busy; there was no time to waste.

She cursed Zheraï's name. The unexpected alliance between the Koreshians and Stormians risked compromising the Mistian strategy, for it allowed the invaders to ignore the Northlands and the Stormlands, making their conquest significantly faster. She had purposefully refused to mention that issue during the council; calculated risks needed to be taken for the war to be won.

After taking some food for herself, she equipped her armour. For a few moments, she studied her helmet. In the polished metal, she saw her own green eyes, their slight glow reflecting on the steel's surface. Never had she feared for her own life; her magic made her unequalled on the battlefield, and her defeat at the Fortress did very little to change her thoughts on the matter. Had it not been for Xelya's own powers, no single Mistian warrior would have defeated her. Yet could she save those in Ksadnivi, Kashpur, Naila?

She left the fort's perimeter, wishing to see the land for herself. She squinted. Nearing the camp was a lone cavalier, riding to the fort as fast as he could. He stopped and dropped from his horse as two soldiers hurried to Syrela's side.

"Unlikely to be a hostile," she said. The two men nodded and followed her up the hill.

"My General!" said Cadmael, saluting.

Syrela took a moment to inspect him. There were no marks of battle, no wounds or dents in his armour that would suggest he had fled in a hurry.

"Me and my men met a group of villagers running to the south," he said. "They gave us some important information, and I thought it was good to tell you as quickly as possible."

She raised an eyebrow and repressed a smile, unsure whether the information truly justified such a hurry. Nevertheless, she listened to his report with a grave expression.

"Is it likely that the city has already fallen?" she asked once he had finished.

"I doubt it," said Cadmael. "But it's going to be a matter of days, at most."

Biting her tongue, she nodded. She was to expect the worst. "Rest for the day. There was no need to risk your own health for a matter of hours. Otherwise, I shall handle the preparations." She knew her words had fallen on deaf ears; Valirian had warned her that Cadmael had a tendency for zeal. In some ways, there was something admirable in his willingness to put his duties above anything else, even if in strange manners. "Nevertheless, this does confirm that we have just enough time. We will depart this afternoon, which is according to our plans."

Once she had returned to her quarters, she unrolled a map of the Grasslands. It would take, at the very least, four days for the Koreshians to reach the defensive positions they would set up. That was if Kashpur had already fallen and if they were to ignore Ksadnivi. A more likely estimate was some eight or ten days, if not more, for it was unlikely that the Koreshians would learn of the Mistians' positions in the immediate future. Though all had thus far unfolded according to plan, there were few reasons to rejoice. The Pearl of Illmeria would fall, ruined, ravaged by the invaders. She shook her head, not daring to imagine what would soon befall the beautiful city. But Illmeria was not lost. The Mistlands would stand and fight. What was destroyed would be rebuilt, or so she repeated to herself.

"If only you had not been so blind, o Lady Adiloka the wise," she whispered. Syrela summoned the two other captains, Zelshi and Akior, and informed them of the situation.

"What are your orders, My General?" asked Akior.

"We will leave this very afternoon," she said. "We need to hurry. It is unwise to waste any time, which is why I requested your presence so that we may instruct each group of their exact destination."

Hunched over a few maps, the three discussed a few details before coming to an agreement. The two captains headed outside, and she followed them shortly after. The camp was soon buzzing with activity as several battalions formed and gathered the supplies they needed, prepared to leave at any time. Syrela allowed herself not a second of rest, constantly shifting from one side of the camp to another as she supervised the captains' work and answered any of their questions. The mere thought of staying put left her uneasy. Soon, four columns of troops exited the wooden fort, heading in slightly different directions, and the next day, all had taken their positions.

And so vanished her need to stay constantly active, as each day seemed identical to the previous. Though there was some pride in seeing the relief of those hundreds of Illmerians fleeing the Koreshian army, she found no peace at night. Often, the refugees brought reports of the invaders' advance, though they were imprecise and sometimes contradictory. Often, she had to fight the urge to call for an attack; the thought of having to wait, far away from the conflict, was unbearable. She was a general. Who, other than the Queen herself, could deny her command? And was she not a warrior, the Blade of Illmeria herself, who had sworn to defend this land? Yet each time, she forced herself to wait. She knew to ignore such instincts, regardless of the frustration or grief. It was a catastrophe the Duchess had caused. Attempting to prevent it would only cause greater losses.

"So be it," she told herself. It had been yet another nightmare-filled rest, with visions of flames and blood, of ruins and ashes. Atop a small mound, she observed the horizon. The hills further north were covered by the dark mantle of the night, yet she saw the shrubs that covered them move with the wind. She had resolved to spend some time alone in meditation, a few minutes away from her camp, every morning. That was a habit she had developed since they had taken their position, yet what had perturbed her that night had kept her awake long before dawn. The refugees of that day had confirmed the fall of Kashpur and the incoming siege of Ksadnivi further south. If it were true, as Ksadnivi was even less defended than the Pearl of Illmeria, then the Koreshian army could approach the Mistian positions in the incoming days. A direct confrontation was to be avoided at all costs; therefore, a tactical retreat to the western hills appeared the wisest solution. Perhaps the Koreshians would attempt to take control of the iron mines in that area. There, she might find an advantageous battleground.

She took a deep breath. It was perhaps two or three hours before dawn, but if she was to be restless, then it was wiser to make use of her time. She returned to her tent, washed her face with cold water, and equipped her armour.

"It has been too long since I last wore this mask." It had been reforged almost identical to her last one, though with a few improvements added. It now protected the top of her head and her jaw correctly, though her mouth was still not hidden behind any metal, according to her wishes: she did not want her voice to be muffled in any way in battle, nor did she wish for her breathing to be impaired.

She headed to the bridge, and greeted the guards there. They seemed surprised to see the War Hero leave the camp alone, so early in the morning, but none dared question her. Her magical eyes would grant her an advantage in the darkness, allowing her to see any danger from afar, if there were any. Having crossed the river, she disappeared behind a few bushes and headed further north to the dark hills on the horizon. They seemed far and tall yet were hardly more than an hour away.

She knew what lay beyond, rather familiar with the region: a road that led north, zigzagging in the valleys and plains between the short hills of the region. She told herself that this was nothing but some scouting, that it was wiser for a general to see the ground with her own eyes. In truth, the repetitiveness of the days had led her there; she hoped that the change of sight would do her some good.

Eventually, she reached the top of the hill, observing the new horizon from there. Everything seemed peaceful. Another hill further away bordered the road on the west, while a small grove bordered it on the east. To the north, another line of trees, or bushes perhaps, had grown alongside the road and followed it. She took a deep breath, letting the cold air fill her lungs with a slight smile, the sensation invigorating. She effortlessly climbed a rock and sat on it cross-legged, closing her eyes for a few moments. For many long minutes, she focused her attention on her breath: slow, controlled. Her eyes only reopened as the first rays of light appeared from the east. She straightened her back and stretched as much as her armour allowed her to before once more setting her sight on the valley below.

Something was odd, as if out of place. She frowned and squinted. What she had mistaken as trees, or bushes, appeared under the daylight as people. Two groups were headed to her soldiers' position. Though nothing seemed unusual at first glance—refugees fleeing the war were nothing out of the ordinary, after all—something puzzled her. All appeared to be in a rush, yet one group was faster than the other—a banner of red and gold! She turned around and ran to the camp, closing the distance in no time. Her men noticed her hurry, and a sergeant rode to meet her in the fields.

"My General!" he said. "Is there danger approaching?"

"Gather the men at once!" she said. "Meet me on the fields and prepare for battle!"

Without waiting for an answer, she turned around, and so did the sergeant. The sound of a horn behind her. Her men were gathering and would soon join her, yet there was no time to waste. The first group, mere refugees, was now two hundred steps away. She went to meet them, shouting at them to continue running. Behind, the Koreshian soldiers were approaching. She alone would have to stand between her people and them. So be it.

"The Blade of Illmeria! We are saved!" cheered the refugees.

She ran past them. They were ahead by hardly more than a few minutes, and the bridge was still too far away; the invaders risked catching up. She climbed the small mound ahead. The Koreshians were now fully in sight. She closed her eyes and waited. Her breath slowed, her heartbeat calmer by the second.

"Fearless before death," she whispered to herself. Before her, some seven hundred invaders, the golden lion of their banner flying high. Behind her, the four hundred soldiers under her command approached. They would be just in time.

"March forwards!" she said. "Maintain the ranks!"

Her orders were repeated by the sergeants, and the Illmerian army prepared for impact. The Koreshians had slowed down. They, too, intended to fight a battle there, and so they formed ranks. None of her men had fought the enemy before, and most had never seen a battle. She could not tolerate hesitation or fear.

"Soldiers, men, sons of Illmeria! As we send back the invaders to their land, let it be known that the War Hero was only a brave warrior amongst brave warriors! Let it be known that the fury of Illmeria shall not end until our land is safe once more! Charge!"

A war cry echoed amongst her men, and she took a step forwards. She pursed her lips and focused on the distance between herself and them: two hundred steps, at most. The blades on her back unsheathed, following her into battle. Behind, her soldiers marched with the caution and discipline she had taught them. She would precede them by almost a minute. Just enough time. She observed the Koreshian ranks as they attempted to reorganise themselves after their chase. She noticed a weak point on her left: the ranks not as tight, a soldier visibly frightened. There, she would strike.

She avoided their attacks, her magic deflecting many of their blows as her spear found the neck of her target, leaving him dead as she pushed further. Her four blades flew in circles around her, forcing many back, striking a few in the weak points of their armours. The Koreshians were unprepared for her powers; none had ever witnessed the War Hero in battle. Their shouts soon drowned out their superiors' commands. Relentless, her spear struck many more times, leaving a dozen soldiers dead, their ranks shattered. The Illmerian first line clashed with the Koreshian vanguard, and the battle truly began. Further in, she was surrounded by enemies. Not one could escape her deadly dance as she unleashed the magic flowing in her veins. It had been mere minutes, yet the Koreshians scattered, lacking the will to fight. Perhaps they had been exhausted by a night spent giving chase, or maybe they were fresh recruits, men that had never fought a battle. Regardless, she could not let them live.

The invaders were fleeing, the Illmerians gave chase, and for a long hour, they pursued. If even one escaped, their presence could be revealed. Eventually, her men gathered: some 360. Amongst the missing men, some twenty had been wounded, while the others had given their lives for Illmeria—minimal losses. Her men cheered, their celebration replacing the echoes of battle, the first victory of what would doubtlessly be a long and exhausting war. No Koreshians, it seemed, had escaped, but she could take no risks. Her position was likely to be the first attacked should the Koreshians send a massive force further south. It was the exact reason she had personally gone there. Yet other positions could very well be under threat, too, especially as the fleeing villagers soon confirmed her suspicions: Ksadnivi had fallen as well. Nothing stood in the way of the Koreshians should they continue southwards, and a battle fought on such grounds was one even her exceptional talents alone would not win.

"Gather the troops, Sergeant," she said. "We will depart as soon as possible."

It was wiser to regroup her men for the time being, for her priority was to avoid unnecessary losses. Soon, messengers had been sent to the three captains, requesting their return to the landing area, and in the following days, her army had regrouped and marched west. Even if outnumbered one to four, Syrela believed in a possible victory. She knew this land; it lacked not in favourable positions. Still, it would not be an easy victory. Alexar, if it was indeed he who once more led the Koreshian army, had doubtlessly learnt from the previous war. But she still had many more tricks to use in battle.

CHAPTER 23

"THIS LAND SHALL BURY YOU AND YOUR MEN"

The maritime breeze carried a smell all too familiar to Valirian, one that conjured countless memories, some he had wished to never relive. Yet he gazed at the Sea of Tranquillity, mesmerised by the sun's reflection on its surface. It was a brief moment of peace for what had been two days of frenetic activity, for all in Mistport prepared for battle: the Koreshian fleet had been sighted near Mistian shores.

He had underestimated the speed of the warships, and that mistake could prove fatal. There was not enough time to evacuate the entire population. The nearby villagers had been able to find refuge in the city, and those further south had been instructed to head to the Fortress for safety. The size of the fleet fit the most pessimistic of scenarios he and Syrela had planned for: easily twenty thousand Koreshians, if not more. Against such a force, the entire city risked becoming a battlefield. In those conditions, his thousand men alone could cause the Koreshians heavy casualties. If only Mistport had been evacuated! He could then gain time, and the fierce resistance would force the invaders to retreat, for they would run out of supplies and suffer too heavy losses. But Valirian knew Koreshian tactics all too well. He could not allow the citizens to be slaughtered. He and Aaposhi had organised the defences, digging two trenches around Mistport, hoping that the tall and thick walls of the city would grant sufficient protection—an illusion, he knew. The Koreshians had mastered siege warfare. Perhaps he could hold against them for a few days, but eventually, he would lose control of the city.

He glanced past the sea and stared at the horizon beyond the mist. His only hope was the War Hero and her men. Earlier that morning, he had sent a letter across the Sea of Tranquillity, hoping it would reach Syrela. She frequently wrote to him, generally once every other day, keeping him informed of the situation across the strait. Thus had he heard of the fall of Kashpur, but also of the capture of Ksadnivi, from her last letter, four days prior. Likewise, it had been three days since the Mistian fleet left Mistport—he had heard not a word from either the fleet or Syrela since. It was unlikely that the army in the Grasslands had been defeated, for he trusted the War Hero's abilities, but he ignored not that war often was unpredictable. More plausibly, Syrela had engaged the enemy, the both of them having underestimated the other's strength, and thus, she had been prevented from returning to the Mistlands.

He sighed and looked down at the amulet around his neck. In his discussion with Xelya that evening, both had shared their concerns for the other, yet neither could do anything more. It was certainly possible that such an impressive Koreshian army could split and lay siege to both Mistport and the Fortress at once in an attempt to capture the cities rapidly. The Illmerians would stand and fight—and die if need be. Hopefully, in their glorious defeat, they would weaken the invaders, and the War Hero would retake Mistport.

A HOME OF MIST

* * *

The day had come. After a troubled night, one filled with nightmares, Valirian hurried to equip his armour and met with Aaposhi on the city walls. The Koreshians had just arrived, or so the captain had told him. In spite of the mist, he attempted to count the enemy troops; they were numerous, as reported by the scouts, but the figure of twenty thousand appeared as a clear overestimation—or his fear of a simultaneous siege of the Fortress was to be soon confirmed. There were a little more than ten thousand, perhaps eleven or twelve thousand invaders.

He sighed. He had wished himself able to warn Xelya, but they had used the amulet's magic too recently. Hopefully, his warnings of the day prior would be enough.

"They are still taking positions," said Aaposhi.

Valirian nodded, though he turned not to face the captain. He, too, had slept very little that night, as shown by the redness in his eyes and the heavy bags under them. Together, they stared at the Koreshian army, just out of arrow's reach. Around them, Illmerian soldiers hurried to the walls and prepared themselves for battle. The seemingly flawless organisation of the invaders was the façade of their fear-induced discipline. A mark of Alexar's command, Valirian knew. He frowned and squinted to better distinguish the shapes on the horizon. There was a voice that echoed: powerful, fearsome, one he had grown accustomed to. A group of Koreshians approached the walls, just enough to be seen through the mist. In the centre, a tall man in a black armour was their leader. There he was, the Butcher of Illmeria.

"Citizens of Mistport," said the Koreshian general, his Illmerian accent far from perfect. "Surrender now and you will be spared. Open your gates!"

For the shortest of moments, Valirian glanced around himself, the thought that his men would listen passing through his mind, yet his fears vanished as he shook his head. The Mistians were tenacious and proud, and many amongst them had seen the destruction Koresh would cause, too. He straightened his back and raised his head, taking slow steps to the crenellations. He took one last deep breath.

"Alexar!" shouted Valirian in Koreshian. "This land shall bury you and your men, for none of you shall survive this battle!" His voice echoed in the plains beneath.

It looked as if Alexar leaned forwards on his horse. Valirian smiled, and a chuckle even escaped him as the Koreshian general turned around and returned to his camp. The joy was short-lived. The battle would soon begin, for Alexar's voice would certainly call for an assault in mere instants. Yet there was silence, silence for a long hour.

"Careful!" shouted a sergeant.

The Koreshian war machines had fired their first projectile, but the thick walls of the city stood strong. The invaders had formed ranks, not so far from the fortifications, yet seemed hesitant at their siege weapons' lack of impact. Doubtlessly, they had expected the walls to crumble, much like those of the northern Illmerian cities. The war machines fired quite a few more projectiles at the wall in hopes of creating a breach, but they soon realised that such would not be the case quite yet. A call in the distance: Alexar's powerful voice commanded his men, and the Koreshians charged the walls with debris and whatever they could find.

"They want to storm the city walls!" said Valirian. "Aaposhi, bring pikemen up here, now!"

A few orders were shouted, and several groups of Mistian soldiers rushed to the fortifications. In spite of his hurry, Valirian had to repress a smile. Storming the city walls was foolish. The Koreshian attack had been too early, for the Mistian archers rained arrows onto them at their approach. It was only as the invaders filled up the trenches that they could bring tall ladders, and the few that successfully reached the fortifications were met by the tip of a pike. Certainly, Alexar had underestimated the number of troops garrisoned in Mistport, and Valirian would make him pay dearly for that mistake.

"Fight on, men!" said Aaposhi. "Cut them down! Let's send those dogs back to their masters!"

The captain let out a war cry as his blade found the neck of a Koreshian soldier, and at the head of a small battalion, he rushed to a section of the wall occupied by a group of invaders. When one section had been cleared, another seemed overwhelmed. Hours passed all too quickly in this frenzy, but the trenches were filled with the bodies and blood of the enemy.

Valirian's blade pierced the heart of the soldier before him when the Koreshians called off the assault. Alexar's stubbornness had been his weakness once more, for he should have understood long ago that such a frontal attack would fail. The war machines ceased not firing at the walls, however, but it gave the Mistians time to render unusable the enemies' ladders and reorganise.

"This city shall not fall!" said Valirian. "Let your arrows make each of them regret the day they set foot on our land!"

It was good that arrows were unlikely to run out before the end of the battle. The supplies were such that they could last a long week, at least, without the slightest of worries. It was not the ability to sustain a prolonged battle that troubled Valirian. Food, water, ammunition: all were in sufficient quantities. Rather, he knew Alexar would eventually break the city's defences, and then how much longer could they hold? Yet time had passed more rapidly than Valirian had thought: the afternoon neared its end already. Mistian losses had been minimal, about a hundred soldiers, especially compared to the countless Koreshians who had died, but they were still heavily outnumbered.

"They are bringing battering rams this time," said Aaposhi.

Valirian frowned, yet he was quite unsurprised. "If that's the only hope of the Koreshians, then perhaps Mistport can indeed be saved. Our gates can last for many hours."

"Ladders!" shouted a soldier nearby.

What was Alexar doing? If he hoped to divide the Illmerian forces, he would need to send more than just a few more soldiers as arrow fodder. Had his pride been hurt by the initial failure of his plan? It was with a slight smile that Valirian watched the sun set on the horizon. Alexar had wished to take the city rapidly, no matter the cost, but that had proved impossible. The walls still stood strong, unbroken, and the invaders' losses were great.

"Take the lead of our defences on the wall," said Valirian. "I will head to the gate and—"

"My General!" called out a soldier. "My General! Koreshian warships have been sighted approaching the port! The enemy is trying to land directly into the city!"

Valirian's expression darkened. He glanced at Aaposhi, and the two men nodded. The enemy had used nightfall and the mist to their advantage and intended to attack the harbour. There was no time to waste. Valirian jumped on his horse, cursing his own short-sightedness as he rode to the north of the city, followed by some six hundred men. Swordsmen, pikemen, archers, and many militiamen with axes, pitchforks, and scythes: all those available and willing to defend the city. The battle was far from over—such was Alexar's message. The Mistian defences were split successfully; that was the reason behind the Koreshian general's stubbornness. The warships were minutes away from the docks. Their number only warned of the size of the incoming force.

"Build a barricade!" said Valirian. "Grab whatever you can!"

With the help of the citizens rushing out of their homes to help, they began forming a tall barricade of crates, wheelbarrows, stones, and planks. All that could be used was soon piled at the harbour's two entrances. Yet there was not enough time. The ships had arrived, and the barricades were far from constructed. Had Valirian foreseen the possibility, he could have easily prepared a trap and caused heavy casualties to the first wave of Koreshians. He clenched his fist on the hilt of his sword, biting his tongue as he shook his head. This was not the time to regret his own mistakes. Gathering his men, he formed ranks and prepared a charge against the landing Koreshians. He still held the advantage for the time being.

"Now! Charge!" he said, his men following him in his assault. The first Koreshian wave was left disorganised, and many fell to the Illmerian attack, yet Valirian had to call for a retreat. The invaders had gained enough time for two more warships to land, and the defenders were outnumbered, the odds now against them. The battle had to be fought smartly. Gaining time was crucial if the Illmerians were to stand any chance.

"Soldiers, tight ranks!" shouted Valirian. The Illmerian formation created a wall of pikes and shields, his men intent on slowing down the Koreshians. The invaders attacked, and though many perished to the Mistian phalanx, the defenders were losing ground.

"Fire!" shouted a man. Above, hundreds of commoners had gathered on the walls. Hunters had taken their bows, lumberjacks their axes, others their knives or even mere rocks, and threw them at the Koreshians. Valirian glanced to his right and his left. It had been enough; the gates had been partially closed and the entrances barricaded.

"Retreat behind the barricades!" he said. At the head of a small group, he would cover the retreat of his men and give them the time needed to take positions. "Fight on!" he said to his elites. "Fight for Illmeria and what is ours!" He glanced at the gates again: they had been closed, for the enemy had neared them dangerously. He turned around. There was still an escape, their last chance before he and his men were surrounded. One of the towers nearby had a small door heading up the walls.

"Soldiers, to me!" said Valirian. He had to fight through the line of Koreshians that separated him from his objective; a passage had to be made. Those who had already retreated to safety soon realised the situation, and focused their fire to help their general. Valirian would not relent. Thrice he swung his blade, and thrice he found the weak point of his enemy. He thanked Syrela, Cadmael, and all the spirits of Illmeria as a fourth enemy fell to his blows, grateful that his training had borne fruit in the end. They were mere steps away from the door, yet a fifth opponent stood in his way. A tall Koreshian sergeant thrust his spear at Valirian. The weapon's tip narrowly missed the Advisor's arm, and he repositioned himself, striking back at the man's neck. Yet as the man collapsed to the ground, a sharp pain in his right leg brought Valirian to his knees. He screamed; a Koreshian spear had found its way to his armour's weak point, and he could not move.

"Help the general!" said a soldier nearby.

Valirian's cry had doubtlessly saved him. Soon, his men dragged him through the passage, sealing it behind them. They had escaped.

CHAPTER 24

OPPORTUNITY OF AN END

"Your wound doesn't seem life-threatening, My General," said one of the soldiers.

Using cloth as a bandage had been enough to stop the bleeding, and though Valirian was impaired in his movements, the pain had begun to fade away. "Bring me to my horse. Help me onto it." The battle was far from over, and he would not abandon his men in such crucial moments. Using the shaft of a spear as support, and helped by two of his soldiers, he limped to his mount. "Sergeant, hold the position and keep firing arrows from the walls. We have halted their progress. Let us make them pay now."

It had taken quite some time to secure the harbour. It was already an advanced hour of the night, a comforting thought as he galloped to the southern gates. Throughout the day, hundreds of militiamen, if not over a thousand already, had joined the battle, helping stabilise the situation, and news from the walls was good: Aaposhi had successfully repelled every attack by the Koreshians, and the main gates still stood. The battle was at a stalemate for the most part, but Valirian knew that the invaders would eventually breach the defences; they were still far too many. From there, the outcome would be uncertain.

"Have the Koreshians attempted to climb the walls recently?" asked Valirian.

The captain shook his head with a shrug. "Not recently. I think they hoped for the attack on the harbour to weaken us more on this front than it actually did. They suffered heavy losses attempting to climb up here many times earlier, though."

At the main gates, not too far away, the invaders' attack did not relent. There had certainly been a change of tactics; however, Alexar had not yet called a retreat but instead committed to the assault. That meant he still had more than enough men to send into battle—hardly a positive sign.

"What do you think their losses are so far?" asked Valirian.

"We've maybe killed two or three thousand here," said Aaposhi. "Even if that's a lot, we've had losses of our own, and I don't know how much longer the main gates will hold. Good thing is that we aren't heading for a prolonged siege. It's victory or death—and now."

Valirian nodded. He knew where to head next. He had let himself be caught unaware once. Such a mistake he would not repeat. On the large plaza behind the main gates, his men hurried all they could find to a large barricade, hoping to delay the breach for as long as possible. Though all knew the Koreshians would eventually break through, the disposition of the defences was such that any forces entering the main plaza would be stuck between a labyrinth of barricades ahead of them and a rain of arrows from the walls above—the Illmerians would make the invaders pay dearly for each step. Was there truly any hope for reinforcements? Maybe a quarter of the Koreshian army had been defeated, while his losses numbered perhaps two hundred, at most. But the situation was bound to turn less favourable once the battle was fought in the streets instead.

"Prepare traps," said Valirian. "Gather as much rubble and stone as you can. We can make it fall on the invaders as they enter the plaza." From the roofs of the houses around, simple mechanisms were prepared for when the fateful moment arrived; the more chaotic the battleground, the more it would favour the defenders. Any tactic, any way to undermine the enemy's morale or gain the slightest of advantages, be it a second, was to be used. If the city could be turned into a living hell for the Koreshians, then it would be.

"My General!" said Aaposhi. "They have almost breached the gates!"

A quick glance at the sky: the first rays of the sun pierced through the mist. Dawn had come. Valirian called his men into position. There was no reason to leave any of them exposed. Soon, the next stage of the battle would begin. A loud crash, followed by another. Boxes and carts fell from the barricade onto the ground, breaking and scattering onto the plaza, and yet another crash followed, louder than the previous ones. The gates had fallen.

Hundreds of Koreshians poured into the city, their war cries soon replaced by their screams of terror as rocks and rubble fell on them from the sides. Arrows soon followed. Pressed by those behind them, the survivors were forced to charge forwards into the Illmerian barricades, yet as they were dealt with, more joined the fray. They were innumerable, an uninterrupted flow of invaders pouring into Mistport.

"This city will not fall!" said a Mistian sergeant nearby. His shout was echoed by the soldiers around him.

Yet in spite of the casualties they had suffered, the Koreshians eventually overran the defensive positions, and the Illmerians were forced to retreat further into the city. It was wiser to cede ground than to lose men, or so thought Valirian, yet he seemed unable to prevent either. While more enemies seemed to fall, his losses were too heavy to carry on for too long. There needed to be a breakthrough of some sort.

"Men, soldiers of Illmeria, to me!" said Valirian.

For a second, there had seemed to be the glimpse of such an occasion. If not now, then never. Even wounded, he would fight. On horseback, his lance in hand, he led a hundred of his soldiers in a charge. The Koreshians had been distracted, their ranks briefly disorganised. If he could deal with the twenty invaders before him quickly, then he could isolate and surround a larger group.

His lance broke, but the tip lodged itself in a Koreshian sergeant's heart. The attack had been too sudden for his enemies, and the timing was impeccable: the flow of enemy reinforcements that passed through the gates had just stopped. His sword in hand, he and his men quickly dealt with the small, scattering group—even faster than he had hoped. There was still much fighting in the plaza; the entire zone had not yet been overrun, and his position was perfect. He trapped another battalion of Koreshians between his group and another in an adjacent street, as planned, then claimed victory in two other skirmishes. Those few successes were the occasion to turn the tide and retake some ground. He would defeat scattered groups of Koreshians and rally his men behind him. He charged into the plaza, forcing many of the invaders to retreat to the gates under Illmerian cheers.

Yet the celebration was short-lived—there he was. At the head of a hundred grey giants, Alexar entered the plaza and rallied those two hundred Koreshian soldiers still in the area. The next fight would decide the outcome of this siege. All could end now. For once, the Illmerians outnumbered their enemies, but even then, Valirian knew not to overestimate his odds, for each grey giant posed a significant threat, and defeating any was worthy of rejoicing. He glanced at his men, then at the Koreshians, who were gathering some thirty steps away. There was no time to waste; he could not allow them to form ranks.

"Attack!" he said, leading his men into another charge.

The semblance of order on the plaza was short-lived. In mere seconds, the two forces had entered a chaotic brawl that scattered them all into smaller groups.

Valirian's sword had found its target quite a few times throughout the first day and night of the battle, yet all he had fought were mere footmen, peasants turned soldiers by the Koreshians. Now he faced a grey giant. From a nearby barricade, he grabbed a spear and gripped its shaft tightly. His horse raced, galloping as fast as it could. The impact was seconds away; it was now or never.

His vision blurred. Something had collided against his breastplate, and he was out of breath. Another shock—this time, it was the paved ground beneath him. He had been knocked off his mount. He hurried to stand up, in spite of the sharp pain in his leg, and drew his sword from his belt, but he was surprised to see the grey giant on the ground. Next to the dead soldier, his horse agonised; his mount had been in the trajectory of his enemy's pike. Valirian cursed. The pain in his leg was getting worse, making him wince, but he could not afford to stay still. The battle raged on all around. In spite of the grey giants' might, the Koreshians were slowly getting pushed back, but Valirian could not allow them to retreat.

He scanned the plaza; his target could not be that far. There he was! A group of grey giants had engaged a larger troop of Illmerians, and from the brawl, Alexar attempted to flee. In spite of his wounds, Valirian gave chase. It was an occasion he could not let pass; it was the time to strike. "This battle ends here!" he shouted in Koreshian.

Alexar turned to face him. A chuckle, muffled by his black helm. "You have always been so rash when angered, boy. You stand no chance against me, nor do you stand a chance against Koresh. Turn around and run away while you still can." In spite of his warning, Alexar raised his two-handed sword. He certainly knew words were futile.

Valirian was the first to attack. As he suspected, his blade was easily blocked by the Koreshian. Yet he struck once more at his old master's shoulder, hoping to tire him as his blow was also likely to be parried. Alexar's counter-attack came soon after, and a step to the right sufficed to avoid it, but Valirian understood his weakness all too well: he could hardly move his left leg, even less so lean on it.

Another attack from Alexar: a thrust forwards that kept the two of them at a distance. But the Koreshian had a greater reach. Valirian cursed. He could not fail, not now. It was too crucial of a moment. Leaning on his right leg, he dashed forwards, ignoring his painful wound. His enemy was once again within his reach; this was perhaps his last chance. With a thrust of his blade, he hoped to find his enemy's neck, yet the Koreshian stepped to the left at the last moment.

Valirian's eyes widened. Too late did he understand: Alexar had noticed his wound and lured him into the simplest of traps. The Koreshian's sword was the last glimpse Valirian caught. He had been too obvious in his weakness, too reliant on his ability to jump to the right. Alexar's strike came from that side, an attack that could not be parried.

A sharp pain. A scream escaped Valirian's throat, and his vision blurred as he hit the ground. He had never stood a chance. He had been foolish. How could he have ever hoped to defeat Alexar, alone and wounded? The blow had pierced his armour, and he felt blood pouring from the gaping wound. A second passed, yet he still breathed. He glanced at his opponent; his shape was blurry, but he stood a few steps away. Alexar had hesitated for a brief moment but once again raised his sword. Valirian tried to reach for his weapon, a step away from him, but his right arm ignored any command. The wound had been too severe. He crawled and, with his other hand, grabbed his weapon, but as he turned to face his opponent, he found Alexar running away.

"Help your general!" shouted Aaposhi.

It had been just in time. A sigh escaped Valirian's lips as he collapsed on the ground.

CHAPTER 25

A FURIOUS CLOUD

Never would Aaposhi have imagined witnessing such a carnage. On the plaza, a thousand bodies lay on the ground, most lifeless—and amongst those still breathing, few would survive to see nightfall.

"Give chase!" he said. "Let none escape!" A few stray grey giants were cornered, and the captain led his troops into a charge. He parried a strike, and his counter-attack added his enemy to the casualties of the brutal assault.

Soon, the Koreshians had retreated from the plaza entirely, doubtlessly regrouping outside the gates to prepare another attack. Two hundred Illmerians gathered what they could to rebuild a barricade, hoping to gain some time. Aaposhi bit his tongue. The sight of his city in ruins was one all too familiar. Never would he forgive the invaders.

He knelt next to his general: a heartbeat. The cut was deep; it was a miracle that the Koreshian general had not severed the Advisor's arm. A few soldiers rushed to Aaposhi's side, carrying cloth, bandaging the wound the best they could. "He should hopefully survive," said the captain. "Remove his armour and carry him out of here."

Slowly, to the soldiers' surprise, Valirian's eyes opened. A cough escaped his lungs, and he spat out some blood. The men removed his helmet, revealing a few bruises, a nosebleed, and a small cut on his lips. He winced at their touch. Thankfully, nothing vital seemed to have been hit.

"It will take just a second, My General," said a soldier, helping him out of his armour. The Advisor sighed, attempting to ignore the pain by biting on some cloth.

"It looks like the Koreshians have been repelled, for now," said Aaposhi. "The plaza is once again under our control, and the walls have not fallen in spite of their attempts."

Valirian glanced around, as if to confirm with his own eyes the captain's words. He knew Aaposhi meant to encourage his men, above all, and give some reasons to be positive, but the situation was no less dire. Their numbers were shrinking. For how much longer could they hold the fortifications?

"We will continue fighting bravely," said Valirian. "Mistport, the unconquerable, shall not fall." He believed not his own words. Alexar would certainly not endanger himself again, and eventually, sheer numbers would triumph.

His wounds bandaged, he was helped onto a horse once again and rode to the top of the walls. Even through the mist, he could count the Koreshians. While he had lost half his troops, including hundreds of brave militiamen who took up arms to defend the city, the invaders still numbered in the thousands—at least five or six thousand, he estimated. At two hundred steps from the gates, some more Koreshian battalions gathered, preparing for another assault. Valirian gazed at the horizon, at the hills behind the Koreshian forces. The mist was clearing, slowly, which meant the sun was close to its zenith. More than a day had passed since the battle began.

"Is a storm approaching?" asked Aaposhi, pointing at the sky.

Valirian squinted. A strange, dark cloud had formed, barely perceptible through the mist.

* * *

Seven thousand men, almost exactly. Very few soldiers were missing, reported the captains, a sign of a successful operation. Silently, Syrela observed her troops as they marched on: quick, disciplined, determined. They marched westwards. There was smoke in the distance, the only sign she needed to know the situation in Mistport.

What if they were too late? She shook her head. She would avenge her fallen brothers and sisters. She would slaughter each and every Koreshian in the city. Her thoughts went to Valirian. She knew he sometimes walked the fine line between bravery and recklessness, for she had seen it herself. He had been wise to send her a message; any later and her troops would have been terribly out of position. She had been marching westwards from the wooden fort for three hours when his courier reached her. In spite of her calm, stern expression, she felt her heart race. Each second mattered, or so it felt, and so she rode to the head of her army. They were less than an hour away, and more than once did she have to fight the thought of galloping ahead, of joining the fray immediately.

She let out a silent sigh and glanced at her captains. Zelshi and Cadmael nodded to one another. Akior studied the smoke in the distance.

"Behind the hill," said a scout. "The Koreshian war machines are just there."

Once at the top, she closed her eyes, sighing yet again. Mistport was not yet lost! The mist still hid their presence for a few moments; the cloud of dust following them would appear as an approaching storm, giving them just enough time to position her troops. She would leave the invaders no chance of escape. Dropping from her horse, unsheathing her blades through her magic, she glanced one last time at Cadmael and gave him a nod. The Koreshians were preparing an assault on the main gates. It was now or never.

She took a step, and her troops readied themselves. She took another, then a third. Her pace increased. Soon, she was running, her men following her example. Illmeria would be victorious on this day.

* * *

"My General!" shouted a soldier. "Reinforcements! The War Hero has arrived!"

In spite of his wounds, Valirian rushed up the stairs. Leaning on the crenellations to keep himself stable, he gazed at the hills—a purple flame on a field of black flew high in the sky. At the army's head, a warrior charged alone, preceding the vanguard by a half minute. "The Blade of Illmeria has come to the rescue."

Around him, his men cheered. He held back tears. He allowed himself a smile as he saw the Koreshians scatter before her, the invaders too fearful to fight back, fleeing to the sea as fast as they could. Alone, Syrela engaged a group of grey giants. Further to his right, Cadmael led some six hundred cavaliers in a charge.

"Let us join the War Hero's army for the final strike," said Valirian.

His men drew their swords and hurried to the gates. Staying in the back line on his horse, he followed them outside the city as their battle cries joined those of their brothers. Even wounded and far from battle, he shouted orders, encouraging his men as the invaders were pushed further and further from the walls. The Koreshians were stuck between the city to the east and the Illmerians to the south and west. Their only escape was the sea, but neither the Mistian cavalry nor the War Hero spared them.

"Run to the ships!" the invaders shouted. A warship left, then another. There ended the success of their attempted retreat. The third one was damaged by a captured Koreshian war machine and sank. Many others were damaged; some were even boarded and captured. Illmeria was victorious.

"General Valirian," greeted Syrela as their eyes met. Seeing him struggle, she helped him off his horse, surprised to see him without armour, before noticing his wounds.

"General Syrela, your arrival saved the lives of thousands," he said. "This is a glorious triumph!"

She removed her helmet, and they met for a short embrace. Some hundred steps away, their soldiers defeated the last of the Koreshians.

"Spirits be honoured, you are safe," she said as they broke the embrace. For a moment, she studied his wounds, yet she showed no emotion.

"The last few Koreshians in the harbour should easily be dealt with," he said.

"Indeed," she said. "I shall let Captain Cadmael and Captain Zelshi handle the situation." The captains exchanged a few words, then left, and Valirian followed Syrela to the castle.

"I fear that the Fortress is currently under siege, too," he said. "My scouts reported a much larger force than what was defeated here."

"Do you think the Queen was caught unaware?" she asked.

He shook his head, and all worries vanished from her expression. "I warned her in advance." He showed her the silver amulet around his neck.

Syrela raised an eyebrow but nodded. Xelya was ready; that was all that mattered. She helped him take a seat in his chamber and sat next to him. "Then I shall lead our army there as soon as possible. Prepared, the Fortress can hold for weeks, at the very least. I will arrive in time."

About to answer, he winced as he felt a sharp pain in his right arm. Syrela moved to his side and carefully lifted his arm. "May I?"

With his permission, she removed the bandage and studied his wound, whispering to herself a few inaudible words. "Leading your men into another charge was very unwise. Your wounds are quite severe. A little more and you could have lost your arm for good."

He felt his heart skip a beat at the thought, but he shrugged. "I will not die because of a cut on my arm."

Syrela stood up. Her frown made him lean further into his seat. "Does your life have so little value in your own eyes that you would risk it so carelessly? Your voice is needed in this war. Losing you would be a dire blow to Illmeria. Do not risk the fate of a continent with your foolishness!"

He looked down to avoid her glare, and she knelt at his side again. Her hand softly lifted his chin so that he looked into her eyes.

"Valirian, in the name of our friendship, I demand of you to stay back in the next battle—until your wounds are healed," she said. "No soldier would dare think of you as a coward. You fought bravely. You saved them. Please, do not waste your life for naught."

He sighed. His left hand took hers, and he forced a smile. "I am sorry, Syrela. I will let you lead our army into the next battle." He helped himself up with the armrests, and she took him in her arms, an embrace he reciprocated.

"Let us find you a healer," she said. "Afterwards, I will leave for the Fortress. You may follow so long as you stay in the back."

"It is wiser for me to follow," he said. "My presence will be needed at the Fortress after the battle."

She nodded and disappeared for some minutes before returning with two healers. An hour later, the Illmerian army had gathered before the gates of Mistport and headed southwards. Valirian glanced behind, looking at the city one last time. Alexar had escaped yet again, he had learnt. He bit his tongue. The vile dog would not escape forever, but it was his hatred of the man that had almost cost Valirian his life. For his survival, he had to thank Aaposhi, yet that defeat had made him realise his own weakness. If he was to triumph over his old master, he must better control his emotions.

"Koresh will now see that this war is far from over," said Syrela.

CHAPTER 26

UNSEEN, UNLEASHED

The wind caressed Xelya's visage, her long hair dancing as she observed the horizon; the gusts were particularly powerful, even for the top of her Tower. The shy sun of a spring morning still hid behind the tall mountains of the Fortress, giving a red tint to the mist that blurred the city below her. If she were to focus her magic again, she could hear the echoes of war, the footsteps of a marching army. The Koreshians were near.

She whispered a word and squinted, confirming what she had thought: a scout, on the hilltops to the north. She tightly gripped the ledge of the balcony. It would not be long before those fields turned into a battlefield. The preparations for this battle had been exhausting, as her attention was constantly demanded everywhere, yet she allowed herself no doubts. Victory would be hers. Her people would be safe: some had fled further south to Ilmassar, and those too far north had sought refuge at the Fortress. There would be enough food for everyone, including the thousands of Northerners who had fled the war.

Instinctively, her fingers reached for the amulet around her neck. A coldness seized her heart as she gazed into the purple gem. All attempts to contact him the previous night had been fruitless. The battle of Mistport had certainly begun; what dangers would he face? She sighed, shaking her head. If only her powers were such that she could lay waste to both Koreshian armies alone. She hated this uncertainty, this powerlessness. She hated having to wait. Footsteps, coming from the stairs behind, startled her out of her reflection and made her turn around.

"My Queen," said Xilto. "The enemy is here."

She glanced at the city, far below. They had done all they could to prepare. The tall walls would protect them, and the gates, though still doubtlessly the weak point, had been fortified by her Advisor. Fire was her only preoccupation, for it could spread throughout the city and kill more than the Koreshians would. Measures had been taken, but there was no certainty of their success. "Is everything ready according to my plans?"

"Yes, My Queen."

She turned to observe the hills to the north once more: the red and gold banner, the first lines of the Koreshian army, and many war machines. Nothing unexpected. "Then every available man shall head to the northern wall at once." She paused and counted twenty-four banners, each of five hundred men, and there were doubtlessly more behind the hill. "They appear more numerous than what I had first envisioned. Excellent. More shall be buried here, and Koresh will know my wrath."

Xilto moved to her side, observing the army from the balcony. "Do you believe in our chances, My Queen?"

For a moment, she studied the captain. His features were marked by a deep frown, and he looked down at her inspection. "Captain, it is not the first time this land faces war. It is not the first time the Mistlands, our home, must fight against an unjust oppressor. Our spirit is unbreakable, and I shall never let a tyrant rule over the Fortress again. Such is my duty as your Sovereign and Queen."

She noticed a smile as he bowed low. Then he headed to the stairs, leaving her alone. She summoned a servant, who helped her out of her regal dress and into her armour. The Koreshians had arrived rapidly, too rapidly to attack the city from the north and south simultaneously, just as she had hoped. Supposedly, the Koreshians cared not if the Illmerians fled their cities, for all that mattered was whether they could capture Mistport and the Fortress. The remnants could be dealt with after.

"Here, My Lady," said the servant. She was perhaps sixteen years of age, one of the orphans who had fled Mistport after the first invasion. A tear rolled down her cheek as she bowed and left. She had lost everything once already. Could she bear losing it all again? To each person in the Fortress was a similar story. Fears, doubts, loved ones.

Xelya pursed her lips, fists clenched. She glared at the war machines. Soon, they would attack the walls. They were positioned precisely where she wanted. She took a deep breath and closed her eyes. It did little to calm her racing heart—on the contrary, the weak embers in her chest turned into blazing flames, spreading into her blood. She could no longer hold back.

Her lips moved. A raised hand, and a whisper echoed in the valley. A deep rumble, the earth itself shaking. The sharp cliffs on either side of the Koreshian army growled. The whisper turned into a command, a word spoken loudly in an unknown language. The same magic that had shaped the walls of the Fortress an eternity ago now caused an avalanche of rocks from the mountains around the Koreshian army. The invaders panicked as many of their comrades were buried or crushed, as several of their war machines were broken by the rockslide.

Then, silence. For a moment, not even the survivors dared speak, as if any of their words could provoke another storm of stones. Long minutes had to pass before the Koreshian sergeants dared give orders once more.

Out of breath, Xelya collapsed on her chair. Her magic had killed hundreds, maybe a thousand, and destroyed half the war machines, but now her legs could hardly support her own weight. Footsteps, again. She frowned. She expected no one, and she was in no capacity to help if her attention was needed anywhere.

"My Lady!" said the servant, the same young woman of minutes before.

"Is there some pressing matter?" asked Xelya.

The girl hesitated but was speechless as she simply bowed. "Does My Lady need anything?" she eventually said. "I heard . . . something."

With a hand gesture, Xelya showed the battlefield, and the servant's eyes widened. "I would like some tea. And please bring some apple shortbread with them, too." All she needed were a few moments. Soon, she would join her men on the walls.

* * *

The sound of a war horn. Xelya rushed down the stairs and ran to the walls of the Fortress. Even Valirian's elite, the men he had hand-picked to guard her, struggled to keep pace. The battle had begun. The soldiers repeated the rumours to one another, about she who had unleashed her fury, but made way and turned silent at her arrival, for none dared whisper before the Queen of Mists. Below, the Koreshians approached, weapons and shields raised, the shouts of their sergeants and their comrades behind pushing them ever closer to the walls.

"Prepare yourselves," said Xelya.

The first wave would be a disaster for the Koreshians. They were too few, and the path was too narrow, yet they rushed to the gates with a battering ram. With eight hundred Illmerians on the wall, the rain of

A HOME OF MIST 223

arrows took the lives of dozens of invaders. There were still some thirteen thousand Koreshians left, Xelya estimated, even though many had already perished to her magic. The battle would certainly be long, but she was prepared to fight it. The Fortress would not fall.

The remaining war machines fired flaming projectiles at the wall. Behind her back, her fists clenched. Around her, the soldiers braced for impact. The loud crash was almost deafening, yet twice did she need to blink—the rock had disappeared! The Illmerian troops cheered; the impact had barely been felt. Another projectile was approaching, and this time she carefully observed; as it crashed, it was reduced to dust and sand, producing a sound similar to a colossal bell. Some hitherto undetected magic had been activated. Judging by their reaction, her soldiers seemed not to hear that odd and powerful sound—unsurprisingly. It was magical in nature, and even she had failed to detect those enchantments in all those years spent in the Fortress. While with each crash she winced and bit her tongue, her soldiers would rejoice, certainly attributing the feat to their Queen. But stranger was this odd tingle she felt within her heart at every activation; never before had she felt so alive, so aware of everything around her.

"They have ladders!" said a sergeant nearby.

Xelya looked for Xilto, and they exchanged a nod. The captain hurried in the opposite direction with some troops. "Stand ready!" she said.

A thought crossed her mind, more and more pressing as it lingered; there was a strange tingle at the tip of her fingers. She leaned over the crenellations, and her hand reached for the wood of a ladder nearby. In a whisper, it was set ablaze as if it were a dry stick, and she pushed it back into the Koreshian army.

The day would be exhausting. Already, she had a headache, one that only worsened as she repeated the process many more times.

She did not expect the invaders to simply run out of wood, but with each ladder destroyed, they were fewer to reach the walls, allowing her men to better focus their attention. The rampart was turned into a battlefield, one where the few Koreshians successful in their race to the top were rapidly defeated. Once more, her magic set ablaze a ladder, but this time, her knees gave in. Helping herself with the crenellations, she fought to keep herself standing.

"My Queen!" said Xilto, rushing to her. "My Queen, the situation is under control."

She struggled to catch her breath. With the captain's help, she managed to stabilise herself. She was grateful his help had hidden her weakness from her men; her display of power had given them courage and hope. They needed to hold on and keep faith, even against a much larger army. "You're right," she managed to whisper. "Fight on, Captain."

"This wall shall not fall, My Queen," said Xilto. "On my honour, we will hold."

She forced a smile, then struggled down the stairs. Her personal guard rushed to her side.

"My Queen, are you wounded?" asked the sergeant.

"Worry not. Escort me back to the Tower. I need some rest." Many minutes after, and with the assistance of a servant who helped her up the stairs, she was back at her balcony. She collapsed on her seat with a loud sigh but clutched the armrests. The fray was so far away, now. She worried not about the outcome—or tried not to, at the very least—but could not help but watch. What had been this strange noise, this hidden enchantment? Did she not know this city by heart, to its most insignificant stone? Yet again, rocks were fired by the war machines and certainly disintegrated on impact as the sound—albeit much more distant—still echoed to her, now comparable to two crystal glasses lightly clanking.

Xelya rubbed her temples, hoping to alleviate her headache. Once this battle was over, she would uncover that mystery. She glanced over the mountains to the west. A halo of orange crowned the snowy peaks. The first day of this siege had passed, and the Koreshians had been unsuccessful.

* * *

A sudden gust of wind awoke Xelya. Something unnatural accompanied it—a roar, a crackling. Still struggling to open her eyes, she felt something within urging her to scan the room.

"My Lady!" shouted a servant, just outside her door. "The Tower is on fire!"

Xelya jumped out of her bed and hurried to the antechamber. The flames were spreading all too rapidly, blocking the way to the stairs. She and her servant were stuck. She needed to act quickly. Whispering a few words, Xelya picked up the servant and carried her in her arms, yet the protections she set up did little against this unnatural heat. The fire was magical! She cursed. Her spells could protect her from natural fire, yet against magic, there was nothing she could do. Koresh had sent sorcerers in its army.

"My Lady . . ." whimpered the young woman.

To be defeated by another mage was unimaginable. It was no ordinary magic, certainly, but Xelya could not stand there and let herself be consumed. With a word, she slammed the door wide open and dashed through it shoulder-first; it was now or never. The heat was more and more pressing, and she could no longer breathe, yet she had to continue down the stairs. An echo, an almost identical sound to the one she had heard the previous day: a gentle tapping on crystal. One level below her bedchambers, the flames had been stopped alongside a clear line. Above, the fire consumed the wood, but below, the construction was intact. Now that both she and her servant were safe, Xelya stared at this strange separation.

"We need to continue, My Lady!" urged the servant. "The Tower is still burning!"

"Look."

The young woman stared at the unnatural line, and her eyes widened. "Is this of your doing, My Lady?"

"This magic is ancient," replied Xelya. "Even I do not fully grasp it." Together, they stood near the entrance, prepared to leave at any moment if the flames began to spread, but on the contrary, the fire seemed to only weaken.

Eventually, the young woman bowed low. "Thank you for saving me earlier, My Lady. Allow me to find some food for you in the kitchen."

Her eyes not moving from the magic at work, Xelya answered with a nod. She herself had been unable to stop the fire due to its magical nature, had she not? She whispered a few words, trying to create the same wards as earlier, but her magic failed yet again. Her eyes widened. This enchantment—similar, if not identical, to the one protecting the walls—was so powerful it could manipulate and absorb the magical energy around itself. It required an affinity so powerful that even she, the Sovereign of the Fortress, was unable to achieve such a feat—or was she?

Her hand caressed the unburnt wood, and she closed her eyes. The spell was ancient, as she had suspected. Never had she noticed it, though not because this enchantment had surrounded her for so long it had become imperceptible—no, it had been hidden by its creator, and only now, as it took action, could she notice it. Another outstanding feat of the powerful mage at its origin.

"My Queen!" said Xilto. "Come down!"

She had to repress a smile at his bewildered expression. Certainly, he questioned why she was unafraid of the flames rather than running away. "This magical fire will burn all the wood through until nothing is left. Except below this line. It is not as dangerous as it appears."

"So, the situation is under control?" asked Xilto, taking hesitant steps forwards as he kept an eye on the fire.

"Indeed," she said. Above, already, most of the upper level had been turned to cold ashes which the wind blew away. A few minutes after, the highest floor entirely destroyed, the fire stopped, leaving a clean separation. "The sorcerers who cast that spell must now be quite exhausted."

She headed to her throne, at the end of the large table, and shrugged. For as long as it stood, the Tower would be a target for attackers, and though it was quite unfortunate that it suffered such damage, it was hardly surprising.

"I was deathly worried when I saw the flames spreading, My Queen," he said. "But I'm glad to see that you are safe. No projectile was fired this way, though! How did this happen?"

"The Koreshians have brought sorcerers with them," she said. "A handful of them, or perhaps just a particularly powerful one. Regardless, the fire was magical in nature. It does not need a projectile to start."

With a grave expression, Xilto nodded. He walked to the Queen's side and watched the battle from above. "They are innumerable," he said, "and they have sorcerers, too. This war is a never-ending nightmare." The slight smile the Queen's lips formed made his eyes widen— how could the Sovereign be so calm when outnumbered ten to one, at least?

"Be not afraid, Captain," said Xelya. "Dawn is soon to come."

CHAPTER 27

VIRTUOUS GAMBLE

A column of black smoke and echoes of battle. Valirian's fears were confirmed. Syrela glanced behind her, and the soldiers began whispering. She feared not for their morale; the victory at Mistport had been grandiose enough to make them believe that another would soon follow. Could the Fortress's tall walls hold? That thought crossed her mind a few times; it was more difficult to ignore than she had at first imagined. Whispering a few words, she begged all the spirits of Illmeria to protect the city and its inhabitants.

As she pressed on, the men behind followed her example. There was no time to waste. Noon was long behind them when the Fortress was finally in sight.

"The city has held on!" said Cadmael. "We got there just in time."

She let out a sigh of relief and nodded, silently thanking whichever power had built those colossal walls. "Stay on the hill," she told Valirian. "Wait for the battle to be over before approaching any closer, but the Queen will want to know that you're safe."

He refrained from protesting. Would he be capable of facing Xelya in such conditions? He hoped she would not learn of the details of the battle; she would see his actions as foolish recklessness. He looked down. For a second, he dared imagine her reaction if he had never returned to her. With each different scenario, his heart felt heavier. His fingers reached for the amulet around his neck, and he tightly clutched it as he sighed. Around him, his men followed Syrela into battle. Soon, he was alone on the hill, watching the War Hero unleash her storm of steel in the Koreshian ranks. The battle of Mistport could have—should have—been his last.

* * *

"Cadmael!" said Syrela. "Lead a breakthrough on the right flank!"

Her orders were answered with a nod, and moments after, the Mistian cavalry pushed through the Koreshian lines and encircled a large portion of their army. The Illmerians' initial charge had been remarkably successful, yet the enemy was now cornered between them and the tall walls—they would fight fiercely. The Koreshians were numerous. The battle would doubtlessly be long, yet this victory was crucial.

An explosion. Screams reached Syrela's ears. In spite of the surrounding chaos, she felt that some magic had been unleashed nearby. A few of her men fell, consumed by some deep red flames. Some Koreshian sorcerers were nearby. The fire spread, burning some ten soldiers as it rushed for her.

She needed to take cover. She dashed to the left, and her blades returned to her. Her own protections were powerless against this magical fire. Her heart raced, and she clenched her teeth as she hid behind a rock.

"My General!" said Zelshi. "We have to find the source!"

To Syrela, his voice was barely audible, deafened by a strange rumble that sounded both near and distant at once. The group of sorcerers was not too far yet still out of her reach. The little protection the rock offered was just enough to save her. She felt the heat of the flames. How long would her cover last? Her vision blurred. Then everything turned black, cold, silent. Her heart sank—was it over?

Her body jolted, still struggling to recover. The strange rumble had knocked her to the ground, into the mud, but the red fire was no longer. She glanced at the walls of the Fortress, and it felt like her eyes met the Sovereign's, in spite of the distance. Her legs still struggling, Syrela used her spear to help herself up. Another explosion, just as powerful as the first, almost knocked her back down. Purple flames were now spreading in the Koreshian ranks.

"The Queen of Mists has joined the battle!" said Syrela. "Victory is ours!"

A roar arose from the Illmerian army. The invaders had been too disorganised; their forces were soon separated, then scattered. A few hoped to flee. None were successful. The carnage continued for two long hours, yet not for an instant did it appear as if the Illmerians could lose. When all fighting ceased, not one Koreshian had survived. The gates opened, and the Queen herself led a small battalion out to meet the army of relief.

"My Queen," said Cadmael, "I hope that reinforcements were not too long to come." The young captain dropped from his horse and bowed low as the War Hero took slow steps towards the Sovereign.

"The Koreshian strategy was hopeless," said Xelya. "The invaders can stand neither against the will of Illmeria nor against the ancient magic that protects this land."

It indeed was clear that the Koreshians had failed to even break through the gates, much to Syrela's relief. This second victory against Koresh had cost little. The captains left to handle the aftermath of the battle with their men, yet the Queen rejoiced not; instead, she frantically scanned the battlefield.

"Where is my Advisor?" she asked. As the War Hero's answer was not immediate, she paled.

"He is alive and safe," said Syrela. "There is something we must discuss privately, however."

Xelya sighed, feeling as if her every muscle had relaxed. "Follow me. I know where we shall discuss." She led the War Hero to the old temple, and neither spoke another word until well out of sight from all.

"Valirian was wounded during the battle of Mistport. I suppose you guessed that much," said Syrela. "His wounds are quite severe, and though he is not at death's door, it is rather the conditions under which he was wounded that are of concern. Captain Aaposhi was a witness to his actions. In fact, had it not been for him, we would certainly be mourning Valirian at the current moment. I first thought his wound to be just an unfortunate consequence—we are, of course, constantly exposed to some risk, after all—but it seems that he was quite inexplicably foolish in his behaviour."

Repeating the account Aaposhi had told Syrela in secret, the War Hero narrated the duel between Valirian and the Koreshian general and explained the situation in Mistport as it unfolded. Finished, Syrela let out a sigh. Even if she doubted not his good intentions, he had risked his life, and possibly all of Mistport, through this foolishness.

"This is cause for concern," said Xelya. "It appears I must prevent him from leading the army directly if he is to be so rash and unwise."

"I agree," said Syrela. "He does not quite realise the danger his life was in, and he is of too great importance to be lost in such a stupid way."

Xelya knew Valirian to be brave, for it was bravery that had made him stand between the War Hero and her during the Battle of the Fortress, after all, yet no man could cheat Death forever. "I thank you, my friend, for sharing this information with me."

Syrela bowed her head as her only answer. They had arrived at the old temple, and each took a seat in the Queen's room.

"Let us wait here for him," said Xelya. In her hands, she had the silver amulet. She toyed with it, vigorously biting her tongue. How could he risk his life so carelessly? It took many deep breaths to keep her from storming out of the temple in search of him. A thought came to her, and her eyes widened. She turned to the War Hero, who raised an eyebrow. "Did you recognise the Koreshian general at Mistport?"

Syrela hesitated, digging deep into her memory, and kept her silence for almost a minute. "I only saw him from a distance, entirely armoured, and did not hear his voice. He wore an armour of black, likewise to the Koreshian general at Kashpur, but I do not know whether that is the standard in the invaders' army."

"Was he not killed or captured?" asked Xelya.

The War Hero shook her head. A disappointment, certainly, but it seemed that Koresh was prepared to sacrifice everything except their generals, having certainly lost too many in the first invasion.

"Let us at the very least find some reason to rejoice after these two major victories," said Xelya. "Though there is still much left to do, I cannot say I had great confidence in our ability to defeat the Koreshians on an open field the way we did twice."

* * *

The temple was now in his sight. He had wished to avoid what was to come for as long as he could. It was by no mere coincidence that both Syrela and Xelya had so suddenly left the battlefield. Yet he had no other choice. They both knew; neither would understand. He glanced at the wide-open door, some twenty steps away, and took a deep breath before dropping from his horse. Even as he landed on his right leg, he winced at the pain and had to limp to the entrance. His wounds were too severe to be hidden—he could not even move his right arm, though the bleeding had stopped—but he had still refused to ask for any help getting to the temple. Cadmael had offered his assistance, and though he appreciated the thought, he had declined.

He entered the building. Above him, Xelya and Syrela were sat at the table. He bowed the lowest he could. "My Queen, Lady Syrela."

Xelya stood up, while Syrela took a deep breath. The Queen's neutral expression made him shiver.

"Advisor," said the Sovereign, "were you afraid of facing your Queen?"

He looked down for a brief moment, then forced a smile as he bowed again. "No, My Lady. I was delayed because I oversaw the aftermath."

Xelya shook her head. With her hands behind her back, she stared at her Advisor from the platform up the stairs. "Advisor, do you believe me a fool?"

Her calm voice turned his blood to ice, and he looked down again.

"Do not hide behind technicalities, Valirian," she added. "That might have been the truth, but you and I both know your presence was not needed there."

He sighed. Eventually, he slowly nodded. "I knew you had heard of what happened, My Lady."

"Thank you for your honesty," she said.

"My wounds are not that severe," he said. "There is no need to worry."

Syrela jumped from her seat and slammed her clenched fist on the ledge of the platform. "Valirian, you know very well that it is not only a matter of how severe they are. You are not only lying to yourself in that regard, but you are also denying the fact that you almost lost your life in that duel!"

"I did what I thought necessary," said Valirian. "I may not have magic to protect myself, unlike you both, but that does not mean I will allow the land I love to be destroyed before my very eyes!"

"You were already wounded," said Syrela. "Do not be ridiculous. Even I would not go into battle like that! You yourself know that Koreshian generals are experienced fighters. You stood no chance, and only by some crazy luck did you survive."

"Then if that needed to be my fate, so be it! I also know all too well the price one pays for not taking action when need be."

Xelya raised her hand. For a second, nobody spoke. "Do you think yourself more useful dead than alive, Advisor?"

He sighed and closed his eyes. "You wouldn't understand. I do not wish to die, and I am aware I risked my life. Yet I know better than anyone the results of cowardice and the horrors a man too afraid to die can allow." He heard the Queen heading down the stairs, slowly, and the War Hero followed her. As his eyes reopened, Syrela's expression had shifted. He swore he saw a tear in her eye. "I did what I thought would save the city and countless innocents. Without their generals, the Koreshian soldiers would scatter. They fight out of fear. Most importantly, it was unclear at that moment whether we would receive reinforcements. Syrela, you could very well have engaged the enemy, and the gates of Mistport had already fallen. Lasting another day in such conditions would have already been a miracle. That was the only solution I saw."

A long moment of silence passed. Too exhausted to argue his case any further, he looked down. Would they understand his desperation? Was there even any other choice, given the situation? He himself knew not.

"You're too important to risk it all like that," said Syrela. "You're the person who knows our enemy best. We cannot lose you because you charged into a hopeless duel."

"And what good is a leader if he is not willing to sacrifice himself?"

he said. "If you had indeed been delayed, chances are that I would have lost my life in the battle anyway. What good is a man willing to let others die for him just so he may live another day?"

Xelya's hand reached for his chin. Her grip was gentle, merely raising his head so they would make eye contact. "I understand," she said. "Neither of us doubt your good intentions, and I admire that you have set yourself to follow an honourable and righteous example. Neither of us ask of you to give up those principles. Yet understand our position, too, Valirian. You are valuable to Illmeria. Your survival can, in turn, save tens of thousands." She let go of his chin and sighed. "As Lady Syrela said, you know our enemy best. Do not waste this crucial knowledge."

He looked into her eyes and found no anger. He felt his heart slow down, and behind his back, his fists relaxed. Eventually, he slowly nodded. "I understand. I never meant to worry either of you. It was reckless, but I did it because I thought our situation hopeless. I just ask that you understand my motives."

Xelya smiled. "All in Illmeria, from Ilmassar to Naila, shall know of your virtue, Valirian. Worry not."

"Thank you," he whispered. He turned to face the War Hero as she came closer.

"Forgive my anger, Valirian," said Syrela. "I never thought you had bad intentions. I was simply worried for you."

He smiled, though he raised an eyebrow and turned his head as he felt the Lady's hand on his shoulder.

"Now," said Xelya, "I order you to sit while I heal your wounds."

CHAPTER 28
THE DUTY OF EVERY RULER

Chatter and laughter reached Valirian's ears through the door of his room. He stretched and opened his dry eyes. Just outside, Xelya and Syrela exchanged pleasantries. He washed his face with some water, hoping the cold would help in waking him up after that long night of sleep, and headed out of his room, where Xelya and Syrela had just finished their breakfast.

"Good morning, Advisor," said Xelya. "I had just thought of waking you up. Three hours have passed since dawn."

"Good morning to you two," he said, reciprocating the War Hero's smile. In spite of the late hour, he refrained from worrying; that day would be an exception, after all. He joined them at the table and had a light meal, not wanting to linger too long. "I can't remember the last time I slept so well. Admittedly, a welcome change to the past few nights."

"It's the relief that comes with victory," said Syrela. "I also feel well rested."

Standing up, Xelya invited the two to follow her. "Let us head to the council room. The captains are doubtlessly waiting for us already."

* * *

"We still have six thousand men," said Akior. "That is if we count all the regulars that survived the battles and gather them all. I'd bet that many amongst the refugees are willing to take up arms and join us."

Such results were remarkable. Though it meant that a third of the Mistian army had perished in battle, or had been too gravely wounded to continue fighting, comparatively, the Koreshian losses were immense: over thirty thousand, with many warships and siege engines lost in battle, too.

"With those willing to fight, we should easily gather over ten thousand," said Xilto. "I have already sent sergeants in the refugee camps in the south to recruit those who want to fight."

"A wise initiative, Captain," said Valirian. He glanced at Syrela, and the two nodded to one another. "The Blade of Illmeria and I are in agreement," he continued. "We must seize the opportunity before us and strike back while the enemy is weak. We have at the very least some ten days before the enemy can react at all. Two or three weeks is a more likely number, as it will take them some time to gather an army again."

Syrela took a few steps to the round table, on which lay an unrolled map of the Grasslands and Heartlands. "It will take us some four days to cross the Sea of Mists, five if we are to take some time to equip the volunteers. That will give us a week during which we should face little to no resistance, as we know from the refugees that only a small fraction of their army stayed behind to occupy Illmeria."

"What about the Stormians?" asked Cadmael. "I don't remember seeing any of them in either battle, which means they all stayed behind."

"Though they certainly stayed behind," said Valirian, "their numbers should be rather negligible. Koresh is unlikely to trust them to the point of making them the majority in any garrison."

"The Stormians are competent fighters," she said. "They should not be underestimated, naturally, but their numbers are unlikely to exceed three thousand, split throughout the entire region. I would estimate the Koreshian garrison to add up to four thousand, shared between all the major cities and other strategic points. The worst case still gives us a significant numerical advantage, and with their general's retreat, it will be difficult for them to coordinate their defences. The only challenge we will face shall be Kashpur itself."

Valirian leaned over the map and shared a glance with Syrela. Moving a few of the wooden pieces they had scattered over the table, he formed two groups. "Let us divide the army. One force shall head east and retake the villages, towns, and bridges from the Koreshians, then head to Ksadnivi, while the other force shall head west and retake the mines, destroy the Koreshian fort on the western shore, and rejoin with the first group near Ksadnivi."

Syrela scanned the room, studying the captains' reactions. Some nodded, some observed closely, but none objected. Likewise, she had no disagreements with the plan.

"Since it would of course be unwise to leave the Mistlands completely undefended, Captain Xilto can stay behind," he continued. "He can coordinate the defences, if need be, and inform us in case of a Koreshian army heading there. Since the Fortress has proven capable of holding against an army significantly larger, we should have little to worry about."

A slight smile formed beneath the captain's grey beard, and he bowed. He thought himself more useful in the Mistlands anyway, for he grew old. Confident that, under his leadership, the Fortress would hold against any force, he approved of the plan.

"The others shall follow us to the Grasslands," said Syrela. "Captain

Zelshi and Captain Akior, you shall follow me. I will take control of the western force."

"Then Captain Cadmael and Captain Aaposhi will follow me east," said Valirian. The two had agreed without a word, as if everything had seemed obvious to the both of them, but there was one who had yet to speak, and so both generals turned to the Queen, seeking her approval.

From her seat, Xelya stood up. She scanned the room, her lips slightly pursed until she nodded. "For it is the duty of every ruler, I shall lead my army to the Grasslands. I shall fight alongside my people."

A heavy silence fell on the room. None, it seemed, knew how to answer. Syrela bowed low, and all followed her example. "The invaders will know to fear the Queen of Mists."

"As you wish, My Lady," said Valirian. In truth, could anyone have expected the Sovereign herself to stay back, to cower before battle? He, more than anyone, had seen what she was capable of, and the thought made him smile. Her place was on the battlefield—nowhere else. He had no chance of convincing her otherwise, anyway, had he disagreed.

"There are some logistics questions we gotta answer," said Aaposhi. A long hour was spent discussing such matters. Once they all concluded that no details had been neglected, the Queen dismissed the captains, who returned to their duties.

"I must say that your announcement was a pleasant surprise, My Lady," said Valirian. "It is good to know that your magic will assist us on the battlefield."

With a smile, Xelya sighed. She gazed into his eyes and chuckled. "I could not tolerate the idea of my Advisor risking his life so far away from myself, especially as I hold the power to protect you. I shall accompany you on this campaign."

He looked down, nodding slowly. Regardless of how embarrassing the thought was, how could he blame her after the events of the past days? "I hope your protection won't be needed, My Lady. Though please be assured that I will show more care in the future."

Her expression shifted to a slight frown. She took his right hand in hers. "I meant not such a decision as an insult, Valirian. Our foes are powerful, and there are sorcerers amongst the Koreshian army. You have your importance. It would be foolish not to take precautions."

He sighed. He knew she meant well, but the thought threatened to weaken his resolve. Perhaps he did underestimate the dangers he would face, but what other solution did he have? "I have seen what magic is capable of. I have seen what either of you two are capable of. I have even glimpsed the Koreshian Emperor's aura. Yet if I fear any of it, I will truly be powerless. Do not scare me away from my duties.

"I know that I have an important role within this army, yet I cannot let my lack of magical affinity shape how I must act, else I would see myself cower, dooming many to a fate I could have protected them from. This is why I fight, regardless of how insignificant I would be before such power."

"Your courage is admirable," said Xelya. Her mouth opened, as if she were to say more, but no sound escaped.

"It's easy for us, who have some affinity with magic, to forget how we seem to others," said Syrela. "Though I still want you to show some care, you are right. Do not be afraid of the enemy. The Queen and I will do our best to defeat their sorcerers."

"I trust in you both to lead our men to victory," said Xelya. "We must rely on each other to triumph—and twice already, we have triumphed over them."

* * *

Valirian smiled, remembering how he had once judged the activity at the Fortress overwhelming. Those times, the days that followed his arrival, felt like an eternity ago, yet only months had passed. He observed the activity from the tall walls above; thousands were in a rush, bringing supplies, weapons, and horses to the northern gates, while others carefully supervised the last preparations before they would depart that very afternoon. "What folly it was to think that any semblance of calm would follow our victories," he told Syrela.

Next to him, she observed the hills to the north and the army that gathered just outside the city. His remark made her laugh, yet her eyes moved not. Never had she imagined witnessing such a spectacle, as thousands of battle-ready men had formed ranks in the recently harvested fields. Only a day had passed since their victory at the Fortress, and already were they ready to leave, as thousands of volunteers had joined the army some mere hours after the battle's end. It was good that they had wasted no time, for the advantage was theirs for at least a week, after which not even the spirits of Illmeria would know.

"Do you think the Koreshian generals would approve of their Emperor sending another army to Illmeria after losing so many men already?" asked Syrela. Even though she had been victorious against Koresh many times now, it felt as if their empire was endless, ready to send soldiers until Illmeria bent—or broke.

"It is not the Emperor who would defend such a proposition," answered Valirian. "See, it is the same general who led both invasions, and that is no coincidence, nor is it a strategic decision, either. In their internal politics, success means status, and status means power. Until now, Alexar, that Koreshian general, had been highly successful, and as such, he had Tarasmir's trust. His voice in the high council mattered greatly, and each of his words was listened to by his peers and subordinates. Failure is a grave blemish, but it can easily be forgotten about if it is followed by another success."

"So, in your opinion, Alexar will continue to support an invasion until he is personally successful?" she asked. "Does he not risk his voice at the council?"

"He would," he said, "had he not gotten some partial success to boast of. Sadly, most of Illmeria is still occupied. It is something he can easily hide behind. For the rest, well, most of the councillors do not even know of the existence of the Mistlands. A defeat there can be hidden, minimised, or depicted as a partial success."

With a sombre expression, she shifted her attention to the army below before returning to Valirian. Could there never be peace? "Let us hope that he makes the mistake of returning to Illmeria," she said. "Then I will make sure he does not return to his homeland, if such is the only way to end this war."

He moved to her side and watched the army with her. He could only hope to see Alexar fall to her blade. That sight would be one to greatly enjoy.

"Make way for the Queen of Mists!" announced a voice from the plaza below. Surrounded by her personal guard, and riding a black horse, Xelya took the lead of her army.

"We shouldn't make her wait," said Valirian.

In the early afternoon, a large army of some nine thousand men left the Fortress, marching north to the city of Mistport. Never had an Illmerian ruler gathered an army of such size—not in recorded times, at least—and with the help of the few Koreshian warships captured during the battle of Mistport, all could cross in a day and reach the shores of the Grasslands.

"The fortifications we built should not be very far away," said Syrela. "From the fort, we will split according to plan."

All three judged unlikely an enemy attack in the near future—the terrain was too equal, and the Illmerians would most certainly have the numbers' advantage on their side—yet the soldiers were on high alert; this land, after all, was occupied by the Koreshians. To the west, the sun was setting. Soon, scouts reported that the fort built weeks prior was still intact and that the handful of men left behind had nothing of note to report. It was therefore decided that they would stay there that night and leave shortly after dawn the next day.

"It seems that our estimations were correct so far," said Syrela. She, Valirian, and Xelya all looked at maps while sharing some food together.

"Indeed," said Valirian. "And if there is nothing too unexpected, we should be able to reach Ksadnivi in five days, from both sides."

"Good luck, Lady Syrela," said Xelya. "Long days await us, doubtlessly."

CHAPTER 29
GHOSTS OF WAR

The grey fields beneath were a grim sight. The entire area, where a village once stood, had been set ablaze by the Koreshians. It had been mere hours since Valirian had led his men eastwards, away from the fort, yet already did he see scars from the invasion. A year before, already, he witnessed so much destruction in the Grasslands. Would Illmeria ever heal? Across a small river, on a nearby hill, a temple lay in ruins, yet he knew it to be a more ancient scar, one of the many temples destroyed during the first invasion.

"Is this a place you know, Advisor?" asked Xelya. As he answered not, she nodded, understanding all too easily his thoughts through his silence. The stray groups of Koreshians they had met were easily defeated; they were small patrols at most, never more than thirty men, yet nothing behind them was ever left standing.

"My General, there are no survivors here, either," said a soldier.

The young man before him struggled to contain his anger. His traits showed Valirian that he originated from the northern parts of Illmeria rather than the Mistlands. Perhaps he once lived here, or perhaps he had relatives who once inhabited this region. "All the more reasons to make the Koreshians pay," he answered to the soldier. This grim spectacle only strengthened his men's will to fight, much to his relief, yet there was hardly any reason to rejoice. "Set up camp on this hill, nearby."

The day had been long. Hardly any pauses had been taken, but for Valirian, no rest was to be found that night. Nightmares would wake him up, over and over. The sight of Kashpur set ablaze dragged him out of his sleep with a cry. A mountain of skulls made him open his eyes, cold sweat on his forehead.

Dawn was nearing. He stood up from his bed, whispering a handful of curses as he washed his visage with some cold water, hoping it would make his headache vanish. He gazed into the mirror. He no longer was the young man, scared and docile, who followed Alexar without a thought, yet so many questions were left unanswered still. Would he truly have spared this land through his sacrifice?

Footsteps approached his tent, and he let out a sigh. What could require his attention so early in the morning? "Yes, what is it?" he asked, massaging his temples as he turned to face the entrance. No answer. The sound was too unlike a wild animal, too. He frowned. A thought crossed his mind, and he hurried to his sword.

"Good morning, Advisor," said Xelya.

He let out a sigh and nearly collapsed onto a chair at the centre of his tent. "Good morning, My Lady."

For quite some time, she studied him, until she sat to his side. "You look as if you have not slept in days."

He slowly nodded, arching his back and rubbing his temples once more. She stood up and set some water to boil. Opening a small box, she took some leaves and prepared some tea for both of them.

"This night has not been the most pleasant," he said, earning a sympathetic smile from her.

"Sometimes, I wonder if I will ever sleep again. Perhaps there is no rest other than death for the likes of us." She placed her hand on his and felt his muscles relax.

Soon, the delicate perfume of tea filled the tent, and his lips formed a smile. "Did you need me, My Lady?"

She laughed softly, taking a sip from her cup. "Am I not allowed to visit my friend and discuss with him?"

He chuckled and leaned back in his chair with his eyes closed, slowing down his breath.

"Tell me, what is bothering you, Valirian?" she asked.

Twice did his mouth open, but he seemed unable to speak.

"Your nights are filled with nightmares of old memories," she said. "Before, already, you were witness to horrors committed on this land, and you feared seeing it again for yourself."

He closed his eyes. Slowly, he nodded. "I thought I had defeated that ghost, long ago, but it still haunts me, it seems. I saw the wounds of the first invasion still wide open, yet the second one is bringing just as much destruction." His eyes wandered, studying the ground aimlessly. He held back a shiver as her soft hand caressed his shoulders. "I still ask myself, 'Could I have avoided it all?' I sat in the Koreshian general's tent. I was tasked with sharpening his weapons. He was defenceless. Could I have saved them all?"

Her hand moved to his chin. Gently, she made him look at her. "You no longer are the young child you were back then. I know not what Ayun told you. I ignore how he saw in you what is so clear to all of us today, but never forget him."

"I won't. I promise." He took a deep breath. The storm in his mind vanished; his headache seemed almost painless now. "We have a say in Vinmara: 'Ashes are fertile and grow the next harvest, and so is death the herald of life.' I will help you rebuild Illmeria once this war has been won."

She smiled. With her tea finished, she stood up. "I doubt it not, though do not expect peace to leave you any more time to rest, either."

He laughed. She turned around, prepared to leave, and he stood up. "Xelya," he called.

She turned to face him, raising an eyebrow.

"Thank you," he said. He caught a glimpse of a smile as she disappeared behind the fabric of his tent.

She let out a sigh. She understood all too well how he felt. It was good that her words made him regain courage: his men would be inspired by it. She lifted the red fabric of her own tent and collapsed into her armchair. "What a shame it is," she whispered to herself. "Why must I keep such a distance, wear such a mask at all times?" She shook her head. This barrier she felt unable to break through, did it stand a reason to exist? They faced death all too often; perhaps it was better that way—each day could be their last. She remembered the battle of Mistport, the tale she had been given by Syrela, and she shivered. The outcome could have been much worse. And if it had been so, that feeling of loss that would have inevitably overcome her, would it have been made any less painful by this mask?

* * *

Rarely were the battalions of invaders significant enough to hold their positions for longer than a few minutes, and never did they resist for more than an hour. Most had fled in a hurry. Perhaps rumours of an Illmerian army from the south had spread, or perhaps they had been given orders. Regardless, they would be crushed to the last. Even should they retreat to the more defensible positions of Kashpur, they would be heavily outnumbered, especially as more and more joined the Illmerian army. It surprised Valirian to see pockets of resistance scattered throughout the Grasslands, hurrying to celebrate the Mistians and their arrival. He could only imagine the celebrations Syrela would be met with. He had doubtlessly underestimated the Illmerian spirit, unconquerable and proud, and with each skirmish, the army grew larger.

"By now everybody's heard of the invaders' defeat in the Mistlands," said a peasant to Valirian. "They're running away north, I guess to Kashpur."

On the fifth day, a letter from Syrela reached him, informing him of their victory against a significant Koreshian force at a fort they had established on the western coast. That night, heavy rain poured over the land, and the next morning, a bright sun was in the cloudless sky. In spite of the devastation, the Grasslands were beautiful. All would regrow, in time. On the field he walked, green plants had grown out of the ground. "Illmeria, I make you this promise," he whispered. "This land will grow prosperous once more, freed from the Koreshian blight."

Valirian glanced behind. Most of the territory occupied by Koresh had been reconquered, and many who hid in forests or hills returned to their homes. South of Kashpur, only Ksadnivi still lay under enemy control. It would be the next objective. He knew Alexar's tactics too well, however. Just how many had escaped or survived the Koreshian siege? As scouts reported the city to be in sight, his heart raced. He needed to see with his own eyes. Only then would he know for certain.

"I feared much worse," said Xelya.

There were few reasons to rejoice, but Valirian responded with a nod. The walls of the city, normally the height of a person and a half, had been for the most part destroyed, and most of the outskirts had been severely damaged. Otherwise, the rest of the city seemed rather intact. Did Alexar judge sufficient the destruction of Kashpur?

"Lady Syrela has not yet arrived," said Xelya. "Let us hope that she has not been delayed."

"It is still early in the day," said Valirian. "I would be surprised if we had to wait for more than a few hours."

Xelya's horse trotted a few steps forwards so she could study the city more closely. Silent, she reflected. "Given their lack of fortifications, do you not believe that we could attack immediately? She would reinforce us as the battle is ongoing."

He frowned. That was a possibility he had considered, and their success was likely, yet something kept him from agreeing. "Though I suspect the Koreshians to gather their forces in Kashpur, rather than in Ksadnivi, there is still a chance for a trap. We can't know exactly how many soldiers guard the city, as most are hidden inside."

"Very well," said Xelya. "Let us wait, if you so judge it wiser."

Valirian commanded his men to surround the city while awaiting Syrela's arrival. The War Hero was not long, for two hours after, a scout reported sighting of her troops.

"Today, the banner of Illmeria shall be raised high above Ksadnivi once again!" Syrela's voice echoed in the plains. Even Valirian's troops roared at her announcement. As her forces joined Valirian's in surrounding the city, the War Hero rode to meet him.

"Just in time," he said. "Do you intend on attacking the city today?"

They both glanced at the sky: the sun was past its zenith, but far from the horizon still.

"We should try," she said. "I can lead our troops into a charge and break the Koreshian defence, I am quite certain. I worry far more about the possibility of Koreshian reinforcements and the chance of a tough battle in Kashpur."

"Do you not fear a trap?" he asked.

She paused, studying the city for quite a few minutes. Her expression shifted to a frown. There was something strange; the city was too silent. "I would not say that Ksadnivi is the best location for a trap. It's too small, even if the Koreshians tried to hide in houses. But there is something unsettling about this situation."

They both approached the city, joining Xelya's side some two hundred steps away from the ruined walls. Not a Koreshian banner in sight, not an invader spying in the distance, at least as much as they could see.

"You are right to have concerns," said Xelya. "It seems as if the city is deserted. Entirely."

Nearby, Cadmael rode to join the three of them. "Do we start the assault?" asked the young captain. A hand gesture from Valirian made him keep silent as his attention turned to a major street of the city. A small group approached, perhaps some forty soldiers, the tall man leading them carrying a white flag.

"Wait here," Valirian said to Cadmael. Followed by a few men of the Queen's guard, he went to meet them. They were no Koreshians. Rather, the group consisted exclusively of Stormians. Recent marks of battle were seen on their armours, blades, and exposed faces, as none wore a helm, rather carrying it against their chest. Now only five steps separated the groups, and their leader, a captain of some sort, knelt before Valirian, holding his flag high.

"I, Captain Kuthaï, of the Kinshaï clan, surrender with my men. The city of Ksadnivi is now under the control of the Queen of Mists and her army. I only demand that my men be spared."

Though it was uncommon for the Stormians to surrender, yet not quite unheard of, Valirian frowned and glanced at the city. Did the Koreshians not know that they would be killed to the last? "The Stormians amongst your men shall be spared," he said. "Know that we demand the head of each and every of the Koreshians within, however, for justice demands it." He expected the man to refuse, or for his men to hesitate, yet the captain stood up and nodded.

"My Lord," he said, "the Koreshian soldiers within the city have all been executed by my command, to the last of them. Do you wish for me to bring their bodies before you?"

Valirian's eyes widened, and he found himself speechless. He glanced behind, relieved to see Xelya approaching. Was the alliance between the Koreshians and the Stormians that fragile that the Duke had already broken it, or was it an independent act by the captain and his men? "My men will verify your claims and ensure that this is no trap."

"What is the situation, Advisor?" asked Xelya telepathically.

He explained the situation to her as claimed by the warrior. The Lady raised an eyebrow, then dropped from her horse.

"How many of you are defending the city?" she asked the captain. "Is that all of your men?"

Kuthaï knelt before the Queen and bowed his head. His answer was not immediate. Certainly, he feared stumbling on his own words before her. "Your Grace, six hundred of us were sent by the Duke to capture Ksadnivi after the fall of Kashpur. We were to be followed by some five hundred Koreshians, which we slaughtered to the last throughout this past night. The invaders wished to burn the city to the ground and flee with all the supplies they could gather, o Queen of Mists. We refused such orders, and out of the six hundred Illmerians, only us and some thirty others survived the battle."

Through the link that connected them, Valirian felt that she repressed a smile—it was good that the Stormians had acted as such.

"They have more than earned their right to live," said Xelya. *"They will be spared."*

"The Koreshians wish to slow us down, and demoralise us, by burning all they can to the ground," said Valirian. *"Thankfully, our supplies are more than enough, even without those in the city."*

They nodded to one another, and Valirian gave orders for Syrela

A HOME OF MIST

to hurry to the scene and for Cadmael to carefully enter the city. A thought crossed his mind, and through the telepathic link, Xelya heard his idea. She paled. Her attention turned once more to the Stormian captain.

"Tell me, Captain, of the fate of Kashpur," asked Xelya.

The man abruptly raised his head, as if startled, then looked down with a sigh. He stood up and glanced at his men before looking at the Queen of Mists once more. "My Lord, Your Grace, what happened in Kashpur is the reason we meet on this day, for I personally asked the Duke to send my men and I to Ksadnivi so that we may spare it from sharing Kashpur's fate. The Koreshians agreed under the condition that three hundred of their men would follow us, though later another two hundred arrived from the countryside, south-west.

"Thankfully, as most of Lady Adiloka's army had already been defeated, the battle was quick and the majority were spared. It was no easy task to keep those drunken barbarians under control, but some threats kept them from causing any further damage." He sighed. The War Hero approached, and Kuthaï bowed before her, recognising her familiar silhouette, which he had seen more than once on the battlefield. "Such cannot be said of Kashpur. We once named the city the 'Pearl of Illmeria,' yet beyond a few hundred of my kinsmen, there is not a living soul left there, for the Koreshians are soulless vermin."

Valirian's breath became heavy. Alexar had warned him, told him in great detail, what would be done, but he had been unable to stop it. What he feared most had happened.

"Many had fled, from what I could see," said Kuthaï, "but death is certainly the most pleasant fate one could have met in Kashpur, and those that were not killed were taken into slavery. There are horrors I witnessed that night that I dare not speak of."

The Queen's irises turned brighter. There were sparks of pure magic that escaped her eyes. The telepathic link still partially open,

Valirian shivered as his mind grazed Xelya's. He glimpsed at her aura, yet the storm was too dense for him to see anything. His knees felt weak, and he battled to keep himself on his horse.

"Have all the Koreshians left in Illmeria gathered in Kashpur, then?" asked Xelya.

There was a deep echo to her voice. Perhaps the magical link between the two of them was the cause, but Valirian swore the sky itself turned darker.

The captain answered with a slow nod.

"Let it be known, then," she said. "You and your soldiers shall be spared."

CHAPTER 30

BLOSSOMS

The city had been freed. The Queen's banner was flown high above its tallest buildings, just as Syrela had promised. Kuthaï had not lied: indeed, all the Koreshians had been killed by his order, and the rare few who had escaped did not hide from the Illmerians very long, as the locals were more than glad to rid themselves of the invaders. Night had fallen. To Valirian, finding Syrela had proven particularly difficult. She had allowed herself no time for rest, handling or supervising all sorts of matters after the capture of the city, to the smallest of details.

"Lady Syrela," he said. Startled, she raised her head. He had found her overseeing the delivery of supplies to the citizens of Ksadnivi—stone, timber, and all sorts of material to help them rebuild their city.

"I had not expected to see you here so late," she said.

"I was unsure of your whereabouts," he said, "though I cannot say I am surprised to find you here."

"Is working so unusual for you that you are surprised to find your fellow general busy with her duties?" she asked.

They laughed, and he stepped to her side. Together, they watched citizens carry construction materials to a large plaza in the centre of Ksadnivi.

"I originally came to invite you for dinner," he said. "The day has been long. I figured a meal would do all of us good."

She shrugged. She did not feel hungry—or, more exactly, she had lost her appetite. "I'm afraid I have to decline. Maybe I will eat something light in the middle of the night."

"Well, perhaps would you enjoy a drink?"

The proposal made her laugh. "Drinking wine before a battle wouldn't be the wisest for me. I can't risk it affecting my magic."

His eyes widened for a moment. Could alcohol, even in such small quantities, truly affect her? But before her refusal, he found nothing to say and simply nodded. As he turned around, she sighed and looked down.

"But since you so wish for my presence," she said, "perhaps I will follow to enjoy the company. Lead the way." The smile on her lips, albeit weak, was no less a heart-warming sight, and together, they headed to the Illmerian camp, set just outside of the city, to the north. Entering the large red tent that served as their headquarters, they joined Xelya at the table.

"Ah, so you found her!" said Xelya. "You doubted your own abilities, Advisor."

"So it would seem," he said. "I suppose you were right to insist. I owe you an apology."

"I am hardly to blame for the city's size," said Syrela. "Neither is it my fault that the streets are particularly narrow in Ksadnivi." With a slight smile, she poured all three of them a glass of wine, which they shared with an occasional joke.

In spite of this jovial ambiance, often did the shortest of pauses turn into a heavy silence. They spoke not of it, for all three knew what traversed one another's minds in such times. The fall of Kashpur, the horrors that happened there, had been grim news that none of them had stomached quite yet.

"Justice shall be served, my friends," said Xelya after a minute-long silence. Though Syrela and Valirian both nodded, neither answered. What was there to say?

"The surrender of the garrison here did gain us some precious time," Syrela eventually said. "Kashpur is less than a day away."

"And now we know that not all amongst the Stormians approve of the alliance," said Valirian. "Perhaps that is something we can use against the Duke." The prospect seemed to raise their morale, and they finished their light meal shortly after.

"I am confident that we can defeat the Koreshians before an army of relief arrives," said Syrela. "There should not be a prolonged siege at Kashpur. The walls of the city are just not tall enough for a defence of that kind."

Valirian rubbed his chin. Perhaps Syrela was right, but how would they then defeat said army? Yet if she was confident, then perhaps so he should be, too. "There is a lot we need to discuss, Syrela. Perhaps we should meet tomorrow morning before our army leaves for Kashpur."

She agreed, then stretched, fighting against herself to stay awake.

"Let us all find some rest now," said Xelya. "Tomorrow shall certainly be a long day."

"I shall try to do so," Syrela said with a sigh. She stood up and wished the two a good night before disappearing.

"I can only imagine the pain she must feel," said Valirian. "Kashpur was her second home."

Xelya sighed. Syrela would doubtlessly struggle to find any rest that night. "Let us hope she does not feel any guilt. I had hoped to bring her some comfort by inviting her here, but all of us were too affected by the news."

"We share the grief. It is understandable. I am sure she appreciated our company in some way."

One could only hope. With a whisper, Xelya blew out the candles lighting the tent, letting only the pale light of the moon inside. "Have you seen Kashpur with your own eyes?"

"From a distance only," he answered. "The Koreshians did not get to enter the city during the first invasion."

Never would she witness the city in its full glory. The thought felt heavy, crushing, in her mind. She clenched her fist. *There had to be a way!* A way to return to the past or undo what had been done—but there was not. She knew it. She bit her tongue and shook her head before letting out a loud sigh. "As selfish as those words will sound, I regret that I will never lay my eyes on the beauty of Kashpur. That I will never be able to witness the glory of the Pearl of Illmeria. So many treasures have been lost and might never be recovered."

How he understood her. He tried to recall the sight of the city from the hills around, of the white temples and impressive palaces he caught a glimpse of from far away. It was such a distant memory, now. "It is worse to never witness the blossoming rose than to watch it fade."

"Indeed," she said. A silent minute passed before she proposed they both head to sleep.

Alone. Xelya removed the silver locket from around her neck. "Never will I lay my eyes on the beauty of Kashpur . . ." she whispered to herself. It had been a dream of hers, to see for herself the white city, yet never had she once imagined it would be destroyed. It was as if she had thought the Pearl of Illmeria would last for all eternity. Now that the treasures of the city had been lost forever, how she missed them. She wished to have dared visit it during her youth, even against the will of her masters.

"One should indeed admire the rose in its full glory while it lasts," she said, looking at herself in the mirror. Nothing was eternal, and those things beautiful, pure, and worthy of attention deserved to be cherished and appreciated for as long as they would last. She sighed. The fear of loss could only, ultimately, tarnish the beauty of what was to be loved. Never could it prevent its loss. Perhaps she did not truly appreciate the things she cared for. Perhaps she should allow herself to enjoy rather than fear.

* * *

The red rays of the sun covered the green hills of Illmeria, the early morning of a summer day. Valirian could not stay in bed any longer. Filled with energy, he hurried to get dressed and equip his armour. Then he headed to the red tent.

"Good morning, Valirian," said Syrela.

Deep in his thoughts and not having expected to see the War Hero so early in the morning, he was startled, which made her chuckle. "Good morning," he answered. Her visage was pale. There were dark circles around her eyes, making him look down as he stepped to her side.

"It's ... tough," she said, letting out a sigh. "But I will be fine. Sadly, it is only a confirmation of things you had warned about long ago."

He said not a word and simply placed his hand on her shoulder.

"You seem to know this general's tactics very well," she said. "Did you spy on him as a slave? Or perhaps were you a servant of his?"

He nodded with a joyless smile. "I was not the most honest in that regard. I was his scribe, though I hid it from you and Xelya for fear of your reaction."

She raised an eyebrow. "You feared losing our trust? You know better than all of us that slaves do not choose their masters." As he sighed and sat on a chair, further into the tent, she frowned yet followed him. Something perturbed him, she could tell.

"I'm sorry," he said. "I am not entirely innocent in the fate of Kashpur." Valirian expected a reaction from her, but she kept her silence. "I could have ended it all. But I feared. I was in his tent, sharpening his sword, just before your victory at Kashpur. He spoke of burning the city and leaving nobody alive. But I knew that if I took the chance to do the right thing, I would have paid for it with my life."

She took his hands in hers, clutching them as her lips pursed. "I cannot, and will not, condemn you. You were never meant to be there in the first place. But I do believe the spirits of Illmeria have guided you to the here and now so that you may save this land. There has to be a reason."

"Do you believe there is a reason for everything?" he asked.

She looked down with a shrug. "That is what my father used to say. I naively agreed, until a year ago. I do not think Evil has a purpose for Good, else I would have to think that there is some good in the murder of thousands of innocents, but I do think Good always rises to face Evil." A tear rolled down her cheek and fell onto the ground. She closed her eyes, her arms trembling. "I, too, could have prevented that disaster."

He wrapped his arms around her, and she hid her face in his cape. "Syrela," he said, "if you had been defending Kashpur, Xelya and I would be mourning the death of a dear friend."

"But I chose to go to the Mistlands. I could have—should have—refused Adiloka's orders. My oath to the spirits commanded that I not attack, but I caved to her demands. I could have prepared an army to defend against this invasion, and together, we would have defeated Koresh."

He knew not how to answer. His embrace tightened, and she reciprocated.

"I cannot explain the emptiness I felt when it dawned on me that the spirits no longer approved of my conduct," she said. "When I broke my oath to Nav by attacking the Fortress, I felt so cold. I felt like no hearth could have warmed me ever again. Now, with the loss of Kashpur, disgust fills me at the mere mention of my titles. 'The Blade of Illmeria,' 'the War Hero,' 'She Who Has Never Lost a Battle.' Looking at my own armour was unbearable this morning."

"Why would the spirits allow me a second chance," said Valirian, "even though I knew I acted out of cowardice, and not to you, even though you meant well, even in your mistakes?" She answered not. Valirian bit his tongue. His heart raced as his mind hurried him to say more. "What makes me deserving of your respect? If even I could amend my own faults, let me assure you, you already have done the same for yours."

"I can't help but feel I could have saved them."

"As do I," he said. "Yet neither of us could. I will let none, not even the spirits, judge you for things that were impossible to you. Do not let what is outside of your control determine your honour." He stood up, his hands reaching for hers. In spite of her heavy armour, he helped her up.

She took a deep breath. Her lips formed a weak smile, and her expression relaxed. "Thank you. I don't know if there was another way, but all I can do from here is my best. May the spirits approve of us and bring us victory." Her worries turned to Lady Adiloka. What had been her fate? She shivered at all the horrors her mind conjured and preferred to hope that, somehow, the Duchess had escaped, that she would appear from some ruins or secret hideout.

He smiled. "Shall the mighty War Hero let the guilty go unpunished?"

"Let us stand against evil together and deliver justice upon the invaders. They have awoken Illmeria's fury." She headed to the table nearby, where a map of Kashpur had been unrolled. "They are fewer than us, even with the most pessimistic of estimates. Kashpur was built in the flattest area of the region, and the river that passes south of the city is too shallow at that point. They will find little to hide behind outside of ruins. Are there any chances they run away?"

"It would be foolish for them to run away without supplies," he said. "If they take their supplies with them, they will be slowed and exposed. We may very well catch up to them."

She moved a few pieces on the board, simulating how a possible flight from Kashpur could unfold for the Koreshians. "Given their only reasonable escape route, it would be a slaughter, indeed."

"I worry more about an army of relief. It could arrive in the following days. That is worrying."

"That is my fear, too. We have to approach things methodically, but the battle of Kashpur could be resolved in a day," she said. "Then, hopefully, we will have dealt with them before an army of relief arrives."

"Then our plan should be to lure that army of relief into an unfavourable battle. Do you have any location in mind?"

She paused to think. Though ideal in theory, the Mistlands would be unreachable with an army on their tail. The Northlands, on the other hand, while reachable, were too risky: the Koreshians would have the ability to starve them out, for the enemy would know not to fall for the same trick twice. "The only reasonable place would be the Grasslands. Perhaps we can make it to the hills to the south-west, or perhaps we can lure them over a bridge, where we would have the advantage."

He nodded. It was their best option, even if the battle would be rough. He turned his attention back to the map of Kashpur. "They will have certainly erected a palisade around the city and dug some ditches. Those should not be insurmountable obstacles, however."

Syrela moved a few pieces to the north-west of the city. An idea had arisen in her mind. "We have a large enough cavalry. Though it is quite unusual to use cavalry inside a city, I believe that this is an opportunity not to be missed. See, there is a particularly large avenue that connects Kashpur to the road and goes all the way to a large plaza. They will have certainly barricaded the entrance, but if we are to send footmen first, we may give our cavalry an occasion to charge."

"If you are confident that the area is clear enough, the idea might have some merit," he said. "On that, I shall trust your judgement. We can have Zelshi lead the footmen into battle there and hide Cadmael and his cavalry behind the hills while the rest of the army attempts to take over the main streets."

Taking some charcoal, they highlighted a few of the major streets of the city: the objective was to split the Koreshians into smaller pockets that could more easily be crushed.

"I fear that they will have enough time to retreat deeper, to the eastern parts of the city, and establish a defence around the palace," said Valirian.

"They might," she answered. "However, that should not worry us. We should still be able to isolate some of their forces, which will later give us an edge. Defeating the remnants gathered around the palace should not be the most difficult part."

He shrugged, but for lack of a better plan, he did not object. "I hope so. It is never ideal to fight a battle inside the ruined streets of a city. Too many things will be unaccounted for, and there is always a place for the enemy to hide."

"I share your fear that we shall face considerable resistance. If we fail to take the invaders' positions before an army of relief arrives, the danger will be great."

He nodded. He feared, too, suffering too many losses. They needed each and every man fighting on their side, as many more battles would certainly be fought. But was there any other choice?

CHAPTER 31
THE LAST ROAR OF THE STORM

It was late in the afternoon that the scouts reported their sighting of the ruined city. Soon, the Illmerian army had taken positions, according to the plan. Cadmael and his cavalry had been particularly cautious in not revealing themselves to the invaders and had reached the hills north-west of the city shortly before the first siege engines were positioned.

"We were correct on the palisade," said Syrela. "The western part of the city is particularly damaged, but the streets strangely do not seem encumbered."

It was not so long ago that Valirian had gazed upon the city from that very same hill; yet the sight now was incomparable to the one a year prior. Hardly a house was left standing to the west, and to the east, most of the major buildings—temples, palaces, and various towers—had suffered heavy damage.

"The war machines are in position, My Generals," reported a sergeant.

After exchanging nods, Valirian and Syrela parted ways, for the

War Hero would lead the assault from the north while he would lead from the south-west.

"Is all in place, Advisor?" asked Xelya.

Quickly, he glanced behind, then nodded. The battle would begin any second.

The Queen dropped from her horse. Taking a few steps forwards, she climbed a rock and watched the city for a moment. Symbolically, this would be Illmeria's greatest victory. She turned around. Her men stood ready; all looked at her, eager to liberate what was theirs.

"Sons of Illmeria," she said. "Today, we show the will of our land and of our people, the desire for freedom that has brought us to triumph over the enemy again and again. To you, I give this one order: spare any Stormian wise enough to surrender, for they are our brothers, even in this war. But to the Koreshians, the invaders, show no mercy, for they showed none to our brothers and sisters. Let none survive!"

From the ranks, loud cheers and war cries erupted, men slamming their shields against their weapons.

"Let none survive!" she repeated. The battle cries loudened, doubtlessly echoing to the city. She glanced at her Advisor.

Valirian whispered a few words to a sergeant nearby, and the war machines fired at the Koreshian palisade. The soldiers marched on, slow at first so as to allow the siege engines to destroy the defences. Further north, the battalion led by Zelshi had been quicker to enter battle. Already, combat raged on as the Illmerian footmen pushed back the Koreshians, clearing a large path for Cadmael and his men. A simple signal, a blue flag raised by one of Zelshi's sergeants, and the Mistian cavalry charged into the ruins of Kashpur.

"Charge!" said Valirian. Now was the time: the Koreshians must be engaged on different fronts so as to assist Cadmael in his assault. By Xelya's will, a powerful gust of wind sent the thick black smoke into the Koreshian ranks as Valirian led his men into an attack on what remained of the palisade. "Victory is ours!" he shouted. "Let this battle be remembered for ages!" His blade was the first to find a target, then again as he struck another.

The invaders' formation was disorganised. A push through the centre isolated two groups of Koreshians that were soon dealt with, and a third was isolated by a building collapsing quite suddenly. Valirian glanced at Xelya, unsurprised to find her as the cause. To the Queen, such a battlefield was ideal: little effort was needed to make a ruin collapse the way she desired. She would not even need to unleash her full powers quite yet. The battle would doubtlessly be long and exhausting. It was wise that she kept her strength.

"Form ranks!" shouted a Koreshian sergeant. The first Illmerian assault had caused heavy losses on their side, but the Koreshians knew that there was no chance to escape. They would fight to the bitter end.

"Aim!" said another Koreshian.

Some ten steps away from Valirian, a group of archers had positioned themselves on some rubble and aimed at him. For a second, he felt his heart stop; he was out in the open. He raised his blade. If he were to perish, he would rather die fighting. His legs moved on their own as he ran to them.

"Fire!"

Arrows flew around him. He was so close to them. How had they missed? Three strikes, and three Koreshian archers died. The others were dealt with by his men, and Valirian glanced behind. His eyes met Xelya's, and he understood. It was good that she fought by his side.

"Captain Cadmael has taken the plaza," said Xelya. "The invaders are trapped. Fight on!" A part of the cavalry charged into the large street from the other side. If they could join forces, all Koreshians positioned westwards would be trapped.

"Soldiers, to me!" said Valirian. That was an opportunity he could not pass up. A push from the centre broke the enemy lines once again, and some Illmerian soldiers who had stayed back to defeat a few pockets of Koreshians joined the fray. "Let us send these demons back to their pits!" A Mistian cavalier helped defeat a Koreshian spearman, and the two battalions connected. The invaders were trapped.

"Help the general!" said Cadmael. "To the right, charge!" More of the young captain's cavaliers poured into the street and the Koreshians were soon all dealt with. "My General! It's good to see you."

"Hurry and return to the plaza," said Valirian. "We can trap all the Koreshians to the west." Without a word, Cadmael gathered his men behind him and rejoined Zelshi's battalion. Further away from the combat, Valirian had taken over the western plaza, his men engaging in a few skirmishes as some Koreshians attempted to retreat eastwards.

"Excellent," said Xelya. "Perhaps, after all, it is not impossible for us to retake the Pearl of Illmeria in a single day."

"This was a remarkable success, so far," he said. "And in a matter of minutes, we will defeat those that we have trapped. This could not have gone any better."

* * *

"My General, the battle has begun to the south and north-west."

Syrela equipped her helmet. They were to await a specific time, one she had to observe to the best of her abilities. From the slight elevation to the north of the city, she could hardly tell how the battle would unfold, though she preferred to trust Valirian, Xelya, and the other captains. "Akior, lead your divisions slightly further east. Aaposhi, follow my battalion and enter the city shortly after us."

Following her orders, her troops approached the ruins. She was at the head of the less experienced men of the Illmerian army, amongst which many were peasants and refugees who had joined the day of the departure, along with those who had joined the army as they recaptured the Grasslands. For her attack to stand any chance, the Koreshians needed to be distracted. Only small, and rare, groups of invaders defended the northern area of the city, offering little to no resistance to the overwhelming Illmerian numbers. Was it a trap?

"My General, my group, led by Captain Akior, has discovered an area guarded by Stormians," said a young soldier. "Captain Akior thinks it's too dangerous to continue without reinforcements."

Were the Stormians tasked with defending the northern front? That could explain the lack of Koreshian presence but not the lack of resistance. Were they refusing to fight?

"Inform Captain Akior to stand his position," she said. "I will arrive with the rest of our forces as soon as possible." As she knew Aaposhi to be following her, she led her group to meet with his, and she informed him of the situation.

"So we regroup with Akior and see how to deal with the Stormians?" said the captain. "Well, let's not waste any time, then. I don't know whether to trust, laugh at, or fear them."

She hurried her troops, worried that Akior's forces had engaged the Stormians, but to her surprise, he had been allowed to take position around the area.

"There are three pockets of Stormians in the nearby district," said the captain. "However, the pockets all seem to be connected in different ways. What's the most surprising is that they know our positions, but they have not made any attempts at attacking us—or anything."

She frowned, rubbing her chin as she studied the map. They had taken position in the artisan district. There was hardly anything of note that made the area more dangerous, or prone to traps, than any other. It was, admittedly, less damaged than the southern and western parts of Kashpur, yet something felt off. "You said the three pockets are connected in some ways?" she asked.

"Well, according to the maps we have," said Akior, pointing at streets and small plazas. "We don't have control of the area, so we don't know how usable those are."

A thought came to her mind, something that could explain this bizarre situation. "Send scouts to those positions. Monitor any Stormian movements. I have my suspicions." The major flaw of the Stormian army had always been the same: a lack of coherence, as clan allegiance often trumped loyalty to the Duke—clans that were often feuding. Zheraï had attempted to overcome it by separating clansmen from one another within his own army, but if his authority had eroded as a result of the Koreshians' failures in the Mistlands, those tensions were at risk of reigniting. So she was hardly surprised when the scouts' reports came: barricades, arrows fired, and frequent skirmishes between the three Stormian groups.

"Do they not know that there is a battle going on at the same time?" asked Aaposhi.

"They probably don't see the battle as their business at all," said Akior. "Do we just ignore them?"

The idea was not as unreasonable as it seemed. There were hardly any reasons for the Stormians to attack the Illmerians. It would take quite some time before the tribal feuds were resolved, and by then, the battle could very well be over, too. "What are the estimated strengths of each group?" she asked.

"We can't tell for sure their numbers, but we know that the group to the north is significantly more numerous," said Akior. "Perhaps as big as the other two combined."

"That must be the Mehakaï," she said. "The Duke's clan." She nodded to herself and straightened her back. It was all she needed to know. "Gather our troops. Let us meet these groups head-on."

At her command, the men hurried to form ranks and followed her through the streets in tight formation. The silence gave a threatening air to every street, as if an ambush awaited them at every corner, yet Syrela marched forwards without any fear, ahead of her men by several steps. The Stormians seemed to hide at her approach, for the plaza that served as the headquarters of the northern group was empty, only a few movements in some of the ruined buildings around giving any hints of life.

"In the name of Lady Xelya, Queen of Mists and rightful ruler of Illmeria, I, General Syrela, demand your immediate surrender!" she announced. Her voice echoed in the ruined streets, and for a long minute, she stood still, her eyes not moving from the mansion before her. It had been damaged during the Koreshian attack yet kept relatively intact otherwise, and from the broken windows, one could see silhouettes hiding, moving, spying.

The Stormians who showed themselves were few, maybe some twenty or thirty, though none left the mansion to drop their weapons, nor to fight. They formed lines to prepare for their leader's arrival rather than forming ranks for battle. From inside the building appeared a tall man, with long black hair tied behind his head by some twine. He studied the War Hero for a moment. His eyes had a deep blue glow, the blue of a cold ocean, and he nodded to himself, a frown on his visage, as he approached her, some thirty steps separating them. He was without a doubt one of the Stormcallers, powerful warrior-mages of the Stormlands, capable of calling thunder down at will, or so the legends said—an elite few that were generally high ranking amongst their clans, if not at their heads.

"I, Kirethi, wishes to fight you, o Blade of Illmeria, in a duel to the death," he said. "My troops will surrender to you should you win. Should you lose, however, I demand that my men be allowed to return to the Stormlands."

She frowned and studied his men for a moment. All bore the symbol of the Mehakaï, yet Kirethi had not declared his affiliation with them. "Which clan are you part of, Kirethi?"

"I no longer have a clan," he said, "for I shall no longer stand with the one that once led us."

The answer surprised her not; such she had guessed from their feuds with the other groups. She considered his offer. In the past, Syrela had already fought and defeated a Stormcaller. In truth, that fight only gave her little knowledge of her opponent's possible abilities, for each had a unique fighting style, making their powers translate in various ways. The man wished no more than to eternally cement his legacy, for the one who defeated the Blade of Illmeria herself could certainly claim honours for generations to come—a vain goal that was far from uncommon amongst Stormcallers. Was it truly wise to grant him such an opportunity? Even if she defeated him, it would be an honourable defeat. She glanced at the Stormians. They stood no chance against the Illmerians, who heavily outnumbered them. If she so wished, in mere minutes, they could all be dealt with.

An idea crossed her mind. "Do you believe this offer to be to my advantage?" she answered. "My time is precious. Your petty demands are meaningless to I. We outnumber you. You stand no chance. Surrender now, and you will be spared." She took a few steps forwards, leaving her men a good distance behind.

Kirethi frowned. The blue glow of his eyes darkened, and he drew his weapon. "Has the famed War Hero of Illmeria lost her courage? Perhaps the lives of your men are less valuable than your time. You would rather sacrifice them!"

"The city has been retaken, and your Koreshian masters are defeated. Your pride is of no matter to I, and I will not grant you your wishes of vain glory."

"Fight me now, or be remembered as a coward!" he shouted.

She smiled and turned around, taking a slow step towards her own soldiers. Footsteps, behind—precisely what she had been waiting for. His war cry echoed in the ruined plaza, and at the last instant, she dashed to her left, avoiding the Stormcaller's attack. Her spear blocked his sword while her four blades unsheathed from behind her back.

He dashed backwards, then slashed the air. A powerful shock wave destabilised her, leaving her staggered. Worse, her blades had been sent flying far behind; manipulating them from such a distance was impossible. Only her own magic protections had prevented her from being blown away by the warrior's magic, who now prepared for an assault.

"I will have your head, War Hero!" he shouted before leaping forwards.

She was still armed with her spear, and some of her magic still protected her. She was far from defenceless. She dodged and aimed at the man's arm. The tip of her spear found the armour's weakness, leaving a cut, unfortunately one too small to bother the warrior. Even with his unexpected magic, she had been able to lead him where she wanted and have him strike first. The battle was far from over. She could wait for his next assault, then disarm him, for her reach was greater than his.

He leaned forwards, ready to attack at any moment, and she slowly circled him. If she could gain just enough time to get closer to her blades, she could call them back. He had not used his powers again, a sign he would probably struggle in doing so during the same fight.

"You can still save your life and surrender now," said Syrela.

The man was predictable. Those were all the words she needed to utter to get him to attack. She jumped backwards, avoiding his blade, before thrusting forth with her spear, hoping to send her opponent's weapon flying. A shock wave. Her ears were ringing, and her vision blurred. She had landed on her back and her head had hit the ground. It was weaker than the first blast yet still strong enough to send both weapons flying far away. She had barely recovered her senses, but before she could react, the man had jumped on her. Though he was weaponless, he would not relent. She could not avoid the first blow to her face, but even with all of his strength, it was not enough to knock her unconscious; her magic had absorbed part of the blow. Just in time, she blocked the next punch—but what was she to do? The man was above her, blocking her movements.

She looked around. There had to be something. She retaliated, hoping to get some time, and her punch landed on the man's jaw, feeding his anger. His hands wrapped around her neck—there, she spotted it! Her spear, some five steps away.

"Men, help your general!" said Akior.

No! They mustn't! She gathered all the energy left in her body. He turned his head to glance at the Illmerian soldiers approaching. This was her chance! A slight smile appeared on her lips as the man began to suffocate her—suddenly, he gasped. His grip tightened, then loosened, and his eyes rolled to the back of his head. She pushed him off and stood tall. With a gesture, she made her men stop, then pulled her spear out of Kirethi's back, staring at the Stormian soldiers who had formed ranks nearby. "I have won."

Slowly, she stepped towards the Stormians, the tip of her spear down. "Surrender now, and you will be spared." She was a mere step away from them. The soldier before her had his blade raised, yet he trembled. With two fingers, she pushed down his sword. Still shaking, he dropped his weapon. The other Stormians soon followed. "Treat our Illmerian brothers with respect," said Syrela. "Gather them and bring them out of the city."

Akior and Aaposhi gave a few commands to their men as Stormians exited the surrounding buildings. One of the Mehakaï warriors brought his clan's banner to the War Hero, bowing low before her as he, too, dropped his weapons.

"Are there other Stormcallers in Kashpur?" asked Syrela.

The soldier shook his head. "No, o War Hero. The other two clans in Kashpur are minor clans and have very few men here."

The buildings empty, the plaza retaken, Syrela turned to her two captains. "Let's hurry. We can deal with the other pockets of Stormians with ease, and if we are fast enough, we might arrive first at the palace."

Indeed, the two other groups were quick to surrender, for news of Syrela's victory against Kirethi spread rapidly. Only an hour after, they had retaken most of the northern districts.

"What is the plan now, General?" asked Akior.

"We try to reconnect with General Valirian's army," she said. "The centre and the eastern districts are where the Koreshians will give the greatest resistance, so let's be careful on the way."

CHAPTER 32

FLAWLESS PURPLE

"No progress, I'm afraid, My General," said Zelshi. "Our losses are minimal, but they have built a really thick wall, and we can't get our siege engines here easily. The streets around here are too narrow."

The report was worrying. After their initial success, Valirian had hoped for a swift victory, yet he was met with unexpectedly fierce resistance. How had the Koreshians built such a wall so rapidly? It was at least two steps thick and three or four men tall. All that was left to be retaken was the harbour, the palace district, and the areas in between. It was a fraction of the city, yet it could hold on for far too long, especially if an army of relief was indeed on its way.

"Bringing the siege engines would not be wise anyway," said Valirian. "We would have to clear the rubble, move them, and fire at the walls for many hours, if not days. We cannot risk time we do not have."

Syrela's success had brought a wave of hope, as if her presence alone would make the walls crumble, but it appeared that only an assault with ladders could stand a chance. A costly attack that they could not afford, either.

"What are our chances if the Koreshians send an army of relief and we fight them in the ruins?" asked Valirian.

Syrela shrugged. "It wouldn't be an impossible battle, but it would be very unwise. We would have no escape, and if they choose to sacrifice the men inside, they will starve us to death. We would be playing a risky game."

If only the Illmerian fleet had been positioned outside of Kashpur's harbour! Much like how the Koreshians had attacked Mistport from the sea, a simultaneous landing would split their forces and could help grant them victory. Yet the fleet was days away, in the Mistlands.

"We have to take a risk," said Valirian. "Either we sacrifice some men to overcome those defences or we sacrifice time to bring the war machines into the city itself. The only other option is a tactical retreat."

Syrela looked down, nodding to herself. There was no right solution. "My instincts would always tell me to prioritise safety above all else. We are flipping a coin in any other case, and the wrong result means the end."

He sighed, and they parted ways with a nod. He met with the other captains. Each of them told the same story, and all reached the same exact conclusion. Three possibilities, none desirable. He cursed. He had allowed himself to be overly enthusiastic about their early successes. All hope was not lost in this war; they could not allow themselves to be hopeless, but what were they to do?

As he sat on some rubble with a frown, still deep in thoughts, Xelya's silhouette caught his attention. She was alone, though at a safe distance from the walls, just far away enough not to be noticed by the Koreshians. She observed, otherwise immobile.

"My Queen," he greeted her.

"What is the news, Advisor?" she asked.

"Unfortunately, we are at a crossroads," he said. "Lady Syrela and I have discussed the situation. Three options are before us. First, we could assault the walls, which would be terribly costly. Second, we could bring some siege engines here, but we would need to clear some of the rubble, and it might take days before a breach is made in the Koreshian walls. Or we could retreat."

She turned to face him, studying him with a slight frown, and her purple eyes squinted.

"Lady Syrela suggests the path of safety," he continued. "If we choose to wait and we are caught in the city by an army of relief, we are unlikely to win, and there would be no way of escape. If we lose too many men by attacking the walls right now, we risk finding ourselves incapable of defeating the army of relief."

"And so you wish for I to give the order?" she asked. He nodded, then bowed low. She grabbed his chin and raised his head, staring into his eyes. "And I trust that you will follow my commands, then."

His heart raced, but he chuckled and nodded. "Of course, My Lady."

"Gather my cavalry and have Cadmael lead them," she said. "Gather them in the largest street, west of the wall."

"My Lady, using cavalry within a city is unwise. I suggest—"

"I care not about your lesson on basic tactics," she interrupted. "I ask of you to obey my command." Her grip loosened, and the hint of a smile formed on her lips.

He nodded and turned around to give Cadmael the Queen's orders.

Slowly, she headed there, to the street she had mentioned. When careful plans and strategies failed, sometimes boldness and audacity could triumph instead. Valirian had been wise enough not to contest her orders—or perhaps he had understood her thoughts.

"Captain Zelshi, keep your troops ready, too," said Valirian.

Many minutes had passed, and Cadmael had gathered his cavalry.

"My Queen, are you sure that you want us to use cavalry?" The young man stuttered as he spoke, not knowing how to voice his concerns to his Queen.

"Worry not," said Valirian.

Alone she stood, some forty steps away from the wall. She had climbed some rubble, her eyes not moving from the recently built fortifications before her, and Valirian stepped to her side. She closed her eyes. Strangely, she felt odd palpitations in her chest, and she turned to him. She opened her mouth, wishing to speak, but no words escaped.

"At your command," he said. "You have all my trust, My Lady."

She glanced behind. No soldier could hear them. "I might feel weakened. I might collapse or lose consciousness, even. Stand by me as I use my magic."

He nodded. They both turned to the Koreshian fortifications. Behind, the streets had been mostly cleared. The Illmerian troops had formed ranks. A strange warmth, a breeze around Xelya. Soon, a faint whisper escaped her lips, and for a long minute, there was little more. A small orb of purple, the size of an eye, formed in her palm. Slowly, it grew to the size of an apple, the whole world silent before the mage's mysterious whispers. On the wall, the Koreshians hurried. A few gathered to observe the scene. Others attempted to fire arrows—they turned to ashes two steps away from Xelya. Suddenly, the faint whisper turned into a powerful speech, given in an odd and foreign tongue, the orb tripling in size. The Queen's eyes had turned entirely purple, the glow turning into beams of light, and the breeze turned to strong gusts.

". . . sa'ar!" she shouted, a conclusion to her speech, hurling the orb to the wall. She fell forwards, Valirian barely catching her in time. Behind, Cadmael's war cry led his men into a charge. The wall had crumbled.

"So much effort . . . for a mere pile of stones . . ." she whispered, out of breath, forcing a slight smile. The breach was wide, almost as wide as the street, and four horsemen could enter the plaza behind at a time. Illmerian footmen followed the cavalry charge, Syrela at their head, as the first echoes of battle reached their ears. He helped her stand up straight, making her lean on his shoulder.

She glanced at her work and at the soldiers who joined the fray. "I had hoped for a more evident weakness in their fortifications. Unfortunately, such was not the case."

"Are you feeling fine?" he asked. He, too, glanced at the battle nearby. The Illmerian soldiers seemed not to struggle entering the plaza—a good sign, as it meant the Koreshians were unprepared for such an assault. How could they have been?

"I am," said Xelya. "And I am most thankful for your help." After a deep breath, she took a step on her own. Her body was still trembling, so he left not her side, but the sight brought him a smile. "I suggest that you join your men in the fray. Your presence will be more needed there than here."

The last traces of her magic had vanished, and seven of the Queen's bodyguards approached, so he nodded, confident she would be in no danger. Unsurprisingly, the heavily outnumbered Koreshians struggled holding on to the plaza; the attack had been too sudden. Better, even, were the Illmerian battalions to the north and south of the plaza that launched an assault soon after, as they noticed the Koreshians being distracted. The invaders were pressured on all sides but the east.

"After them!" shouted Akior. "We will pursue the invaders to the end of the world if need be!" His battalion followed a group of Koreshians retreating to the harbour, while in the plaza, Cadmael's cavalry helped Syrela and her men surround a large portion of enemies.

"Leave none alive!" she said. "Victory is ours!"

Never before had Valirian seen his own troops so enthusiastic, energised. The plaza was covered in bodies, yet very few were Illmerians, a miracle.

"Lady Syrela," greeted Valirian.

"Ah, Valirian," she said. "I suppose from your expression that the Queen is feeling alright." She removed her helmet and wiped the sweat off her forehead. She had a black eye, many bruises, and a few superficial cuts on her visage, yet she smiled as she glanced around. The battle had been won; only a few remnants would need to be dealt with overnight.

"Indeed she is," he said. "I can only imagine how taxing such a feat must have been." He glanced at the large opening in the fortifications behind, and they shared a laugh.

"You have no idea," she said. "Even I, taught in the arts of magic, can hardly believe what I saw with my own eyes." She turned. Behind was the great palace of Kashpur. Its exterior had been damaged, most specifically the decorations and statues that surrounded it, but the edifice itself seemed otherwise unharmed. "The palace is still ours to take. It's a symbolic step, more than anything else, but it would give a clear message to the few Koreshians still alive. Maybe you could lead a few soldiers there. It would also give the Queen a safe place to rest for the night. Wiser than to risk going through all the dark alleys to return to camp."

He answered with a nod. From the breach, the Lady approached, surrounded by her guard.

"Allow Captain Zelshi to follow you, alongside two hundred men," said Syrela. With a hand gesture, she commanded the captain to her.

"What is the situation, Generals?" asked Xelya.

"Captain Zelshi and I will lead a battalion to clear the palace," said Valirian. "It will also give you a place to rest for the night."

"I am far from defenceless, even when exhausted," she said. "But still, I shall listen to your advice. Lead the way, but do not expect me to simply wait outside aimlessly."

He chuckled. There was little he could do to prevent her from joining the battle for the palace, but she risked little: she would have guards protecting her.

"I will be able to take care of everything outside," said Syrela. "It will take some time, but it is simply a matter of eliminating the few pockets of resistance left in the city."

They parted ways. Then, with two hundred men, he entered the palace, exchanging only a few words with Zelshi to agree on a strategy. They knew little of the building. All they could establish was what appeared obvious at first glance: it was large, divided into wings, and at least two levels high. All Valirian knew otherwise was that the ducal quarters were on the upper floor, in the western part of the main wing, just above the plaza they had just retaken, for the ruler of Kashpur often gave speeches from one of the balconies to the local population. Valirian and his troops would head there while Zelshi cleared the rest of the ground floor. The battalion sent inside proved more than enough, for only a few Koreshians had taken refuge in the palace—indeed, fleeing to the harbour appeared wiser in every respect. Only half an hour after, Valirian's men reached the ducal quarters. The Queen's guards inspected the area. It was empty.

"Protect the ducal quarters, but do not enter unless absolutely necessary," said Valirian to the guards. "The Queen needs to rest."

Some ten men guarded the large double door of a dark brown wood, one that complemented nicely the red of the palace walls. Though the ground floor had been ravaged, with little recognisable, as Koreshian soldiers had pillaged all that seemed to have value, the upper floor had been spared by comparison. No particularly luxurious item had been left, naturally, yet the doors were for the most part intact, and the large and colourful tapestries on the walls still hung from the ceiling. On both floors, most of the windows had been broken, though more had been left intact on the upper one. In particular, the ducal quarters had mostly been spared. Certainly, Alexar had temporarily taken residence there after his conquest. This was where Lady Adiloka had once lived. The rooms were large, the door handles made of gold, and golden engravings in varying patterns were on the red walls. Many chandeliers, candelabras, and oil lamps—often decorated with pearls, rubies, and opals—normally lit the rooms.

"Worthy of the Duchess's ambitions for grandeur," said Valirian, "but quite bittersweet now that her fate has been sealed." On their left and right were four doors, two on either side, which led to smaller bedrooms, while in the centre was a large double door.

Xelya led the way, entering the large room that was once the bedchamber of the Duchess herself. "She certainly had good taste." She sighed, forcing a slight smile. Everything was mostly intact, beyond the shards of a broken vase under a wooden table near the entrance. "I do feel a bit of sympathy for Adiloka. She was unwise, and in the end, she made mistakes that cost her everything, but in some ways, she meant well for her people."

He nodded. There was something he dared not disturb in this room, so he spoke not. Having found some bedsheets in a wardrobe, she used the little magic left in her to make the bed in the blink of an eye.

"You shouldn't spend yourself like that," he said. "I could have done this for you."

She turned to him, the hint of a smile on her lips, and snapped her fingers. The lantern he carried was put out, making him chuckle. There was a large and wide-open window, opposite the bedroom's entrance, that allowed in the calm summer breeze and the pale blue light of the full moon. With slow steps, she headed there. Taking a deep breath, she closed her eyes, letting the air caress her skin—yet she suddenly turned around. She observed Valirian, her mouth open yet not saying a word. He had not noticed, focused on studying the details of a tapestry under the moonlight. Her attention turned to the city below. There was something so strange: the sight was grim, for Kashpur was little more than ruin, yet she felt so light, unburdened, filled with an exhilarating sensation. What had been lost would be rebuilt, even if she would never witness the beauty of the Kashpur of old.

She turned around, again. He raised an eyebrow and bowed, about to leave, but she instead invited him to her side with a hand gesture.

Her heart raced faster, and an idea imposed itself in her mind. She once again opened her mouth and closed her eyes but felt unable to speak. For weeks now, she had ignored this thought. Fear, denial, even guilt, sometimes, had made her push it away. She glanced at the city below, a slight smile on her lips. "Never will I lay my eyes on the beauty of Kashpur . . ." she whispered.

Had the sight of a ruined Kashpur not been painful to Valirian and her, too, though they had never set foot in the city? Was the loss any less meaningful? Fear, denial, guilt—all would only harm her in the end. It was wiser to embrace what was temporary, to enjoy it for as long as it could last.

"Valirian," she said.

"Yes, My Lady?"

He had moved to her side. How would she finish that sentence? She hesitated, but he stayed silent, waiting for her to continue. "Never before have I found the strength within myself to speak of this," she said. "But I have to admit the shame and guilt I still feel for having attempted to control you with magic, that day, so long ago."

For an instant, he almost answered, about to reassure her and repeat that all was forgiven. Yet he refrained. He smiled and nodded.

"I would like to apologise to you, sincerely," she said.

"You are forgiven, Xelya," he answered. He slowly nodded, and he bowed his head. "I forgive you," he repeated in a whisper. He felt her hand on his breastplate. Gently, she pushed him against the wall. There was a wide smile on her lips, and she untied the knot behind her head, letting loose her hair. Their eyes met, and he felt a rush—what was that daring sensation?

She took a step forwards, and her lips met his. She felt him jolt at the touch, and so she moved back. His arm wrapped around her waist, and they once more met in a loving embrace. After long minutes, they parted, for a brief moment, immobile as they looked at one another in silence. They kissed once again, more confident, more passionate, the notion of time so far away. Only an eternity after did she take a step back. She looked down and, with the help of her magic, removed her armour.

Even in her nudity, there was something mysterious about her, something grandiose. His eyes were unable to look away, admiring her flawless, silky, fair skin and her graceful figure. Her body was fit, giving her delicate and harmonious proportions an air of nobility, of elegance, even in her simplest attire.

"You are flawless..." he said, finding no other words for the beauty before his eyes, magnified by the blue light of the full moon.

With a smile, she tilted her head slightly, making her white hair scintillate in the pale light, a spectacle of pure silver. With his help, she began undressing him. His body was one of a warrior, of the Illmerian general he had become. His strong and wide shoulders, his well-defined torso, yet his otherwise lean and slim figure gave his body a statuesque appearance. His skin had tanned over the days spent outside fighting and training, giving it a golden colour. Powerful and lively.

She took his hand and guided him to the bathroom nearby, more than glad to clean themselves after the difficult battle they had fought that day, yet they hurried to bed mere minutes after. Valirian gently pushed her onto it. They thought themselves out of reality as they got lost in their passion. As if in the sweetest of dreams, nothing seemed real except the love they felt for one another.

"I love you, Xelya," he whispered in her ear. He kissed her neck, then every inch of her body, holding her hand tightly, feeling his heart race like never before as he brought happiness to the woman he loved.

Her soft breath growing more and more irregular, she pushed him on his back. "I love you, too, Valirian." Their fingers intertwined once more, and they became one. They spared one another no caresses, held back no loving words. Her purple eyes were like two flawless gems in this blissful night, and their lips united in one last kiss.

CHAPTER 33

BURNT

Her eyes still closed, Xelya smiled. Instinctively, her hand reached to her side and caressed Valirian's shoulder. He was still asleep, but he deserved to rest a little longer. It mattered not that quite a few hours had passed since dawn. She sat on the edge of the bed and rubbed her dry eyes before getting ready for the day.

"Good morning, My Lady." Valirian was just opening his eyes.

She moved to the edge of the bed and sat next to him. "Allow me to reassure you, last night was not a dream. Such formality is unneeded, Love."

He chuckled, then rested his head on her shoulder. There, they both stayed, not saying a word for many long minutes. Some noise outside made Xelya turn her head—nothing much, certainly, just a sergeant or one of the captains giving orders. Yet her eyes moved not from the wide-open window, even as calm returned to the large plaza below.

"What is on your mind?" he asked.

For a few moments, she only observed the sky. Did she even truly understand the thoughts on her mind? For many weeks she had felt paralysed by her own fears, hiding behind excuses, content in her own denial, yet all of that had vanished in a single night spent with the one she loved. It felt so surreal. It mattered not to her what the nobles, the army, the commoners would think. Would they not celebrate their union, as the two saviours of Illmeria became one? "I feel unstoppable. I did not have the strength to admit what I truly felt for far too long. Now I truly understand the beauty of spring blossoms."

He took her hand, and together, they glanced outside. Did he not share how she felt? He had convinced himself that his love for her would disappear if he forgot himself in his duties, fearing her refusal. He sat behind her, hands reaching for her shoulders, and massaged her. "Danger will exist for as long as Koresh threatens Illmeria, but I promise you that I will not allow our love to end tragically."

She turned her head, and their lips met for a brief kiss. It all seemed out of time, and neither wished to think of what could be happening just outside. Nothing existed beyond their room.

* * *

"Scouts have looked through the entire district. There doesn't seem to be any pockets left," said Akior.

Syrela removed her helmet and let out a sigh. The night had been long and exhausting, yet it was finally over. "Spirits be honoured. Victory is ours, and little time was lost. This is no small success."

"What are your orders, General?" asked the captain.

She looked around. The soldiers were equally as exhausted. It had been rage, she knew, rage and a desire for revenge that had given the Illmerian troops enough strength to continue fighting throughout the night. Now that the battle was over, her own anger had been mostly appeased. "Gather the men and let us review the state and numbers of our troops. After that, we will all be able to rest."

She turned to face the troops gathered behind her. They joked with one another. Most had removed their helmets, sheathed their weapons, and many sat on stones and piles of rubble.

"Sons of Illmeria," she said, "I ignore not why many of you fought this battle. I ignore not that many of you, just like I, knew someone in Kashpur or saw this city as their home. I ignore not that, as this battle is now over, as we claim our greatest victory yet against Koresh, you see nothing but ruins around you. Each of you, every single man, from the youngest to the oldest, fought with the bravery and ferocity of a lion. You fought on, knowing it to be your duty, so that life may regrow on ashes, that life may continue in spite of the carnage. Today, I am no longer the only War Hero in Illmeria, for each of you is as deserving of this title as I. This is our home, and we will not abandon it!"

The men cheered. In spite of their exhaustion, they celebrated for a long minute. A heart-warming sight for Syrela. She knew all too well that the battle for Kashpur would be far from the last to be fought.

She turned to Akior once again. "Gather the men outside the city. I will head to the palace. And stay prepared. We can never be too safe."

As she left, she glanced behind. The harbour, too, had been mostly destroyed. The calm ocean, further, gave the sight a grim look. The palace was not too far, surrounded by a few patrolling soldiers, which reassured her. It was quite unlikely that something had happened, yet her tired mind could never be quite sure. With pressing steps, she traversed the many corridors and halls of the palace, for she knew it quite well. In search of Zelshi, she found many of his soldiers keeping watch over various access points that the captain had judged of strategic importance.

"General!" said Zelshi. "You could not arrive too early."

She raised an eyebrow. The captain seemed agitated, incapable of staying put as he looked around various piles of paper. "What is the situation in the palace, Captain?"

"The palace has been cleared, and the last Koreshians here have all been killed." He bowed, which made her frown. What was the meaning behind his worries?

"Then what troubles you?" she asked. "Do you have anything else to report?"

He nodded and, with a gesture, invited her to follow him. They navigated a few corridors until they arrived before a large door, guarded by two men. It led to an office, rather spacious though quite messy, for papers, books, and parchments were scattered about the floor. A fierce battle had taken place here, doubtlessly. In the centre of the room, next to a desk that had visibly suffered a few blows, a young Illmerian soldier seemed to piece together a torn paper, as if it were a puzzle. At the War Hero's arrival, he stopped in his activity and bowed before taking a few steps back, away from the desk.

"This is where one of the Koreshian captains had his office," said Zelshi. "Captain or whatever equivalent. I don't think he was a general, though. Me and my men arrived just as he got there with a few of his own soldiers. He tried to defend the room, and I felt like something was wrong. Before we could kill them all, he had already shredded the letter and started burning some of the bits. He was quite panicked."

She began to piece the story together. The Koreshian officer was trying to hide some military intelligence, perhaps too late. It was quite ironic, she thought. Given Zelshi's tale, the Mistian captain would have never suspected a thing had the Koreshian officer not shown such worry. In his precipitation, too, he had torn the letter before trying to burn it, which was outright stupidity.

"I sadly can't read whatever language it's written in," said Zelshi. "I thought maybe you could, My General."

She hunched over the letter. In spite of the damage it had suffered, it did not take her long to realise it was written in Koreshian, though her knowledge of the language was too limited to make anything of it. The message did not appear to be coded, a relief in itself, for they would otherwise lack time to decipher it.

"There are two things that I can clearly understand," she said. "The message has a date, and those are military orders. I may not be able to read it, but I know who can. I need to see the Advisor, right now." With swift steps, she turned around and left, leaving Zelshi to hesitantly follow her.

"Do we need to prepare the army?" he asked.

"There is no need to make a decision immediately," she answered. "Keep our men ready for anything, however."

Zelshi bowed and quickly left, not wanting to underestimate the situation, whatever it might be. Syrela wasted no time and hurried up the palace's impressive stairs to the ducal quarters. The two guards before the doors saluted her yet seemed surprised to see her in such a hurry—already, she had disappeared behind the doors. Yet once inside, she stopped herself in her race. Never before had she entered the ducal quarters. Any of her discussions with Lady Adiloka had been held in a more public setting or in the gardens. The large door in the centre was certainly the Duchess's room—and thus where Xelya had, most likely, elected to sleep.

Enough time had been wasted. She opened the other four doors, one by one, expecting to find Valirian, fully awake, but he was nowhere to be found. Had the Queen also woken up, then? But, clearly, none of the four rooms had been used in weeks. Had they rested in another part of the palace? Carefully, she knocked on the large double door, leaning in closely to listen. Whispers, yet she could not make out what was being said.

"You may enter," said Xelya.

Syrela found herself speechless as she pushed the door open. In the back of the room, Valirian adjusted his shirt, both of their armours near the window.

"Good morning, Syrela," he said.

She rubbed her eyes, gathering her thoughts, and bowed. "There is something you have to see, Valirian. Captain Zelshi has found a letter in one of the offices, written in Koreshian. I believe them to be military orders." There was a slight stutter in her words, which made her tense up.

Valirian frowned and exchanged a brief look with his Lady.

Standing up from the edge of the bed, Xelya nodded. "Lead the way, Lady Syrela, though allow us to equip our armours first. We can never be too sure, even in the palace."

Syrela glanced at the armours, then at the large bed nearby, before closing the door and waiting outside, in the hallway. She let out a slight sigh, shaking her head. It was all too easy to guess. She had intruded, without a doubt. Thoughts conflicted in her mind, and she said not a word as she led them through the many corridors and halls of the palace to the office.

"The invaders tried to destroy the letter, My General," said the young Illmerian soldier. "I spent most of the night and the morning trying to piece it back together." The young man bowed and made way.

A frown appeared on Valirian's visage. Twice did he read the letter. The handwriting was all too familiar. Had Alexar been unable to find a scribe to replace him, after all this time? Yet there was no time for mockery and no reason to rejoice. "As we feared," he said. "The Koreshian high command called for the return of all their men to Kashpur and to defend the city until an army of relief arrives." He straightened his back and turned to face both Xelya and Syrela. "That army is certainly on its way. Given the dates on the letter, they might land tomorrow or the day after. We are lucky for such an oversight by the Koreshian officers."

"Then we need to summon all the captains, urgently," said Syrela.

"We've got to discuss the situation and decide what to do right now or we won't have the time to prepare."

All three nodded, and Valirian led the way out of the palace. They called for the soldiers to gather outside the city and for the captains to report to the red tent at once.

CHAPTER 34
A CANVAS OF SAND

Many long minutes had passed, too many for Valirian. Beyond Syrela and Xelya, sat around the large table, the red tent was empty. From her seat, the War Hero studied a map. Curious, he moved to her side. Before her was a map of the western coast of Illmeria. Finally, Zelshi arrived, soon followed by Cadmael. Syrela paid them little attention, at first, still focused, and only as Akior and Aaposhi arrived, some two minutes after, did she stand up to greet them.

"Not a moment too soon," said Xelya.

"Captains," said Valirian. "You may have guessed that the situation is quite urgent. In the palace, Captain Zelshi found Koreshian military orders indicating that an army of relief is to arrive soon at Kashpur. The letter was dated, and an estimated time of the army's arrival was also given. I believe it should reach Kashpur in the following days. In two or three days, to be precise, if not tomorrow or today."

The captains looked at one another. Aaposhi was the first to take a step towards the table. "Are we sure the letter is not a trap? We fought hard over Kashpur, and though we were able to take control of the city, if we abandon it and a Koreshian army comes to take it back, it will be really hard to retake afterwards."

"If it's a trap, they tried their damned hardest to prevent us from walking into it," said Zelshi. "I saw how panicked that officer was. He knew he'd made a mistake and was trying to cover it up."

"Captain Aaposhi does bring up a fair point, though," said Akior. "Retaking the city will be quite hard if we abandon it to the Koreshians and retreat."

"The greatest issue we faced in the battle for Kashpur was that the Koreshians could receive reinforcements at any moment," said Valirian. "Our suspicions were proven correct, but if the Koreshians are foolish enough to trap themselves in the city and let us besiege them, it is to our advantage in many ways. We were racing against time until now, but in such a siege, time will be in our favour instead."

The captains looked at one another. Some whispered a few words to themselves or to their companions, but in seconds, they had all turned their attention to the generals once more.

"What is the current state of my army?" asked Xelya.

"We did suffer some losses in Kashpur," said Aaposhi, "but much less than anticipated. We'd be at around eight thousand men, currently."

"I have lost some twenty cavalrymen," said Cadmael. "Hardly anything, and each and every single one of my men are ready for another fight."

Syrela's eyes widened. Certainly, an idea had come to her mind, yet she only smiled, making Valirian raise an eyebrow.

"So you suggest we abandon Kashpur and get reinforcements, My General?" asked Akior. "Then we besiege the Koreshians as they go back in the city and starve them out?"

"That will depend on the size of their army," answered Valirian. "We can't risk that if they outnumber us too heavily. At best, we will be reinforced by some two or three thousand men. A siege, by nature, means that our troops will be spread out, which would leave us too vulnerable if we are outnumbered."

"Why not just keep the city and try to hold it?" asked Aaposhi. "We could do what we did in Mistport, or at the Fortress, again. And unlike in those battles, where we had to defend the civilians, here we can turn every single stone into an obstacle. We even have their own fortifications we can use!"

"Never use the same strategy against the same enemy twice," said Syrela. Knowing that she had their attention, she unrolled the map she had studied for many long minutes before. "If we are to abandon Kashpur and they prove to have too big of an army, we will be unable to besiege them. We will have lost much ground, and who knows if Koresh will not send another army—and another after that. If we are to stay in Kashpur, we are using tactics the Koreshians will expect. We will fight a battle they have already fought. They will prepare for it. We know that their general survived the battle of Mistport. Let me remind you, our greatest advantage in Mistport was surprise. Never did the invaders expect to be met with such an army. No, I suggest a different strategy. Let us meet them head-on as they land."

The tent turned silent. Yet it had been the War Hero, the Blade of Illmeria herself, who had proposed such a daring plan.

"The Koreshians hoped to gain enough time for an army of relief," she continued. "We know that this was their plan. Depending on favourable or unfavourable winds, they will arrive in the following days without a doubt. We know that much. But where will they land?" With a dagger, she pointed at one location, and all approached the table and leaned over to see: it was a large beach, on the edge of the Northlands, directly west of Kashpur. "The Koreshians know the land enough. The Northlands are too forested to comfortably land there. Plus, the Koreshians would not be so foolish as to expose themselves to an ambush by traversing the forest. South, there are cliffs and the mouth of the River of Pearls. That would not only slow them down; landing there would also be difficult. It's a safe bet to assume that they will land on that specific beach, 'the Beach of Grey Sand,' as we call it in the Northlands."

"You suggest meeting them head-on?" asked Valirian. "The ground does not seem particularly advantageous, unless you plan to lure them into the forest."

"Our advantage will be surprise," answered Syrela. "We cannot risk staying in Kashpur, no matter what, but if we are fast enough, we can ambush them as they land, and that will be a significant enough advantage."

"And if they are not there, we risk nothing, for we need to leave Kashpur anyway," said Valirian, "while on the other hand, we can send scouts ahead to see if the Koreshians are already here and then deviate southwards instead if need be. Smart plan."

Xelya stood up from her seat, and Valirian gave her some space so that she might observe the map, too. "I approve of this plan. We have shown our enemy much carefulness: we defended our cities, we fought only on our terms, and we never risked an unfavourable battle. The time has come to surprise them."

Turning to the captains, Valirian found Akior and Aaposhi nodding to themselves, while Zelshi studied the map in greater detail. Cadmael, on the other hand, seemed already prepared to leave. "Gather the men and give them the order to break camp," said Valirian. "We are leaving immediately. This is a race to the beach, one we could still win."

"Yes, My General!" they answered. In a matter of seconds, they had left to execute the order.

"I need some time to gather my thoughts," said Xelya. "Allow me a few minutes of calm. I shall find you at the head of the army."

Syrela collapsed into her chair. All had left but Valirian. She rubbed her eyes and let out a sigh. The bruises and small cuts on her visage no longer felt painful; she was too used to them by now.

"You should take some rest, at least for the little time you can," said Valirian.

"No," she said. She stood up from her chair and stretched. She was pale, yet her red lips were pursed as she shook her head. "No. There is too much left to do."

"You did not sleep at all last night and barely slept the night before!" he said. "There might be a battle tonight. You cannot reasonably go for another sleepless night!"

"I will rest once we are victorious," she retorted. "There is too much at stake for me to just sit idly." Her reaction took him aback. Her expression changed, her traits relaxed, and her frown disappeared. She looked down and sighed.

"You cannot take such risks, Syrela," he said. "It could get you killed on the battlefield. Your magic could fail you at a crucial time."

"Then I will die for Illmeria," she whispered.

He sighed and shook his head. Instead of answering, she took him in her arms. His eyes widened. There was something off. Yet without hesitation, his arms reached around her, and he held her close.

"Promise me you will take some rest," he said.

With the little strength she had left, she nodded.

* * *

The time had come. Two hours had passed, and the Illmerian army had gathered in a long column. At its head, Xelya and Valirian, side by side, looked westwards. Syrela was to rest, then catch up to them on her horse, hopefully before any battle would occur. The Lady glanced behind. Her troops had suffered some losses, but the battle of

Kashpur had been a resounding success, both strategically and symbolically. No, what worried her was different. Much like Syrela, who had exhausted herself during the battle, the men looked tired, and their march seemed slower than usual.

"I hope we made no mistake in our judgement," said Xelya. "If the Koreshians were to have landed already, I cannot be certain that our men would be capable of running away from them."

Silently, Valirian nodded. The thought of changing plans, of commanding his men to head southwards rather than westwards, had crossed his mind more than once already. Yet each time, it was as if a silent voice deep within, a faint whisper, told him, *Do not*. He had placed his trust in Syrela. It would not be easy, far from it, but they had to take risks.

"Let us hope that Lady Syrela's expertise will win us the war," she said. Her eyes met his, and they smiled at one another. She remembered that very morning, how invincible she felt, and in that, she found strength. Each time an Illmerian scout appeared on the horizon and galloped to her, she felt a clenching in her chest; each time they would bow, she felt her hands grip even more tightly around her reins. Yet each time, the report was the same.

"No sightings of a Koreshian army, My Queen."

Each report would be followed by a sigh of relief. She dared hope that the Koreshian high command had changed their mind, that there would be no army of relief. They had lost tens of thousands of men. Could they really muster yet another force? But each time, she silently shook her head. She knew all too well what would inevitably come. Peace, it seemed, would not return to Illmeria just yet.

The sky turned to a beautiful mix of pale oranges and reds as the sun hid behind the horizon. It was at that time, near the end of the day, that Syrela caught up to them. Her return gave the men some hope, and they cheered as she galloped to the head of the army. She gave a nod to Valirian and Xelya, yet their attention was to the west. A scout, the last of those sent ahead, approached.

"There are warships on the horizon," he said. "They won't be able to land until late at night, that is for sure."

The news brought a strange relief to Valirian. Perhaps it was Syrela's return that gave him hope. Perhaps it was knowing that her prediction had been correct. A battle was still to be fought, but it would be the Illmerians who would decide its terms. "Captains, set camp here," he said. "We have little time, but it may be just enough." The gentle breeze carried the smell of the sea, making Valirian frown as he galloped to the cliff just south, following the scout. It took many long minutes until the Koreshians, having lit some torches, inadvertently revealed their presence, yet he could now see for himself: the warships would arrive in some eight hours, before dawn. "Our troops need some rest. We should have just enough time. Give them four hours of sleep, and then we shall prepare for battle."

The captains allowed their soldiers to sleep, knowing the War Hero, the Advisor, and the Queen would all keep watch. Together, the three climbed a small mound nearby, just high enough for them to oversee the whole battlefield. There was little Valirian could see. Often, he relied on the guiding words of either Syrela or Xelya. The moon, hidden behind dark clouds, left the glow of their eyes as the only source of light.

"You two have an advantage over me," he said. "What do you see?" They both observed the area, he knew, taking long minutes before they turned to him.

"The beach is bordered to the south by a steep cliff," said Syrela. "Further north is where the Northlands begin. The hills are taller and partially wooded. In between, the beach is quite wide and flat. The only elevations are further to the east, where we stand, but it is hardly usable in combat."

He nodded. The mental picture was clear enough for him to imagine how the battle could unfold, and he had an estimate of how many Koreshians would land.

"I see them," said Xelya. "A few hours separate us from yet another crucial battle, though I fear not. Thrice already we have triumphed, and again we will."

"We have time," said Syrela. "We can explore the terrain as much as we need to and then decide how to fight this battle."

* * *

The camp, which had been asleep minutes prior, woke up into a silent activity. Men shared a light meal together, or sparred, as they awaited orders, yet all knew not to be too loud, nor to light any fires. Their camp was hidden behind a few small mounds. It was unlikely that the Koreshians would suspect anything, so far away, but no risks would be taken.

"There would be some twenty thousand," said Syrela. "At least that seems a reasonable estimate given how many warships we can see."

Under the red tent, all eyes were on a sketch of the area, drawn with charcoal by Syrela and unrolled on the large table. After the War Hero's words, none dared speak.

"Good thing we didn't try to trap them in Kashpur, then," eventually said Akior.

"That's hardly comforting," said Zelshi. "They still outnumber us heavily, and our troops are exhausted."

"The situation is not hopeless," said Syrela. "The cliff to the south plays in our favour, even if the terrain does not allow us to position archers there. Our current position is slightly elevated compared to the beach, and we have enough men to surround them." Moving a few wooden pieces as she spoke, Syrela had soon established a strategy:

the Illmerian archers would be located on the more elevated areas to the south-east, while two battalions would hold off the Koreshians and keep them near the sea, making them a perfect target for the archers.

"I fear that our army is too exhausted to risk fighting a drawn-out battle," said Valirian. "Under normal circumstances, we would be able to set up basic defences, some barricades and trenches to slow them down and break their morale, but the Koreshians will eventually overrun our position."

She frowned. About to disagree, she had stopped herself. There was some truth in his words. They were at least outnumbered two to one, if not three to one—or more. The fight was not hopeless, but holding on to defensive positions was no easy task.

"Do you have an idea, then?" she asked.

Her frown vanished as a slight smile appeared on his lips. He glanced at Cadmael, and the young captain raised his chin and put his chest forth. "I believe I do," said Valirian.

CHAPTER 35
A THUNDER FROM THE MISTS

From the tallest hill, Xelya observed the Illmerian army. With the little time at hand, they had established defences to the best of their abilities: barricades, palisades, and trenches—rudimentary, but enough to gain some time. Valirian had proposed that she stay in the back line so that she might use her magic from there while also keeping a global view of the situation. It would be her task to command the archers. She would wait for a large enough number of Koreshians to have landed. It was hoped that even if the invaders were to retreat, they would only do so by sacrificing many of their troops, a victory at hardly any cost. Otherwise, this battle would be the Illmerians' best chance to triumph over the Koreshians.

"Here shall the fate of Illmeria be decided," she whispered to herself.

Further north, Valirian led a large battalion of footmen. Once the first volley of arrows struck the Koreshians, it was expected that they would be drawn to his group. Xelya had protested against him taking such a risky position, yet as Aaposhi swore to defend his general, with his life if need be, she reluctantly accepted. Zelshi, too, accompanied her Advisor, and that helped bring her peace of mind, for the captain was an exceptional warrior. In spite of the darkness, her magic allowed her to distinguish their groups: all three led a large portion of the Illmerian army and would certainly be targets of the fiercest Koreshian assaults, in spite of the barricades and other defences.

Beyond, further north and partially hidden behind a hill, Syrela led another battalion, Akior under her command. Xelya could only guess the outline of the War Hero's group. She turned to the sea, squinting as she tried to more clearly distinguish the Koreshian warships. They would soon land. Her heart raced, yet she remained still. Perhaps the invaders hoped the night would give them cover, for dawn was some three hours away. She glanced around. Some of her archers were trembling; none dared to speak, not even whisper. It was not out of fear of alerting the invaders, she knew.

She glanced at the warships, and her heart raced even faster. The first Koreshians were landing. If only she could give her men some words of encouragement. She breathed in deeply, eyes closed, hoping to calm herself, yet to no avail. She was all too limited in her magic, too exhausted from the spells cast the past days. How could she feel in control? Silently, she cursed the invaders and their Emperor. Many had now stepped onto the grey sand, yet she withheld the command. She would wait for the perfect moment.

Now! An orb of purple formed in her hand, and she threw it into the Koreshian ranks. Hopefully, it had taken the life of an invader, but above all, it served as a beacon for her men. "Fire!"

Following her spell were hundreds of arrows. The first volley left the Koreshians disorganised, and their screams echoed. For a brief moment, she thought the warships retreated, that they would turn around and leave, disappear behind the horizon and never return, but under the orders of their sergeants, the invaders had formed ranks and marched forwards.

"Send those dogs back home," she said, pursing her lips.

She glanced at the cliff and nodded to herself. She might not have within her the power to change the course of this battle, but she could give her men some hope. Her whispers echoed. Soon, large rocks were detached from the cliff and crushed doubtlessly many Koreshians. She panted—that was all she could do for now.

She glanced at the barricades, not so far away. "May the spirits of Illmeria come to your aid, Valirian my dear."

* * *

"The time has come," said Valirian.

Zelshi and Aaposhi nodded and drew their swords. Briefly, they inspected their men. The sight left them few reasons to rejoice. All knew this battle would claim the lives of many of them. The survivors would lose brothers, friends, sons. How could he blame them?

"Brothers," said Valirian. "I ignore not the fear in your hearts. Together, we have fought many battles, yet again and again we have triumphed over the invaders! Once more, we shall fight for the land that is ours and for those we cherish! To battle!"

To his right, Zelshi let out a battle cry, his sword high in the air. All followed his example as the Koreshian lines approached rapidly. The captain was the first man to strike. The breaking of spears and the clashing of swords and shields drowned the war cries in their tumult, and Valirian joined the battle at Zelshi's side. The captain's heroism had renewed the vigour of his men. It mattered no longer to any that the Koreshians were innumerable. Each strike seemed to bring victory closer.

"We won't let this vermin into our land!" screamed Zelshi. Around him, a hundred elite Mistian soldiers, amongst them veterans of the very first campaign. Covered by the volleys of the Illmerian archers, they seemed invincible. They fought bravely, and not an inch of ground was given without bitter resistance, yet the first barricade was overwhelmed, and to the north of the battlefield, the Koreshians threatened to cut off the Illmerians from their retreat. "Give your brothers time to retreat!" said Zelshi. His words were followed by a roar and a swing, claiming the life of another Koreshian. With his men, he led a breakthrough, carving his way through the enemy's ranks to the north, stopping the Koreshian advance and giving the larger battalion time to retreat. But more invaders arrived from the south-west.

"Zelshi, retreat!" said Valirian. "Your men are going to be trapped!"

He nodded, not even turning to face his general. As they moved back, they took every occasion to strike, giving their enemies no respite. Zelshi led his men through the palisades and the Koreshian ranks, relentless in his fighting. A scream. A Koreshian spear had found its way to his flank. With a grunt, he retaliated, cutting off the head of his attacker. Just as his legs started to give in, two of his men carried him to the second line of defence. His vision blurred. "No . . ." The wound was nothing; he needed to fight on! Then, all turned black.

"He is still alive, My General! His wound is deep, however."

"Take him to the camp," said Valirian. "His bravery has gained us precious minutes, and his heroism defeated many of our foes." The situation was quite dire. More and more ground was being lost, and though the initial blow to the invaders' advance had certainly gained much time, the battle was far from won. The melee turned into a bloodbath, yet the Illmerians refused to yield. Under Valirian's leadership, they kept a tight formation, and supported by archer fire, they made the enemy pay dearly for each inch of ground.

"We've made a breach, in their centre!" said Aaposhi.

A nod from Valirian was all the captain needed. At the head of a few elite soldiers, he broke the lines and established a spearhead. Now was the time. Valirian blew his war horn once, and the powerful sound echoed throughout the battlefield. The tactic was perilous, but he trusted Syrela.

* * *

Syrela shook her head. It was a dangerous game that Valirian played. This time, at least, she would personally intervene. Her grip around her spear tightened, and she clenched her teeth. The sounds of battle had reached her ears for many long minutes already, yet she was to wait. What if he had perished? What if he could no longer sound the horn? Those thoughts had crossed her mind many times.

She glanced behind. Akior stood ready by her side, and they shared a brief look. No doubt, the captain battled with those same thoughts. She shook her head again. With her eyes, she could see the battle, not far away. It was foolish of Valirian to wait any longer!

"We must act," she said.

Akior nodded silently and, with a gesture, commanded the men to march forwards. She took the lead of her battalion, some ten steps ahead of them. Her swords unsheathed from her back, and her march turned into a trot, her trot into a sprint. The war horn echoed. Perhaps he was not as reckless as she had thought. The Koreshians expected not the reinforcements, even less so for the War Hero herself to lead the charge. Her spear and blades broke the Koreshian lines. It was too late for them to reorganise. A spear, thrusting to her left. A few arrows, flying at her. A sword, striking to her right. None hit. Her magic deflected many of the attacks and her swift feet avoided the others. Her mind was empty. No longer did she need to think. It was her against an army, and she would triumph, no matter the numbers.

Around her, the soldiers led by Akior poured into the wide gap in the Koreshian lines, using to their advantage the havoc caused by her assault. She paid them no attention. She would carve a path to the spearhead formed by Valirian and his men. Her own troops would follow.

"The War Hero has joined the battle!" she heard from the Illmerian lines. The men cheered, and soon their cheers turned into battle cries. A large group of Koreshians, maybe a few hundred men, were isolated, cut off from the rest by the Illmerian army, then promptly dealt with. Yet though the invaders had lost some ground, the Illmerian success was met with a grim realisation, one Syrela only now truly grasped: they were too heavily outnumbered. As the battle carried on, the battalion Syrela and Akior had led began to be surrounded from the north.

* * *

Well over an hour had passed since the battle's beginning. It seemed never-ending. Valirian glanced around. His soldiers had held on to the best of their abilities, but they were exhausted. The position was unlike the advantageous battleground of Mistport or the Fortress. Despite the Illmerians' defences, and though they still held the high ground, the Koreshians were making some dangerous progress. The invaders suffered greater losses than the Illmerians, doubtlessly, but in the darkness, in the chaos of battle, and as the Koreshians continued gaining inches of ground, it certainly appeared otherwise to the invaders. For quite many minutes, the Illmerians had kept the battle a stalemate, in no small part due to Syrela's prowess, yet there was no time to waste. The Koreshian troops to the north slowly surrounded them, cutting off their retreat. If this battle was lost, the war would be over and Koresh would triumph. In the east, far on the horizon, the first rays of the sun. He would never accept defeat. Never would Alexar get the triumph he wished for. Never would Valirian allow for those who lost their lives in Kashpur to be unavenged. He looked north, to the forested hills, and blew his horn twice. All hope was not lost.

* * *

A horn echoed, far in the distance. The battle had begun. Cadmael toyed with a small rock beneath his horse, moving it around with his spear. Every now and then, he would glance to the beach, downhill. There was little he could see, yet he glanced again and again, gripping his spear tightly each time. The wait was insufferable. He let out a sigh and glanced at his men. The Mistian cavalry had formed a brotherhood, a remarkable kinship marked by discipline—or so, at least, he liked to describe it. Each of them stayed immobile, as unmoving as the forest around them. Unnaturally silent, the trees rarely moved, even in the slight breeze. They were hidden from the Koreshians' sight. Such was the plan.

"As I twice sound the war horn, only then will you charge," Valirian had told him.

That he had sworn to follow those orders made it no less painful. The echoes of battle made his heart palpitate. If only he could see for himself the battle unfolding! He turned around, again. In spite of the darkness, he briefly inspected his men. He took great pride in their perfect ranks, their identical uniforms, the strict training they went through every morning. He saw it a great honour, bestowed by the Queen herself, to lead those men, each a veteran of previous campaigns.

Cadmael made his horse trot forwards, grinding his teeth as he once more attempted to catch the slightest of glimpses of the battlefield, in vain. The only signs of battle were the echoes and the weak lights of the torches in the distance. Lost in thought, worried for his brothers in arms, he almost came to forget what he awaited. The sound of the war horn startled him. The adrenaline rush was intoxicating. He gripped his lance tightly, hoping to hear it ring once more. The war horn echoed once again.

He smiled and turned to face his men. "Brothers! The time for battle has come. Victory is calling. Justice demands it be brought upon those invaders. Illmeria begs for our help! Deliver the rage of every spirit, until none stands against Illmeria, our home!"

In a thunder of hooves and armours rattling, soon drowned in war cries, the trot of the cavalry turned into a gallop. The battlefield drew nearer, the first rays of dawn shining on their armours. "Victory comes from the Mists!" shouted the cavalrymen. With their lances couched, only seconds separated them from the enemy. Their weapons shattered and they trampled the Koreshians, who expected not the sudden assault.

The first charge left the invaders disorganised, the perfect occasion for Syrela. The War Hero led her men in a breakthrough, isolating yet another group of Koreshians while the cavalry, having drawn their swords, charged at the enemy archers.

"Victory is ours!" shouted Aaposhi.

The exhaustion and discouragement that, minutes ago, had filled the Illmerians' hearts had vanished, replaced with renewed bravery. The numerical advantage of the invaders mattered no longer to the Illmerians—and neither to the Koreshians, who retreated in a panicked hurry to their warships, hoping to escape the slaughter. A first warship set sail, followed by another, until six had left the shores. The others, however, were boarded, as the last of the Koreshians on the beach were dealt with.

"Those are easily three or four thousand men that escaped us," Valirian said.

To his right, Aaposhi squinted. They had not yet gone very far. "Should we give chase, My General?"

The option was tempting, but after long seconds of silence, Valirian shook his head. "It is too dangerous. Our men are quite inexperienced in naval warfare, and they are still exhausted from all the fighting." He shrugged and let out a sigh, his eyes unmoving from the warships that sailed further and further away. He stuck his sword in the sand, resting his hand on the pommel.

"Are these all the warships that escaped?" Xelya asked.

Her voice nearly startled him, and he answered with a nod.

Slowly, she stepped into the sea, until the water reached her knees. The warships were still within arrow's reach. She took a deep breath and closed her eyes. To her side, she felt Valirian's presence, wise in knowing what she would soon attempt. Whispers escaped her mouth, an orb of magic forming between her palms. With a shout, she hurled it at the nearest warship. The orb rippled on the water's surface and, as if carried by the waves, rolled to the ship's hull. The impact created a burst of flames and splinters. The large hole left behind allowed water to pour in. Soon, the ship began sinking. Her sight was blurry, and she felt weak, but supporting herself on Valirian, she overcame it, in spite of a few hesitant steps back to the beach.

"This victory is one to be remembered for centuries," she said. "A reminder that Illmeria cannot be broken, that we shall never bend to invaders."

Under cheers, songs, and laughter, they both observed the aftermath. Finally, it was over. Syrela had disappeared without a word—certainly, she had returned to the camp—yet Valirian couldn't help but feel disappointed; he wished to see her and celebrate their accomplishments together. Still, in the end, he felt relieved, and he walked to the Lady's tent with great happiness. They could rest easy, for now. The hardest battles were behind them. As Xelya poured them both some tea, he removed his helmet and rested his head against the back of his seat.

"Let us rest after this drink, shall we?" she proposed.

He mustered the strength to answer with a slow nod, then brought the cup to his lips. Neither said much. The silence and peace, one another's company, a few gentle caresses, and a parting kiss before he left her tent. That was all they wished for.

CHAPTER 36
GAPING WOUNDS

The three hours of rest passed all too rapidly. Valirian stretched his sore muscles, struggling to open his dry eyes as Cadmael entered his tent. The young man seemed hesitant but dared to step closer as his general grabbed a coat and drank from his waterskin. "What is the situation, Captain?" he asked.

"This battle is a resounding victory," said Cadmael. "We did suffer losses—nearly three thousand of our men gave their lives for Illmeria—but the enemy lost some twenty-five thousand soldiers. We also captured five warships, and eight were too severely damaged by the fighting."

Valirian nodded at the numbers and sighed. "That is nevertheless three thousand Illmerians that will not return home." He stood up and headed to his mirror. There were a few scratches on his skin and a superficial cut on his right cheek, but nothing troubling.

"My general," said the captain, "every Illmerian made this sacrifice willingly. If we had not, we would have no home to return to, even if we saved ourselves."

Perhaps he was right. Perhaps he had been too negative. Yet it did little to appease Valirian. Those were four victories against all odds. How much longer until they made a mistake? Would there be a second chance? And a thought forever returned to his mind, making him clench his fist. "What of the Koreshian generals? Is the fate of any of them known to us with certainty?"

The young captain shook his head in response, making Valirian frown. He clenched his jaw.

"We haven't found the body of a high-ranking Koreshian officer," said Cadmael. "They either escaped or sunk with the warship destroyed by the Queen."

Though Valirian nodded, neither possibility satisfied him. If Alexar was to die, he wished to be certain of his fate. He wished to see the Koreshian's final breath. Nothing else would satisfy him. "Thank you," he still said.

The young captain bowed. Knowing it unwise to stay much longer, he soon disappeared.

Valirian barely had time to get himself into proper clothing before rapid footsteps approached his tent. He let out a sigh and shook his head. "What is it this time?" The footsteps stopped, and an instant of silence passed, making him frown. Had the person turned around and left or simply hesitated to enter? As he took a step forwards, the fabric of his tent was lifted, and Xelya appeared. He bowed. "My apologies," he whispered.

She took his hands and caressed them. "What is tormenting you, dearest?"

He sighed again. "I should have been more mindful, sorry." Before he could move, she had wrapped her arms around him. He reciprocated, pulling her closer and closing his eyes. His breathing slowed, and his muscles relaxed.

Gently, Xelya pushed him onto his bed and sat next to him. "Tell me everything."

His anger had not yet vanished. But why should he hide the source of it from her? "I suppose I should have told you this earlier. I did not lie about my arrival to Illmeria, but I hid some details, in fear that it would change your decision to keep me alive." The suddenness of his admission made Xelya frown, but his weak smile was enough to reassure her. "I was no common slave. Already have I alluded to this, but I was a scribe to no other than Alexar, the Koreshian general who led the invaders' army to Illmeria." He shook his head, his smile vanished, and he bit his lips. Tightly, he gripped the edge of his bed. "The wise Illmerian philosophers have written a great deal about this internal fight against evil we must all wage to stay on the path of righteousness. They speak little of the absolute opposite, of those who relish evil and destruction. There are men devoid of any honour, compassion, or sense of justice, and never in my life have I met anyone more cruel and atrocious than Alexar. And yet again, he has escaped me. I know I am not responsible for the horrors he committed, yet I still feel a duty to bring justice."

She looked down. Many times before had he spoken of the man, and never positively. That he had directly served him explained much. Xelya wrapped her arms around him once again. "You may have come here as his slave, but you have grown to become his most feared enemy. Time for justice will come."

He took a deep breath, and it felt as though a weight had been lifted off his chest. He hoped Alexar had not forgotten who had denied him victory at Mistport. He hoped the Koreshian had grown to hate his former slave as much as Valirian hated him.

"Forgive my curiosity, but if you were a scribe, were you considered above other slaves?" she asked.

"In many ways, though not simply because of my role as a scribe. Koreshian society is extremely hierarchical. Everyone has a superior, and everyone has subordinates. At the top is the Emperor, of course, and at the bottom, the weakest slaves of the iron mines, the Kennels. I was the most powerful slave under Alexar. The luckiest of the damned."

"Why was such a position given to you?" she asked. "Surely, you mustn't have served under Alexar for very long. Why did he entrust you with such a position so rapidly?"

"I suppose it was due to my noble origins, unfortunately. Natural, non-magical green eyes are unique to Vinmaran nobility, and even amongst them it is a rare occurrence. Children born with green eyes have royal blood, dating back to the first kings of Vinmara, and are said to have been blessed by fate, or so go the legends. Alexar recognised my noble origins and as such thought me valuable. Now, as to why he entrusted me with those responsibilities, I suppose he wished to corrupt me in some way." He stood up. His hand reached for Xelya's, and he helped her off the bed. "I hope you understand now. I will not let Alexar go unpunished for his crimes. I can tell from experience why the Koreshian troops seem so desensitised. Everyone is afraid of punishment."

She looked outside the tent and allowed herself a smile. The thought of their recent victory eased her mind. There appeared to be no immediate threat, for even the Stormians and their Duke seemed weak and defeated. "Even after such a victory, there is much left for us to do."

"Indeed. I will see Zelshi. I hope he recovers from his wounds rapidly. After that, we should gather the captains and Syrela to discuss our course of action."

"You should be the one to see Syrela, too," she said.

He turned to face her. She, too, had seen it: something was off with Syrela. "I will. You are right."

They parted ways afterwards. In the camp, the soldiers had finished a frugal meal, yet the time was for celebration. The little alcohol still available had been distributed, and the men drank and laughed and sang. Even the stern sergeants had joined the festivities, and none seemed to care about the light rain. The sight made Valirian smile. It had been an exhausting task, but he and Syrela had led those men to victory. He lifted the fabric of a white tent, where wounded soldiers were being cared for.

"My General!" greeted Zelshi. The captain tried standing up from his bed, and two soldiers rushed to keep him still.

"Easy there," said Valirian. "Your wounds are serious."

"I know, My General," he said. "But I'll recover soon. I don't think I'm bleeding any more. The spear hit nothing vital."

Valirian turned to the soldiers with a slight frown.

"He's right," said one of them. "It barely missed the lungs, thank the spirits. Otherwise, we'd be mourning him."

"A relief, then," said Valirian. "Though I suppose I understand now the worry of the Queen and the War Hero regarding my wounds at Mistport."

Zelshi chuckled. He struggled to get up, using only his left arm, the heavy bandages keeping his right arm against his chest. "It's part of being a warrior. Of course, we don't want any of our companions to die. I saw the fear in my men's eyes, and I knew I had to be prepared to sacrifice myself for Illmeria."

Valirian smiled. He helped the captain stand straight, and the two soldiers helped him walk. "You understand better than I the fine difference between bravery and recklessness. Nevertheless, I am thankful the spirits chose to spare you."

The captain chuckled again and shook his head. "You think the great spirit of death would want my company? He's trying to keep me here for as long as he can because he knows the moment I die, he has to deal with me."

Valirian laughed. Together, they slowly headed to the red tent.

"That is certainly a way of seeing things. In the end, you have more than largely contributed to this great victory."

At the sight of their wounded captain, the men cheered and bowed. Many raised their cups.

"As they have, My General," answered Zelshi. "Some are entrusted with lots, others with little. So long as everyone does their part, then there is no reason to feel ashamed."

Valirian observed the scene for some time. Zelshi barely moved, yet many more arrived to celebrate and bow before the captain. It was a heart-warming sight. Many minutes passed before the soldiers thought it appropriate to make way.

"The Queen and I decided to discuss the aftermath with the other captains and Lady Syrela," he said.

"Then go and gather the rest. I'll meet you there," said Zelshi. "I'll take my time, but I'll eventually make it."

* * *

"May I enter?" asked Valirian. No light, nor sound, left the War Hero's tent. After the battle, Syrela had simply vanished. She who would normally join the men in their celebrations, albeit in a more reserved way. Should he turn around? Syrela's absence was easy to justify. If she answered not, perhaps she wished not to be bothered.

"You may," she said. There was something strange in her voice. Her tone was abnormally formal. He lifted the fabric and entered. The tent unlit, Syrela sat in the only chair, immobile aside from her eyes, which glanced at him for a brief second. She stood up and saluted him. She stood straight, towering over him, appearing even taller than usual.

"The Queen and I have gathered the captains to discuss our course of action from here," he said. He knew not whether to demand her presence or offer that she join. At that moment, he noticed her armour. She had not removed it since the battle had ended.

"Understood," she said. She turned around and returned to her seat.

Valirian looked down. How was he to react? A thousand thoughts battled in his mind, each attempted explanation weirder and less likely than the previous. "Lady Syrela," he said. "I want you to know that, without you, we would not have won this battle. I admire your bravery and your wisdom."

She looked down and forced a slight smile as she stood up. "Thank you for your kind words."

CHAPTER 37
"LET US REMEMBER THEM"

The walk to the red tent was silent. The men had finished celebrating; too exhausted, they had gone to rest. Syrela was ahead of Valirian by a few steps. He had hoped for his words to comfort her, only to find her more silent. Had he made a mistake? In spite of his best efforts, he failed to silence those thoughts.

"Just in time," said Xelya.

They both entered the tent, and the captains saluted them. Not without a smile, Cadmael removed his helmet. On the large map of Illmeria at the centre of the table, the Koreshian pieces had been removed. Only a few Stormian pieces remained in the opposing forces, largely outnumbered by the Illmerians.

"Twenty-five thousand less of them," said Zelshi.

"What is the status of our army?" asked Valirian.

"Our footmen have suffered the most," said Akior. "We lost some twenty-six hundred of them. Otherwise, we lost some one hundred cavaliers."

"Barely any losses amongst the archers. Am I correct?" asked Valirian.

"None reported," said Akior.

Valirian found no reason to rejoice. Each and every cavalier lost was significant; they were the most experienced and best-equipped soldiers of the army. "We have a little less than six thousand men, then."

The captains confirmed with a nod. Many of them were hardly more than militiamen, peasants who had taken up arms against the Koreshians. Those would return to their farms or their cities and rebuild what had been destroyed. Yet there was no longer any need to take risks, and a more prolonged campaign against the Duke could be considered. Even with fewer men, victory could be achieved.

"If we are to trust any of our sources, we still outnumber the Stormians quite heavily," he said. "If we do not make the same mistakes as the Koreshians, we may be able to take back most of the land lost."

"There are no threats from within," said Syrela. "We do not need to leave troops behind. The Koreshians have been dealt with, and we can count on at least some reinforcements from the Mistlands. By now, Captain Xilto must have trained a sizeable force back at the Fortress."

"Agreed," said Valirian. "Let us position our troops near Kashpur and wait for reinforcements. Then we shall go on the offensive."

Cadmael glanced at both generals. His eyes met the Queen's. Nervously, he bowed.

Xelya stood up from her chair. Slowly, she approached the table. "It seems Captain Cadmael has an idea. Speak your mind."

"My Queen, My Generals," he said. "If you allow it, I have a suggestion."

Syrela and Valirian glanced at one another. She raised an eyebrow but turned to face the young captain.

"A big portion of the Stormians has been defeated or was captured in Kashpur," he continued. "And in Ksadnivi before that. I think we should press our advantage and retake Naila now, then push into the Stormlands while they are still recovering from our victories."

"Most of our men are exhausted," said Syrela. "As the Advisor said, we should not make the same mistakes as Koresh. The Stormlands cannot fight a long-term war."

"Then allow me to lead the cavalry there," said Cadmael. "We are still enough to fight battles, and none of us are exhausted beyond the need for a day or two of rest."

That the young captain knew no fear made Valirian smile, yet Syrela was doubtlessly the voice of reason. She sighed and glanced at him, hoping to have Valirian temper the young man's enthusiasm. "Captain Cadmael," he said, "with all the respect and gratitude we have for the Mistian cavalry, and by extension you, as their leader, this is quite dangerous. With how important the cavalry is, and how valuable each and every soldier of your division is, we cannot risk you in such battles."

Yet Cadmael turned to the Queen and once more bowed.

Xelya smiled. That the young captain spoke his mind so openly was admirable. He seemed unwilling to insist any further, however. It was unwise of him to disagree with his superiors when both seemed so sure of their decision.

"Advisor," said Xelya. "Would you affirm, beyond any reasonable doubt, that Koresh will not return to Illmeria in the foreseeable future?"

The question made him think. As if to help himself reach a conclusion faster, he observed the map on the table. "My Lady," he answered, "I fear that it is quite impossible to predict. Though I am quite certain that no Koreshian army will land in the following weeks, their return in the following months is possible." He glanced at Syrela, who nodded in confirmation. Unfortunately, Koresh was unpredictable. The Emperor could consider sending another army, just as easily as he could decide against it. And that was without considering that Alexar could gather, or attempt to gather, an army without Tarasmir's permission.

"As such," said Xelya, "it is very possible that in merely a month, Koresh will have returned with an army of a similar size as the one of last night. Am I correct?"

The possibility depended on whether Alexar thought it possible to find a scapegoat. If he thought it possible to recover from his situation politically, then he would not risk another invasion; he doubtlessly risked too much. Otherwise, he might attempt an attack once again. If forced to choose between death in Illmeria or dishonour in Koresh, Alexar would certainly choose the former, though it would not be easy for him to gather an army without imperial support.

"You would be correct," said Valirian. "Koresh lacks not in manpower or equipment." He had guessed what she meant, and she had made him doubt. There was a risk, and not a negligible one.

Xelya turned to face Syrela. The War Hero had not said a word since the Queen had spoken, yet she thoughtfully observed the map. "Lady Syrela, would you define Naila as a heavily defended city? Would it take several weeks, or months, to capture it?"

"No, My Lady," she said. "It is in a valley, and it lacks proper fortifications. This is why my men and I had to abandon it during the first invasion."

Xelya nodded. Her hand on the table, she moved a few of the pieces around. "Therefore, one could expect a properly organised army to capture the city in days, in all likelihood. The Koreshian defeats were doubtlessly caused by overconfidence, yet overconfidence alone does not explain them." She turned to face Valirian once again. "From you, Advisor, I have heard those same words, repeated many times—'the real enemy is Koresh'—even though we had just fought a hard battle against the Northern Alliance. The correctness of your words I will not allow anyone to doubt, yet let us remember them once again, and let us not underestimate the stubbornness of our real enemy.

"We are to defeat the Duke, yet the longer we wait, the more likely we are to be forced into a war on two fronts as Koresh once more returns. If there is some time to be gained, if we are capable of dealing a major blow to the Duke's power, then we are to seize the occasion, for the faster we unite Illmeria, the greater our chances of victory will be against a future invasion. Risks are part of any war, and the real danger is no other than the invaders' return." Xelya turned around and returned to her seat. Her generals and the captains looked at one another, and exchanged a few words.

"I shall lead the army going to Naila," said Syrela. "I, and too many Northians, have been waiting for an occasion to return home, even if only for a few days."

Valirian nodded. How could he refuse? He turned to Cadmael. The young captain struggled to hide a smile, proud to have received the Queen's support. "Captain Cadmael, as you asked before, you will lead the cavalry, as well as a few battalions of Mistian footmen, to the Stormlands. You are to take control of the Blue Ford and establish a bridgehead, cutting them off from Naila and preventing them from reinforcing the city."

They discussed and then agreed on the exact distribution of the remaining troops and decided that Akior would follow Syrela, Zelshi would stay in Kashpur, and Aaposhi would follow Valirian and Xelya back to the Mistlands.

"I shall then return to Kashpur with reinforcements, join Cadmael's positions, and lead a campaign in the Stormlands," said Valirian. "Capturing Asharsaï within a month and a half should be possible."

CHAPTER 38
A GUESSING GAME, A MATTER OF TIME

The news of the Koreshian defeat and the reconquest of Kashpur had rapidly spread. Already a brave few souls had returned to the city's ruins from the Grasslands where they had taken refuge. Those hundred Illmerians would doubtlessly be followed by more, an encouraging sight to the soldiers and militiamen who had returned to the city. In the following days, most of the rubble had been cleared as all took part in the reconstruction.

However, Syrela had been strangely absent, spending most of her days and nights in her room, locked and alone, surrounded by nothing but books. Whether she even ate worried Xelya and Valirian. They were only reassured as they once heard her late at night in the palace's kitchens.

"It is most unusual of her," said Xelya.

How could he disagree? He had spent most of his time with his love, in the beautiful gardens of Kashpur—the green leaves had turned to ambers and reds, and the last fruits of summer were ripe—yet he had not spoken a word with Syrela since the day after the battle. "Something is clearly troubling her," he said.

She caressed his hands and glanced through the window of her room. The sun was setting over the city. "Perhaps all that we must do is simply wait. Let us give her some time. She will always be welcome by our side."

He raised an eyebrow, which made her smile. "You speak as if you knew what bothered her."

"Only vague guesses," she said. "Yet it would be unwise to speculate too much about our friend's well-being."

He shrugged. He knew not whether she spoke the truth or not. He had hoped she would share her thoughts with him, but as to her habit, she preferred a vague answer. He knew it unwise to press the matter, however.

* * *

The fire crackled in the hearth, the light of its red flames dancing on the book in Syrela's hands. For many hours she had held this book, yet no progress had been made. She counted the pages she had already read—too few, maybe a quarter of the work.

She sighed and, without much enthusiasm, closed the book and threw it on her bed. Admittedly, this *Account of the Wars between Vinmara and Koresh* was hardly an enthralling read, even to her. Yet she had trained her mind to focus on whichever task was expected of her, regardless of her own desires. How come she struggled now with something so trivial? She knew why. She glanced at her door. She had not left her room since last night. She headed to her window and repressed a shiver. How was it so cold in this end of summer? The ninth month had barely begun. No, the air was warm. Everything felt cold, rather.

She glanced at the grey city beneath. It was far from a beautiful sight, yet she had come to terms with what had happened here. The guilty had been punished. For now, Illmeria would be safe, and she feared not the invaders' return; she had seen the Illmerians' ability to unite before such a threat. In fact, all Illmerians, barring the Stormians, had come to accept Xelya's rule, making her realise a truth she had once refused to accept: to the people, it mattered not who ruled, so long as they were protected, so long as the ruler brought peace and prosperity. Mistian or Heartian, the Queen of Mists or the Duchess of the Pearl—that mattered not to them.

The smell of roasted meat dragged her out of her reflection; only then did she realise her hunger. She would resist. She would wait until all were asleep. Her heart ached. She remembered the day she found Valirian and Xelya together. To the loss of Naila and the loss of Kashpur, to the destruction the war had brought, was now added that.

Syrela sighed and rubbed her forehead. How long would she have to avoid him until what she felt for him disappeared?

* * *

The palace had turned perfectly silent. The wooden floor creaked. The normally quiet sound felt almost deafening to Xelya, yet it awoke no one. She continued her walk through the dark corridors of the palace, needing neither lamp nor candle, for her magical eyes and the blue light of the moon proved more than enough. She arrived in the kitchen. Just as she had hoped, noise: someone was in there. Xelya pushed open the door and promptly closed it behind her, startling Syrela.

"My Lady," stuttered the War Hero.

"Oh, Lady Syrela," answered Xelya. "I am glad to see you here."

Syrela had made herself a meal—a simple one, with cold cuts of meat, some rice, and a few grilled vegetables—and had intended to leave, but, hesitant, she instead sat at the table.

"I found myself restless and wished to make some tea," said Xelya.

"It's understandable," said Syrela. "I imagine this is far from the first time you have found yourself unable to sleep. Ruling must leave your mind with countless unsolved problems."

Xelya laughed and offered her a cup, which the War Hero gratefully accepted. "Valirian has this wonderful capacity to bring peace to his mind and can seemingly sleep regardless of the situation. I must say I envy that of him."

Syrela chuckled and picked up the cup of tea. For a few moments, she stared at the reflection of her two green eyes, deep in her thoughts.

"There was quite no right time to speak of that matter before," said Xelya, "but I suppose you have by now understood the new nature of my and Valirian's relationship."

Slowly, Syrela nodded. "It was quite unexpected, and I feared to be intruding, but I guessed so on the first morning."

"I thought so," said Xelya. "I had not intended to keep it secret anyway."

"Will he be your consort once peace has returned to Illmeria?"

The question made Xelya think; she kept her silence for many long seconds. "I am not quite certain that all the old traditions must be kept as they were." Her response made the War Hero look down, hiding a wince. Briefly, Xelya frowned.

"I wish you both happiness," said Syrela.

Xelya had a slight smile as she finished her tea. Then she leaned forwards. "I make you this promise, my friend: I will do all I can to rebuild Naila into a prosperous city, no matter what." Her words made the War Hero smile, and for a second she seemed to relax—but her sombre expression soon returned. "I understand that you miss your homeland," continued Xelya. "If you find it necessary, stay in Naila for some time. I dare hope that no battle is to be fought in the near future. The time to rebuild what has been destroyed has come. If your presence is needed at my council, you shall be informed."

"Thank you, My Lady," said Syrela. "This means a lot." With her meal finished, she stood up and bowed, then headed to the door.

"I wish you a pleasant night, Lady Syrela," said Xelya.

"Likewise, My Lady."

Silence, again. Xelya sighed, glancing at the closed door behind her. Her suspicions might have proven more correct than she wished.

* * *

The low sound of hooves on the pavement, a few whispers. Those were all that disturbed the silence. At the sight of their generals and their Queen, the men's discussions ceased, and each of the captains bowed. As he inspected them, Valirian could not hold back a smile. Contrary to his previous fears, the events of the past days had kept them well-organised. Each and every man was expected to tend to his armour and weapons, and beyond the few blades or plates of armour that had suffered significant damage from the battles, none had failed in their duties. Their numbers had dwindled, and for a second, that darkened Valirian's expression, but he ignored the thought the best he could. After all, more than their losses, hundreds of men had returned home to rebuild the villages and towns of the Grasslands and Heartlands.

"May the spirits of Illmeria guide your blade, Lady Syrela," he said. "May your victory be swift as you free your home from the accursed betrayers."

She nodded, though with a slight frown.

His lips forced a smile. "I wish for your home to have escaped the fate of Kashpur," he said, lower so only she could hear.

She looked down, trying to hide a sigh he very well heard. "Thank you," she said, her voice just as low. Wasting no more time, she called to her the men that were to fight by her side. Soon, her army was marching northwards.

Cadmael passed Valirian, and the two exchanged nods. The young captain trotted out of the ranks to approach his general.

"Remember," said Valirian. "Let neither early successes nor possible setbacks obscure your judgement. Excess of zeal alone can be your downfall. I also wish for you to remember this: those you will fight may be enemies, but they are above all fellow Illmerians. Show mercy. The enemy of today may fight by your side tomorrow. Fight to bring peace, not destruction. The Queen wishes to rule this land, not ashes and ruins."

The young man stood still for many long seconds, no doubt reflecting on the advice. After a moment, he bowed and rejoined his men.

Valirian glanced at Xelya, surprised to see her smile.

"Were you to order him to charge off a cliff," she said, "I have no doubt he would listen to you without thinking twice."

He held back a chuckle. "He is a smart and promising young man. He would know better."

"I doubt not his intelligence, but his loyalty to you is quite unparalleled."

Finding it hard to disagree, he smiled. The last of Syrela's army had disappeared behind the tall ruins of Kashpur, and so he turned to face the men still on his right. Many of them were wounded, though rarely too gravely. Others were Mistian peasants who had taken up arms in the past weeks yet wished to continue the fight. Quite a few had not suffered any significant wounds but had their weapons or armour too damaged to continue fighting. In a few weeks at most, they would certainly be able to return to battle.

"It feels as if an eternity has passed since the Tower last appeared before my eyes," said Xelya.

He glanced southwards, then turned to Aaposhi. "Are our men ready?"

"Yes, My General."

"Let us depart, then."

CHAPTER 39
COLDNESS AND OLD RUINS

The green, steep hills of the Northlands. Syrela dropped from her horse. Everything seemed identical to when she had last seen her home. The tall trees hardly bothered by the gentle breeze, the shallow rivers and streams which reflected the green leaves above, the light grey stone often covered in moss—all as if frozen in time.

Only three days had passed since they left Kashpur, and already Naila was hardly more than an hour or two away. Having expected to reach the city in at least four, Syrela was quite surprised. Perhaps her men had regained courage at the thought of returning home. Although she did not expect the Stormians to be caught by surprise—her army was too large to go unnoticed, and they had doubtlessly heard of the reconquest of Kashpur—she had dared hope that her speed could deny them the time to properly prepare.

"Captain Akior, what are the scouts' reports?" she asked.

"It seems that the Stormians have abandoned the western hills to strengthen their position in the east," he said.

She glanced around, observing the forest. An ambush was unlikely, but she could never let her guard down. She had approached the city from the east, meaning her men were closer to the Stormians than imagined. Perhaps that was to be adjusted. She took a few steps forwards, giving her a better view of the area surrounding Naila. A small valley and its river, a few fields—that was all that separated her forces' camp from the city.

"That would be an indication they lack in numbers," she said. "Otherwise, they would know not to give up the western hills. Their control over the city would be greatly diminished if they gave us such a position." Had she been in their situation, she would have concluded that her best chance of success was to take a fight at this exact river crossing, then retreat to the western hills, contesting each and every inch of ground if need be. Yet there was no Stormian soldier in sight. Perhaps their intention had been to retreat eastwards all along, in hopes of fleeing to the Stormlands.

"Are your orders to send our forces to the western hills and capture the position, My General?" asked the captain. He seemed ready to turn around in an instant and call the soldiers into formation, yet for many long seconds, she stood immobile, rubbing her chin, until she shook her head.

"If they are as few as they seem to be, then a frontal assault on their position would be faster and be less risky for those inside the city," she said. "If they are numerous, their position is still hardly favourable, and we'll have more than enough time to adapt." She turned to face the captain and nodded. "Gather our forces and prepare them for battle."

Akior bowed and had soon turned around. His voice echoed mere instants after, and the silence in the camp was replaced by the sergeants' orders and a familiar tumult.

She watched them hurry into formation with a slight smile, and a short hour after, they had forded the river at a shallow point not too far. Still no enemy in sight. Yet even if they were to attempt an escape to the Stormlands, their retreat would be cut off by Cadmael and his men. Perhaps that was the reason for their lack of organisation: the Stormians had realised the young captain's presence all too late. Whatever the answer, it mattered not to Syrela. Less than a hundred steps separated her from the first temple in sight, which had visibly been fortified to the best of the defenders' abilities, barricaded with crates, carts, and large rocks.

"Sound the charge," she said.

Akior blew the large horn he carried, echoing on the plateau. A handful of Stormian spearmen were positioned at the front, the rest certainly hidden behind the short walls. A few arrows were fired, hardly enough to deter the War Hero and her army. Syrela's blades unsheathed. Her spear in hand, she took rapid steps, and at her approach, a few of the defenders retreated inside. Those who dared to stand in her way were left lifeless before the temple's broken gates. The positions taken by the Stormians were visibly damaged in previous battles. She charged further in as her men, behind her, climbed the barricade. Before they could join the fray, those twenty men outside the small temple had been dealt with.

"Akior," she called. "Enter the temple from the west wing!"

This first skirmish was soon over. The first of a handful, doubtlessly, but the Stormians posed little resistance. The next temple they had barricaded was hardly a tougher challenge, for the defenders lacked the manpower to hold those positions. Split and outnumbered, they stood no chance. By the afternoon, some hundred Stormians had tried to escape to the east, hoping the forest would give them cover—in vain. They were swiftly flanked and surrounded.

"Lay down your weapons and your lives will be spared!" shouted Syrela. Her demand was met with silence, yet none of them dared move, either. She felt her heart race. She vigorously bit her tongue. The thought of leaving none alive traversed her mind. After all, had they not captured her city and brought her people under their yoke? But for now, she would hold back the order. One of the Stormian sergeants dropped his spear. His men followed his example. Soon, all had surrendered.

She felt a strange fire burning within her. Her temples were beating loudly, and she tightly gripped her spear. Thoughts of what might have happened in Naila clouded her judgement. Something inside demanded justice, almost overwhelming her, but she closed her eyes and took a deep breath. "Round them up, and let not one escape."

She had held back her own desires for vengeance, and her men had followed her orders, but soon, she would herself be in Naila. She would see with her own eyes what had happened. The survivors would share their stories, and may the spirits come to the occupiers' aid if that awoke her anger once more.

She left behind a group of soldiers to guard the prisoners, and the rest of her men followed her to the southern gates. The two columns before the entrance were still standing. They were some sixty feet in height and built in a rare red wood that grew only in the northernmost parts of the Northlands. Painted and decorated richly, they had visibly not suffered any damage. Between them, some twenty steps above ground, there was a rope, support for the Duke's banner: a black and gold eagle on a field of blue. The sight made her chuckle. Soon, it would be cast down, horses and cattle trampling over it. It would be torn to shreds and never again be flown above her city.

"The walls have suffered some damage," said Akior in a low voice.

He was right. The short wall that surrounded the city was hardly more than a pile of rubble, though it was nothing remarkable to begin with: hardly taller than a man and a half on average and barely two men in height at its highest point. Some of the damage was not always the Stormians' fault; the city had not fully recovered from the

Koreshians' first invasion, and quite a few of the ruined buildings had simply not been rebuilt since.

"I think we will soon have all the answers we need," said Syrela.

Further inside the city, a small crowd had gathered. The echoes of battle had certainly reached them, and the bravest dared to see what was happening with their own eyes. Even from the distance separating them, she could see more and more people gathering. She could hear a murmur. As she and her men passed the gates, the loud voice of one of the elders told the crowd to make way for the Blade of Illmeria and her army. The city had seen better days, and the war had visibly resulted in food shortages, but a disaster had narrowly been avoided. The citizens cheered, throwing flowers at their passage. Young boys were in awe before the Mistian soldiers' uniforms, and adults were both surprised and curious at such a sight never before seen, their imposing armour and long pikes leaving them whispering about their origins.

"Your people celebrate your return, o Blade of Illmeria," said one of the elders. "The land that is yours rejoices, and the spirits are honoured by your presence."

Syrela removed her helmet and looked around for a quick moment. A smile was her first answer, and having dropped from her horse, she bowed before the elder. "I am likewise honoured by your words, o Elder Fahj. The joy I feel in returning to the city that saw my birth is incomparable."

Beneath the wrinkles on the short man's face, a smile appeared, and he bowed, the other elders following his example. He wrapped his arms around her, and she reciprocated. In spite of his age, much strength was left in his body. "We mourned the news of your capture, my child, and had thought you would never return." Behind, Akior dropped from his horse. Fahj glanced at him and raised an eyebrow. "Who are those warriors fighting so loyally at your side?"

The captain bowed before the elder, and Syrela gave him a nod.

"They are soldiers as loyal to Illmeria as I," she said. "May we head to the hall? There is a lot we need to talk about."

The old man wasted no time. He turned around and the other elders all followed him. Behind, the crowd dispersed, and only a few Mistian soldiers followed Fahj and the War Hero to the base of the largest hill in Naila.

"You may not follow us up the hill," said Syrela. "Only the Blade of Illmeria is allowed to carry weapons to the city hall."

Akior glanced at the stairs behind her. Of a polished white stone, they seemed to go on forever, and he struggled to hold back a smile. "As you wish, My General. I can't lie, I'm relieved that I don't have to climb those."

The remark made Fahj smirk, and the old man led the group up the hill, Syrela at his side. It was sunset when they reached the top. They entered the council hall, a large building entirely made of white and red wood and hardly decorated beyond a few tapestries depicting the myth of Naila's foundation, centuries before, by the first Blade of Illmeria. Servants brought them some tea as they took seats around the large table of red wood at the centre of the room.

"Forgive my prolonged absence," said Syrela. "I know that my duties are, above all, towards Naila, that protecting my city is my first mission before any other, and I failed to be present in times of need."

One of the elders, an old woman, stood up. Her hand on her heart, she bowed with a smile. "You need not apologise, my child. None would dare question your honour, nor your loyalty. War is unexpected and terrible."

Syrela looked down, forcing a smile. Silently, she let out a sigh. "How was Naila treated under the Duke's rule?"

A few elders whispered, but none answered, until Fahj, to her right, stood up from his seat. "We were forced to pay tribute to the

Duke, which included a significant part of our harvest. Food supplies are low, and heavy restrictions have been imposed for a month now, but with your return, there is hope for a solution. Otherwise, most of the combat happened outside the city. Their occupation was strict but rather peaceful. We, the elders, were stripped of practically all of our powers, but I think it was clear that neither side wished to continue fighting after the battle."

It was what she had deduced, but the confirmation lifted a weight off her heart. "It is good, then, that Naila avoided the fate of Kashpur. I suppose you have all heard what happened there, have you not?"

Lips pursed, Fahj looked down as he nodded. The other elders bowed their heads. Most, if not all, had seen the Pearl of Illmeria with their own eyes, for they had taken refuge there during the first invasion, and many in Naila knew someone who lived there.

"We mourned the fall of Kashpur for a week as we learnt the news," he said. "The Stormians did not prevent us. I doubt any of them approved of what happened anyway. We can only be thankful that justice was served and the guilty were punished."

For many long seconds, they all bowed their heads, until a frail old lady stood up. "What about the Duchess?"

By Syrela's silence, all knew the answer. "May she find peace amongst her ancestors."

In unison, the elders repeated her words. What might have gone through Adiloka's mind in those last days, as she saw her inevitable defeat approach all too rapidly, Syrela could never comprehend; and what cruelty she would have faced in her final moments, Syrela had never dared imagine. Alone, in a hopeless fight, her husbands dying one after the other. The thought made her shiver.

"Who, then, will unite and lead Illmeria?" asked one of the elders.

"Lady Syrela," asked Fahj, "are the rumours about your allegiance to the Queen of Mists true?"

"They are, o noble elder," she said, "and those men that fought by my side are Mistians. Now she, alone, may unite us against our enemies."

"In your own words, you were mistrustful of her," said Fahj.

She chuckled. It felt so long ago now. "It is true. But she has proven my judgement of her to be wrong and earned my trust. It is her army that was triumphant against Koresh, four times already. Without her, Kashpur would still be in the hands of Koresh."

To her surprise, Fahj nodded, a gentle smile on his lips, and he sat down. "Then we shall follow the Queen of Mists."

For a moment, her thoughts wandered. She repressed a sigh. She yearned for some solitude and tranquillity. "What has become of the Temple of Iron?"

Fahj took some time to answer. He clearly wished to be careful with his wording. "The temple was quite contested by the Stormians and defended to the bitter end by the Duchess's troops. It has been abandoned since, but the main building is still standing."

* * *

Syrela had wasted no time. The elders had agreed to end the discussions, for all that was important had been said. Now, in front of her eyes, stood the ruins of the Temple of Iron. Reality proved less saddening than the description given by Fahj, for in spite of the damage, the temple seemed rather intact. Some of the smaller buildings had their roofs damaged, and the walls had partially collapsed, certainly from the Stormians' assault—little in comparison to the ruin that had greeted her after the first Koreshian invasion. Yet even then she had not given up: this temple had been the house of her ancestors, and for countless generations, the Blades of Illmeria had resided there. Amusingly, of the two banners usually flown before the gates, only one had been torn, as if on accident. The other, though slightly damaged, still displayed quite clearly her family's coat of arms.

She stepped inside and let out a sigh at the sight. The garden had been abandoned for months. Quite a few of the green roof tiles had fallen off into the courtyard, scattered amongst the wildflowers and herbs, and grey moss had grown from the fissures in the walls. Even though the damage suffered was indeed hardly comparable to the destruction left in the wake of the Koreshians' passage, this time, her return felt different. Everything was lifeless, abandoned. Vast holes in the walls of some of the buildings let the damp air circulate, a result of some fire. As she approached the large double door of the main building, she felt something hard beneath her boot: an arrow tip, one of many, as a few broken spears were also scattered around. To her relief, there had been no bodies left behind, neither outside nor inside, yet some of the furniture on the lower floor had been damaged. A broken chair, a table with a large dent, or a torn curtain. The battle had been remarkably fierce, for each inch of ground had been defended, it seemed, though the defenders were too few to hold. The upper floor was left relatively untouched, and though she had to climb over another broken chair to enter what had once been her bedroom, she found it just as she had left it, beyond the layer of dust on the furniture.

Syrela reached for the leather pouch on the desk and brushed it with the palm of her hand. Slowly, she untied the knot that kept it closed and pulled out the book it contained. She let out a deep sigh, finding some relief: once again, her work had survived. It was her duty, as the Blade of Illmeria, to continue her line's legacy, and she had dreaded having to rewrite everything she had noted so far. That it had escaped the Stormians' attack surprised her relatively little—destruction was clearly not their goal, after all—yet how it had survived the fire provoked by the Koreshians the year before still eluded her. She had found it, perfectly intact, in the cellar of the temple, in this leather pouch. Someone must have protected it, but who? It could not have possibly been a Koreshian soldier. How she wished to know the answer, to thank the one who, in such horrible times, had valued something seemingly so mundane yet so important to her.

She forced a smile as she placed the book back into its pouch and the pouch back onto the desk. She removed her helmet, instinctively finding the mannequin in the corner, then her armour, for the first time in days, and collapsed onto her bed. Massaging her temples, she winced as she touched one of the sore bruises next to her left eye. For a moment, she chose to forget everything. After all, had she not given all the necessary orders to Akior?

Her eyes closed, and she stayed there, immobile. She was away from everything and everyone, yet this strange coldness in her heart seemed to not leave her. She felt a tear on her cheek. She did not bother to wipe it.

CHAPTER 40
WHAT PRIDE BRINGS

A storm gathered in the distance, its powerful rumble echoing from the dark clouds into the valley. Such occurrences were far from rare in the Stormlands, yet this spectacle impressed Cadmael. Never had he witnessed such a storm so clearly, as they were relatively rare in the Mistlands. A flash nearly startled him, yet his eyes widened. A second one soon followed, and for the first time, he witnessed a lightning arc with his own eyes.

"We're in position, Captain," said a sergeant in a low voice.

Cadmael answered with a nod. Regardless of the sight's beauty, he had to focus on his duties. He glanced at the narrow gorge below, and all seemed calm. Above, he and his troops had taken positions, waiting patiently for a small convoy of Stormians that a scout had located and would doubtlessly pass through the gorge. Such ambushes had been Cadmael's preferred tactic over the past week, part of a plan to weaken the enemy before any significant battle, in accordance with the lessons Syrela had taught him: avoiding a direct confrontation and using superior mobility. In that regard, he was fortunate, for he never had to chase after the Stormians. They were forced to use those strategic gorges and roads to supply their troops in Naila or those positioned in various outposts alongside the strait separating the Northlands and the Stormlands.

"Here!" whispered a scout.

Cadmael raised his hand, a sign he had understood. None of his men dared move even an inch. Some hundred soldiers, protecting a caravan. Their leader, on horseback, appeared first from behind the rocks. They entered the gorge not without some fear, certainly, but it was too late. Arrows flew, the leader was killed, and the Mistian soldiers descended upon their prey. A few minutes of bloody combat, and the skirmish was over. In an instant, the Stormians had been dealt with.

"Alright, boys, you know the drill," said Cadmael. "Take what you can. Burn the rest. Let's not waste any time." Leaving behind a column of smoke, he led his men back to a camp an hour away from the gorge. To a large army, one using more traditional tactics, the Stormlands were certainly difficult to conquer. There were too many narrow and dangerous ravines and paths and hardly any flat plains on which roads could be built. Having turned that to his advantage made Cadmael smile with pride. Each passing day meant his troops were more familiar with the region.

"Second Battalion, reporting a resounding success, too, My Captain," said a sergeant. In the following hour, the various divisions scattered in the region regrouped, all reporting similar successes.

"Yet," said Cadmael, "this is probably the last day we meet no resistance. They'll answer sooner or later. We have to stay careful."

"Do we stop operations, then?" asked one of the sergeants.

"We've dealt quite a good blow to their war effort," said another. "We could retreat and finish taking control of the outposts to the west."

For long minutes, the sergeants discussed, but Cadmael could not bring himself to make a decision yet. "Night will bring counsel," he said. In truth, he hoped for an occasion, a mistake the enemy would make, to strike a severe blow.

Early in the morning, the scouts reported activity on the nearby plateau, where passed the road leading to Aremaï. The Stormians were visibly fortifying the position and would not be done before a few days at least. Was it the occasion he had dreamt of, or had he convinced himself he needed to attack? He repeated Valirian's advice to himself, whispering those words as if they alone would bring him the right answer. Aremaï was the second largest city in the Stormlands. That assault would draw them dangerously near it—but also give them a particularly advantageous position.

"What are your orders, Captain?"

Cadmael clenched his fist and bit his tongue. His mind felt blurry, unable to focus. What was he supposed to do? "Lead me to the location. I need to see it. Then I'll make a decision."

The three scouts guided their captain between the sharp rocks and dry bushes of a hidden mountain path, and a short hour after, they had reached a position above the Stormians. Below, some three hundred men camped. Palisades were being erected, trenches dug. It was a large area they had to cover, and it would take them some time. The answer dawned on him. Should the Stormians fortify the location, taking it from them would prove costly, even for a large army. It was now or never. With only a nod to the scouts, he turned around and rushed back to the camp.

"Gather the men," he said. "We'll attack and take that position from them."

The sergeants wasted no time. Soon, the Mistian army was on the march. Unfortunately, the Stormian position, up the hill, protected them from a cavalry charge; still, it was worth the risk. The sun had reached its zenith when the large slope leading up the plateau was in sight, and though the Stormians sounded the alarm, they struggled to keep order in their ranks. They were outnumbered five to one at least; they had certainly underestimated the size of the Mistian army. Cadmael led his men up the hill, yet only a few men, disorganised and retreating, were left on the plateau. The others had fled. From the elevated position, one could see Aremaï, hardly more than an hour away. It was where the two hundred Stormians would seek refuge, for the city was well-fortified, with tall walls and a moat filled with seawater. For a moment, he considered pursuing them, yet it would draw him all too close to Aremaï, and success was hardly guaranteed. No, he had another idea on his mind. "Half of you, return to our camp. Then return here with everything and everyone. We will lay siege to the city."

* * *

The rest of the day had Cadmael staring at the city's gates. The thought of seeing them opening, when he was at his weakest, kept him on edge. Even if some eight hundred men were still by his side, he had sent the same number back to their previous camp. They had set up defences, using whatever the Stormians had left behind in their panicked retreat, in case a counter-attack was to be launched from the city, yet he was thankful that such had not been the case. It was at dawn, the next day, that he truly realised the size of the walls, however. Having led some six hundred footmen down the plateau, Cadmael found himself some hundred steps away from the fortifications, yet their shadow already covered his group. He had imagined his army capable of simply surrounding the city and depleting it of its supplies or possibly storming its walls and gates with ladders and battering rams—a foolish thought, he now realised. Stretched, his entire army could barely surround the city, and the walls were comparable to those of Mistport, as Valirian had warned, though perhaps not as thick. He considered retreating and cursed himself for his recklessness. The general would have shown much more carefulness in such a situation. His hope was for the Stormians to make a mistake. Perhaps they would try to attack his group, in which case his cavalry would charge down the hill and deal with the defenders. Otherwise, reinforcements from the west would eventually arrive; Naila had certainly been retaken by now, and in time, even Valirian would arrive with a sizeable army.

"Citizens of Aremaï!" he said. "In the name of Lady Xelya, the Queen of Mists, I demand your immediate surrender. Your lives will be spared and your homes left intact if you open the gates and lay down your weapons!"

His voice echoed. His words had doubtlessly been heard by the defenders, yet all that followed was silence. Not even for an instant did he think the Stormians would comply, but it made him appear in a position of force—hardly the truth. The handful of archers he saw positioned on the walls seemed deaf to his request, immobile as though he did not even exist, simply content in knowing that no attack had been ordered. Cadmael turned around, prepared for a long wait of days, weeks even, until reinforcements arrived to his position.

The gates opened. Eleven men, all clad in heavy armour, stepped outside the city. The man leading them, at the front and centre of the small group, was strong and tall, taller than any of his followers or any of the Mistians. He held his helmet against his side, revealing a visage marked by harsh traits, rough skin, and deep wrinkles. Though none were too severe, the man had a few scars, the largest of which was on his left cheek, just above his trimmed grey beard. Yet as he got closer, what struck Cadmael was the deep blue glow of his eyes, all too familiar to him. Rare, too, were the Illmerians with an eye colour different than the browns, dark oranges, or hazels, leaving no doubt in his mind.

Only a few steps separated them now. For a moment, Cadmael

doubted the man would stop, but he did, and the warrior studied him for a brief instant before looking far behind, as if he expected to see something, or someone, behind Cadmael. Letting out a humph, he frowned. His attention returned to the young captain, though neither said a thing for a long minute.

"As a matter of honour, I refuse to surrender," he eventually said. "Do not dare ask again, young one."

The strange, unnatural echo in the warrior's voice almost startled Cadmael. He fought to keep his mind focused and control his fears; he bit his tongue and raised his head. The warrior was a Stormcaller. He recalled a talk with Syrela about her supposed fight with one such warrior at Kashpur, and she had mocked his doubtfulness. Perhaps he had been the fool all along—or perhaps it had been some form of jealousy.

"Where is your War Hero, young one?" asked the tall warrior. "Where is the Blade of Illmeria, the Saviour of Kashpur?" The Stormcaller had waited without a word until then, but the frown on his visage turned more severe. Visibly, his patience was running out.

Cadmael's lips pursed. His chest filled up as he took a few steps forwards. Who was this warrior who dismissed him so quickly? To that Stormcaller, he barely seemed to exist, as if he were an inconvenience in his way to fight Syrela. "General Syrela and her men are retaking Naila from your forces. I am the commander of this army. It is only a matter of time before your Duke is defeated. Why risk your life and those of your men for a lost cause?" His response made the warrior chuckle deeply, making Cadmael grip the shaft of his spear tightly.

"Young one, I care not about who leads this army, nor do I care about the Duke," he said. "I am Kshashil, of the Zulshi tribe, and leader of the Onoraï clan. I am undefeated and invincible, and I demand for your War Hero to come so we may fight. Should she defeat me, then my clan will respect her and bow to her, else your armies will leave our lands. I care not about this war between your Queen and the Duke, however." Having expressed his demand, the warrior turned around.

Who was this warrior, so obsessed with Syrela? Cadmael sighed. He remembered Valirian's words, but no matter: he could not extinguish this fire within his heart. "I am Cadmael, captain of Illmeria and hero of Mistport. Many times have I fought and defeated Koresh, and never have I been defeated, either. In fact, I am also the one who captured the Blade of Illmeria herself at Fort Seaguard and brought her in chains before the Queen of Mists. As such, I demand to have a duel against you, Kshashil, as you wished to have one against the War Hero."

The man stopped in his tracks and turned around. Wide-eyed and silent, he observed Cadmael. A slight smile on his lips, he chuckled again. "So the rumours were true. And you would be the one to have defeated the Blade of Illmeria? You're barely old enough to grow a beard. But if you are so eager for a fight, so be it." He unsheathed his sword and, with it, pointed at a field not too far away. With a nod, the warriors following him headed there. "Tradition would normally dictate that ten of your warriors would fight against ten of mine, while we fight one another, until none are left alive. I understand you are a foreigner; therefore, I will be content with a mere duel. I promise your men will be spared."

"Likewise," said Cadmael. "I will forbid my men to lay a finger on you or your clansmen. You have my word."

The old warrior chuckled but bowed his head. "I appreciate your sense of honour, young one."

Silently, the soldiers followed Cadmael and Kshashil to the field. The young captain sent one of his men back to the camp to inform the sergeants there of the situation.

"Your clan, rather than the Duke, is what you fight for, is it not?" asked Cadmael.

With the hint of a smile, Kshashil nodded. "Is it not what all warriors fight for? Dukes, queens, emperors, they are all meaningless titles when compared to kinship, to the ties formed by the blood of birth or the blood of oath, that each and every man shares with his family, tribe, and clan."

Cadmael looked down. How could he not have some sympathy for the old warrior's views? Defending his home from the Koreshians—that was the reason he had taken up arms, and it was for peace that he fought. His heart longed for nothing else. Perhaps, in time, he, too, would find a wife and have a family, in an Illmeria where they needed not fear for their lives. Why had he felt hurt when the warrior had demanded to fight Syrela and no other? Was he fighting for himself, after all? For his own glory, fame, and recognition? The thought made him frown. He had a bitter taste in his mouth. He nodded to himself and turned his attention to Kshashil, some forty steps away. They had allowed one another some time to warm up, and Cadmael had briefly sparred with one of his sergeants, but Kshashil seemed content with a simple jog and a few basic movements with a wooden sword.

"The time has come, young one," said the Stormcaller. "Let this duel be remembered for ages."

Only some twenty steps separated them now, and Cadmael studied his opponent once again, to reassure himself. His foe would be a fantastic warrior, certainly his toughest challenge, for if an Illmerian were to be so determined to fight Syrela herself, then either foolishness or the quest for an eternal legacy motivated them. What worried him was his ignorance of the old man's powers. It was too great of a disadvantage. In the countless tales he had been told, never did the Stormcallers have a similar set of abilities. Each certainly used their powers to their advantage, in accordance to their strengths and weaknesses. If he were to triumph, he would need some creativity, for his talents alone might not earn him a victory.

For a few moments, the two circled one another, Cadmael's spear ready in his hands as he noted the weak points in Kshashil's armour. One of the major flaws of the more traditional style of Illmerian armour was its weakness on the flanks and the armpits, perhaps the very first thing the Advisor had fixed in the Mistlands, and the Stormcaller's armour was no exception. The other flaw he noticed was the weak spot behind the old warrior's knees, yet exploiting such a weakness was quite a challenge—but Cadmael was not without ideas.

He was the first to strike. Keeping his opponent far away with his spear, he leapt forwards and targeted his opponent's left flank. The old warrior was unbothered by the attack, deflecting the blow with the flick of his wrist, and before either could strike again, a few steps separated them once more. Another thrust, yet this time the Stormcaller's blade directly parried the tip of Cadmael's spear, causing an explosion of blue sparks and a shock wave that he felt all the way in his shoulders.

He stepped back. Immobile, he studied his opponent again, trying to make sense of what he had just witnessed. He could not lose focus; there was too much at risk. He considered his odds, and he realised he could not risk being hit, not even on his armour, after what he had witnessed. And so, thankful for the wooden shaft of his weapon, he took another step forwards, followed by another thrust aimed at the old man's right flank, yet with little more success. Why was the Stormcaller so passive? Kshashil clearly aimed to have his blade block the tip of his spear, for that happened again and again. Cadmael suspected something. His shoulders were getting sore. If he could feel that, if the energy released every time was such, then his spear was certainly damaged by it and there was no doubt that the old man had only shown a glimpse of his powers.

After one last parried attack, Kshashil seemed to have grown tired of that game, and after deflecting another of Cadmael's thrusts, he stepped forwards, dangerously close. Defending against the Stormcaller's strikes was more painful than he imagined. Every time he blocked with the shaft of his spear, the young man would feel his shoulders getting more numb from the powerful shock wave. He needed a plan. Anytime now, his weapon would break before the warrior's magic. He bit his tongue, blocking yet another attack, ignoring the pain and pushing his opponent's blade away. He stepped to the right and struck at the old man's neck. It was only with a swift movement backwards, and by blocking the strike with his shoulder, that Kshashil lived. Yet he had been hit, and Cadmael smirked.

"That was your last chance, young one," growled Kshashil.

His retaliation was swift. Though his powerful blow was blocked by the shaft of Cadmael's spear, the energy released by the impact broke the weapon in half. Even after, as the tip of Kshashil's blade grazed his armour, Cadmael struggled to keep his balance. He had just enough time to jump back and draw his sword. He would get no more chances. In spite of his first weapon breaking, he could continue to fight, but he could not allow himself to be intimidated. He would need to strike fast and end this combat soon, for he stood no chance fighting in a traditional manner.

Cadmael braced himself. A few steps away, Kshashil readied another attack. The blue glow of his eyes seemed darker than before, a slight trickle of blood on his left shoulder.

Cadmael feared not. He knew what his opponent was capable of now. He feigned being prepared to block the attack but instead dashed to the right at the last moment, letting his opponent's blade strike his left arm, numbing it entirely. It mattered not. He was at the perfect angle. With a swift movement, he struck Kshashil behind his knees, almost severing the old man's left leg. They both let out a scream, and in a last attempt, the Stormcaller pivoted and struck again. There was no other option than to parry it. The shock in Cadmael's arm made him wince and drop his weapon, and as he jumped back, he could not feel his right hand. The pain had numbed it and his vision blurred for a few moments, but he stayed conscious. A few steps away, Kshashil struggled to stand up. Cadmael hurried to pick up his weapon and lunged. He struck the Stormcaller on his right wrist, wounding and disarming him. The duel was over.

"You are a deceptive warrior, young one," he said, "for what appears as inexperience and recklessness hides your strengths well."

The victorious smile on Cadmael's lips vanished at the remark. Had it not been recklessness and pride that led him to this combat? He sheathed his sword and removed his helmet, looking down with a slight frown. "There is no deception, venerable one. Only harsh lessons that I should learn, and only now have I started to do so."

"You are a remarkable warrior, then," said the old man. "I have much respect for you, and I expect the same from my men." Not without struggle, the old Stormcaller removed his helmet. His wounded wrist covered the silver decorations of his armour in blood, and a few drops fell on his beard. "I have been defeated, and I am old. I have seen too many battles, and I had hoped to die at the hands of the War Hero herself. A fitting end for a legendary warrior. But I do not doubt that, in time, your legacy will be as great as the Blade of Illmeria's, for my name and my own renown shall be tied to yours from this moment on."

Glory, triumph, and fame were all meaningless before death, in the end, and that thought made this bitter taste return. This quest for admiration would lead him nowhere, just how it had led Kshashil, a warrior certainly without equal in all the Stormlands, to his end.

"Bring me a swift death, young hero," he said, bowing his head and presenting his neck.

Cadmael knew his duty; he knew such would be the outcome of this duel. With a heavy heart, he lifted his blade and prepared to strike. The old man had an inexplicable smile as he waited, his eyes closed. Not daring to make a sound, Cadmael sliced his neck, and Kshashil's head rolled.

A dozen steps behind, the Stormians knelt as they watched the end of their clan leader. Only after many seconds had passed did one of them stand up. The pommel of his sword towards Cadmael, the warrior knelt. "We recognise your victory," he said, his voice deep and calm.

Following the customs of the Stormians, Cadmael grabbed the pommel and nodded. The man removed his helmet, revealing the blue glow of his eyes, almost identical to Kshashil's, though perhaps slightly fainter. He was much younger than the Stormcaller, though certainly quite older than Cadmael himself; his traits showed some experience, his eyes some wisdom. "I am Shireï. As the oldest nephew of Kshashil, the Onoraï clan is under my protection for the foreseeable future, until a new clan leader is chosen by our warriors. Work with me, and let us ensure that no further bloodshed is needed."

CHAPTER 41
INTOXICATING, IRRESISTIBLE

Barely an hour after Cadmael's victory, the Queen's banner was flown above the walls of Aremaï. It was with an odd peacefulness that the defenders laid down their weapons and opened the gates. Cadmael had expected some form of resistance after the death of their clan leader, but instead they cleaned and bandaged his wounds. Had they expected Kshashil's defeat, or was he heading into a trap?

"Is there no one in Aremaï who wants to see me dead?" asked Cadmael.

Shireï shrugged. He turned to the city beneath them, and the young captain stepped to his side. It seemed surprisingly small when seen from its fortress of blue slate, an impressive construction built on the north-eastern side of the city, alongside the river. "I would be a little cautious around Zeya, his eldest daughter," answered Shireï. "She was always so protective of him, but it is unlikely that she will take action against you. I will also ensure that she gets no such occasion."

"What about you?" asked Cadmael. "Had you wished to kill me, you would have done so when I was weak, back in the fields, and had you chosen to defend your city, you would have held on for weeks, if not more."

"Many of us in the Zulshi tribe are experienced and talented warriors," said Shireï. "We know that death is part of a warrior's life. My uncle's death is something I was prepared for. Taking revenge for fighting a battle he accepted is pointless." He turned to Cadmael and, with a hand gesture, invited him to sit at the table nearby. A servant had brought some drinks but soon disappeared behind the door. "See, neither he nor I wanted to fight the Illmerian army. I had suggested negotiating with the Queen of Mists weeks before, when the news of Kashpur's reconquest reached us, but in his quest for glory, he refused, just so he could have a chance to fight the Blade of Illmeria. A quite vain objective, in the end."

Cadmael brought the cup to his lips as he listened to the warrior. It was filled with a transparent liquid, yet its perfume reminded him of the musakin or other wildflowers. He winced as he swallowed the liquid, for he felt a burn in his throat, which made Shireï chuckle.

"It is quite a strong alcohol. I should've warned you," he said.

Cadmael joined him in his chuckle and took a second sip, this time much more ready for the strangely pleasant sensation.

"In the end, what I value is my clan's safety," said Shireï. "Had you been defeated, I would have again insisted for negotiations with your army regardless. As my uncle said himself: we do not care about the Duke. He lost our respect the moment he allied himself with the Koreshians, and he lost our support at the battle of Kashpur. Likewise, the men you nearly fought on the Derhkaï plateau were not part of our clan. They were soldiers under the Duke's command and are currently locked safely in our prisons. The Duke hoped to fortify the border and gain himself some time as he deals with the current situation in Asharsaï."

Cadmael frowned and leaned in.

Once more, Shireï chuckled, yet this time he stood up and slowly headed back to the balcony. "The Duke has lost much of his support and most of his warriors at the battle of Kashpur. During the Battle of the Blue Ford, which preceded his rise to power, the Mehakaï, his clan, was absent. It was the heavy losses of the other clans that saved the Stormlands from the first Koreshian invasion, but in the aftermath, the Mehakaï were too numerous and too powerful. Most clans were quite resentful but too weak to oppose him."

"I take it that you will side with us against him, then?" asked Cadmael.

"Why else do you think I am telling you all this? If we are with you, it will be a revolt helped by the Queen of Mists rather than an invasion. We will overthrow the Duke and negotiate with Lady Xelya on our future and the autonomy given to us, which would be beneficial to everyone."

"Let me warn you that I don't have the authority to negotiate in the Queen's name," said Cadmael. "But I will appreciate some military support nevertheless." With his drink finished, he stood up. "Tomorrow, I intend to push eastwards, directly to Asharsaï. I would like to count on your clan's support."

Shireï contemplated the city for a few seconds. Cadmael knew his plan to be daring, but with the promise of reinforcements from the War Hero's army and his victory that day, he could surprise the Duke by acting swiftly.

"That is a bold plan," Shireï eventually said. "While I feel quite obliged to offer you my support, I suggest carefulness. The war is lost for the Duke. He stands no chance in the long term."

"It is bold, and already before, I allowed my arrogance to lead me into unnecessary battles," said Cadmael. "My men were never meant to go so far east, and it's only by pure arrogance that I fought Kshashil. But this time, I believe this move to be strategically correct. If the

Duke still believes that he holds the Blue Ford, to the point that he sends men to fortify the position, then he will not expect an army of this size so deep in his land. We have a day or two where we will not meet any resistance."

"Smart, though no less bold," said Shireï. "I advise against an assault on Asharsaï, so long as we do not know the situation there in any greater detail at least, but otherwise, I will trust your instinct."

"How many warriors can your clan gather?"

"Some three hundred," he said.

"And those Mehakaï warriors you captured, how many are they?" asked Cadmael.

Shireï's lips pursed, and for a quick instant he looked down. "A few hundred, too. But I ask of you to spare them. There is no need to cause unnecessary bloodshed."

Cadmael bowed low, his helmet held against his left flank, and closed his eyes. "You have my word, I will not do anything to those prisoners. I simply asked for strategic reasons."

"Thank you. I will follow you eastwards, tomorrow. I know the region well, and my knowledge of the various clans, the tensions between them, and their history will certainly prove useful."

With an agreement reached, Shireï offered to make Cadmael visit his city. Though heavily fortified, it was quite significantly smaller than those he had seen before. Compared to the Fortress, the architecture was simpler, but the city had been built on multiple levels, with the roofs of the lower levels serving as terraces—to help in case of battle, Shireï told him, as archers could be positioned there if an enemy entered the city. Nevertheless, there was something elegant in the bluish tints of the taller buildings' roofs and the brown-red wood of their walls. The streets were narrower than those of the Fortress, and the port was more for fishermen to sell the fish caught that day than anything else, but the city was no less buzzing with activity.

A few Onoraï warriors guarded them during their visit, but Shireï's worries proved unfounded, for it was curiosity above all else that seemed to gather a small crowd around Cadmael. A few words would sometimes reach him, often mentioning his "strange uniform" or his "impressive armour," making him smile. Shireï showed him a local brewery, where this strange, transparent alcohol was made, the name of which, "nakra il," roughly meant "scorching water" in the Stormian dialect.

"Will you honour my tribe with your presence at our table tonight?" asked Shireï.

There was no hesitation from Cadmael. As the afternoon went on, their discussions had turned to lighter subjects, and as they returned to the blue fortress and patiently waited for food to be brought, they shared stories of battles with one another. Shireï seemed to be particularly intrigued by the young captain's narration of the battle of Mistport and his heroic charge at the beach of grey sand. Likewise, Cadmael attentively listened to the warrior's account of the Battle of the Blue Ford.

"When the Koreshians ordered a third charge, thinking they had broken our ranks, is when we surrounded their vanguard, and Kshashil carved his way to their general," said Shireï. "He made quick work of him, which left them disorganised, and after another hour of combat, they retreated."

Those words were the last Cadmael remembered of his long discussion with Shireï, for alcohol flowed generously. He came to regret that most of his soldiers, untrusting of the Stormians, preferred camping outside the city, but it hardly prevented him from enjoying the tribe's hospitality. He laughed and joked with the Zulshi warriors until late at night, until most of them had fallen asleep on the floor.

He found himself in the pleasant company of a young woman, a true beauty, with her blue robe, her long black hair, her orange eyes.

Shireï had been the one to introduce her to Cadmael. She was one of his nieces, and with a shy smile, she had followed the young man to his bedchamber. Perhaps it had been the sweet alcohol the two had shared together that filled them with such courage, or perhaps the two were meant to unite, but as the door closed behind them, they forgot the world outside, for nothing but the other mattered.

CHAPTER 42
A PLEA FOR HONOUR'S SAKE

It was the warm sun of dawn that awoke the two lovers. They found themselves speechless, absorbed in the other's wide smile.

"Perhaps it is wiser if I do not stay for too long," she eventually said.

He wrapped his arms around her and kissed her neck. She held him tightly against her body, her eyes closed. "I will return, Meila," he said. "After the war is done, I will return and ask for your tribe's blessing. I want to have you as my wife." At her bright smile, his heart felt ready to burst.

Her embrace around him tightened, and for many seconds, she refused to let go. "I will wait for your return," she whispered. Once at the door, she turned around one last time, her smile still wide.

Cadmael fought the urge to take her by the hand, to keep her close to his heart forever. A second after, she had disappeared in the corridor, and already he let out a sigh. He would ask for her hand, and he was certain Shireï would not refuse it, and neither would her parents. On that day, he swore to fight for Meila, to protect her and keep her safe from Koresh.

He returned to the large hall, where Shireï and a handful of his most trusted warriors shared some food. With a warm welcome, they invited him to join them, which he gladly did. Soon, the small group was headed to the Illmerian camp just outside the city.

"Captain Cadmael! I didn't expect you to go so far to the east, but it looks like that was the right decision." The voice was familiar, almost startling Cadmael. Akior had arrived!

The two men burst into laughter as they greeted one another with a hug. "I didn't think reinforcements would be that quick," said Cadmael. "But that's good news. We've made some allies against the Duke, and I don't think he'll see us coming."

"Seems like you have at least a story or two to share," he said.

A more serious expression returned to Akior as he turned to Shireï, and both warriors bowed before one another. After a quick introduction, all three gathered their men and broke camp, then took the road eastwards, to Asharsaï.

"I was doubtful of our chances to besiege the Duke in his city," said Shireï, "but with those reinforcements, there might be a chance." His lips pursed, and he took the lead of his men, his horse trotting alongside Cadmael's. "Justice has come, Zheraï," he added in a whisper. "Your reign shall soon end. I'll make sure of it."

Cadmael would narrate his many anecdotes to Akior, speaking in great detail of his duel against Kshashil. There was little for them to do, in truth, for even the occasional fortified temple or stray patrol of the Duke's men posed little trouble. Often, they attempted to hide, surrendered, or even defected at their approach. Cadmael's army was simply too large. Those few that betrayed their allegiance to the Duke told the same tale as Shireï, however: too many distrusted the Duke, or the Mehakaï, whatever the reason might be. They spoke of infighting, and often were the old clan rivalries mentioned. The Illmerians soon witnessed it for themselves, as on quite a few occasions they encountered groups of Stormians from different clans fighting one another.

"Battles between clans and tribes are highly codified," said Shireï. "A tenth of the warriors of each clan, tribe, or group will fight to the death in a series of duels, until there are no warriors left on one side. That is how a lot of disputes are solved, often for matters of honour or for plots of land more than anything else."

"Are there never battles, then?" asked Cadmael. "As in combats involving all the warriors of a clan, regardless of anything else?"

"Not amongst Stormians," said Shireï. "It would be too deadly. The first Koreshian invasion was the first occurrence in two centuries, according to tales. Rarely will clan leaders agree to rally against a common threat."

"How come your people were able to unite so quickly during the first invasion?" asked Akior. "The Mistlands were disunited, and the Duchess took months to react and gather an army. If not for the Stormlands, the War Hero would have stood truly alone before Koresh."

"It is quite a miracle," said Shireï. "But first and foremost, rumours spread rapidly. This is how we caught wind of it. Truth is, my father is the one who convinced the other clan leaders to take precautions. Coincidentally, the leaders of six major clans had gathered just outside Aremaï for negotiations about the inheritance of some land. Since they had been discussing for almost three weeks, they agreed to solve the issue peacefully after dealing with the Koreshians.

"As I briefly mentioned, a few clans did not join. The six present there at the time did, but the Mehakaï did not, alongside a handful more, though all were minor clans beyond the Mehakaï. Most did not join as they were still recovering from recent battles, or due to ongoing battles, but the Mehakaï did not out of personal gain. As we all discovered, too late, the battle had exhausted us, and most of our warriors had perished, but Zheraï was at the peak of his power."

Neither captain thought it wise to ask any more questions, and Shireï had told them much already, more than enough to better understand their enemy. They would sometimes put an end to those ritual duels they met on their way, taking as prisoners the participants, but Shireï kept their attention focused on more pressing matters. It was, according to him, impossible to put an end to those ancient traditions—at least, not so quickly—nor was it desirable, for it had kept a semblance of order in the Stormlands, preventing clans from destroying one another.

"It is an agreed rule here that no clan shall attempt to destroy another," he said. "Doing so would be dishonourable and would draw the ire of all the other clans."

"Has it happened, in the past?" asked Cadmael.

"On rare occasions, though those parts of our history are rather taboo," answered Shireï. "The perpetrating clans are often dissolved or destroyed, too, but I shall not speak more on that subject."

And so Cadmael asked nothing more, though there was much he was curious about. Those two days had, in truth, given them many occasions to talk, for there had been little action otherwise. As expected, the Duke had not anticipated the surrender of Aremaï, and with the tensions at his capital, his attention was sure to be elsewhere. It allowed the Illmerian army to take much land, capturing temples, garrisons, and outposts on their way with great ease. The third day was rainy, though Shireï guaranteed that no thunderstorms would be on their path, visibly reassuring the Mistians.

"There is one major fort still on the road," said Shireï. "After, we will have reached the plains and farmlands preceding Asharsaï."

That fort would appear on the horizon during the afternoon. A large wall with a gate, controlling the road, with four large towers.

On the one side, it reached a cliff, and below was the sea, while on the other side, one of the four towers had been partially built inside the hills.

"In position, soldiers!" ordered Akior.

It was unclear how many soldiers were defending the position, but the gates had been shut and barricaded, and archers rushed to the battlements, though none fired quite yet.

"Could we avoid them by going through the hills?" asked Cadmael.

Shireï shook his head, though he studied the cliffs and mountains to the east. "Not with an army of this size. A small group could take a detour of a few hours, but we'd risk being ambushed. The only other way would take days, four or five perhaps."

Cadmael shrugged. Slowly, his horse trotted closer to the walls, just in arrow's reach. "The army of the Queen of Illmeria has arrived! You are outnumbered and stand no chance. Surrender now and you will be spared."

The only answer was an arrow, though it landed quite a few steps to his left. Soon, a few others followed, but already Cadmael had turned around. He frowned. Those men, even if more numerous than he had first imagined, still stood no chance. Were they willing to die just to follow orders? "Why are those fools resisting to the bitter end? We outnumber them thirty to one. They'll be dealt with in no time!"

"Those men are part of the Mehakaï clan," said Shireï. "We are fighting on their land. They will not surrender unless they are surrounded and their captains are dealt with, I fear. It is a matter of honour and principle, first and foremost."

A sigh escaped Cadmael. They discussed a plan with Akior: the heavily armoured footmen would approach the walls with ladders and a ram, while the archers would build wooden towers on the more elevated positions to clear the walls.

The Illmerian soldiers took positions. Cadmael had to be

convinced not to charge into battle, for the wound to his arm was still recent. As such, he stayed in the back. He nodded to Akior, who led the men in the assault. With shields raised, they slowly approached the walls, battering down the gates and drawing the archers' attention.

"I'm convinced I could have led the charge," said Cadmael.

His confidence made Shireï chuckle. A few steps away, the Mistian archers had built towers as tall as a man, just enough elevation to properly fire at the Mehakaï still on the walls.

"But you don't need to, either," said Shireï. "Akior is doing well enough, and giving yourself one more day of rest before Asharsaï is far from unwise."

Cadmael moved his left arm to see for himself: he felt a bit of pain, but it was hardly a bother. He could not help but feel that he had narrowly avoided a broken bone, given the strength of the impact, but the wound had not turned out too severe in the end. In a week, it would be nothing but an old memory. "You might be right," he said.

Under the cover of their own archers, the Illmerians climbed the walls. Akior's commands echoed in the valley, and soon the gate was opened from the inside. Hardly an hour had passed. The Stormians who had surrendered were brought outside, but most had lost their lives or fled. Only some twenty men stood there before Cadmael.

"You inflicted no casualties to us, gained no time, and your stubbornness brought many of your clansmen to die," said Cadmael. "Why did you fight such a hopeless battle?"

The Mehakaï kept their silence. Cadmael had not expected an answer; it was more surprise that had made him ask. As he ordered them to be brought to the back of the line with the other prisoners, only one man stayed behind, falling on his knees before Cadmael.

"My Lord, I beg of you!" he said.

With a gesture, Cadmael stopped his men from taking him away with the others. He dropped from his horse and stepped closer to the prisoner.

"My Lord, Asharsaï is a battlefield!" said the man. "My family is there. Please put an end to this. I beg of you!"

CHAPTER 43
AN INESCAPABLE BATTLEFIELD

The man could tell him no more; he himself knew little of what was going on. Shireï arrived not a second too late, and Cadmael hurried back on his horse.

"Shireï," asked Cadmael. "How many clans are there in Asharsaï?"

"Well, the Mehakaï is by far the largest clan in Asharsaï. It is their city, after all. But as a result of Zheraï's ascension to power, a few tribes of other clans have sent representatives there." He thought for a few moments, staring at the man being taken away. "The Tulsaï and the Kinshaï clans have a significant presence in Asharsaï, too, if my memory is correct. What is the matter?"

"According to this man, the clans in Asharsaï are fighting one another," he said. "We can waste no time here."

Akior shouted some more orders, and soon the soldiers had formed a column and were headed south. Shireï stood immobile for a moment. He watched the prisoners being brought to the back of the column with the other captives. Cadmael glanced at him and raised an eyebrow but shrugged as he got out of sight.

"What's the plan?" asked Akior.

"If the clans are fighting in Asharsaï, we have a duty to end any combat there," Cadmael answered. "After the past weeks, I don't think any will pose a real threat."

"It will be combat in a city. We can't be too careful. Trust me on that one. I fought the Koreshians in Mistport, the first time around, and that's how we got them. Just like us back then, they got nothing to lose."

"But . . ." Cadmael stopped himself. He frowned and rubbed his chin, and he glanced at the soldiers behind him. "What do you suggest, then?"

"Ground can be retaken. Men can't be brought back from the dead. Slow and steady. We have the advantage."

"Alright, we'll do that, then."

Shireï galloped to the head of the army, rejoining the two captains. Lips pursed, he studied the horizon for a long minute, then turned to Cadmael. "We will reach Asharsaï tomorrow at noon or shortly after."

"Do you know the city?" asked Cadmael. "Any information you can give us on the layout or its fortifications?"

"If the clans are fighting inside, the walls and fortifications aren't anything to fear," he answered. "It's more the narrow streets, the risk of fire in a city built almost entirely of wood, and the palace itself that I worry about."

Perhaps Akior's caution had been wise, for Cadmael, too, began to doubt. Should he renounce his plan and wait for his general to arrive? "In a matter of weeks, the Advisor, Lord Valirian, will arrive with some fresh troops from the Mistlands. We can wait for him and ensure our victory."

"And leave hundreds, if not thousands, to die," said Shireï. "We must act now, though not foolishly or rashly. Believe me, if clans are fighting in a city, they have discarded all the rules and traditions of our people, and they will target everyone, not simply the other clans' warriors."

Shireï's expression made Cadmael shiver; the blue glow of his eyes seemed more intense, and he could only be thankful that he was not the target of his anger. "So you fear a fire, and you are certain that the clans have abandoned all traditions. Zheraï knows our army is coming, so we can expect some sort of last-resort trap from him, perhaps something like trapping our troops in the burning ruins of his city. I can't risk so many men's lives, but you are right in saying that we can't wait. What do we do?"

Shireï looked down. He glanced at the soldiers in orderly ranks behind the three of them. Many of the Stormians, most of them his own clansmen, joked and laughed with the Mistian soldiers. "Cadmael, Akior, do you trust me?"

The two captains looked at one another. There was a slight smile on Cadmael's lips as he nodded.

"Then I have an idea."

* * *

The following morning, the city was clearly visible on the horizon. They had marched a few hours past sunset under Shireï's advice, not wanting to take any risks. Asharsaï was still a few hours away, but they would reach it before noon, or so Shireï seemed to think, at least.

"Today's the day," said the Stormcaller.

"Indeed." Cadmael chuckled. He stretched and warmed up with a stick, leaving Shireï to observe him with wide eyes, surprised at his optimism.

"Do you never fear going into battle?" he asked.

"Always," said Cadmael. "That's why I smile and joke and laugh.

Each could be my last. I've led charges against the Koreshians many times, I've fought the War Hero herself, and I've even fought a Stormcaller now. They weren't all wise decisions, but I always fought for the same goal, so I try to remember that."

Shireï chuckled. Akior joined them soon after, and they hopped on their horses.

"So, I'll stay outside with the footmen, just in case?" asked Akior.

"You're free to join us," said Cadmael.

Akior laughed, a joyless smile on his lips, and his head turned to the city. "I'm not as brave as you. I could try to hide behind excuses, but I've been deathly afraid of fire ever since I almost burnt alive in Mistport. I just hope we're overthinking this and he doesn't have that sort of twisted plan."

"I hope so, too," said Shireï.

They resumed their march, and as they neared the city's tall walls, echoes of battle reached them, confirming what they had been told.

"The walls have been deserted. Breaking down the gates shouldn't take too long," said Akior.

"Then let's get to it," said Cadmael. He gripped his spear tightly, jaw clenched, and glanced at Shireï, who gave him a nod.

Under Akior's command, a small battalion of Mistian soldiers forced the gates open with a battering ram, and for a long hour, the two watched, not saying a word, not daring to look left or right at the other cavalrymen. A loud crack startled Cadmael. He almost jumped forth and rode his horse forwards but realised the gates hadn't been opened quite yet. Another one made him jolt—still, the gates stood, though not for much longer, doubtlessly.

A third one. Now was the time! Cadmael led his cavalry inside the city, letting out a war cry that his men all echoed. The plaza behind was empty. Even there, the fighting seemed distant. Shireï took the lead and guided Cadmael and his men through the city. First through a large avenue, then around a turn, then another turn. Their charge forced the Stormians to the sides, interrupting their skirmishes. Some were trampled, others impaled by a lance, but the Mistian cavalry paid no attention to any other than Shireï. Deeper in the city, the large avenues were rarer, and traversing the narrow streets and alleys on horseback was no easy task, but eventually, they caught up.

"The palace isn't too far away now," said Shireï.

They had grouped up in another plaza, smaller and covered with bodies. Many were women, old men, some even children.

The Stormcaller spat on the ground. "We just have to go through here and we'll be practically there." Another street, a little larger than those they had just traversed. Yet a barricade had been put in place.

"Let's dismount and attack it," said Cadmael. "We can't waste any time."

Shireï raised his hand, making the young man frown. "Do you trust me?"

Cadmael glanced further down the street, then turned to his companion. "I do. We'll follow you."

"We can't waste any time. Charge!" Shireï unsheathed his sword and galloped into the street. Some Mehakaï clansmen guarded the barricade, and a few arrows flew. Cadmael followed, and soon after, all the cavaliers entered the street, charging straight into a wall of wood and spikes.

Everything turned darker. A low chant echoed. Cadmael looked up, and a strange orb formed in Shireï's hand. The chant became louder and louder. In only a matter of seconds, they would crash head-first into the barricade, yet none stopped. A cry. Cadmael froze and looked up. Had Shireï been hit? A flash of blue blinded him, and a loud crash followed. When his sight returned, a second after, the barricade was no more; all had been blown away, broken, or burnt.

"Go through!" shouted Shireï.

Cadmael's blade found the neck of an archer nearby. He made his horse gallop faster than ever, hoping his men could follow. He let out a sigh as he glanced behind. Even Shireï, though he was no longer in the lead, had made it through. Minutes passed, the street curved in odd ways, and Cadmael's heart raced. Often he looked up, keeping the palace in his sight. Almost! He could see the end of the street, where it led into a final plaza. He sheathed his sword and gripped his lance in his right hand. "Ready yourselves!"

The plaza was less defended than he had anticipated. Rather, he soon realised its defenders had for the most part been killed, for a battle had recently occurred there: the bodies of countless warriors covered the paved ground. Those who remained aimed, then fired.

A scream. Shireï! Cadmael's eyes widened, and he killed one of the enemy archers with a growl. An arrow had found a weak spot in the Stormcaller's armour and had pierced his left shoulder deeply. As the last of the defenders were dealt with, Cadmael rushed to him.

"We're there," said Shireï. "That went better than I thought."

"Are you able to fight?"

"It's too deep for me to fight, I think," he answered. "That and I spent all I had for that damned barricade. You go on without me. I'll be okay."

Screams from within the palace made them turn. Shireï dropped from his horse and, with his foot, turned over the body of one of the warriors on the ground. "That's a warrior of the Tulsaï. Both clans will fight to the bitter end inside. Be careful."

Screams, again. Yet this time, they came from deep within the city. Shireï dropped his sword. Smoke. Tall columns of black smoke, from multiple areas. The fire spread rapidly, too rapidly.

"You hurry into the palace," said Shireï. "Your men will be safe there, and the others are outside. That's all we can do now. I'll find a place to hide."

Cadmael grunted. Already his horse was going up the stairs of dark grey stone and into the wide-open gates. His men followed, but he had already engaged the enemy. "For the Queen of Mists!" he shouted.

In every hall, every room, every corridor, the Mehakaï and the Tulsaï fought one another, and everywhere, the Mistians would put them to the blade. No warrior was to be spared.

"Captain, the Duke's trying to escape! Some of us are holding him off in the throne room!"

"Time to end this, then!" He rushed through the corridors, down a set of stairs, and into the throne room. What the soldier had described had turned into a bloodbath. On one side of the room, the Mistian soldiers held on to the gates. On the other side, warriors of the Tulsaï poured in. Between them, the Duke and his men, surrounded. In his armour of blue and gold, he fought, in spite of the fate that doubtlessly awaited him. He swung his blade and struck at the necks of many Tulsaï warriors.

"There you are," Cadmael whispered. Many soldiers separated them, but he would not let any obstacle stand in his way. He swung, he lunged, and warriors of both clans fell to his attacks. Zheraï was in a duel against another Tulsaï warrior. Cadmael was almost there.

A war cry, followed by a laugh. "I killed the Duke!" shouted the warrior. "I killed him!" Above him, he raised the severed head of his slain opponent as he laughed. The young Mistian captain was approaching him, but the warrior did not even raise his blade as his throat was sliced. The few Tulsaï and Mehakaï that remained stopped fighting soon after.

"In the name of Lady Xelya, the Queen of Mists, drop your weapons!" said Cadmael. Amidst the curtains of red silk, the furniture inlaid with gold, and the rich tapestry, he observed the carnage. One by one, the remaining warriors dropped their weapons before him. He gripped his sword tightly. Each time, he fought the urge to behead them, right then and there. In the end, he told himself, the massacre had been stopped. The Duke had been defeated, for good. "Bring everyone outside," he told his men. "Search the palace and bring anyone hiding outside, too. The plaza should be safe from the flames."

A heavy, pouring rain greeted them outside. Though not enough to stop the fire, it doubtlessly limited the flames from spreading too rapidly.

"Shireï!" Cadmael called. He was nowhere to be seen. Seconds passed, and he called again—nothing. He looked around. His men began inspecting the plaza, searching amongst the dead bodies.

"Captain!" a soldier called.

Cadmael rushed, dropping his sword and removing his helm. In the centre of the plaza, there he was, lying on the ground, motionless.

"I think he's still alive," said the soldier.

He was breathing, yet he had lost consciousness. Had he hidden the severity of his wound? Had he been poisoned? Thoughts raced in Cadmael's mind. Shireï's heart was beating at a normal rate.

"Bring him inside!" said Cadmael. With the help of a few soldiers, they rushed to carry him to the dining hall. "Remove his armour. We need to inspect his wound." The arrow had pierced quite deeply, and though Shireï was still bleeding, the blood loss was not significant enough to have caused him to pass out. Likewise, it did not seem as if an infection had developed in such little time.

"He doesn't even have a fever," said a soldier.

"Keep an eye on him, and make him drink plenty of water," said Cadmael. "We have to do all we can."

"He'll make it, Captain! We'll make sure of that!"

Cadmael's eyes moved not from the wound. He gave a nod to answer his men. He hoped Shireï would reopen his eyes in mere seconds, yet the only sign of life one could see was the slow movements of his chest as he breathed. Otherwise, not a muscle moved.

"Cadmael! Here you are." Akior rushed into the room. His presence brought the hint of a smile to the young captain's lips.

"Good to see you," he said. "You made it through the city? Is there still fighting going on?"

"When we saw the fire, we feared you had been trapped," said Akior. "Quite a lot of civilians fled right into us, and the warriors that escaped the flames dropped their weapons. Shortly after, the rain started pouring, so we cautiously went in. Turns out most of the fighting had stopped, and we helped control the fire. Spirits be praised for that rain!"

"So, the city is under our control, and the fire won't spread?"

"The fire has been stopped, and the surviving warriors have been captured."

Cadmael sighed. He turned his head back to Shireï's still body. "Well, at least we got some good news."

"Do we know what happened? That arrow wound doesn't seem severe enough."

"It is not. He was still conscious and well when we reached the castle, even after he used his powers in combat. Yet when we came out after the battle, he was unconscious, in the rain."

As if to see for himself, Akior reached for Shireï's chest. His heart was beating, albeit rather slowly. "The night will make things clearer. He'll wake up eventually, I'm sure."

"Bring all the important warriors that surrendered to the palace's plaza," said Cadmael. "We have a city to rule, some explanations to hear, and some punishments to deliver."

CHAPTER 44

A WHISPER AND A DANCE

The assembly that had gathered surprised even Cadmael. In normal circumstances, he would watch as the Advisor, or the Queen herself, delivered whatever speech or judgement to such a large crowd, but now he was the one who would talk. The entire city, it seemed, had gathered: the streets all around the plaza were filled with citizens who wished to hear or see what would now happen. Cadmael bit his tongue and glanced at Akior. His fellow captain stood up, and so did he. Before them, some ten steps away, ten warriors, of the Kinshaï, the Tulsaï, the Mehakaï. Some elders, of each clan, had also been brought forwards.

"Step forth and state your name," said Cadmael. With a short blade, he pointed at one of the Kinshaï warriors, who had announced himself as their clan leader.

"I am Akashir, of the Kreshi tribe, leader of the Kinshaï," said the man. "I swear on my clan's honour to speak all the truth as I know it."

"Then, answer: what has brought your clan, alongside the Mehakaï and the Tulsaï, to fight to the death, disregarding your most ancient traditions and putting the lives of countless innocents in danger?"

Akashir glanced behind. On his stern visage, his lips were pursed. He let out a sigh and bowed his head. "There was an attempt to end Zheraï's life, My Lord. One of our tribes accused the Tulsaï of being behind it, and the Tulsaï retaliated by slaughtering every single one of those tribesmen in one night. This brought me to defend our clan by retaliating, but Zheraï saw it as a revolt and executed many of my warriors publicly."

Cadmael exchanged a few words in a low voice with Akior, agreeing they needed to question more warriors to be certain. Then he pointed at one of the warriors of the Tulsaï. "You. Come forth and state your name, then tell us why the Tulsaï fought against the Mehakaï so bitterly."

"I am Azheï, of the Sashï tribe, and warrior of the Tulsaï. As our clan was unjustly accused of the assassination attempt, many of our warriors were publicly executed, and without any proof, by Zheraï."

"Do either of you question the other's words?" asked Akior.

"No, My Lords," they both answered.

Cadmael pointed at one of the other warriors. He was young, much younger than any of the others around him, and the only Mehakaï there. He seemed to struggle staying still and bowed low as Cadmael pointed at him. "What of the Mehakaï? Step forth."

"I am Kelshi, of a tribe now gone, warrior of a clan dishonoured," he said. "The Duke acted out of fear, for rumours of betrayal were plenty. He was almost assassinated by some unknown warriors, some three weeks ago."

"You do not deny their words, then?" asked Akior.

"I do not, though I equally accuse them of conspiring against the Duke."

Cadmael sighed and shook his head. The truth was hardly hidden, but the decision was no easier. To hang them all, to dissolve each of those clans—that thought came to mind, but he could not, lest they plot to revolt against the Queen herself. "No clansman, no single warrior, is innocent in the carnage that unfolded here. What is clear is that the Tulsaï and the Mehakaï suffered greatly from the battles. Give us some time." He sat down, and Akior did so, too.

To all, their discussion certainly seemed to last for an eternity, as they debated the course of action to follow. Eventually, they stood up again.

"This city is now under the Queen of Mists' rule, as are all of the Stormlands," said Akior. "Each and every single warrior of the Mehakaï, the Kinshaï, and the Tulsaï are to join the Queen's army in the war against Koresh."

"As the tribe that spoke against the Tulsaï is no longer," said Cadmael, "we see no ground to punish anyone for those accusations, whether they were baseless or not. Asharsaï is a city under the Queen's direct authority, which we shall represent until she decides otherwise. From this moment on, no warrior of any clan shall be authorised within its walls with any weapon of any sort. Lastly, as punishment for what happened, the clan leader of each clan present in Asharsaï shall be publicly executed, and the clans, all three, will be stripped of any of their authority."

Akashir took a step forwards. Again, he bowed his head and knelt. "You certainly know that the clan leaders of the Mehakaï and the Tulsaï were killed in battle. I am the last of the three. I ask for your mercy, though not for I: spare those that now lead, even if symbolically only, their clans."

Akior and Cadmael looked at one another. For a moment, neither said a word.

"Enough blood was spilt in this war," said Cadmael. "We don't need to kill anyone else."

Akior glanced at the city. A great part of it was now in ruins; only the large palace of grey stone seemed intact from the outside. He shrugged and let out a sigh. He remembered Mistport, his beloved city, burnt by the Koreshians much like Asharsaï had been burnt. "You're right. Zheraï is dead, and the Stormlands are part of the Queen's realm now. Let's not forget why we came here in the first place."

Cadmael nodded. They needed not say more. He jumped off the small wooden platform, built by his men for the occasion, and approached Akashir. "Your wish is granted. Only you shall pay the price."

Akashir bowed his head and closed his eyes. A Mistian soldier approached to keep him still as Cadmael unsheathed his sword. Behind the palace, the sun was setting, its orange light reflecting on the young captain's blade. He took a deep breath and let out a cry—in a swing, it was over.

* * *

How long would that uncertainty last? Cadmael had hoped for the night to be enough, for Shireï to wake up the following morning as if nothing had happened. Yet nothing had changed. The Stormcaller lay on his bed, perfectly still, his eyes closed. He was no paler than the previous day, worrying and surprising at once.

"Do we write a letter to his clan?" asked Akior.

"Too soon," said Cadmael. "As long as we can delay announcing whatever it is that happened, then let's wait."

A few servants of the Mehakaï had been tasked with watching over him, and a few soldiers guarded his room. They had given him plenty of water, tended to his every need, yet the morning had passed, and so had the afternoon.

"It's getting late," said Akior.

Cadmael leaned in. He could feel his heartbeat, and Shireï was still breathing, though neither were easily audible. A whisper made Cadmael jump. He looked behind, and Akior raised an eyebrow.

"Are you okay?"

What had he heard? No, it certainly came from Shireï. He leaned in again, his ear close to the Stormcaller's mouth—there was doubtlessly something.

Akior frowned and moved to the young man's side, leaning in, too. Strange words escaped his mouth, gibberish yet with a semblance of structure. The two captains looked at one another, wide-eyed. Akior shook his head before leaning in again. Gently, Cadmael tapped on Shireï's cheek, as if that would wake him up. He moved not, but neither did this strange chatter end.

"Is he speaking?" asked Cadmael.

"If he is, it's not a language I can speak," said Akior.

Cadmael glanced through the window. The sun was setting, and a cold breeze passed through the room. Shireï's body tensed, making them both jump. Again, they looked at one another. Then both stared at the Stormcaller. He tensed again, gasping for air, thrashing around, yet his eyes were still closed. He let out a cry, and his eyes opened. Cadmael and Akior stood up, and Shireï backed off, protecting himself with his arms.

"Where am I?" he asked. He studied the faces of the two men before him, then let out a sigh. His body relaxed, his arms fell to his side, and he tilted his head back.

"Is everything okay, Shireï?" asked Cadmael.

"My limbs are numb, my head hurts, and I feel terribly weak," he said. "How long have I been gone for?"

"A little over a day," said Akior. "We were worried. Cadmael said he found you just fallen on the ground like that. Your wound was really not that bad. What happened?"

"I . . ." He rubbed his temples, shaking his head.

"Let's get you some food," said Cadmael.

"That would help. I shall try to recollect my thoughts in the meantime."

Some meat, bread, and beer were brought to him, and he ate to his heart's content, barely pausing as he devoured an entire loaf and half a ham. Once he had eaten most of the food, he leaned back in his chair and sighed.

"So, do you remember anything?" asked Akior.

"Mostly," he answered. "I remember . . . I felt my knees get weak, and then nothing. I took a risk, but I had never imagined what would result of it."

Cadmael's eyes widened, and he leaned forwards. "A risk? Did someone attack you?"

With a gesture, Akior told the young man to give Shireï some time, yet Cadmael's enthusiasm seemed to make Shireï chuckle.

"Not quite," he said. "I saw the city burn, I saw my wound, and I just felt . . . anger. Something was building up within me. I knew you and your men would be safe, for the stone palace of the Duke would not burn, and I feared not for Akior and the rest of the army, but I could not tolerate this feeling of powerlessness. Watching thousands die by the flames was unbearable. I was wounded, and had used my powers quite extensively already, but I felt the need to try anyway. I gathered the little power left in me to gather nearby clouds in the sky in hopes that rain would fall on the city and help stop the flames."

Akior's jaw dropped, and he shook his head. He let out a laugh. "You called the rain? I thought those clouds were moving fast, but I just thought it was a lucky coincidence!"

"Well, I did not call the rain per se," he answered. "I would not have been able to. I just helped the clouds gather above us."

"Still, there always needs to be a bit of luck to any good story," said Akior, "but that doesn't make it any less impressive. Admittedly, I cannot believe half of what I have seen the Queen do."

"That would have certainly been trivial to her, from what I have heard," said Shireï. His eyes widened, he shivered, and his visage paled. He brought the beer to his lips and drank. "I wish I had forgotten what happened afterwards."

Cadmael frowned. He had tried to make sense of this strange whispering, but he simply could not. "Why did you collapse, then? And what exactly happened afterwards? You were unconscious for a day."

Shireï finished his beer and shook his head, shivering again. He looked at the meat before him and took an eager bite. "When one uses too powerful magic, such as for a task too difficult to achieve or when one is already too exhausted, then magic may cause one to collapse. Sort of." He winced and let out a sigh. "It is not like when you collapse out of exhaustion. You pushed too far for your body to handle the effort, indeed, but you also pushed your spirit too far. Legends of old speak of a race of wizards, the Mahïrs, whose magic duels would often end in the collapse of one of the participants. They would die simply because they pushed themselves way beyond their limits."

"What's so different, then, apart from the fact that it's possible to die from it?" asked Cadmael.

"It is hard to explain," said Shireï. "I definitely neared death. I have no doubt about that." He leaned in and looked around, ensuring nobody else was in the dining room; nobody else could hear. "I saw things," he whispered. "Things I cannot explain with words. I saw Nav, the great spirit of death."

The two captains shivered. They looked down, and Akior nodded. "Sometimes I do not envy those capable of using magic."

"So you were in this sort of . . . dream?" asked Cadmael.

"Dream, nightmare, vision, I don't know," he answered. "A bit of all three. Things felt real; there is no doubt. I felt an ominous presence, at first. Something creeping, all around me. Then a shadow appeared, with purple eyes. He spoke to me, but I couldn't look at him." Shireï finished the rest of his food, and many minutes passed. The slightest of noises would startle them. Slowly, the candle on the table, their only light, grew weaker.

Akior grumbled. "This is why you never mention the great spirit's name! It's enough to get everyone paranoid."

"He's supposed to be the protector of life," said Cadmael. "I don't understand what is so terrifying about him."

"Truth is, we should all go to sleep," said Shireï. "There is much we need to talk about tomorrow. I hope I didn't miss too much."

* * *

The three met again around the same table the very next morning. Rested, and with plenty of food to share, they laughed loudly and told jokes as they ate. As their meal neared its end, though, Cadmael and Akior told Shireï of the aftermath of the battle, of the events leading up to the revolt, and of the execution of Akashir.

"It is in our hands to make sure this does not happen ever again," said Shireï. "Please, trust my advice: the stronger the clans, the more likely it is to happen."

"This is why we limited their actions in Asharsaï," said Cadmael. "They have no say in the governance of the city, and none of their warriors are allowed with weapons within the walls."

"Those are good ideas, but they do not go far enough," said the Stormcaller. "See, you are limiting the scope to Asharsaï. The city doubtlessly needs to be ruled by a Mistian administrator chosen by the Queen, but we need to go further. The main problem is not the clan structure; it is more exactly the warriors within those clans and the way matters of honour are solved. Here is my solution: since the

Stormlands are now ruled by the Queen of Mists, then all warriors are to join her army, and for so long as they are in the Queen's army, they no longer are part of any clan. Once their service is over, only then will they be able to return to their clan, though not as warriors any more. In parallel, we need a system to address all matters of honour and justice other than through the warriors."

"You suggest we strip the clans of all power regarding war," said Akior. "Won't that result in resistance from the clans?"

"The Mehakaï are no longer, the Kinshaï and Tulsaï are in no position to refuse, and I would not oppose a proposition I myself made, so the Onoraï will follow. With that, not many of the other clans will disagree, believe me."

Akior and Cadmael looked at one another and hesitantly nodded. "We can only really apply short-term solutions here," said Cadmael. "We don't have the authority for that sort of reform. But the Queen's Advisor, Lord Valirian, or the Queen herself will probably be interested in what you have to say."

Shireï smiled. He stood up and invited the other two to follow him. "I would very much like to meet the Advisor."

"I'll write a letter to Kashpur," said Cadmael. "It's about time we tell them of our success. It's also a good occasion to send back the troops that are not needed here alongside the remaining Kinshaï, Tulsaï, and Mehakaï warriors."

CHAPTER 45

WITHIN ONE'S HEART

A sergeant shouting orders, another counting aloud the number of crates. All the while, citizens watched the scene, interrupting their sale of fish to observe the thousands of men that landed in the harbour. Seeing Kashpur so full of life, in spite of the horrors the city had suffered, brought a smile to Valirian's lips. Certainly, some of the activity was exacerbated by his arrival, alongside Zelshi and some seven thousand men, yet there was no denying that the resilient citizens of Kashpur had been quite remarkable in how quickly they had rebuilt the eastern part of the city.

"You said the plan was to stay in Kashpur for a few days, My General?" asked Zelshi. "Why not immediately reinforce Cadmael's army?"

"We are only to stay three days. First, to allow our scouts to give us reports on all that might be of interest. After all, we do not know for certain if Koresh is stubborn to the point of returning so soon. Second, I need to ensure that we will receive all the supplies we might need while we are in the Stormlands." Valirian turned to Zelshi and placed his hand on his shoulder. The captain could not help but repeatedly glance at all the cargo being unloaded. They had not heard from Akior, Cadmael, or Syrela since the news of Naila's reconquest. "Worry not. Captain Cadmael has my trust and enough experience not to fall into any obvious trap. He should have a solid position in the western Stormlands."

"Understood, My General."

The captain returned to supervise his men while Valirian headed to the palace. There were many letters that needed to be written, yet upon entering the ducal quarters, he let out a loud sigh and struggled getting to work. They had barely returned home to the Fortress when he was ordered to leave again.

"Xelya . . ." he whispered. He toyed with the amulet around his neck, fidgeting with it for a few minutes before he looked at the unwritten letter on his desk. His room was getting darker as the sun set, and he shrugged. He would have time to write the next morning, he thought, yet the following morning was hardly any easier. Still, most of the work was done by noon. He merely needed to find some soldiers to carry the letters to the right people.

"My General!" Zelshi opened the door and rushed in. Out of breath, he bowed.

"What is the matter, Captain?"

"A young farmer reported sightings of a large army marching to Kashpur," said Zelshi. "Maybe two or three hours away."

Valirian frowned. How could a sizeable army have gone unnoticed for so long until it was too late? "Koreshians? Or Stormians?" Without waiting for an answer, he stood up and headed outside the palace, Zelshi behind him.

"He did not know," the captain said, "but the army 'comes from the forest,' from the Northlands, so I dare assume Stormians."

"Most likely Stormians, then," said Valirian. "Prepare our men, but they may not be as hostile as they appear."

The soldiers gathered in ranks under the sergeants' shouts behind Valirian. He led his men uphill, Zelshi to his left; the captain had already drawn his sword. The enemy was surely not too far away; they might even come into view once Valirian and Zelshi reached the top. Indeed, in the valley below, one could see the army spotted earlier by the young farmer.

Valirian laughed. "Hold."

Struggling to hold back a laugh, Zelshi repeated his general's order with a shout. The banner carried by the army below was now fully in sight: a purple flame on a field of black.

"My General!" said a sergeant from the other army. "We bring news from Captain Cadmael. What we have to report will be most pleasing to you."

Next to the sergeant, a tall man removed his helmet, revealing to Valirian his glowing blue eyes. The man bowed and handed him a letter. "I am Shireï, of the Zulshi tribe, and leader of the Onoraï clan. We wilfully submit to the Queen of Mists and her rule."

"As the Queen's Advisor, I welcome you into our ranks, Shireï, you and your clan," said Valirian.

"My Lord, I have been a companion of Cadmael during much of his campaign in the Stormlands," he said. "There is much to tell and much I wish to discuss with you."

Valirian dropped from his horse. Behind, Zelshi joined his side. "Tell the men to set camp outside the city, for now," he told the captain. "If they have nothing to do afterwards, make them help in the reconstruction works."

As Zelshi gave some orders to the sergeants and led them to the city, Valirian opened the letter Shireï had given him. His eyes widened as he read the tale as narrated by Cadmael. "All the Stormlands?"

"Not all the clans have formalised it," he answered. "But those who haven't will follow soon. It's a trivial matter to get them to agree."

Valirian nodded. He rubbed his chin, still unsure if he believed what he had just read—it all felt too surreal. "You said you wished to discuss some matters? I suppose you have a request in exchange for your loyalty."

Shireï bowed low. "Not quite, My Lord. I have suggestions, in order to keep peace in the Stormlands. Allow me to tell you more about what happened in Asharsaï."

"I will hear you," said Valirian. "But let us share a meal. That will be a more appropriate setting."

* * *

A strong gust of wind made the flames of the campfire dance; it crackled as Syrela added a few more branches to it. She smiled. Dusk bathed her city in a pale orange light. The sight of Naila from just outside her temple rivalled the view Xelya had of the Fortress from the heights of her Tower.

She headed to the well in the temple's courtyard. Making it usable again, alone and without many tools, had been quite a challenge, but she had all the water she could need. She filtered it and poured it into the kettle above her campfire, biting into a grilled hare's leg. Elder Fahj had proposed to bring her food and water, but she had refused. At first, he often came to visit her, doubtlessly fearing to find her malnourished. His visits were short, but not unwelcome, and though they had become less frequent, she appreciated sharing some tea with him.

She turned around and let out a sigh. She knew how foolish it was to imagine herself capable of rebuilding the Temple of Iron in its entirety, all alone, but she could smile at her progress. The garden had been cleared of all the broken spears, arrow tips, and shattered shields but also of the weeds. The main building had still quite a few broken windows, but some of the furniture had been repaired.

She stopped in front of one of the side buildings. She again tried to push the door open, but something blocked it on the other side. "Guess there is no other choice." She stretched and took a deep breath. She pushed again, using her magic to aid her. A loud crack startled her, and she jumped back. The door was now open. She scanned the room. Nothing moved. A beam that had fallen from the roof was responsible for blocking the door, but she had managed to dislodge it. She looked up: the entire roof had collapsed, and a heavy rock lay on the cracked wooden floor. That one would bother bringing siege equipment to attack such a small temple surprised her. She let out a slight chuckle at the thought.

She shrugged. It was too late in the day to work any more, so she poured herself some tea and watched day turn to night. For weeks, she had been far from anything; no longer did she need to worry about politics and battles and wars. Even Elder Fahj spoke not of those matters with her, preferring philosophy and poetry to any other subjects. Yet against the coldness within her, this void, all she had tried seemed powerless. All that time alone had not been enough to completely erase what she felt for him. She had a duty towards Xelya, her Queen—yet the thought of it only made this cold sensation worse. The guilt that had come with Naila's fall had been hard to handle; the guilt that had followed the massacre at Kashpur had been crushing. It had taken her too long to understand that one's value depended not on the ability to achieve but on one's righteousness of heart. Yet how could she call herself righteous while she desired her liege's husband? Did Xelya's friendship mean nothing to her? The thought of such dishonour made her shiver. She would distance herself from him. What other choice did she have? Her own pain was preferable to becoming a betrayer.

"Lady Syrela." Elder Fahj's voice echoed in the hills, startling her. A visit from him, at such an hour, was quite unexpected. What could he want?

"Lady Syrela!" called out another voice. It was a young man's voice, nothing like the elder's.

She stood up and went to meet them. She could guess the reason for their presence. "I am here. What do you need?" Next to the elder was a young soldier. Weaponless, he carried a letter in his hand. She reached for it, and the young man bowed.

"My General, a letter from Lord Valirian," he said.

"You may return to the city and rest," she said. "Thank you."

The campfire gave her just enough light to read. The style was doubtlessly Valirian's. Direct and elegant, each word as if chosen with great care. She was asked to return to Kashpur and, from there, head to the Fortress, for the Stormlands had been conquered and the Queen wished to discuss the course of action to follow with her generals. Though she was surprised by the speed of the Advisor's campaign in the Stormlands, having to return to Kashpur bothered her less than imagined.

She felt a raindrop on her cheek and instinctively returned to her room. It felt like an eternity since she had last worn her green gambeson or felt the weight of her armour's plates on her shoulders. She had been alone for far too long. Why wait? She equipped it, gathered her few belongings, and rushed to her horse, outside. Quickly, she caught up to the elder and the soldier.

"I must leave for the Mistlands," she said. "Rebuild the Temple of Iron while I am gone. I have already done some of the work, as you have seen." She left him no time to answer. Already, she was galloping away as he wished her good luck. She allowed herself little sleep and only rested once she had entered the cover of the forest; likewise, she woke up early the following morning.

* * *

Valirian sighed. The day was grey and rainy, again. In those conditions, would the letter even reach Syrela? Why hadn't he gone to Naila to meet her himself? He had many times considered the option. Why hadn't he? He shook his head. He worried far too much. He found comfort in knowing that, soon, he would return to the Mistlands. He would not be separated from Xelya for too long. He stepped on the balcony. Eyes closed, he let the raindrops fall on his visage, and he took a deep breath. A horse galloping below made him frown. He looked down. In disbelief, he blinked: Syrela had arrived. It had been nearly a month since he last saw her. Thoughts raced in his mind as he fought to stay calm. What had troubled her when she left all those weeks ago? He wished for her heart to have found the peace she yearned for.

The door to his room opened wide, and Syrela bowed low.

"Dear friend," he said. "I am glad to see you again, after all this time."

There was the hint of a hesitant smile on her lips as he walked closer. She froze as he wrapped his arms around her, but after a second, she reciprocated. "Likewise, General." For a moment, they stayed there. Many long seconds passed before they broke their embrace. "I'm glad to see you, too," she added. In spite of a weak smile, she looked down. "Let's not make Xelya wait."

About to speak, Valirian stopped himself. Together, they prepared themselves for their travel back to the Fortress and their departure in just an hour. His thoughts wandered to Xelya and the future. From great struggle and perseverance, they had brought peace to Illmeria, but would it truly last? He feared knowing the answer, and both Syrela and Xelya most certainly shared his perspective on the matter. This age of war had not quite yet ended.

The story continues in the third and final book of The War of Obsidian and Mist: The Lion of Obsidian.

If you enjoy my work, share about my books and leave a review online! That's the easiest way to support me.

Let's connect on social media:
X: @c_r_burgundy
Instagram: @charlesrburgundy

Go on my website and subscribe for free to my newsletter to keep updated and find all the information about my books:
charlesrburgundy.com

ACKNOWLEDGEMENTS

How could I not say thank you to the amazing family and wonderful friends who supported me since the very first day? You have all been invaluable to me through every step. Thank you a thousand times.

I want to also say thank you to my editor, Bodie, who is always a great pleasure to work with. I also very much appreciate your love for history, which I share, and your book recommendations!

Alexis, your art never misses. It's always incredible to work and think with you on how to create the best cover every time.

To my readers, thank you! Our love for stories connects us, and I may not know you all, but I nevertheless want to thank each of you.

To my Lord, thank you for your guidance and solace.